AFTER THE STORM

Center Point
Large Print

Also by Linda Castillo and available from
Center Point Large Print:

The Dead Will Tell

**This Large Print Book carries the
Seal of Approval of N.A.V.H.**

AFTER THE STORM

Linda Castillo

CENTER POINT LARGE PRINT
THORNDIKE, MAINE

This Center Point Large Print edition is published in the year 2015 by arrangement with St. Martin's Press.

This is a work of fiction. All of the characters, organizations, and events portrayed in this novel are either products of the author's imagination or are used fictitiously.

The text of this Large Print edition is unabridged. In other aspects, this book may vary from the original edition. Printed in the United States of America on permanent paper. Set in 16-point Times New Roman type.

ISBN: 978-1-62899-715-6

Library of Congress Cataloging-in-Publication Data

Castillo, Linda.
After the storm : a Kate Burkholder novel / Linda Castillo. — Center Point Large Print edition.
pages cm
Summary: "When a tornado tears through Painters Mill and unearths human remains, Chief of Police Kate Burkholder is tasked with the responsibility of identifying the bones and finds herself plunged into a thirty-year-old murder case that takes her deep into the Amish community to which she once belonged"—Provided by publisher.
ISBN 978-1-62899-715-6 (library binding : alk. paper)
1. Burkholder, Kate (Fictitious character)—Fiction.
2. Women police chiefs—Ohio—Fiction.
3. Cold cases (Criminal investigation)—Fiction.
4. Amish—Ohio—Fiction. 5. Large type books. I. Title.
PS3603.A8758A69 2015b
813´.6—dc23

2015023890

This book is dedicated to the first responders: Police officers. Firefighters. Emergency medical personnel. Disaster relief workers and volunteers. Thank you for everything you do and for being there when you are needed most.

Acknowledgments

Once again, my deepest appreciation and heartfelt thanks to my publishing family at Minotaur Books. Charles Spicer. Sally Richardson. Andrew Martin. Jennifer Enderlin. Sarah Melnyk. Jeanne-Marie Hudson. Kerry Nordling. Hector DeJean. April Osborn. David Rotstein. And many thanks to my friend and agent, Nancy Yost. I sincerely love working with all of you!

Seek, and ye shall find; knock, and it shall be opened unto you.

—*The Holy Bible*, King James version, New Testament, Matthew 7:7

Prologue

August 29, 1985

The old barn had a history. Nine-year-old Sally Ferman had heard all of the stories, and every single one scared her. Her dad told her that the farm was originally owned by a young German immigrant by the name of Hans Schneider. He built a cabin and married a French woman, Rebecca. They had three sons, and over the years, Hans and his boys built the barn, raised cattle and sheep, and grew tobacco and corn.

Then one snowy night in 1763, a band of Delaware Indians raided the settlement. Hans was shot dead as he stood by the window with his muzzle-loader. His wife was dragged from the cabin and scalped. The three boys—all armed and prepared to fight to the death—were burned alive when the Delaware set the cabin ablaze. Rumor had it, if you came out here at night you could still hear Rebecca screaming as her scalp was being hacked from her skull.

Sally didn't know if the story was true; she'd never heard anything out here except for the coo of the pigeons and the occasional squeal of the hogs. The one thing she did know was that the old barn, with its stone foundation and dark windows, was the creepiest place she'd ever seen.

From her house next door, it looked like a normal barn, with faded red paint and a rusty tin roof. But up close, the place was falling down and spooky. Grass and weeds grew shoulder-high at the crumbling foundation. Last summer she and her best friend, Lola, had sneaked over. They'd nearly talked themselves into going into the barn, when the Amish guy came out and they'd had to hide in the weeds. It had been scary but exciting, too. All he did was pee out the back door. Despite their momentary terror, they'd laughed all the way home. Sally had had a tough time explaining the cockleburs in her hair to her mom.

The memory made her sigh. Lola had been so much fun. She'd moved away last Christmas because of her dad's stupid job. Sally missed her bunches. Lately, she'd been hanging with Fayrene Ehrlich, who'd just moved to Painters Mill from Columbus. Fayrene was pretty and popular (her mom let her wear lipstick and shave her legs), and she'd already scored a place on the softball team *and* the girls' glee club, two things Sally hadn't managed, and not for lack of trying. Everyone thought Fayrene was the best thing to hit Painters Mill since the new ball diamond out by the middle school. Sally thought Fayrene was a bigmouth and a know-it-all. And she knew for a fact Fayrene wasn't that smart, because she'd copied Sally's homework twice already.

But with Lola gone, Fayrene was the only

friend she had. The truth of the matter was Sally needed to up her game. Prove her courage and her worthiness for fifth grade. Her mom had told her to stay away from the Amish people next door; they didn't want English kids sneaking around in their barn. But that was exactly the thing Sally needed to do to show everyone she was a lot braver and twice as interesting as Fayrene Ehrlich. All she had to do was come back with a cool story for the lunchroom and maybe with a souvenir to prove she'd done it.

"Easy peasy," she whispered as she made her way up the rise from the creek. In the back of her mind she wondered what Fayrene would do if Sally came back with Rebecca Schneider's scalp. That would shut her up for good.

Making sure the coast was clear, she darted across the dirt path to the barn. It was built on a slope, with the front on the uphill side. The downhill side faced the pasture, and there were stalls tucked underneath and a bunch of hogpens outside. There was a big sliding door in front, where the Amish people backed up their wagon to unload hay. But Sally couldn't go in that way because she'd be visible from the house. There was no side door, so she was going to have to go in through the stalls in the back.

Keeping an eye out for someone approaching from the front, listening for voices, she sidled right. She could smell the pigs now, that nose-burning ammonia stench her mom and dad complained about every time the breeze carried it over to their house. Back pressed against the foundation, Sally peered around the corner. The row of stalls on the underside of the barn had dirt floors, and a foot or so of manure was built up at the rear. There were holes where ground-hogs had dug burrows. Those things creeped her out, too, especially the big ones. Her mom said they looked like giant rats.

Not giving herself time to chicken out, Sally slipped around the corner and looked up. The barn was two stories high, three if you counted the stalls underneath. There was only one way to get up to the second level: through the hay chutes cut into the ceilings of the ground-level stalls. All she had to do was shove one of the hatches aside and climb up.

Taking a final look around, she ducked into the first stall and, keeping an eye out for groundhogs, made her way to the rear. The ceiling was low with cobwebs hanging down like dirty cotton candy. She could hear the pigs grunting and moving around in the pens outside, their cloven hooves tapping like heels against the concrete. She reached the nearest hay chute. A quick check for spiders, and she pushed on the heavy wooden hatch with both hands. Dust and dirt and bits of hay floated down to land on her face and shoulders, but she muscled the hatch aside and, standing on her tiptoes, poked her head through the opening.

The barn's interior stunk badly. There was just enough light for her to make out the pile of loose hay ahead, a lone bale of alfalfa, and some burlap bags full of cracked corn stacked against the wall. Heaving herself through the chute, Sally got to her feet, dusted off her jeans, and looked around. The door that looked out over the pig-pens was to her right. To her left was the big sliding door at the front of the barn. There was a flatbed wagon parked just inside. Farther, a window looked out toward the house. She couldn't believe she'd come this way all by herself. All she had to do now was find some sort of souvenir and then get the heck out.

Her sneakers were silent against the plank floor as she started toward the door that looked out over the pasture and the hogpens below. She caught a whiff of horse sweat and leather as she passed by a harness hung on a nail driven into a beam. Rounding a wheelbarrow full of horse poop and straw, she reached the door and peered out. From where she stood, she could see the mossy green water of the pond and, beyond, the creek. Twelve feet down, dozens of pigs—Hampshire hogs and big red ones with black spots—milled about, packed together by steel pipe fencing. A few of the animals looked up at her, beady eyes beseeching, and she looked around for some hay or corn to toss down.

"I bet you guys are hungry," she whispered.

She was tugging a tuft of alfalfa from a bale, when the sound of voices spun her around. The big sliding door began to roll open. Gasping, she darted to the hatch, sat down, and stuck her feet through. She was in the process of dropping down, when some men entered the barn. Sally landed on her feet. Quickly, she stood on her tiptoes and poked her head back through the chute, grabbed the hatch, and dragged it back into place, ducking down as she lowered it over the hole.

But she didn't close it completely. Resting the hatch on top of her head, she peered through the two-inch gap. She couldn't see much, just three sets of legs, men's work boots, and trousers.

"*Sis alles eigericht,*" one of the men said.

Heart drumming with a combination of excitement and fear, she crouched, keeping the hatch open as far as she dared. If they looked her way, they might spot her. But Sally didn't think they would, because they were busy talking. Or arguing.

She was about to close the hatch and make a run for home, when the shouting began. She didn't know Pennsylvania Dutch and she couldn't see their faces, but she didn't need either of those things to know they were angry. Her mom had always told her Amish people were religious and gentle, never partaking in any kind of violence. But there was nothing gentle about the conversation they were having. She almost couldn't believe it when one of the men shoved the other one.

She nearly yelped when they shuffled to within a few feet of her hiding place, boots scraping against the floor, kicking up dust. She heard the wet-meat slap of a fist against flesh. An angry shout. More scuffling as they struggled and danced back to the door. Growling like an animal, one of the men bent and charged the man near the door. Sally saw booted feet leave the floor as the man by the door reeled backward. Then he was falling. He twisted in midair and seemed to look right at her. She caught a glimpse of his face, arms outstretched, mouth open in a silent scream. And then he was gone.

A whimper escaped her when she heard his body clang against the fence and land on the concrete below. Slapping her hand against her mouth, she ducked down so fast she lost her balance. The hatch clattered shut.

Sally landed on her butt in the dirt. She couldn't believe what she'd just seen. "Ohmigod," she whispered. "Ohmigod. *Ohmigod.*"

Was the man dead?

Above her, the men had gone silent. *Had they seen her?*

She darted to the front of the stall and glanced left toward the hogpen. Through the steel rails and a mass of hogs, she spotted the man lying on the concrete. He was moving, head raised, dazed, but looking around. Relief swept through her because she'd thought for sure he was dead.

Her relief was short-lived. The hogs were squealing and running around. Several of the larger animals surrounded the fallen man. Squealing, one of the pigs darted in and rooted the man with its snout. The man shouted something and smacked the animal with his fist.

"Help him," she whispered, looking toward the ceiling where the men standing above could surely see him. *Why weren't they helping him?*

Sally got a sick feeling in her stomach. A big white boar bellowed, rushed in, and slashed at him with its tusks. The man made an awful sound. She saw a tear on his shirt sleeve. The shocking red of blood. Her teeth began to chatter.

She closed her eyes. "Help him," she whimpered. *"Please."*

The pitch of the hogs changed. Sally opened her eyes. The animals were excited and moving fast, darting close and then retreating. She watched in horror as a big sow latched on to the man's shoulder and shook violently, the way a dog might shake a squirrel. The man twisted and tried to roll away, but a second pig lunged and bit down on his arm. Sally covered her face with her hands, but it didn't block the sound of the scream that followed.

"Ohmigod! Ohmigod!" Choking back sobs, she

ran from the barn. She knew if the men looked they would see her, but she didn't care. She didn't slow down. Didn't look back. She reached the fence, squeezed between the wires, tearing her shirt on a barb, cutting her arm. But she felt no pain. Then she was on the path, sneakers pounding dirt. Arms pumping. Legs burning. Terror in hot pursuit.

Her own screams chased her all the way home.

August 30, 1985

She arrived at the covered bridge twenty minutes early. She hadn't told a soul where she was going, and she was so nervous she felt as if she might crawl right out of her skin. But she was excited, too, and glad they'd chosen this place to meet. The Tuscarawas Bridge was special. They'd met here dozens of times over the summer. It was a place of first kisses, whispered promises, the laughter of young lovers, and dreams for the future. Or, if you were alone, it was the kind of place you could just sit and think.

This afternoon was so quiet she could hear the red-winged blackbirds swooping from tree to tree down by the deep pool, and the bees buzzing around the yellow tops of the goldenrod that grew along the muddy bank of Painters Creek. Hefting her satchel, she entered the shade of the covered bridge where it was marginally cooler. She'd worn her best dress today and the black

17

kapp normally reserved for preaching services every other Sunday. Gathering the skirt of her dress, she sat down beneath the window that looked out over the meandering creek. It was so peaceful. She wished for that same peace in her own heart, but it was not to be.

She'd never experienced so many conflicting emotions as she had this past week. The thought of starting a new life with him made her so happy she could barely contain it. Yet the thought of leaving her family behind filled her with sadness. Oh, how she would miss Mamm and Datt and the little ones! How would she get through the day without the love and wisdom of her parents? How could she go to sleep at night without the hugs and kisses of her brother and sisters? Did they know how much she loved them? Would they always remember her?

The alternative, of course, was living the rest of her life without the man she loved—the man she was going to marry—and that wasn't an option. It didn't matter that he was *Mennischt*—Mennonite—and New Order, to boot. He was a good man, kind and hardworking. Most important, he loved her. He wanted to marry her. What did it matter that he loved God in a slightly different way or that his belief system included modern conveniences and driving a car?

It mattered to her parents. She'd tried to explain to them that he would be a good husband. That he would work hard and provide for her and their children. But they were Swartzentruber, the most conservative of all the Amish groups. Her parents were *demutig*, meaning "low" or "humble," and they adhered to the strict traditionalism of their forefathers. They drove windowless buggies with steel-clad wooden wheels. Not only did they spurn electricity, but their home was devoid of indoor plumbing and even linoleum flooring. Her *mamm* wore a bonnet and a dress that reached nearly to her ankles. Her *datt* never trimmed his beard.

Her parents believed those values promised them a place in heaven. But she knew those staunch values also meant they would never listen to her. They would never understand. And they would never, ever approve. In the end, they'd left her no choice but to choose. Her family—her very *Amishness*—or a future with the man she loved more than her own existence.

They'd met most recently two days ago at this very spot. She'd laughed when he'd gotten down on one knee and proposed. Rings aren't exchanged when an Amish couple becomes engaged, but she'd felt like a princess when he told her he'd put one on layaway—a real diamond set into a simple gold band—and he'd be picking it up when he got paid. Her joy was dampened only when she reminded him that her parents would never give their blessing. She was only seventeen years old, but she'd already been baptized. She would be put under the *bann.* Excommunicated. No one would speak to her. No one would take meals with her. Worst of all, they would forbid her to see her brother and sisters. How the thought hurt her heart!

Last night, after everyone went to bed, she'd pulled out her satchel and packed. Underwear. Socks. A change of clothes. A bar of her *mamm*'s lye soap. A copy of *Martyrs Mirror.* She didn't have room for the nearly twelve-hundred-page book, but it was the one item she couldn't live without. No matter how troubled her soul, the old tome, with its accounts of the Anabaptists who'd died for their faith, both horrified and inspired her to love God even more. In the coming days, she was going to need every ounce of strength and faith she could muster.

This morning, after Datt left, she sneaked into the bedrooms of her brother and sisters for final kisses, her tears leaving their soft cheeks nearly as wet as hers. "I love you little ones," she'd whispered. "Be good." She'd hoped that in a few weeks or months, her parents would realize how much they missed her and welcome her back. But she didn't think so, and that made her cry even harder because deep inside she knew she'd never see them again.

It took her two hours to walk to the covered bridge. She'd broken a sweat every time a car or buggy passed. She was terrified someone she knew would see her and tell her parents. Of course, it didn't matter really. They would find out soon enough. Even if they tried to stop her, she wouldn't change her mind. Nothing could stop her now. Nothing.

Slipping off her shoes, she strolled over to the place where he'd carved their initials into the wood. It was a silly thing, but the sight of it made her cry again. Finally, after months of sneaking around and fearing exposure, they'd be together, only now as husband and wife. There would be a wedding. A home. Children. Her chest swelled with love, and not for the first time she asked God how something so right and pure and good could be bad.

Finally, emotionally spent, she went back to her satchel and sat down. He was late, as usual, and she couldn't wait to see him. She could picture his face. So handsome. Such kind eyes. The secret smile he had only for her. He'd be here any moment in that old car of his, elbow out the window, radio blaring, hair blowing in the wind. All she had to do was sit and wait. She figured she could wait forever if that's what it took.

"Hurry, my love," she whispered. "Hurry."

Chapter 1

Present day

I was eight years old when I learned there were consequences for associating with the English. Consequences that were invariably negative and imposed by well-meaning Amish parents bent on upholding the rules set forth by our Anabaptist forefathers nearly three hundred years ago. In my case, this particular life lesson transpired at the horse auction near Millersburg and involved a twelve-year-old English boy and the Appaloosa gelding he was trying to sell. Add me to the mix, and it was a dangerous concoction that ended with me taking a fall and my father's realization that I saw the concept of rules in a completely different light—and I possessed an inherent inability to follow them.

I never forgot the lesson I learned that day or how much it hurt my eight-year-old heart, which, even at that tender age, was already raging against the unfairness of the *Ordnung* and all of those who would judge me for my transgressions. But the lessons of my formative years didn't keep me from breaking the same rules time and time again, defying even the most fundamental of Amish tenets. By the time I entered my teens, just about everyone had realized I couldn't conform and, worse, that I didn't fit in, both of which are required of a member of the Amish community.

Now, at the age of thirty-three, I can't quite reconcile myself to the fact that I'm still trying to please those who will never approve and failing as miserably as I did when I was an inept and insecure fifteen-year-old girl.

"Stop worrying."

I'm sitting in the passenger seat of John Tomasetti's Tahoe, not sure if I'm impressed by his perceptivity or annoyed because my state of mind is so apparent. We've been living together at his farm for seven months now, and while we've had some tumultuous moments, I have to admit it's been the happiest and most satisfying time of my life.

Tomasetti, a former detective with the Cleveland Division of Police, is an agent with the Ohio Bureau of Criminal Investigation. Like me, he has a troubled past and more than his share of secrets, some I suspect I'm not yet privy to. But we have an unspoken agreement that we won't let our pasts dictate our happiness or how we live our lives. Honestly, he's the best thing that's ever happened to me, and I like to think the sentiment runs both ways.

"What makes you think I'm worried?" I tell him, putting forth a little attitude.

"You're fidgeting."

"I'm fidgeting because I'm nervous," I say. "There's a difference."

He glances at me, scowling, but his eyes are appreciative as he runs them over me. "You look nice."

I hide my smile by looking out the window. "If you're trying to make me feel better, it's working."

Good humor plays at the corner of his mouth. "It's not like you to change clothes four times."

"Hard to dress for an Amish dinner."

"Especially when you used to be Amish, apparently."

"Maybe I should have made an excuse." I glance out the window at the horizon. "Weatherman said it's going to rain."

"It's not like you to chicken out."

"Unless it's my brother."

"Kate, he invited you. He wants you there." He reaches over, sets his hand on my thigh just above my knee, and squeezes. I wonder if he has any idea how reassuring the gesture is. "Be yourself and let the chips fall."

I don't point out that being myself is exactly the thing that got me excommunicated from my Amish brethren in the first place.

He makes the turn into the long gravel lane of my brother Jacob's farm. The place originally belonged to my parents but was handed down to him, the eldest male child, when they passed away. I mentally brace as the small apple orchard on my right comes into view. The memories aren't far behind, and I find myself looking down the rows of trees, almost expecting to see the three Amish kids sent to pick apples for pies. Jacob, Sarah, and I had been inseparable back then, and instead of picking apples, we ended up playing hide-and-seek until it was too dark to see. As was usually the case, I was the instigator. Kate, the *druvvel-machah.* The "troublemaker." Or so my *datt* said. The one and only time I confessed to influencing my siblings, he punished me by taking away my favorite chore: bottle-feeding the three-week-old orphan goat I'd named Sammy. I'd cajoled and argued and begged. I was rewarded by being sent to bed with no supper and a stomachache from eating too many green apples.

The house is plain and white with a big front porch and tall windows that seem to glare at me as we veer right. The maple tree I helped my *datt* plant when I was twelve is mature and shades the hostas that grow alongside the house. In the side yard, I catch sight of two picnic tables with mismatched tablecloths flapping in the breeze.

I take in the old chicken house ahead and the big barn to my left, and it strikes me how much of my past is rooted in this place. And how much of it is gone forever. When you're Amish, there are no photos. There are no corny albums or school pictures or embarrassing videos. My parents have long since passed, which means everything that happened here, both good and bad, exists only in my memory and the memories of my siblings. Maybe that's why I can't stay away. No matter how many times my brother hurts me, I always come back, like a puppy that's been kicked but knows no other place to be, no other comfort.

I want to share this part of my past with Tomasetti. I want him to stand in the shade of the maple tree while I tell him about the day Datt and I planted it. How proud I'd been when the buds came that first spring. I want to walk the fields with him and show him where the fallen log was that I took our old plow horse over when I was thirteen years old. I want to show him the pond where I caught my first bass. The same pond that saw Jacob and I duke it out over a hockey game. He might have been older and bigger, but he didn't fight dirty; not when it came to me, anyway. I, on the other hand, was born with the killer instinct he lacked, and he was usually the one who walked away with a black eye or busted lip. He never ratted on me, but I'll never forget the way he looked at me all those times when he lied to our parents to protect me and was then punished for it. And I never said a word.

Tomasetti parks in the gravel area behind the

house and shuts down the engine. The buggy that belongs to my sister, Sarah, and my brother-in-law, William, is parked outside the barn. As I get out of the Tahoe, I see my sister-in-law, Irene, come through the back door with a bread basket in one hand, a plastic pitcher in the other.

She spots me and smiles. *"Nau is awwer bsil zert,* Katie Burkholder!" Now it's about time!

I greet her in Pennsylvania Dutch. *"Guder nammidaag."* Good afternoon.

"Mir hen Englischer bsuch ghadde!" she calls out. We have non-Amish visitors!

The screen door slams. I glance toward the house to see my sister, Sarah, coming down the porch steps juggling a platter of fried chicken and a heaping bowl of green beans. She wears a blue dress with an apron, a *kapp* with the ties hanging down her back, and nondescript black sneakers. "Hi, Katie!" she says with a little too much enthusiasm. "The men are inside. *Sie scheie sich vun haddi arewat."* They shrink from hard work.

Irene sets the pitcher and basket on the picnic table, then spreads her hands at the small of her back and stretches. She's wearing clothes much like my sister's. A blue dress that's slightly darker. Apron and *kapp.* A pair of battered sneakers. *"Alle daag rumhersitze mach tem faul,"* she says, referring to the men. Sitting all day makes one lazy.

"Sell is nix as baeffzes." That's nothing but trifling talk.

At the sound of my brother's voice, I glance toward the house to see him and my brother-in-law, William, standing on the porch. Both men are wearing dark trousers with white shirts, suspenders and straw summer hats. Jacob's beard reaches midway to his waist and is shot with more gray than brown. William's beard is red and sparse. Both men's eyes flick from me to Tomasetti and then back to me, as if waiting for some explanation for his presence. It doesn't elude me that neither man offers to help with the food.

"Katie." Jacob nods at me as he takes the steps from the porch. *"Wie geth's alleweil?"* How goes it now?

"This is John Tomasetti," I blurt to no one in particular.

Next to me, Tomasetti strides forward and extends his hand to my brother. "It's a pleasure to finally meet you, Jacob," he says easily.

While the Amish excel at letting you know you are an outsider—which is usually done for some redemptive purpose, not cruelty—they can also be kind and welcoming and warm. I'm pleased to see all of those things in my brother's eyes when he takes Tomasetti's hand. "It's good to meet you, too, John Tomasetti."

"Kate's told me a lot about you," Tomasetti says.

William chuckles as he extends his hand. *"Es waarken maulvoll gat."* There's nothing good about that.

A giggle escapes Sarah. "Welcome, John. I hope you're hungry."

"I am."

I make eye contact with Tomasetti. He winks, and some of the tension between my shoulder blades unravels.

Neither woman offers her hand for a shake. Instead they exchange nods when I make the introductions.

When the silence goes on for a beat too long, I turn my attention to my sister. "Can I help with something?"

"Setz der disch." Set the table. Sarah glances at Tomasetti and motions toward the picnic table. *"Sitz dich anna un bleib e weil."* Sit yourself there and stay awhile. "There's lemonade, and I'm about to bring out some iced tea."

Tomasetti strolls to the table and looks appreciatively at the banquet spread out before him. "You sure you trust me with all this food?"

Jacob chortles.

"There's more than enough for everyone," Irene says.

William pats his belly. "Even me?"

A gust of wind snaps the tablecloths, and Jacob glances toward the western horizon. "If we're going to beat the storm, we'd best eat soon."

Irene shivers at the sight of the lightning and dark clouds. *"Wann der Hund dich off der buckle legt, gebt's rene."* When the dog lies on his back, there will be rain.

While Tomasetti and the Amish men pour lemonade and talk about the storms forecast for later, I follow the women into the kitchen. I'd been nervous about accepting today's invitation from my brother because I didn't know what to expect. I had no idea how they would respond to me and Tomasetti or the fact that we're living together with no plans to get married. To my relief, no one has mentioned any of those things, and another knot of tension loosens.

The kitchen is hot despite the breeze whipping in through the window above the sink. Sarah and I spend a few minutes gathering paper plates, plastic utensils, and sampling the potato salad, while Irene pulls a dozen or so steaming ears of corn from the Dutch oven atop the stove and stacks them on a platter. We make small talk, and I'm taken aback at how quickly the rhythm of Amish life returns to me. I ask about my niece and nephews, and I learn the kids walked to the pasture to show my little niece, who's just over a year old now, the pond, and I can't help but remember when that same pond was a fixture in my own life. I'd learned to swim in that pond, never minding the mud or the moss or the smell of fish that always seemed to permeate the water.

Back then, I was an Olympian swimmer; I had no concept of swimming pools or chlorine or diving boards. I'd been content to swim in water the color of tea, sun myself on the dilapidated dock, treat myself to mud baths, and dream about all the things I was going to do with my life.

Brandishing a pitcher of iced tea and a basket of hot rolls, I follow the two women outside to the picnic tables. Out of the corner of my eye, I see that Jacob has pulled out his pipe to smoke, a habit that's frowned upon by some of the more conservative Amish. But then that's Jacob for you. He's also one of the few to use a motorized tractor instead of draft horses. In keeping with the *Ordnung*, he only uses steel wheels sans rubber tires. A few of the elders complain, but so far no one has done anything about it.

Within minutes we're sitting at a picnic table, a feast of fried chicken and vegetables from the garden spread out on the blue-and-white-checked tablecloth. At the table next to us, my niece and nephews load fried chicken and green beans onto their plates. I glance over at Tomasetti and he grins at me, giving me an I-told-you-everything-would-be-fine look, and in that moment I'm content.

"Wann der Disch voll is, well mir bede." If the tables are full, let us pray. Jacob gives the signal for the before-meal prayer. Heads are bowed. Next to us, the children's table goes

silent. And Jacob's voice rings out. *"O Herr Gott, himmlischer Vater, Segne uns und Diese Diene Gaben, die wir von Deiner milden Gute Zu uns nehmen warden, Speise und tranke auch unsere Seelen zum ewigen Leben, und mach uns theilhaftig Deines himmllischen Tisches durch Jesus Christum. Amen."*

O Lord God, heavenly Father, bless us and these thy gifts, which we shall accept from thy tender goodness. Give us food and drink also for our souls unto life eternal, and make us partakers of thy heavenly table through Jesus Christ. Amen.

Upon finishing, he looks around, and as if by unspoken agreement, everyone begins reaching for platters and filling their plates.

"The kids have grown so much since I saw them last," I say as I spoon green beans onto my plate.

"It seems like yesterday that Little Hannah was a newborn," my sister says with a sigh. "They grow up so fast."

Jacob slathers homemade butter onto an ear of corn. "Elam drove the tractor last week."

Sarah rolls her eyes. "And almost drove it into the creek!"

"Like father like son," William mutters.

Irene pours a second glass of tea. "Katie, do you and John have any plans for children?"

I can tell by the way the pitcher pauses mid-pour that she realizes instantly her faux pas. Her

32

eyes flick to mine. I see a silent apology, then she quickly looks away and sets the pitcher on the table. "There's tea if anyone's thirsty."

"Maybe they should get married first," Jacob says.

"I love weddings." Sarah shakes pepper onto an ear of corn.

"Any plans for one, Katie?" Jacob asks.

In the interminable silence that follows, the tension builds, as if it were a living thing, growing and filling up space. I'm not sure how to respond. The one thing I do know is that no matter what I say, I'll be judged harshly for it.

"Let's just say we're a work in progress." I smile, but it feels dishonest on my lips because I know now that this Pandora's box has been opened, it's fair game.

"Work?" Jacob slathers apple butter onto a roll. "I don't think getting married is too much work."

"For a man, anyway," Irene says.

"A man'll work harder to stay out of the house." William doesn't look up from his plate. "If he's smart."

"I think Kate's placing the emphasis on the 'in progress' part." Tomasetti grins at Irene. "Pass the corn, please."

"In the eyes of the Lord, the two of you are living in sin," Jacob says.

I turn my attention to my brother. "In the eyes of some of the *Amisch*, too, evidently."

He nods, but his expression is earnest. "I don't understand why two people would want to live like that."

Embarrassment and, for an instant, the familiar old shame creeps up on me, but I don't let it take hold. "Jacob, this isn't the time or place to discuss this."

"Are you afraid God will hear?" he asks. "Are you afraid He will disapprove?"

Tomasetti helps himself to an ear of corn, sets down his fork, and turns his attention to my brother. "If you have something on your mind, Jacob, I think you should just put it out there."

"Marriage is a sacred thing." He holds Tomasetti's gaze, thoughtful. "I don't understand why you choose to live the way you do. If a man and woman choose to live together, they should be married."

All eyes fall on Tomasetti. He meets their stares head-on and holds them, unflinching and unapologetic. "With all due respect, that's between Kate and me. That's the best answer I can give you, and I hope you and the rest of the family will respect it."

My brother looks away in deference. But I know that while he'll tolerate our point of view for now, he'll never agree with it—or give his blessing. "All right then."

I look around the table. Everyone is staring down at their plates, concentrating a little too intently on their food. Across from me, Irene scoots her husband's plate closer to him. "Maybe you should eat your food instead of partaking in idle talk like an old woman."

Sarah coughs into her hand but doesn't quite cover her laugh. "There's date pudding for dessert."

"That's my favorite." Irene smiles at her sister-in-law. "Right after snitz pie."

"I haven't had snitz pie since Big Joe Beiler married Edna Miller," William says through a mouthful of chicken.

I barely hear the exchange over the low thrum of my temper. Don't get me wrong; I love my brother and sister. Growing up, they were my best friends and, sometimes, my partners in crime. There were many things I loved about being Amish: being part of a tight-knit community. Growing up with the knowledge that I was loved not only by my family, but by my brethren. But this afternoon I'm reminded of two things I detested: narrow-mindedness and intolerance.

As if reading my mind, Tomasetti sets his hand on my arm and squeezes. "Let it go," he says quietly.

I'm relieved when my cell phone vibrates against my hip. "I've got to take this," I say, pulling out my phone and getting to my feet.

I walk a few yards away from the picnic tables and answer with my usual: "Burkholder."

"Sorry to bother you on your afternoon off,

Chief. Just wondering if you've been following the weather."

It's Rupert Maddox, but everyone calls him "Glock" because he has a peculiar fondness for his sidearm. A war vet with two tours in Afghanistan under his belt, he's my most solid officer and the first African American to grace the Painters Mill PD.

"Actually, I'm not," I say. "What's up?"

"Weather service just issued a tornado warning for Knox and Richland Counties," he tells me. "We got some serious shit on the way. It just touched down north of Fredericktown."

Thoughts of my family evaporate, and I press the phone more tightly against my ear. "Casualties?" I ask. "Damage?"

"SHP says it's a war zone," he says, referring to the state highway patrol. "There's a tornado on the ground and headed this way, moving fast. Fifteen minutes and we're going to be under the gun."

"Call the mayor. Tell him to get the sirens going."

"Roger that."

But I know that while the tornado sirens are an effective warning for people living in town and will give them time to get into their basements or storm shelters, Holmes County is mostly rural. The majority of people live too far away to hear the sirens. To make matters worse, the Amish don't have TVs or radios and have no way of knowing there's a dangerous storm on the way.

"Call dispatch and tell Lois I want everyone on standby. If things look dicey at the station, she needs to take cover down in the jail."

"Got it."

"Glock, do you and LaShonda have a basement?"

"Got it covered, Chief. I've got a weather radio down there. And a Wii for the kids."

"Good." I look over at the picnic table to see Tomasetti standing, his head cocked, looking at me intently. "Look, I'm at my brother's farm, and we're about nine miles east of town. Can you give me a hand and help me get the word out?"

"I'll take the west side and go door to door. Sheriff's got some deputies out, too."

"Thanks. Do me a favor and stay safe, will you?"

"You, too."

I hit END and stride back to the table. "There's a tornado on the ground west of here and heading this way."

"I thought it looked bad," Irene says, getting to her feet.

Jacob rises. "How close?"

"You've got fifteen minutes to get the animals turned out and everyone in the basement."

William leaves the table and starts toward the buggy where his horse is hitched. "I'm going to turn my gelding out, too."

"I'll help." Jacob starts after him. "Probably ought to put the buggy in the barn."

Tomasetti leans close. "Saved by the tornado," he mutters, but he's already reaching for his smartphone to check radar.

Sarah has snatched up several serving dishes, still mounded with food, and stacked them haphazardly in her arms. Looking harried, Irene herds my niece and nephews toward the back porch. I know there's a door off the kitchen that will take them to the stairs. The basement is a damp, dark room, but it's their best protection against debris if the storm passes over or near the house.

I address Sarah: "Leave the food. You've only got a few minutes. Gather up the kids and get everyone in the basement."

I turn my attention to William and Jacob twenty yards away, already working in tandem to unhitch the horse. "Ten minutes!" I call out to them.

Jacob waves to let me know they're cognizant of the urgency of the situation.

In the few minutes since I received the call, the wind has kicked up. The sky to the west roils with black clouds tinged with an odd shade of green. The tablecloth whips up. A bag of chips flies off. Holding my niece, my sister goes after it, but I call out and stop her.

"Leave it! Take Hannah inside and get into the basement. Now." I glance toward the barn to see

Jacob and William leading the horse toward the gate. "I've got to go."

Surprising me, Sarah trots over, steps close, and presses her cheek against mine. "Be careful, sister."

I give her my best smile. "You, too."

"Kate!"

I glance to my right to see that Tomasetti is already in the Tahoe. Window down, he's turned the vehicle around and is waiting for me. "We've got to go!"

I dash to the SUV, yank open the door, and climb inside. "Where is it?" I ask without preamble.

The tires spew gravel as he starts down the lane. "It just leveled Spring Mountain."

"Shit. *Shit*. That means it's heading northeast."

"Toward Layland. Then Clark."

"And then Painters Mill." I snatch up my phone and speed-dial Glock. "Where are you?"

"I just hit the Stutz place."

"It's headed this way."

"I know."

"Sirens up?"

"Screaming like banshees."

I think for a moment, aware that the engine is groaning, Tomasetti pushing the speedometer to seventy. The wind buffets the vehicle and yanks at the power lines overhead. "I wanted to get down to the mobile home park on the southeast side of town."

"Too far away, Chief. Gotta let it go."

"Shit." Frustrated, I look out the window to see that the trees alongside the road are getting pounded by wind, leaves being torn from branches. It's not raining, but visibility is down due to dust. "I'm going to hit a couple of farms out this way then head to the station."

"See you there."

Outside the vehicle, the wind goes suddenly calm. The leaves of the maple trees shimmer silver against the black sky. Small debris litters the road. Gravel and leaves and small branches with the leaves still attached. Humidity hangs in the air like a wet blanket. I don't have my police radio with me, but Tomasetti has his tuned to the channel used by the Holmes County Sheriff's Department.

"I don't like the looks of this," he says.

I point to a narrow gravel lane shrouded by trees. "Turn here."

He hits the brakes and makes the turn—too fast—down the gravel lane and around the curve to the rear. I'm out of the vehicle before it comes to a complete stop. The first thing I notice are three Amish children playing with a big lumbering puppy in the side yard. The barn door is open, and I see the silhouette of Jonas Miller inside. I run toward the barn while Tomasetti turns the Tahoe around.

"Mr. Miller!" I'm breathless when I step into the doorway of the barn.

The Amish man drops the pitchfork he'd been using and runs out to meet me. *"Was der schinner is letz?"* What in the world is wrong?

"There's a tornado on the way," I tell him in Pennsylvania Dutch. "Get your family into the basement. *Nau.*" Now.

Lightning flashes overhead, so close both of us duck. The wind has picked up again, groaning as it whips around the eaves. Fat drops of rain splat against the gravel and the side of the barn.

"Danki." He brings his hands together and calls out to the playing children. *"Shtoahm! Die Zeit fer in haus is nau!"* Storm! Time to go to the house now!

I run to the Tahoe, wrench open the door. "There's another farm next door."

"No time," he says. "We have to get to the station."

"Tomasetti, half the people in this town don't know there's a tornado on the way."

"We're not going to be any help to them if we're dead."

The tires spin and grab, and then we're barreling down the lane. Too fast. Tires scrambling for traction in loose gravel. The trees on either side of us undulate like underwater plants caught in a white-water rapid. I glance to the west. A swirling black wall cloud lowers from the sky like a giant anvil about to crush everything in its path.

By the time we reach the end of the lane, the first hailstones smack hard against the windshield and bounce off the hood. Tomasetti hauls the wheel left. The Tahoe fishtails when he hits the accelerator, and then we're flying down the road at double the speed limit.

I see his phone lying in the console and snatch it up. The tiny screen blinks on. He's pulled up the National Oceanographic and Atmospheric Administration Web site with a live radar image of Painters Mill and vicinity. I see the flashing red of TORNADO WARNING at the bottom of the page and the magenta-colored mass of the storm moving across the map.

I set down the phone and look around. "It's right on top of us."

"Behind us. Close, though."

I swivel, look through the back window, and I almost can't believe my eyes. Rain slams down from a black sky, close but not yet upon us. *It's chasing us,* I think. Beyond, I can just make out the outline of a darker cloud on the ground, impossibly wide, and a quiver of fear moves through me. I look at Tomasetti. "Our place okay?" I ask.

"I think so."

"Tomasetti, this thing's going to get that mobile home park."

"Probably." Looking tense, he frowns at me. "No time, Kate."

I want to argue. Tell him that if we hurry, we can make it. I can use the bullhorn. It'll only take a few minutes. But I know he's right. We're out of time.

Instead, I rap my fist against the dash. *"Damn* it!"

We enter the corporation limits of Painters Mill doing sixty. Outside the vehicle, the emergency sirens blare, a sound that invariably raises the hairs on the back of my neck. The town has a hushed feel, as if it's holding its breath in anticipation of violence. Paper, trash, and leaves skitter along the sidewalk and street, like small animals running for cover. Some of the shopkeepers along Main Street took the time to close the awnings to protect their windows. Judging from the size of the wall cloud, I don't think it will help.

The sky opens as we fly past the city building. Through the curtain of rain, I spot Councilman Stubblefield dashing up the steps two at a time, wrenching open the door. Then the deluge of rain blinds us. The wipers are already cranked on high, but they're useless. It's as if we've driven into a bottomless body of water and we're on our way to the murky depths.

"There's Lois's Caddy."

I can barely make out the silhouette of her Cadillac parked in its usual spot. "Police radio is probably going nuts."

The SUV skids to a stop beside the Caddy.

"Hopefully she's in the basement by now." Tomasetti jams the vehicle into Park, yanks out the key, and throws open the door.

Through the rain streaming down the windshield, I see a large plastic trash can tumble down the sidewalk. I shove open my door. The wind jerks it from my grip. Wind and rain slash my face with a ferocity that takes my breath. Grabbing the door, I slam it shut and sprint toward the station. The wind howls, harmonizing weirdly with the scream of the sirens. Hailstones hammer down hard enough to bruise skin. Tomasetti reaches the door first and ushers me inside.

I'm soaked to the skin, but I don't feel the cold or wet. Lois stands at the dispatch station, headset askew, her expression frazzled. "Chief! All hell's breaking loose!"

"You okay?" I ask.

"Scared shitless. Never seen it like this."

On the desktop in front of her, the radio hisses and barks with activity. The switchboard rings incessantly. On the shelf behind her, a weather radio broadcasts the latest warning from the National Weather Service.

"You got radar up anywhere?" Tomasetti asks as he strides to the dispatch station.

Lois motions to the computer monitor on her desk. "Been watching it for fifteen minutes now, and I swear it's the scariest damn storm I've ever seen."

"Flashlights?"

"There." She indicates two Maglites on her desktop. "Batteries, too."

I come up behind Tomasetti to look at the screen, and I almost can't believe my eyes. A wide swath of magenta with the telltale "hook echo," indicating rotation, hovers west of Painters Mill, moving ever closer with every blip of the heading flash.

"It's almost on top of us," I say.

"Worst of it's to the south," he counters.

"Lots of 911 calls coming in from that trailer park down there." Lois thumbs a button on the switchboard, takes another call. "Yes, ma'am. We know. There's a tornado on the ground. You need to take cover immediately in a storm shelter or your basement." She pauses. "Then get into your bathtub and cover yourself with sofa cushions, a mattress, or blankets." Pause. "Take your son with you. I know it's scary. Get in the tub. Right now." More incoming calls beep, but she shows no impatience.

I can't stop thinking about that mobile home park. A lot of young families live out there. A lot of children. There are no basements. No storm shelters. No place to go.

A few years ago, I volunteered to help with the cleanup of Perrysburg, Ohio, which is about two hours northwest of Painters Mill, after an F2 tornado ripped through the township. There were no fatalities, but many serious injuries occurred, mostly to individuals who tried riding out the storm inside their mobile homes.

"Stay away from the windows," Lois instructs the caller. "Put the older kids in the closet. Cover them with the mattress. Take the baby and get in the tub. Take care."

Tomasetti looks away from the computer monitor. "Any way to forward 911 calls to the basement?"

"I can forward the switchboard to the extension down there." Lois's fingers fly over the buttons. "Done."

"We need to take cover." Tomasetti snaps his fingers at Lois. "Headset off. Now." When she doesn't comply fast enough, he eases it from her head and motions toward the hallway. "Let's—"

The front window implodes. Glass flies inward. Lois yelps. Something large gets tangled in the blinds. The wind roars like a jet engine. Water soaks the floor instantly.

"Let's go!" Tomasetti shouts, grabbing the weather radio.

Lois scrambles from her chair and dashes to the hall. I'm a few feet behind her with Tomasetti to my right. Around us the building shudders and creaks. Behind me I hear more glass breaking. The blinds flap wildly. We're almost to the basement door, when we're plunged into darkness.

For an instant I'm blind, the meager light from outside unable to penetrate the shadows of the hall. Tomasetti flicks on a flashlight, shoves the other one into my hand. I turn it on, yank open the door. We descend the stairs, our feet muffled against the carpet.

The basement is a dank, dark room equipped with a single jail cell, a duty desk, and a couple of antiquated file cabinets. I shine my light on the desk, and Lois goes directly to the phone and snatches it up. "Dead," she tells us.

I grapple for my cell and call Sheriff Mike Rasmussen on his personal number. He answers on the first ring.

"You guys okay up there?" I begin.

"Went to the south of us," he says. "You?"

"Not sure yet. We're in the basement. I think we're going to take a direct hit."

"You have access to radar?"

"Yeah."

"There's going to be damage, Kate. That damn thing's half a mile wide and chewing up everything in its path."

I tell him about the mobile home park. "I couldn't get to them, Mike. If that park takes a direct hit, there are going to be casualties."

"Pomerene and Wooster are on standby," he tells me, referring to the two nearest hospitals. "Electric and gas companies are gearing up for power outages and gas leaks." He sighs. "Soon as we're in the clear, I'll have my guys head down to that trailer park."

"Thanks, Mike. We should be in the clear here in a few minutes."

"Call if you need anything."

I end the call and look at Tomasetti. He's standing a few feet away, dividing his attention between me and his smartphone, watching the radar.

Above us, the ceiling rattles and groans. My ears pop, and I hear the ungodly roar of a train careening down rickety tracks. In the beam of my flashlight, dust motes fly, shaken loose by the vibration from above, and in the back of my mind I find myself hoping the building holds.

Tomasetti looks away from his phone and makes eye contact with me. I can tell by his expression the news isn't good. "National Weather Service thinks it may have been an F3 that touched down to the west earlier."

I recall the level of damage I'd seen in Perrysburg after that F2, and the knot of worry in my chest draws tight.

He crosses to me, his expression grim. "Do you have an emergency preparedness plan?" he asks.

"Of course we do." Realizing I'm snapping at him when he's just trying to help, I take a deep breath. "I should have thought of that." I step away from him, work my phone from my pocket. "I'll call the mayor."

Auggie answers on the first ring. "Kate. Thank God. Where are you?"

"At the station."

"Everyone okay?"

"Fine. You?"

"Except for the damn maple tree in my kitchen, we're just peachy."

Auggie and his wife live in a nice neighborhood of historic homes and mature trees on the north side of town. "Auggie, is there much damage? Did the tornado get your neighborhood?"

"Aside from that tree, I don't think so. But the wind was . . . unbelievable."

"Look, I think we need to activate the emergency contingency plan."

The mayor goes silent for a moment, as if trying to remember what it is. The truth of the matter is, since its inception two years ago, we've never had to use it.

"You've got a copy of the plan, right?" I ask.

"Uh, yes. Here in my file, I think." But he doesn't sound too sure of that, and I don't think he knows what to do.

I have a copy of it here at the station, but Mayor Auggie is the official coordinator. "You probably need to notify the Red Cross first," I tell him. "I suspect we're going to have casualties. Gas leaks. Power outages. We're going to have citizens in need of food and water and shelter."

"Right."

"Our designated shelter is the VFW hall," I tell him. "You might give Rusty a call and have him get things ready. I think they've got some cots and blankets and bottled water over at the Lutheran Church."

"Sure. Sure. I'll call him."

"Look, I've got to get out there. I'll call my officers and get everyone out helping. Phones are down at the station. If you need something, I've got my cell."

I disconnect and look at Tomasetti. "I don't have time to drive back to the farm for my Explorer, so I'm going to have to commandeer your vehicle." I'm only half kidding.

He's already got his keys in hand. "You've got a driver, too, if you want it."

"I do." I look at Lois. "Call everyone in the department. Make sure they're okay. Then I want every officer on duty. Pickles and Mona, too. Unless they're dealing with their own emergency. First priority is the injured, most critical first. We're setting up a temporary shelter at the VFW."

"Gotcha."

"Call one of the guys—T.J. or Skid—and get them to fire up that generator for you so we have power here at the station. It might be a while before we get our power back, and I'd like to get the phones up and running."

"Okay."

I take the stairs two at a time to the top. Tomasetti and Lois bring up the rear. Then I'm through the door, and as I tread down the hall, I feel the cool, damp air coming through the broken window. Outside, the tornado sirens wail their eerie song. Though it's late afternoon, it's nearly as dark as night, so I turn on the Maglite.

I reach the reception area and look around. My heart sinks as I take in the damage. The blinds flap in the wind coming in through the window. Rain sweeps in with every gust. Water glistens on the floor. An aluminum trash-can lid is lodged between the blinds and the sill. Shards of glass, chunks of wood, and other small debris—leaves and twigs and trash—litter the floor. There's paper everywhere.

"Looks like we dodged the bullet here," comes Tomasetti's voice from behind me.

"Computer and radio are dry." It's the only positive comment I can come up with.

"Oh my God." Lois looks a little shell-shocked as she walks over to her desk. "Want me to call that glass guy up in Millersburg about that window?"

Usually we require three estimates on any work done for the township. Since time—and security —are at issue here, I reply with, "Get him down here within the hour. If he can't replace the glass today, I want it secured some other way. Lois, if

51

you smell any gas or smoke, get out and call the gas company and then call me."

"Okeydoke." She rounds the reception desk and gets behind the phone console, which is eerily silent.

"I'm going to go down to the trailer park to see if anyone's hurt," I tell her. "Call me if you need anything."

Outside the window, the rain pours down, slapping against the concrete like a thousand angry fists.

Chapter 2

It's an unsettling experience to drive through a place you've been a thousand times and not recognize it. Tomasetti and I are in his Tahoe heading south on Township Road 18. The closer we get to the Willow Bend Mobile Home Park, the worse the damage becomes, until it's an unrecognizable war zone. Mud and debris cover the asphalt. Power lines dangle like dead snakes from telephone poles that list at a 45-degree angle. The air smells of gas and burning plastic.

Tomasetti slows the Tahoe, his eyes scanning the area to my right. I'm about to ask him why he's slowed down, when I realize we've arrived at our destination. I didn't recognize it because half of the trailer homes are gone.

"Is this it?" he asks.

For an instant I can't speak. I don't know how to put the disbelief roiling inside me into words. I never liked this place; I didn't much care for some of the people I came in contact with here. Willow Bend was the epitome of a neighborhood on the decline. The Painters Mill PD took more calls from this dismal trailer park than from the rest of the town combined. Drunk and disorderly. Domestic violence. Loud music. Loose dogs. The occasional burglary. But I never wanted this. I never wanted it gone.

The maple tree that had stood guardian at the entrance since I was a kid is gone. The only sign that it had ever existed is the jagged-edged stump that juts three feet from the earth like an abscessed tooth that's burst.

As I look out over the land, I wonder if this is what it's like in the aftermath of war. Dozens of mobile homes have been torn apart and lie in pieces. Several have rolled off their foundations. Others have been smashed by trees. Farther in, I see the back end of a pickup truck protruding from the side of a double-wide. An hour ago, this park had housed nearly thirty mobile homes— young couples and families and singles just starting their lives. Children had played in the postage-stamp-size yards. Barbeque grills and hibachis had been set up on decks. Cars had been parked in concrete driveways. Taking in the devastation, I know I'm going to find things I don't want to find. I'm going to see things I don't want to see.

I feel Tomasetti's eyes on me, but I don't look at him. Instead, I snatch up my phone and speed-dial the mayor. He answers on the first ring, sounding harried and stressed.

"Willow Bend is devastated," I tell him. "We're going to have casualties."

"Aw . . . no."

"I need you to get paramedics and the fire department out here. Ambulances." I run out of breath, my lungs fluttering as if the air were suddenly too thin, and I realize I don't even know if there are any survivors. "Auggie, get the sheriff's department out here. Call the gas company. Tell them we've got a leak."

"Okay. Okay. I'll take care of it right now."

I disconnect and look at Tomasetti. "I need to get in there."

He doesn't look happy about it, but he knows better than to argue. Glancing in the rearview mirror, he drives ten yards into the park before our route is blocked by the exterior wall of a mobile home that has been shorn off. I see tufts of insulation and jagged two-by-fours and wooden paneling with a framed picture still attached.

I throw open the door and get out. For an instant, I stand there, frozen and mute because the devastation is so overwhelming I don't know where to begin. Vaguely I'm aware of Tomasetti's door slamming. Of him coming around to stand next to me.

"Watch for live wires," he says. "If you smell gas, if you hear it, back off. Don't go in."

Nodding, I start toward the nearest mobile home. It's a blue-and-white single-wide that's been pushed off its pad and onto a pickup truck parked in the driveway. "Painters Mill PD!" I shout. "Is there anyone there? Do you need help?"

The words feel absurd coming out. Of course, the people who live here need help. The question is: Are they able to ask for it? Are they able to move? Are they still *alive?* I move closer to the wreckage. I hear hissing, but there's no odor of gas. That's when I realize there's a slow leak in one of the truck tires. In the distance, emergency vehicle sirens begin to blare.

A sound reaches me over the cacophony. A tiny cry, like the mewling of a kitten. I glance over at Tomasetti, who's standing a dozen feet away from me. I can tell by his expression he heard it, too.

"What was that?" But I'm already jogging toward a second overturned mobile home. It's a green-and-white Liberty, lying on its side, a heap of twisted metal, busted two-by-fours, and clumps of insulation. The big bay window at the narrow end is shattered, yellow curtains spilling out and soaked with mud. "Police department!" I call out. "Is anyone in there?"

Ever watchful for live wires and the smell of gas, I reach the window. There's glass everywhere. Indistinguishable pieces of metal. Splinters of wood. I wish for gloves as I kneel and peer in the window. I see a vintage refrigerator lying face down against caved-in cabinets. Water trickling from a broken pipe below the sink to my right. Carpet buckled over a floor that's been split. "Police! Is anyone in there? Are you injured?"

The cry comes again, so clear this time the hairs at my nape stand on end. A baby. Not just a baby, but a newborn, gasping as if trying to cry. "Tomasetti!"

I hear him, already on the phone, calling the fire department for assistance. Mud and glass shards forgotten, I drop to my hands and knees. I yank the curtains from the window, toss them aside. Then I'm slithering through the opening. "Police! Do you need assistance?"

Tomasetti comes up behind me, hooks a finger in my belt loop from behind. "The fire department is two minutes away."

"I think the baby is in distress," I tell him.

"Goddamn it." But he releases me.

Glass slices my elbow, but I don't stop. Then I'm inside a kitchen turned upside down. The refrigerator lies in my way, so I rise to a crouch, ding my head on an open cabinet door. Ahead I see a living room. A shattered television. A sofa lying upside down. A playpen, one side crushed.

The cry comes again. The strangled sound of a drowning kitten. *Not right,* a little voice whispers inside my head, and I know the infant is either terrified or injured or both. I move past the cabinet door and stand. The smell of gas makes me hesitate. It scares me because I know if there's enough built up, one spark and the place could explode. But there's no way I can walk away and leave an injured child behind.

"Hello!" I hear fear in my voice now. Urgency pushes me forward. "Police! Is someone there?"

On the other side of the sofa I see a blanket and bed linens. A stuffed animal. A bunny. I start when I see an adult female lying facedown, a coffee table on top of her. "Ma'am?"

No response.

"Shit."

I turn my head, see Tomasetti crawling through the window, his expression grim. "I've got a woman in here," I tell him. "She's not moving."

"Kate, we've got gas in here."

But in the next instant he's standing beside me and we're moving forward, stumbling over a kitchen chair, crunching through broken glass and splintered paneling.

I reach the woman first. She's wearing an Ohio State sweatshirt. Denim shorts. White legs smeared with blood. "Ma'am?"

She groans, a deep, raw sound. When she looks at me, her eyes are dull and unfocused. "Wha—? I don't . . . what happened." Realization kicks in, and then she screams, "Lucy!" She moves, and then, "Oh, God! My leg! Ohmigod!"

I kneel beside her. "I'm a police officer. Try to stay calm. We're going to get you out of here." I run my eyes over her, looking for visible injuries, and wince at the sight of the white-pink bone protruding through the skin at her shin. *Compound fracture. Jesus.* "Where else are you hurt? Are you in pain?"

"My leg!" she cries. "Oh, God! It hurts like a son of a bitch!"

"Ma'am, is there a child here with you? Anyone else?"

"Lucy," she whimpers. "My baby! She was right here. I was holding her when everything just . . . exploded. Oh, God. Ohmigod! Where is she?" She rolls onto her side and lets out a scream that makes every nerve in my body jump.

"I'll find her. You just lie still." I look over at the playpen. Fear swirls in my gut when I see a tiny hand protruding from beneath it. Little fingers curled and not moving. In the back of my mind, it registers that I haven't heard a cry in several seconds. *She should be crying.*

"I see her," I say.

"Where? Where is she? *Where is she!*"

"We've got her." Tomasetti kneels, sets his hand on the woman's shoulder. "What's your name?"

"P-Paula," she says. "Paula Kester."

I don't think about what I'm doing as I stumble past a splintered table. I fall to my knees, set my hands on the playpen rails, and lift it. I choke out a sound when I see the tiny baby. Its face is blue and scrunched up. Mouth open and quivering. I see pink gums. Eyes that aren't quite right. Blood on its chin. Glass shimmers on a little onesie that's been nearly torn from its tiny body.

Holding the playpen up with one arm, I reach for the infant. Her skin is wet and cool to the touch. I know better than to move an injured patient. If they have a spinal injury, any kind of movement could do more harm than good. But with the smell of gas present, I don't have a choice.

"Come here, little one." Grasping the baby's ankle, I pull her toward me as gently as I can manage. "I've got you, sweetheart. You're okay. You're safe now."

"Lucy?" comes the mother's voice. "Why isn't she crying? *Why isn't she crying?*"

When the baby is clear, I lower the playpen and carefully lift her into my arms. "I've got her."

I glance over to see the woman propped on an elbow. Her face is bleeding and red, her expression twisted in pain, tears streaming from her eyes. "My baby! Oh, my baby! Is she hurt? *What's wrong with her?*"

"We need to get you out of here. Both of you. Right now." Tomasetti's voice cuts through her panic. Deep. Authoritative. No room for argument.

I glance over to see him shoving debris aside, his eyes on the woman. "There's a gas leak," he tells her, "so I'm going to lift you and carry you out through that window over there. That all right with you?"

"Oh, God. Gas. Please! Just take care of my baby."

I hold the child against my chest. I make eye contact with Tomasetti as I brush past him and start toward the window. The smell of gas is stronger now. Building inside the small space. I quicken my pace.

Behind me, I hear the woman moaning. Tomasetti reassuring her as he moves her. I stumble past toppled furniture, the buckled floor, the overturned refrigerator. The baby is limp and soft and frighteningly quiet in my arms as I drop to my knees and scrabble through the window. Holding her against me with one arm, doing my best to protect her from the glass and splintered frame, I crawl through. All I can think about is getting the baby out.

Then I'm free of the trailer. On my knees, holding the child against me. I turn, relieved to see Tomasetti a few feet behind me. He's carrying the woman. I see exertion in his face. Stress in the way his mouth is pulled tight. A moan of pain tears from her throat with every step he takes.

Sirens blare all around. I look over to see a Painters Mill fire truck next to Tomasetti's Tahoe. Clutching the baby, I jog toward the firefighter as he disembarks. A tremor of fear moves through me when I glance down and see that the baby's face is purple.

"She's not breathing!" I scream. "I need a paramedic!"

Tossing his hat onto the ground, the firefighter sprints toward me, arms forward and reaching. "Is she choking? Is her airway clear?"

"I don't know! She was beneath a piece of furniture."

Gently, he takes the baby. His face tightens at the sight of her. Without speaking he moves her farther from the mobile home and drops to his knees. He lays the child on the ground and checks for a brachial pulse. He glances up, shakes his head at a second paramedic approaching. Then, using two middle fingers, he begins rapid chest compressions. "How long has she been quiet?" he asks me, without stopping.

"A minute," I say. "Maybe two. At first she was crying and then . . ."

Thirty compressions, and he sets his hand beneath the infant's neck, pinches her nostrils.

Sealing a tiny rescue mask over the infant's mouth, he gives two short breaths.

The second firefighter reaches us, a stretcher in one hand, an AED kit—a defibrillator—in the other. He drops to his knees beside the first responder, opens the kit, removes the pads. "I need her dry," he says, yanking a paper sheet from the kit.

Quickly, he dries the child. The other paramedic tugs off the infant's onesie. I see a tiny torso. Blue-tinged skin. Unmoving arms and legs. Vaguely, I'm aware of the woman screaming from somewhere nearby. Of sirens and the incessant blare of the tornado warning system. There are a hundred other things I should be doing; there's a gas leak and downed power lines and undoubtedly more casualties. But I can't move. I can't look away from that baby and the two men working to save her life.

The second paramedic removes two electrode pads from the kit, placing one on the infant's chest, the other on the baby's back, sealing them tightly against the skin. All the while a mechanical voice from the AED intones instructions. "Analyzing rhythm. Stand clear. Shock advised."

"Kate."

Tomasetti's voice reaches me as if through a fog. I feel his hand on my arm. I want to say something. Let him know I'm okay. I can handle this. I want to reassure the mother, take her hand and tell her the child is going to be all right. But I don't know if any of that is true. Despite our efforts, I don't know if the baby is going to make it.

Vaguely, I'm aware of my phone vibrating against my hip. Tomasetti pulling me away from the paramedics. "Let them work," he tells me.

Finally, I look at him. Even in the midst of all this chaos, I realize, his worry is for me. Illogical anger burgeons in my chest. I want to rail, tell him this isn't about me. My small world and petty emotions and discomforts don't matter. The only thing that matters is a tiny heart that's stopped and a young life that must not be lost.

Around us several more responders arrive. Men in pickup trucks who are volunteers for the fire department. I hear shouting. Voices filled with urgency and stress. Orders being given. A second ambulance pulls up, and two more paramedics disembark. Twenty yards away, a large truck with the electric company logo emblazoned on the door pulls up to a downed telephone pole where a transformer crackles and pops. In the midst of it all, I can still feel the echo of warmth where the tiny body was pressed against me.

"Kate."

I turn my attention to Tomasetti, blink at him, pull myself back.

"I just heard from Glock," he tells me. "The Maple Crest Subdivision got hit, too."

In the back of my mind a little voice demands to know, *Isn't this enough?* "Casualties?" I ask, instead.

"He didn't know. Plenty of damage, though."

"Shit." My phone has been vibrating nonstop. I yank it out and snap my name.

"Chief!"

It's Chuck "Skid" Skidmore, one of my other officers. He's usually the cocky one, the one who always seems to find some smidgen of inappropriate humor in just about any situation, no matter how dire. Alarm rings hard in his voice. "I got power lines on top of a vehicle out here on Hogpath Road. A woman with a bunch of kids inside."

"You call the power company?"

"They're on the way."

"Keep them in the vehicle, Skid. Tell them to roll up the windows. Don't get too close."

"Roger that."

I end the call and look down at my phone to see I have six messages and a dozen texts. I reach for calm, force my emotions back. Two of the calls are from dispatch, so I press the speed dial for Lois. "You okay?" I begin.

"I'm good." But she's breathless and sounds stressed. "Power's out everywhere. Pickles started that generator, so we got radio and phones and both are going nuts." She takes a deep breath, blows it out slowly. "You heard about Maple Crest?"

"I'm heading that way now," I tell her. "Any word on casualties?"

"I checked with Pomerene a few minutes ago. They have two critical. One fatality. More coming in and lots of minor injuries." A hysterical laugh bubbles up from her. "I just took a ten-fifty-four a half a mile south of town."

The code 10-54 is for loose livestock on the road, a call I always take seriously due to the likelihood of a motor vehicle accident. "Dispatch Pickles."

"Ten-four."

"I'm ten-seventy-six Maple Crest."

"Roger that."

I end the call and take a deep breath. I look at Tomasetti. Behind him I see the ambulance with the baby inside pull onto the road, sirens blaring. I don't let myself think about the tiny newborn I'd held in my arms just minutes ago. The one whose warmth I can still discern. The one who, of all of us, is an innocent and deserves to live.

Chapter 3

I long for my police radio, as Tomasetti and I head east toward the Maple Crest subdivision. Drizzle floats down from a granite sky, smudging the trees and fields into a gothic, impressionist-style painting. The storm that brought the tornado is already past and heading northeast toward Geauga County, where new tornado warnings have been posted.

I've pulled up the weather radar on Tomasetti's phone. The storm track shows the twister plowed a path from southwest to northeast. Most of the affected area was rural, but I know there are farmhouses and barns at risk. As the storm approached Painters Mill, it veered north and gobbled up half of the mobile home park. It then lifted briefly and touched down a second time on top of the subdivision. The homes are sturdier there—brick and stucco, mostly—and while I anticipate plenty of damage, I don't think it will be as bad as Willow Bend.

We've just turned onto Dogleg Road, when I spot a lone figure ahead, walking toward us on the gravel shoulder.

"What the hell?" Tomasetti pulls over several yards from the man.

He's wearing trousers and a long-sleeve shirt

with one of the sleeves torn off at the shoulder. His clothes are soaked and muddy. As he draws closer I notice the suspenders hanging at his sides. No hat. No jacket. One boot on his left foot; the other is bare. The only indication that he's Amish is the long beard. Though I'm certain he sees the Tahoe, he doesn't stop walking. He doesn't acknowledge us. It's as if he doesn't even see us.

"Looks like he's in shock," Tomasetti says.

"I'm going to make sure he's all right." I've got the door open before we've come to a complete stop. Then I'm out of the truck. Rain soft and cold on my face. I can hear the ducks in the pond on the other side of a falling-down fence. The tinkle of the drizzle against the water's surface.

I keep my eyes on the man ahead. But I'm aware of Tomasetti sliding from the truck. The slam of his door as he leaves it to follow me.

"Sir?" I call out. "I'm a police officer. Are you all right?"

The man stops and looks at me as if seeing me for the first time. His face is streaked with mud. The missing shirtsleeve reveals the pasty flesh of an arm that's covered with mud and specks of vegetation. His shirt is shredded, pasted to his body by rain and mud. He's visibly shivering. His beard is clotted with vegetation, flecks of dead grass, and mud.

His eyes peer at me from a pale face smeared with mud. *"Ich sayya Gott,"* he whispers. I saw God.

"Are you injured?" I stop a couple of feet away. "Are you hurt? Do you need help?"

He shakes his head. *"Ich bin zimmlich gut."* I'm pretty good.

"What's your name?" I ask.

"Samuel Miller."

Tomasetti comes up beside me. "What are you doing out here all by yourself without a buggy?"

He looks at Tomasetti, then motions in the direction he was walking. "I was delivering straw to Big Joe Beiler's place. That old mare of his is about to foal."

I look past him, but there's no sign of a wagon. Or a horse. "Where's your wagon?"

"Wind caught it just right. Turned it over. The straw got dumped."

"Is there anyone else with you?" I ask.

"Just me."

"Your horse okay?"

"Sellah gaul is goot." The horse is good. "Spooked. She ran home, like they always do, and left me to walk." He grins. "Just like a female."

"I think you should get yourself checked out at the hospital, Mr. Miller," I tell him. "Maybe you hit your head when the wagon overturned. I'm happy to take you."

The Amish man thinks about that a moment.

"My head is fine. But I'd like to check on my family and make sure they're all right."

I touch his arm gently to get him started toward the Tahoe; all the while I look for signs of injury or confusion. "Where's your farm, Mr. Miller?"

"A mile or so down the road."

"The worst of the storm missed your house," I tell him. "I think you'll find your family just fine."

"I guess it wasn't my day to be called to heaven," he says.

Under normal circumstances, I wouldn't give him a choice about a trip to the ER; I'd take him directly to the hospital despite his objections. Today, however, with Pomerene Hospital undoubtedly flooded with casualties, I decide to comply with his wishes and take him home. I open the door of the Tahoe and he climbs inside.

It's 4:30 a.m. by the time Tomasetti and I pull into the driveway of my old house in Painters Mill. We've spent twelve hours responding to calls, assisting the injured, searching for the missing, assessing damage, and reporting downed power lines and gas leaks to the proper authorities. The last four hours were spent at the Willow Bend Mobile Home Park, helping firefighters with their search-and-rescue efforts. Casualty information has begun to trickle in from the ER departments of Pomerene Hospital as well as Wooster

Community Hospital. So far the two hospitals have reported twenty-six injured, with eighteen hospitalized in serious or critical condition. There have been two confirmed fatalities so far: Sixty-two-year-old Earl Harbinger's vehicle was flipped by the tornado. He died at the scene. And thirty-seven-year-old mother of two, Juanita Davis, was found dead in her trailer at Willow Bend. She was DOA. All but one of the missing have been accounted for. Twelve-year-old Billy Ray Benson was caught in a flash flood, sucked into a culvert, and washed into Painters Creek. Over thirty volunteers—many of whom had their own homes damaged or destroyed—joined Holmes County Search and Rescue. Because of rough terrain, flooded conditions, and darkness, HCSAR called off the search until first light. I can't imagine what the boy's parents are going through tonight.

The damage is shocking, but in light of the loss of life and serious injury, it's easier to keep in perspective. Homes and businesses can be rebuilt. A life lost is gone forever. The east side of Painters Mill—mainly the Willow Bend Mobile Home Park—was devastated. In the Maple Crest subdivision, nine homes were damaged. Two were leveled, reduced to piles of brick and wood and the broken pieces of people's lives.

Tomasetti and I are beyond exhaustion. Facing another grueling day that will begin in a few hours, we thought the smart thing to do was to stay here in town and grab showers and a couple hours of sleep.

I unlock the door, and we step into a living room that's quiet and cool and smells of a house that's been shut up for a long time. I put the house on the market a couple of weeks ago. I've had several showings but no offers. There's no food, and in the seven months I've lived at the farm with Tomasetti, I've moved most of my personal belongings and some of my furniture. But my bed is still here, and I keep some old linens in the hall closet. Since I've never had the electricity shut off, we have light and hot water for showers.

"Kate."

I'm standing in the doorway between the living room and the kitchen. I glance over at Tomasetti, and for the first time I realize I've tracked mud across the living room.

"Shoes." He motions toward my feet, and I notice he had the forethought to leave his at the door.

"Oh." I try to laugh, but it's a strained, tight sound. Mud on the rug is the last thing on my mind.

Clumps of it fall from my boots as I cross back to the door and kneel to remove them. "I feel like I need to be out there, doing something." I have one shoe on, one off, and I shrug. "Anything."

"I know you do," he says.

"There are people who don't have a place to sleep. They don't have dry clothes. They have nothing to eat or drink."

He frowns at me. "You're not going to do anyone much good if you don't get some sleep."

I toe off my remaining boot. "You know, Tomasetti, I really hate it when you make more sense than I do."

"So sue me." Giving me a reassuring smile, he walks into the kitchen.

As I peel off socks that are wet and brown with mud, I find myself thinking of the infant girl we rescued from the overturned mobile home earlier this afternoon. I've thought of her a dozen times throughout the day but never made the time to call and check on her condition.

I hear Tomasetti moving around the kitchen. Water running. Cabinets opening and closing. Pulling out my phone, I go to the sofa and sit, punch in the number of Pomerene Hospital from memory. I'm put on hold several times before I finally reach the ER. In most cases, hospital personnel will not release patient information to non–family members. But because the circumstances are far from ordinary and I'm a public official with a need for statistics, I'm hoping someone will talk to me, at least in general terms.

"Hi, Chief Burkholder. This is Cat Morrow. How can I help you?"

I've met Cat on several occasions over the years. I don't know her well, but we've exchanged pleasantries. "An infant girl and her mother were brought in earlier this afternoon," I tell her. "The baby's name is Lucy. Last name Kester. I'm wondering if you can tell me how they're doing."

"As you can imagine, it's been a madhouse all day. Let me check." I hear the click of computer keys on the other end. "Here we go: Paula Kester and her child, Lucy Kester. Looks like mama is fine. Going to be released in the morning." More computer keys clicking. "And Lucy Kester. Four-month-old female." A pause, then, "Hmmm. Chief, I'm sorry, but the baby passed away two hours ago. . . ."

The news impacts me like a power punch to the solar plexus. Vaguely, I'm aware of her speaking. Something about a possible spinal cord injury. All the while the words I was loath to hear echo inside my head.

The baby passed away two hours ago.

"Chief Burkholder? You there?"

I'm gripping my phone so tightly my hand shakes. I don't know what to say. I'm not sure how to feel. Guilty because I wasn't able to save her. Angry because once again that bitch Fate was unjust to an innocent who didn't deserve it. Hollowed out because I'm too tired to react to any of it.

"Thanks for the update, Cat. You guys keep up the good work."

I end the call before she can respond. I sit there staring at my phone, my pulse thudding. "Goddamn it," I whisper. *"Goddamn it."*

Up until now I'd been operating on adrenaline. Doing what needed to be done and not thinking about any of it. Suddenly everything I've seen— the horrific injuries, the devastating damage, the senselessness of this random storm and the havoc it has wreaked on so many lives—rushes at me, and like so many times before in my life, I rage at the unfairness of it.

I rise abruptly, but I don't go to the kitchen. I don't want Tomasetti to see me like this. I don't want to share this with him or talk to him or let him know how profoundly I'm disturbed by it. I'm a cop, after all. Good or bad, this is part of the job, and if I'm going to continue being a cop, I'd damn well better handle it. Toughen up. Stop caring so damn much.

I'm midway down the hall, intent on a shower and a few hours of sleep, when Tomasetti's voice stops me. "Where do you keep the glasses?"

I stop, take an instant to settle my emotions, and turn to him. "Second shelf in the cupboard next to the sink."

He nods but doesn't go back into the kitchen to do whatever it was he was doing. He's holding in his right hand the old bottle of bourbon I keep above the refrigerator. A kitchen towel is slung over his shoulder. He's staring at me as if he just realized I'm bleeding.

"What is it?" he asks.

Not for the first time I'm reminded that he is my equal, not a man who will be ignored or lied to or misled. "I just called the hospital," I hear myself say. "To check on the baby from the trailer this afternoon. Tomasetti, she died."

Grimacing, he looks away, uses his free hand to rub the stubble on his jaw. "Damn. I hate it when it's the little kids."

I start to turn, but he strides to me and sets his hand on my arm. "Kate, you know it wasn't your fault, right?"

The nurse's words churn in my brain. *Possible spinal cord injury.* "She was only four months old. So tiny. Why her? It's so incredibly unfair."

"I know." He motions to the kitchen. "Come sit with me for a moment."

I muster a smile. "I'm not very good company right now."

His eyes soften. "I think I can handle it."

I follow him into the kitchen. We sit across from each other at the table. I wait while he pours two fingers of bourbon into glasses that are slightly dusty. "I hate bourbon," I tell him.

"Yeah, but it'll do in a pinch." He shoves the glass at me.

I pick it up and take two big swallows. The

alcohol burns all the way down; the taste makes me shudder. Setting the glass on the table, I twirl it and stare into the amber liquid. "In all the years you've been in law enforcement, do you ever wonder if you're cut out for it?"

"No," he tells me. "But only because I'm too old and set in my ways to start a new career."

"Stop making me smile. If it's not too much to ask, I'd like to feel sorry for myself in peace for a few minutes."

He picks up his own glass and sips, watching me over the rim. "Are you having second thoughts?"

"Yeah," I say, injecting a little attitude into the word. "I mean, being a cop is all I know. It's my identity. Most of the time I love what I do." I shake my head. "Then something like this happens, and I wonder if there's something better out there that doesn't hurt as much."

He looks down at his glass, swirls the liquid inside. "I don't know if you've realized this, Kate, but it's the cops who care that have it the worst. The cops that *feel* something. The ones that feel too much sometimes and can't turn it off. I don't know if you realize this about yourself, but you fall into that category. You have an inherent inability to disconnect emotionally. Maybe you care a little too much." His gaze lands on mine. "In case you're wondering, that's not a criticism but an observation."

"I'm glad you clarified that," I say dryly.

"Look, it's tough not to get involved. We wouldn't be human if we didn't feel that way. Some cases get under your skin. You get pissed off. You get your heart torn to bits. It's happened to all of us at some point, and it doesn't mean you're not a good cop." He tilts his head, makes eye contact with me. "But it's a tough row to hoe, Kate. You're the chief of police in a small town. You have family here. Friends. You care about these people. That's a lot of responsibility, and you don't take any of it lightly. Good for the town. Hard as hell for you."

We fall silent. Around us, the house seems to hold its breath as if in anticipation of our next words, the direction in which the conversation will go. The last thing I want to do is cry. It's an innately humiliating experience, particularly if it happens in front of someone I respect and admire. Like Tomasetti. But I can feel the exhaustion peeling away the layers of control. The ones that even in the face of heartbreak I can usually clutch together in desperation because there's something inside me I don't want him to see.

"She had blue eyes," I whisper. "She looked at me. This brand-new little person. It's like . . . I don't know . . . she knew she was in trouble. And she just handed herself over to me. She was counting on me to help her."

"You did your best. That's all any of us can

do. When it's not enough, you pick up the pieces and you move on."

"That's a good speech, Tomasetti, but sometimes life pulls the rug out from under you. Then what?"

His eyes sharpen on mine. I'm aware of tears on my cheeks, hot and unwelcome. I know I'm overreacting and making a fool of myself. I'm exhausted and overwrought, and had I been a smarter woman, I would have forgone the bourbon and conversation for a shower and bed.

Embarrassed, I rise to leave, but Tomasetti reaches out and stops me. "What are we really talking about here, Kate?"

Something that feels vaguely like panic quivers in my gut. For an instant I consider broaching the subject I've been avoiding for a week now. But I'm in no frame of mind. Not tonight.

I glance down where his fingers are wrapped around my wrist and ease away from him. "I'm going to take a shower and get some sleep."

He releases me but holds me immobile with his eyes. "You know you can always talk to me, right?"

"I know." I give him the best smile I can muster. "Thanks for talking me off the ledge, Tomasetti."

"Anytime," he says.

But I feel his eyes on me as I walk away.

Chapter 4

He'd given up baseball practice for this. According to his mom, he was probably going to have to forgo the away game on Saturday, too. Twelve-year-old Josh Pennington loved baseball almost as much as he loved being an Eagle Scout, but his mom had laid down the law: He couldn't do both. It's too much, she'd said. You have to choose. Luckily for Josh, his dad—who'd been an Eagle Scout *and* played short-stop—saved the day and told him as long as he kept his grades up, he could do both.

It was a lot harder than Josh thought. He'd had to get up at 5:00 a.m. this morning and be at the school by 6:00, where he met the rest of Troop 503 for the bus ride to Painters Mill. It was volunteer day, and they were going to spend it picking up trash and debris left by the tornado that hit the day before. First stop was a farm—or what had once been a farm, anyway—on the edge of town. Scoutmaster Hutchinson had instructed them to clean up the area, and boy was it a mess. Big trees had been knocked down. Men with chainsaws had left an hour ago, leaving branches and trash and chunks of crap every-where. Tin shingles and splintered pieces of lumber from the old barn that had been blown down. It was a good thing most of the troop had turned out, because it was going to take all damn day. If they had to camp, Josh was going to miss practice for sure.

His scoutmaster had started two piles: one for deadfall and lumber, which would be burned later; another pile for any type of steel, which would be loaded into a truck and taken to a recycling center. So far this morning, Josh and his partner for the day, Scott, had been concentrating on dragging branches from a felled maple tree to the fire pile. Hopefully, they'd get to have a bonfire later and maybe some hotdogs and s'mores. Mr. Hutchinson was usually pretty cool about stuff like that.

"Hey, Josh, let's get all them boards over there."

Dropping the branch he'd dragged over to the bonfire, Josh walked over to where his friend was standing and looked down at the old wooden siding scattered over an old concrete footer.

"Musta been a hell of an old barn," Josh said.

"Or a big fuckin' outhouse."

Both boys cracked up at that. Josh's mom didn't like Scott. She called him a smartass and said he cursed too much. Josh didn't tell her those were the two things that made Scott so fun to hang out with.

"Let's do it." Josh bent and picked up a six-foot-long plank. One side had once been painted red, but that must have been a long time ago because most of the paint had faded to gray.

For twenty minutes the boys picked up two-by-fours and busted-up siding and a door that had been split in half, and dragged all of it to the woodpile. Josh was thinking about the bonfire and wondered if Scoutmaster Hutchinson would buy some hotdogs. It wasn't yet noon and already he was starving.

He tugged a long plank from the collapsed floor, when something round and white rolled out from beneath it. At first, Josh thought it was a rock, but it was a little too round and rolled easily. Too light to be a rock. Definitely not a soccer ball. Dropping the plank, he walked over to it and knelt, rolling the thing over with his hand. That was when he saw grinning skeleton teeth and the black holes of eye sockets.

"Holy shit!" Josh lunged to his feet and stumbled back so fast he lost his balance and fell on his butt. "Scott!"

Vaguely, he was aware of his friend laughing as he walked over to him. "If you're freaking out over a mouse, I swear I'm gonna tell Missy Hansch, and she's going to think you're the biggest pussy that ever walked—" Scott let out a short little scream. "Whoa! What the hell is that?"

"It's a fuckin' head!" Josh swallowed a big wad of something gross at the back of his throat.

The two boys exchanged looks. Scott's mouth was open so wide Josh could see the cavities in his back molars. "You mean like a human?"

"Well, duh. You ever seen a cow with teeth like that?"

Both boys crept closer, their eyes glued to their macabre find. "I wonder who it is," Scott whispered.

"I wonder why it's here and not buried in a cemetery or something," Josh said.

"We'd better let Hutchinson know." Scott sighed.

"Jeez, I hope we still get to have a bonfire," Josh said.

I'm standing in the middle of a street littered with twisted sheet metal, pieces of vinyl siding, a paneled door, and other unrecognizable debris. A few feet away, a flowered sofa that's remarkably clean sits in the grass near the curb with a young maple tree draped across it. Farther down, a mangled car has been dropped down on top of an otherwise undamaged double-wide. On the lot next to it, someone has pounded a T-post into the ground and raised an American flag.

A dozen mobile homes are crushed as if some drunken giant staggered through, stepping on everything in his path. Several were blown off their foundations. At least two are completely gone, the pieces of which are yet to be found. At the end of the street, a bulldozer pushes debris into a pile that will eventually be loaded into a truck and hauled to the dump. Pieces of peoples' lives gone in an instant.

Tomasetti and I had risen at the crack of dawn, downed a cup of coffee, and then he'd driven me up to our farm, where I picked up the Explorer. We parted ways after that. Neither of us broached the subject of last night's discussion, and we didn't revisit the death of little Lucy Kester.

The American Red Cross, with its iconic red-and-white disaster-relief step van and a small army of volunteers, was already on scene when I arrived, handing out bottled water, serving up hot food, and passing out teddy bears for the traumatized kids.

"Bad as this is, it's a miracle more people weren't killed."

I turn at the sound of Glock's voice to see him come up behind me. His usually crisp uniform is damp with sweat and streaked with dirt. His trousers are wet from the knee down and clotted with mud.

He shoves a steaming cup of coffee at me. "Thought you might need this."

"I do. Thanks." I sip, burning my lip, but it's worth that pain because it's hot and strong and just what I needed. "You been out with search and rescue?"

He nods. "No sign of the kid yet."

"God, I hope they find him. I can't imagine what the parents are going through."

"No one's going to give up."

I nod. "You know I've got you covered with OT, right?"

"Doesn't matter." Looking out over the destruction, he sips coffee. "I'da been out looking for him anyway."

"I know." I've just taken my second sip of coffee when my cell phone chirps.

"Chief." It's my dispatcher, Lois Monroe.

"What's up?"

"I just took a call from a Boy Scout scoutmaster by the name of Ken Hutchinson. He's got a bunch of kids out at that old barn on Gellerman Road that got hit by the tornado, cleaning up, and he says a couple of boys found a human skull."

I nearly spill my coffee. "Is he sure it's human?"

"He seemed pretty adamant."

Gellerman Road demarks the village limits on the north side of town. Everything north of the road falls under the jurisdiction of the Holmes County Sheriff's Department. Everything on the south side belongs to me. This particular property is on the south.

"Notify county, will you?"

"Roger that."

"Doc Coblentz, too." Dr. Ludwig Coblentz is a local pediatrician and part-time coroner for Holmes County.

"Will do."

"Lois, did Hutchinson say if the skull had a body attached to it?"

"He said there's no skeleton, just a bunch of bones scattered all around."

"I'll be there in five minutes." I hit END and dig for my keys.

"You know it's going to be an interesting call when you have to ask if the skull is attached to the body," Glock says.

"That just about sums it up." I start toward my Explorer. "I'll keep you posted."

I've driven by the old farm dozens of times over the years. It's the kind of place you never take notice of because there's not much there: a dilapidated barn, a couple of smaller out-buildings, a rusty silo set among hip-high weeds. It's background noise in a landscape you never look at twice. Back in the 1970s, the house was struck by lightning and burned to the ground. There'd been no insurance, and the elderly owners —Mr. and Mrs. Shephard—moved in with their grown children, who continued to farm the land.

The first thing I notice is the debris, scattered wooden siding and a big black walnut tree that's been stripped of its leaves. I make the turn into a gravel lane overtaken by weeds and clumps of knee-high grass. The lot looks barren without the old barn, which has been reduced to piles of wooden siding, mangled tin shingles, and massive beams. I see the remnants of a concrete foundation that juts a foot out of the ground like an old man's teeth. The Boy Scout troop is still there, but they're no longer working. Mostly preteens, they've congregated into a circle, sitting on logs or rocks or cross-legged on the ground. Someone has given them bottled water. The boys stare in my direction, and I see several point.

I park behind a yellow school bus. A man in a tan scoutmaster uniform is leaning against an antiquated Jeep, legs crossed at the ankles, talking on his smartphone. He spots me as I exit the Explorer, motions me over, and quickly pockets his phone. He's a slightly chubby man of about forty with graying hair, a mustache, and sun-glasses he's pushed onto his crown.

"Ken Hutchinson?"

"Yes ma'am." He strides toward me, looking excited, his hand outstretched.

"I'm Chief of Police Kate Burkholder."

He shakes my hand with a good bit of vigor. "Thanks for coming so quick."

Shouts erupt from the boys a dozen yards away. I glance their way to see most of them standing, pointing to where the old barn had been. "It's over there! Someone's head! It's a skull! Over there!"

I offer a small smile. "The kids okay?"

"More excited than upset, I'd say, but then that's boys for you."

"We appreciate all of you helping out with the cleanup."

"Well, that's what the Boy Scouts do." He laughs. "Sure didn't expect to find a head, though. Damnedest thing I ever saw."

I motion toward the barn. "You want to show me what your boys found?"

"Yes, ma'am."

With Hutchinson leading the way, we walk along a trampled path that takes us through several inches of mud and knee-high weeds. The sun beats down on my back, and I enjoy the warmth against my skin. I can hear the calls of the red-winged blackbirds as they swoop over the small pond at the rear of the property. We round the fallen trunk of a tree, then I spot the foundation twenty feet away, a worn ridge of concrete. Sure enough, just inside the foundation is the white globe of what looks like a human skull.

I stop outside the foundation and raise my hand to prevent Hutchinson from stepping over it. "Probably best if we don't get too close," I tell him.

"Oh. Sure. Of course."

"Did anyone touch or move anything?" I ask. "The boys?"

"The boys that found it turned over the skull.

They thought it was a rock at first. Then they noticed the teeth and those eye sockets." He shivers with exaggeration. "And they got the heck out of there."

From where I'm standing I can see small black scraps of what looks like the remnants of a garbage bag that's badly deteriorated. The ground has been disturbed, by sneakers and perhaps by the storm. Three feet away, I spot the gray-white length of a larger bone. A femur? Part of what looks like vertebrae. Smaller bones of indiscernible origin.

"Is it human?" Hutchinson asks.

"Looks like it," I tell him.

"Wow. Can't believe we uncovered a *body*." He scratches his head. "How do you think it got here?"

"I don't know," I tell him. "But I'd venture to say it didn't get into that bag without some help."

Chapter 5

An hour later, Dr. Ludwig Coblentz and I are standing near where the old barn had once stood, looking down at a human skull. Usually, a call such as this one—the discovery of human remains—would draw a multitude of law enforcement from multiple agencies. Today, however, most cops in the area are occupied with tornado-related issues, many having worked through the night. Glock swung by earlier to lend a hand taping off the scene, but he got called away on a report of possible looting at a gas station that was damaged by the storm. Until I determine otherwise, this area will be treated as a crime scene.

Mr. Hutchinson has rejoined his scouts, who are now munching on burgers and fries from the McDonald's in Millersburg. They've dragged cut logs into a long row so that they have an unimpeded view of the coroner and me.

"I think they're enjoying this more than that LEGO movie," the doc comments as he slips shoe covers onto his feet.

"It beats picking up trash." I pull on my shoe covers and, together, we enter the scene.

The doc squats next to the skull. "It's definitely human."

I motion toward the femur. "What about that? Is it part of the same skeleton?"

"That's a human femur." He turns slightly, indicates the vertebrae scattered a few feet away. "Those are human as well."

"Any idea how long they've been here?" I ask.

Grunting, he rises and goes to the black equipment bag he had set on the ground on the other side of the foundation. He removes two sets of blue gloves and hands a pair to me. "You know you're going to have to get a forensic anthropologist down here to excavate and remove these bones, don't you?"

"Tomasetti recommended an FA who's worked several cases for BCI." I glance at my watch. "He should be here any time now." I slip my hands into the gloves. "I thought maybe you could give me a ballpark."

"Let's take a closer look." He kneels next to the skull and picks it up. "There's no trace of any soft tissue. Even the hair is gone from the scalp. I have no way of knowing if that's due to time or elements or scavengers. That said, taking into consideration the condition of the bones and our climate here in northeastern Ohio . . . I'd say these bones have been here at least a decade." He shrugs. "Depending on the PH of the soil, the bones themselves will eventually disintegrate or even fossilize. So, probably less than thirty years."

"Pretty large ballpark."

"You asked." He frowns, but I see amusement behind his bifocals. "I really can't get you any closer than that."

"Can you tell if the person was male or female?"

"There's no pelvis in sight, *but* . . ." Tilting his head back slightly, the doc lifts the skull, brushing away a bit of soil, and studies it through his bifocals. "This isn't foolproof, Chief, but even with my proletarian eye, I can see that there's a pronounced supraorbital ridge." He runs a finger over the spot above the eye sockets, about where the brow would be. "I can't tell you for certain, but I would venture to say this skull belonged to a male."

"Age?"

He shakes his head. "No clue."

I look around. The dirt is smooth and hard-packed. There are several pea-size pebbles and other debris. A few bones scattered about, some partially buried. "There don't seem to be enough bones here for a full skeleton," I say.

"You're right; there's not."

"Could be buried."

"Maybe." He sets down the skull and looks around. "Or if animals had access to this area, the bones could have been carried off or even consumed over the years."

I indicate the small fragments of what looks like black plastic. "Those pieces," I say, pointing. "Is it plastic? Fabric? Clothing, maybe?"

His shoe covers crinkle as he crosses to one of the larger fragments and bends for a closer look. "Some kind of nonporous material. Quite deteriorated."

I squat beside him. "Doc, it looks like pieces of a garbage bag."

He tosses me a knowing look. "That doesn't bode well for whatever happened to this individual."

Uneasy questions pry into my brain. Did this person suffer some kind of fall and die? Was he crawling around under the old barn and got stuck? Was he working down here and suffered a heart attack? Or did someone murder him, place his body in a garbage bag, and dump it?

I think about the scarcity of bones, and something dark nudges at my brain. "If those fragments are indeed from some type of bag—a garbage bag, for example—we could be looking at foul play."

"Bones always have a story to tell," the doc says to me.

"I suspect the owner of these particular bones didn't have a happy ending."

It takes nearly three hours for the forensic anthropologist to arrive. I used the time to start documenting the scene, taking several dozen photographs, including close-ups of the bones and the scraps of plastic, as well as the surrounding ground. I also walked the immediate area, looking for anything that might offer an explanation for the bones or for additional bones scattered by animals. I'm sipping a bottle of water one of the Boy Scouts brought over to me, when Tomasetti's Tahoe, a Holmes County Sheriff's Department cruiser, and a silver Prius pull in and park in the weeds a prudent distance from the scene.

Doc is sitting in his Escalade, talking on his smartphone. A Holmes County deputy and I are standing near my Explorer, exchanging theories and getting sunburned. Two men I don't recognize get out of the Prius. Sheriff Mike Rasmussen is the driver of the sheriff's department cruiser. The four men approach.

"I heard someone found some bones out here," the sheriff says.

I give his hand a firm shake. "A couple of Boy Scouts found a skull while they were cleaning up."

"Hope they weren't too traumatized."

"More intrigued, I think."

"Dead bodies always make for good ghost stories."

Tomasetti reaches us, looking at me a little too intently. "Chief."

I feel a little conspicuous going through the formality of a handshake; we share the same bed every night, and I'm pretty sure Rasmussen knows we're living together. For the sake of professional decorum, we go through the motions, anyway. "Hi, John."

He turns to the forty-something man at his side. "This is Lyle Stevitch, the forensic anthropologist from Lucas County I told you about."

Stevitch sticks out his hand. "Don't believe a word he told you," he says with a smile.

He's a studious-looking man with wire-rimmed

glasses and a precision goatee that conjures images of Burl Ives. He looks more like a college professor than a forensic anthropologist, but already his eyes are drifting past me toward the caution tape, and I know he's anxious to get started.

"Thanks for coming," I say.

He introduces the young man at his side. "This is Tyler Hochheim. He's a student at Mercyhurst in Erie and interning with me for the summer."

Wearing a wool beanie over shoulder-length hair tied into a ponytail at his nape, Hochheim looks more like a member of the Occupy Wall Street movement than the assistant of a renowned forensic anthropologist. He's carrying a large canvas bag in one hand, a large toolbox in the other.

Doc Coblentz joins us. Once introductions are made, we start toward the scene, with Doc outlining everything we've discovered so far. "There aren't enough bones for a full skeleton, so I suspect some may have been carried away by scavengers over the years."

"Or else they're buried," I add.

Rasmussen, Tomasetti, and I exchange looks, and I know they're thinking the same thing I am. *Or the deceased was dismembered elsewhere, his body dumped in several locations . . .*

Hands on his hips, Stevitch looks out over the scene, giving a decisive nod. "Let's set up a grid, and then we'll begin by collecting everything we find on the surface. Once everything is bagged and labeled and photographed, we'll begin the excavation." He addresses Tyler. "We're going to need soil samples and a thorough sweep with the metal detector, too."

"Okay." His assistant steps outside the taped-off scene and sets the bag on the ground. He removes full-body biohazard suits with zippered fronts and passes one to Stevitch. Tyler then spreads a crisp blue sheet on the ground and begins setting out the tools of his trade: a smaller folding shovel, several different types of brushes ranging in size from a makeup brush to a paint-brush, another tool that looks like a stainless-steel trowel, several picks and chisels of different sizes, a dozen or more plastic containers with sealing lids. He then wraps a tool belt of sorts around his waist. Once he's suited up, he goes back to the canvas bag, pulls out several plastic stakes, a hammer, and a roll of twine and proceeds to mark off a perimeter of the area in which they'll be working.

The process seems oddly unscientific in light of the fact that they're excavating human remains. Tomasetti has assured me Stevitch is good at what he does, and I know the real work will begin once they get everything to the laboratory.

I'm anxious to get moving on the identification process, but I'm well aware it will be a tedious endeavor and could take weeks or even months. Still, Painters Mill is a small town. I know if I take a look at missing person reports, there's a decent chance I may be able to come up with a few names, especially if I can narrow it down by sex and the number of years they've been missing. Unless, of course, this individual was from a larger city and dumped. . . .

"Doctor Stevitch," I begin, "Doc Coblentz estimated these bones might have been here a decade or more, and that the deceased is probably male. Do you agree?"

Bending, Stevitch picks up the skull, weighing it in his hands. "The pronounced supraorbital ridge isn't foolproof, but at this early stage and without looking at the hip bones, I can say with relative certainty that the deceased was probably male." He gives Doc Coblentz a nod of approval. "As far as how old they are . . ." He shrugs. ". . . Ten years is a solid estimate. But until I get them cleaned up and under some decent light, I'm afraid I can't narrow it down any more than that."

I glance at Tomasetti. "What's the usual procedure for manner and cause of death in a situation like this?"

"The FA does the excavation," he tells me. "Then we send everything over to the local morgue, where the coroner as well as a forensic osteology expert will take a look. We've got a guy from Lucas County on our resource list."

"John Harris," Doc Coblentz chimes in. "I know him. John and I went to med school together. He's good. One of the best."

Tomasetti nods. "From there, we'll ship everything down to the University of North Texas Health Science Center in Fort Worth to see if they can extract mitochondrial DNA."

Something sinks inside me when I realize a definitive ID is, indeed, going to take some time. I look at Dr. Stevitch. "Is there any way you can tell me how old he was when he died?"

"Again, anything definitive is premature at this point, but I might be able to give you a range." He runs his finger across the top of the skull, from front to back. "See this squiggly line that runs the length of the skull?"

I move closer. "I do."

"That's the sagittal suture." Using his finger, he taps another barely discernible ridge of bone, this time from left to right. "This one is the coronal suture. Neither are fused, which tells me this person was relatively young."

"How young?"

"Are you comfortable with a guess?"

"If it's a good one." I smile at him.

"I'd say between sixteen and thirty-five." He spreads his hands. "I'm sure Doctor Harris will be able to give you a more definitive answer."

I motion toward the femur. "Height or weight?"

"I'm afraid not, Chief Burkholder." But he grins.

Stevitch goes back to work. I step away from the scene and call Lois.

"Hi, Chief."

"I want you to pull all open missing person reports for Holmes County that are ten years or older. Go back forty years. We're looking for a male sixteen to thirty-five years of age. If you strike out with Holmes County, expand your search to Coshocton and Wayne Counties. If you're still not getting anything, add Cuyahoga County."

"Will do."

I pause. "Everything okay there?"

"Phones are ringing off the hook. Some of the folks without power are starting to get antsy. And people are finding out about the bones and starting to call with questions."

"Word travels fast."

"You know kids and technology. Half the town knows by now."

"Let me know if you come up with a name."

"Will do, Chief."

I've just ended the call, when I hear the crunch of tires on gravel. At first I think it's Steve Ressler, publisher of the local newspaper, wanting a scoop on the remains. It's not Ressler's Ford Focus but an older Thunderbird with wide tires on aluminum wheels, oxidized paint, and a hail-damaged hood. A middle-aged man with sandy-colored hair gets out. He's wearing blue jeans and a black T-shirt. Without looking at me, he crosses in front of the vehicle, opens the passenger door, and bends to help a woman exit.

Something quickens inside me when I spot the crutches. The woman has blond hair that hasn't seen a cut in some time. She's wearing faded jeans and a pink blouse with the sleeves rolled up. The cast on her right leg stretches from just below her knee to her ankle. It's the woman from the Willow Bend Mobile Home Park. The one with the compound fracture, whom Tomasetti carried out. The woman whose baby later died. . . .

Paula Kester.

She's standing beside the car, leaning heavily on her crutches, staring at me. No smile. No spark of recognition or any indication that she remembers me. I don't know why she's here. To thank Tomasetti for saving her life? Thank us for trying to save her child? Or is she here to rage at us because her baby died? I know all too well that when you lose something precious, you always look for someone to blame.

I start toward her, my brain scrambling for words of comfort, but nothing seems adequate. Several things strike me at once as I cross to her. She's a thin woman with a pale complexion. The brown roots showing at her scalp tell me the blond came from a bottle. The cast on her leg looks huge and out of place. I can tell by the way she's shifting around that she's not used to the crutches. That she's probably in pain. And she's been crying.

"Mrs. Kester?" I say as I approach her.

I know immediately this is no thank-you-for-saving-my-life visit. Mentally, I brace because I know it's not going to be pleasant. The woman totters over to me and stops a scant two feet away. A little too close. Invading my personal space. I heed my instincts and step back because I know grieving people can be unpredictable. She looks at me as if I'm something she's scraped off the bottom of her shoe.

"You Burkholder?" she asks.

I nod. "I'm sorry for your loss, Mrs. Kester. What can I do for you?"

Vaguely, I'm aware of Tomasetti approaching from behind me. A few feet away, the man who'd driven her here leans against the fender of the car, arms crossed, staring down at the ground.

"You can't do anything for me." Kester's voice is monotone, her eyes flat. "I just wanted you to know . . . my baby died. Because of you." Propping herself on the crutches, she raises a finger and jabs it at me. "She had an injured neck and you moved her."

I'm usually pretty adroit at deflecting malicious comments. But I feel her words like the sharp edge of a knife against my skin. The death of the child has been a weight on my conscience. I spent most of the night reliving those moments in the trailer home, envisioning what I could have done differently. I spent the rest of the night dreaming of her.

"Why did you have to move her?" Her eyes fill, but there's more anger than grief. "Why couldn't you just leave us alone?"

The need to defend myself is strong, but I don't. Grief is a powerful state of mind, and I know that no matter what I say at this point, it won't help. It won't ease her pain or make her feel better. It sure as hell won't bring back her baby. So I stand there and I take it.

"Mrs. Kester, I'm very sorry—"

Her hand snakes out, connects solidly with the left side of my face. The force of it sends me sideways. I stumble, catch myself. My training kicks in and I reach for her wrists.

"You killed her!" she screams. "Murderer!"

I hear shoes against the ground behind me. Tomasetti moves in, wedges himself between us, grasps her biceps. The crutches fall away as he hauls her back. "Murderer!" she screams. *Baby killer!"*

"Calm down," Tomasetti tells her.

She trips and starts to go down. He breaks her fall, then gently lowers her to the ground to keep her from getting hurt. "Let go of me!"

"Stay down." His eyes land on me. "Are you all right?"

"I'm fine," I tell him.

Rasmussen trots up beside me. "Didn't see that one coming. You sure you're okay?"

"Yup." But my throat is so tight I can barely speak. I'm embarrassed because I let my guard down and got myself sucker punched. On an emotional level, I'm still reeling from the woman's accusation.

Baby killer!

The deputy jogs over to them, his handcuffs out, and kneels next to the woman. She's screaming and crying as they roll her onto her stomach.

"Watch her leg," I remind them.

"Shut up!" she screams. "This is your fault! *Yours!*"

"I'm aware," Tomasetti growls at me as the two men pull her arms behind her back and handcuff her.

It's an ugly scene, painful to watch. Despite her behavior, this is the last thing I wanted to happen to Paula Kester. She's distraught and out of control. Helpless because of her broken leg. But with so many cops present, it's out of my hands. They're bound by law to make the arrest. I figure if I can go to bat for her later, I will.

"Hey!"

At the sound of the male voice, I look up to see the man who'd driven the woman here approach us. He's heavy set, jogging toward us, his face a mask of concern. "What are you doing to her?"

I step toward him, put out my hand to stop him. "Halt right there, and keep your hands where I can see them."

"Okay. Okay!" The man freezes and raises his hands. "I'm cool."

"What's your name?" I ask.

"Carl Shellenberger."

"Show me some ID."

While he digs for his wallet, I jab a thumb at the woman on the ground. "Why did you bring her here?"

"She wanted to see you."

"Why?"

"I figure that's between you and her, ma'am."

"What's your relationship with her?"

For the first time he looks contrite. "I'm her dad."

I can still feel the sting of her palm against my face. The adrenaline beginning to ebb. A gnarly ball of guilt churning in my gut. "Is she on any kind of medication?"

He sighs. "I think the doc gave her something for the pain."

"Did it cross your mind that bringing her here wasn't a very smart thing to do?"

Another heavy sigh. "She was pretty adamant about it."

"Well, now she's under arrest for assaulting a public servant," Tomasetti interjects.

Shellenberger's mouth opens. "Aw, come on! You can't do that! She's got a broke leg and just lost her baby. Not to mention her home. You can't take her to jail!"

"She hit a cop," Tomasetti snaps. "We don't have a choice."

"It's the law," Rasmussen adds.

"Well, she's not thinking right," the man says, looking stressed.

Tomasetti and Rasmussen help Paula Kester to her feet. She's sobbing now, head down, hair hanging in her face. "I can't believe you're doing this to me," she sobs. "It's all her fault."

I want to say something to reassure her. Let her know I'll help her if I can. But I know she's too angry, and any commentary from me would probably make things worse.

She raises her head. Her eyes connect with mine. Her lips peel back. Snarling an expletive, she yanks hard against Tomasetti and Rasmussen. "I'm going to get a lawyer and sue you!" she screams. "I'll sue you for everything you've got, you bitch! All of you! *Fuckers!*"

Rasmussen looks away and shakes his head.

Next to him, the deputy clears his throat. "I've got a cage. Do you want me to transport her and book her in?"

The sheriff nods. "Let's put her in the car."

"What about her leg?" her father cries.

Tomasetti gives him a withering look. "I guess you should have thought about that before you drove her over here, Einstein."

Chapter 6

It's nearly 10:00 p.m. by the time Stevitch and his assistant call it a night. Sheriff Rasmussen left an hour ago. Tomasetti, of course, stayed.

Stevitch and Hochheim spent nine grueling hours going over every inch of the site, running the soil through handheld screens and geologic sieves. All the bones were placed in paper bags, labeled, and stowed in plastic tubs. Once the topsoil had been examined, they turned to their shovels and dug a series of shallow holes. Again, the soil was put through geologic sieves. As darkfall neared and they began to run out of light, I radioed Glock and asked him to bring a generator. I called Holmes County and they sent a deputy out with work lights. The two men continued their tedious work beneath the buzz of spotlights, setting aside bones and fabric and anything else that wasn't indigenous to the site. Finally, once soil samples were taken, Hochheim went over the entire grid area with a metal detector.

Now, while Hochheim packs tools into the canvas bag and carries it to the Prius, Stevitch approaches me. "I think we've extracted everything this site is going to relinquish," he tells me.

"I appreciate your coming out so quickly and on such short notice," I tell him.

"It is the nature of the beast." He chuckles. "This may sound morbid, Chief Burkholder, but we anthropologists live for the dig."

"Any thoughts you can share?" Tomasetti asks.

Sobering, he rubs his beard between his thumb and forefinger. "Interestingly, about twenty percent of the bones are missing. More than likely scavenged by animals."

"Do you have enough for identification?" I ask.

"Fortunately, we have the teeth, which are typically an excellent source of DNA. I'll extract samples and send them off to the lab and get us into the queue."

"Do you think you'll be able to come up with height or weight?" I ask. "Race?"

"Eventually, but it's not going to be a speedy process. I'll get to work on a biological profile as soon as I get everything logged. That includes age, sex, stature, and ancestry."

"What about clothing?" I ask. "Any personal items?"

"A few scraps of fabric, but it's very deteriorated." He lifts a large clear plastic envelope containing several smaller envelopes of different sizes, some of which are paper, some plastic. "Metal detector picked up a couple of interesting items." He indicates a tiny clear plastic envelope inside. "This ring. Small diamond. Band is probably gold."

"Looks like a woman's ring," Tomasetti says.

"An engagement ring?" I add.

"Or a wedding ring," Stevitch concurs. "We'll take a look at it under magnification and see if we can come up with some kind of identifying mark."

"If we can get the name of the manufacturer," Tomasetti says, "we might be able to locate the retailer."

"And maybe the customer." I think about that a moment. "Can you take some photos of the ring and e-mail them to me?"

"Absolutely." As if saving the best news for last, he reaches into the envelope and pulls out a large white envelope. "This is probably the most remarkable item we found. The metal detector picked it up. I believe it could be extremely helpful in terms of identifying the decedent."

He opens the envelope flap. I look inside and see a dirt-caked piece of steel about half an inch wide and four inches in length. Several screws protrude from one end. At first glance, I think he's showing me the hasp from the barn door, but I know it must be more important than that. "What is it?"

"I believe it's an orthopedic implant. A plate, to be more precise. Probably titanium. Judging from the size, possibly for the forearm—the radius or ulna. As you can see, some of the screws are still intact. We also found some additional screws scattered about."

"So at some point this individual broke his arm?" Tomasetti says.

"That would be my guess."

I think about that a moment. "Do those kinds of implants have any sort of identifying number?"

"I believe they do. Of course, I need to get it into a lab environment for a more thorough look. But I'm relatively certain that's the case, and I thought it might be helpful to you in terms of identification."

"Let's hope so," I tell him.

"In the coming days and weeks I'll be consulting with Doctor Coblentz. We, as a team, may or may not be able to determine cause and/or manner or death. I can't make any promises. We don't have a whole lot to work with here, but we'll certainly do our best."

I offer my hand and we shake. "Thank you."

"I must admit I enjoyed every minute." He shakes hands with Tomasetti as well. "This promises to be a challenging and interesting case," he tells us. "I'll be in touch."

Ten minutes later, I'm watching the taillights of the Prius disappear into the night, when Tomasetti approaches. He's left the Tahoe running with the headlights on for illumination while the deputy breaks down the work lights.

"Wanna help me load the generator?" I ask.

"I thought you'd never ask." He flexes his arm. "I never pass up an opportunity to show off my muscles to a woman I'm wildly attracted to."

Rolling my eyes, I bend to the generator, wrap both hands around the handle, and wheel it toward the Explorer. It's not easy; the generator weighs about 250 pounds, and I'm lugging it over clumpy grass, loose gravel, and areas of soft dirt. But I'm glad for the distraction. I'm still thinking about the scene with Paula Kester earlier. Her accusation still stings. I don't want to talk about it, but I'm pretty sure Tomasetti's going to bring it up.

I've dragged the generator only a few feet, when he usurps the handle and takes over. "You're quiet," he says.

"Just thinking," I tell him.

"About Paula Kester?"

"Mostly about the remains."

"Uh-huh." He nods, guiding the generator around a muddy area. "You know Ohio has a Good Samaritan law, right?"

"I'm aware." A statute in the Ohio Revised Code protects anyone who administers first aid to an injured party from liability. "But we both know there's always some lawyer willing to argue the point."

"She's not going to get anywhere with a lawsuit."

I want to tell him the possibility of a lawsuit isn't what's bothering me, but I let it go. "I didn't want her arrested."

"You don't slug a cop in the face and walk away. Yes, there are extenuating circumstances and she may have been overcome with emotion, but she can tell it to the judge."

"Tomasetti, you're such a hard-ass." But I soften the words with a smile.

We reach the Explorer. I fish my keys from my pocket and open the rear door. "She told me the baby had a neck injury," I tell him. "If I hadn't moved her, she might still be here."

"If you hadn't moved her and the gas had ignited, all of us would be at the morgue tonight. You used your best judgment, and I think you made the right call."

"What if it wasn't? I mean, we're talking about a baby's life. Tomasetti, that's huge."

"That baby was in a trailer that had been flipped over and half crushed by a tornado. You know as well as I do that aside from a vehicle, a mobile home is one of the most dangerous places to be during a storm like that. There was a gas leak. You risked your life to get her out."

"I know all of that," I say testily.

"Look, you know as well as I do that when people get caught up in that kind of grief, they say and do stupid things. Paula Kester was dealt a tough hand. She needed someone to blame. So

110

she picks a fight with you and slugs you in the face? What kind of person does that?"

"Someone who's just lost everything, including a child."

He lets my statement stand. "So is she married?"

"I don't know."

"Maybe you ought to check, because if she's still with that baby's father and he's as pissed off as she is, it might be smart to keep an eye on him. Make sure he doesn't do something foolish."

Bending, I grasp the handle of the generator. "Ready?"

He does the same, frowning at me over the top of the motor. "Yup."

We lift the generator in tandem and set it in the Explorer. I step back and Tomasetti closes the door, then turns to me. "You coming home after you drop off the generator?"

"Yeah." I muster a smile. "I'll see you later."

He leans close and sets his mouth against mine. "You sure you're okay?"

"I am." Before I can stop myself, I step into his embrace and give him a hard kiss.

When he pulls away, he's looking at me a little too closely, wondering where that came from. "Don't stay too late."

Nodding, I walk around to the driver's side door, get in, and drive away.

• • •

I didn't have time for lunch earlier, so I swing by the McDonald's in Millersburg for a burger-to-go before heading to the station. I enter the reception area to find my second-shift dispatcher, Jodie Metzger, at her station, headset on, staring at her computer. From the radio on her desk, Foster the People belts out "Pumped Up Kicks."

"Hey, Chief." Rising, she shoves a stack of message slips at me. "I think the entire population of Painters Mill called for you today."

I stop next to her station and take the messages. "Did Lois brief you on those remains found on Gellerman Road?"

She nods. "How awful for those Boy Scouts, finding human bones." She gives an exaggerated shiver. "Lois sent you an e-mail and copied me on it before she left. Oh, and she left this file." She scoops up a lavender-colored folder that's already as thick as my thumb. "She printed several files from NamUs. NCIC's in there, too. And she ran everything through LEADS."

NamUs is the acronym for the National Missing and Unidentified Persons System. It's the largest database of missing persons and unidentified remains in the world and allows civilians to search for missing loved ones and possibly match the missing with remains.

She jabs a thumb at her screen. "I'm working on the National Center for Missing Adults now. Hope to have a list for you within the hour."

I tell her about Stevitch's discovery of the surgical plate. "The deceased may have had a broken arm—the radius or ulna—and had the plate surgically implanted. If you run across anything about a broken bone in any of the profiles, kick it over to me."

"Will do. I'll let Lois and Mona know to do the same." She tilts her head. "Do you have any idea who it is?"

"Not yet." I think about that a moment. "Get in touch with the local Crime Stoppers. Tell them we're offering five hundred dollars to anyone with information that leads to the identification of the remains. All callers will remain anonymous." I pause. "And I'm going to need the name of the owner of the Gellerman Road property."

She jots furiously on a yellow legal pad. "Got it, Chief."

"Skid on duty tonight?"

"Yes."

"Get on the radio and tell him I need help unloading the generator."

"Will do."

I start toward my office, then remember one more thing and turn back to the dispatch station. "Jodie, can you run Paula Kester through LEADS and see if she's got any outstanding warrants?" I spell the last name for her. "If she's married, run her husband, too. I don't have a name, but you should be able to find it."

"Roger that."

After unlocking my office, I let myself inside and make a beeline for my desk. While my computer boots, I quickly unpack my dinner. Experience has taught me that in the course of any death investigation, the first order is always to identify the victim. Without that information, there's no way to build any sort of victimology. At this point, I don't know if I'm dealing with a homicide, an accident, or death by natural causes. But my gut is telling me there was foul play involved, and anyone who's ever worked in law enforcement knows the majority of homicides are committed by someone the victim knew. If I can't name the victim, finding his killer will be next to impossible.

I wolf down my burger as I skim e-mail, responding to the ones that won't wait until morning. But I'm anxious to get to the file. I open it as I pop the lid off my coffee. Not for the first time, I'm impressed by Lois's ability to dig through reams of useless data and get to the pertinent information.

The NamUs reports are on top. The site went live with a fully searchable system in 2009 and contains over eleven thousand unidentified decedent cases and nearly twenty thousand missing person cases. It's a mountain of data, especially when the only information I have right now to narrow my search is location, sex, and the broad age range of eighteen to thirty-five.

My job would be infinitely more difficult if this were a large metropolitan area, where there are many more missing. But since Painters Mill is a small town and the whole of Holmes County is sparsely populated, the numbers are much smaller. Depending on how old the bones are, there may be someone living in Painters Mill who remem-bers something and comes forward.

In the last forty years, for the three-county area, a total of fourteen males between the ages of sixteen and thirty-five went missing and are still unaccounted for. Any one of those missing men could be my unidentified decedent, so I narrow it down to Holmes County.

Pulling a yellow highlighter from my pencil drawer, I mark the six names. Twenty-two-year-old Mark Elliott vanished after a fight with his girlfriend five years ago. Thirty-five-year-old Raymond Stetmeyer disappeared on a fishing trip twelve years ago. In 1997, thirty-one-year-old Ricky Maitland told his wife he was going out for a drink at a local bar and never came home. In 1985, twenty-year-old Leroy Nolt left for work one morning and his parents never saw him again. Seventeen-year-old Benjamin Mullet, an Amish boy, disappeared during his *Rumspringa* in 1978. And Thomas Blaine, twenty-five-year-old father of two from Clark, went missing after a DUI arrest back in 1977. There's no mention of any old injuries or broken bones in any of the cases.

Two of the names, Nolt and Stetmeyer, are familiar. Not because I remember either case, but because Painters Mill is a small town and I happen to know that the families still live in the area. I'm especially interested to find out if any of these missing were treated for a broken arm at some point before they disappeared. Of course, it's too late to contact anyone tonight, so I opt to make the calls first thing in the morning.

The police station is hushed at this hour. The phones have quieted. Jodie has turned down her radio. There's no traffic on Main Street outside my window. It's so quiet, I can hear the whisper of wind against the eaves. The whir of my computer's hard drive. I find myself wishing for the pandemonium I'm usually so quick to complain about. Tonight it's almost *too* quiet. The kind of quiet that sets my mind to work on things I've been trying to avoid all day.

Murderer!

Baby killer!

On an intellectual level, I know the death of Paula Kester's baby was not my fault. I did what any cop would do: I removed the child from a dangerous, life-threatening situation. Yes, I violated the golden rule about moving an injured patient. But I had seconds to make a decision, and I used my best judgment. If faced with the same situation again, I'd do exactly the same thing. Still, I can't help but wonder if that baby would have lived had I not gone into that mobile home. . . .

I think about Tomasetti, waiting for me at the farm, and for the first time I question why I'm still here. Why I haven't gone home to him. I'm avoiding him, I realize. Hiding from him. From a possibility I don't want to face.

I missed my period last month. It should have happened about three weeks ago. I waited, unconcerned, certain my body would not betray me. I made excuses, blaming it on job-related stress, missed meals, too little sleep, even that head cold I had a few weeks ago. As soon as things settled down, I rationalized, it would come and everything would get back to normal. For three weeks now, I haven't let myself think about it. The shrinks would probably call it denial—not an easy feat for a realist like me. But there are some things that are simply too frightening to confront, and, for me, this is one of them.

I've been diligent about birth control. I started taking the pill a few weeks before I moved in with Tomasetti. But as desperately as I want to believe I couldn't possibly be pregnant, there were two or three times in the last few months when I was lax. Once, I got busy and let my prescription run out for two days. The other time I worked around the clock on a crazy case, didn't make it home, and ended up skipping three days.

Tomasetti and I haven't discussed children. We haven't even discussed marriage. Neither of us is ready for that kind of commitment. We're certainly not ready for a family. Honestly, I haven't given it much thought. Yes, there are times when I'm aware of my biological clock ticking—I'll be thirty-four years old this year. Still, the thought of bringing a baby into the world at this point in my life terrifies me.

Sighing, I put my face in my hands and close my eyes. "What the hell have you done?" I mutter between my fingers.

"Chief?"

I startle and look up to see my second-shift officer, "Skid," standing in my office doorway. I clear my throat. "Hey."

He grins. "Long day?"

"I guess you could put it that way." I smile, trying not to be embarrassed. "Help me with the generator?"

"Yes, ma'am."

Coolheaded and experienced, Skid is a solid police officer. But he's not without flaws—nor is he without career problems. Originally from Ann Arbor, Michigan, he was fired from the police department there for an alcohol-related offense. I hired him shortly after becoming chief here in Painters Mill, and so far it's been smooth sailing. He brings a high level of experience to the job, a laid-back demeanor to the occasional dicey situation, and a wicked sense of humor I probably appreciate more than I should.

We cross the reception area and go through the front door. "I heard about those bones out on Gellerman Road," he says as we unload the generator. "You guys figure out who they belong to?"

"Not yet." I tell him about the six missing person cases in Holmes County. "The forensic anthropologist, Doc Coblentz, and another coroner from Lucas County are going to take a look at the remains first thing in the morning. If we're lucky, they'll get DNA."

I hold the door while he rolls the generator inside. "How's your shift going?"

"There're still a lot of people without power, but everyone's behaving themselves. Red Cross is going to be handing out hot meals and water again tomorrow." He grimaces. "I heard you had some trouble out there today with Paula Kester."

"Not my best moment." I let the door close behind us and motion toward the hall. "Let's roll it down to the basement."

He nods. "I had a run-in with her husband a couple of years back, and let me tell you, Nick Kester's a loose cannon."

"He's got a record?"

"Felony assault and possession," he tells me. "Those are the only two convictions I remember off the top of my head. But that guy has a temper. If those two are still together, you might want to keep an eye on him. He likes his meth, hates cops, and he's got a screw loose to boot."

"Bad combination," I tell him.

"Especially if you're Nick Kester and you think someone fucked you over."

Chapter 7

She still thought of him after all these years. More often than was wise for a woman her age. It usually happened in the course of some menial chore, which seemed to be the lion's share of her life these days. Sometimes, when she was hanging clothes on the line or washing dishes or pulling weeds in her garden, she still saw him the way he'd been all those years ago. Laughing eyes the color of a robin's egg. Unkempt hair that was just a little too long. A quicksilver grin that was as contagious as a summer cold. She still remembered the way he'd looked at her. As if she were the only person left on earth. Oh, how the sight of him would make her heart quicken and her palms grow wet with sweat. She knew it was a silly thing—those memories of the frivolous girl she'd been. But a woman never forgot her first love. Even now, a lifetime later, her foolish heart still quivered in her chest when she thought of him.

Feel dumbhaydichkeit. Such foolishness.

She'd lived a lifetime since those days. A good life filled with family and love and God. She had a husband and four grown children now. Her first grandchild on the way. It was sinful to think of a man from her past when she had so much to be thankful for.

Then this morning, after her husband had left the house to feed the livestock, she'd drunk a cup of coffee and skimmed through *The Budget* before starting breakfast. Usually those pages are reserved for news of marriages and births, deaths and baptisms, with the occasional proverb sprinkled throughout. This morning the front page headline had made something inside her go cold: human remains uncovered by tornado.

It was the kind of story she usually didn't devote any time to reading. Why invite bad news into your life? But as she sipped her second cup of coffee, she'd found her eyes skimming, seeking details, looking for things she shouldn't be looking for. And on page six, where the story continued, she'd read a quote from the English police: "We know very little at this point. The only things we do know are that the bones belong to a male between sixteen and thirty-five years of age, and they've been buried in the crawl space of that barn between ten and thirty years. Aside from a few scraps of clothing, the only items found in the vicinity were a metal plate—possibly a medical device for a broken bone—and a woman's engagement ring."

The sound she'd heard had been her own quick intake of breath. She'd closed the newspaper and risen so abruptly she'd spilled her coffee. She'd looked down at the newspaper, her eyes drawn once again to the words she wished she hadn't read.

. . . *a woman's engagement ring.*

. . . *thirty years . . .*

Folding the newspaper, she'd placed it in the paper bag with the rest of the newspapers she'd be using to clean windows later in the week. She was wiping up the coffee spill when her husband came in from the barn.

Brushing bits of alfalfa hay from his coat, he walked to the table and looked down at the stained tablecloth. "Where's the newspaper?" he asked in Pennsylvania Dutch.

"I spilled coffee on it," she told him.

It was the first time in thirty years of marriage that she'd lied to her husband.

I've walked this road a hundred times and yet I don't recognize it. The wind has stripped the leaves from the trees, ripped the cornstalks from the ground, and set the telephone poles at 45-degree angles. The asphalt beneath my feet is covered with an inch of mud and dead foliage. In the distance, the tornado sirens shriek. The storm bears down, a black beast with an insatiable hunger for violence.

I hear the cry of a baby, and when I look down, the child is in my arms. Soft skin warm against my breast. Four months old and crying her heart out. She's soaked from the rain and shivering with cold. Tiny mouth open, chin quivering. Her eyes are on mine, watchful, trusting me to save her.

She's partially wrapped in a white blanket, but it's stained with blood. I'm holding her, running as fast as I can, but the mud is hampering me. The wind is pummeling me, trying to tear her from my arms.

"I've got you," I tell her. "I'll keep you safe."

But when I look down, the baby is being sucked from my arms. I grab for her, but my fingers slide against wet flesh. I hear her high-pitched wail. And then she's gone. When I look at my hands, they're covered with blood.

"Kate. *Kate.*"

Tomasetti's voice drags me awake. I'm lying in our bed, my back against the pillows. My legs are tangled in sheets that are damp with sweat. I'm aware of Tomasetti beside me. I glance down, but my arms are empty. No baby. No blood on my hands. But I swear I can still feel the warmth from when the child was nestled against my chest.

"Jesus," I say. "I'm sorry."

"You okay?"

In the quiet semi-darkness of our bedroom, I hear myself breathing hard. I see the sheets quivering, and it shocks me to realize I'm shaking. "It was just a stupid dream." Throwing the sheets aside, I start to get up.

He stops me. "Kate, hold on. You don't have to leave."

I sit with my legs over the side of the bed. The cool air feels good against my heated skin. I can feel the wet fabric of my T-shirt sticking to my back.

He moves across the bed to sit beside me. "You want to talk about it?"

For the first time I look at him, but I can't hold his gaze and I look away. I'm on the verge of tears. I'm embarrassed because I don't want him to see me like this. "Not really."

He nods as if understanding, but his eyes are digging in to me, prying into places I don't want him to pry.

"Tomasetti, for God's sake, stop staring at me," I say, trying to feign annoyance and not quite managing.

"I'm just trying to figure this out." He shrugs. "Figure you out."

I choke out a laugh that eases some of the

tension. "There's nothing to figure out. It was just a dream. That's all."

"Okay." But he doesn't look away.

I glance at the alarm clock and groan when I realize it's already after seven. "I have to go."

I start to rise but he stops me. "You don't have to tell me what's bothering you if you don't want to, but I'm going to keep asking."

I look down at my hands, which are clasped in front of me. He puts his arm around my shoulder and holds me against him for a moment. It's a kind gesture, not sexual, and he tells me he's here for me if I need him.

"All right," I tell him.

He presses a kiss to my temple. "Just so you know."

I blast through an abbreviated morning routine, forgoing breakfast with Tomasetti for a Pop-Tart and a to-go cup of coffee. My third-shift dispatcher, Mona Kurtz, calls as I pull into my designated parking spot off of Main Street, which is crowded with vehicles I don't recognize, including a news van from Columbus. I let the call go to voice mail and head inside.

In a town the size of Painters Mill, the police department is usually the kind of place someone might go for a little peace and quiet. That's not the case this morning. The instant I walk inside, I'm assailed by a series of camera flashes that leave me half blind. The man behind the camera has hair longer than mine, black rimmed glasses, and enough facial hair to make a rug.

"Blind me with that flash again and you're going to lose it," I mutter as I stalk past.

He snaps two more shots at my back.

At the reception desk, Mona Kurtz is standing, talking to a woman wearing a geometric-print dress. At twenty-five, Mona is one of my more colorful employees. She keeps things interesting with her Lady Gaga–esque wardrobe and a personality that's part rock and roll, part girl next door. But when it comes to her job, all frivolity goes out the window; she's got her eye on an officer position, and as soon as one becomes available—or my budget allows—I plan to promote her. She's not unflappable, though, and as I close the space between us, I see her composure waiver.

She spots me and her relief is palpable. "Chief."

To my right, I see T.J. Banks, my third-shift officer, standing outside his cubicle. It's nearly 8:00 a.m., which tells me he's finishing post-shift incident reports.

The woman in the geometric dress turns, her eyes sweeping over my uniform. "Chief Burkholder?" Even as she says my name she nods at her hairy counterpart with the camera.

Giving her half of my attention, I pluck a dozen

or more message slips from my slot on Mona's desk. "What can I do for you?"

"I'm Bridge Howard with Channel Sixteen out of Columbus?" She ends the statement on an up note, as if she's asking a question.

She's about six feet tall with the requisite blue eyes and blond hair and enough lip gloss to wax an SUV. Her cameraman passes her a mike, which she promptly shoves in my face. "Chief Burkholder, what can you tell us about the bones found here in Painters Mill? Have you identified them yet?"

I glance past her to see that the cameraman is already filming, and I tamp down a flare of annoyance. But while I'm no fan of the media, I've been around long enough to know I might need them at some point and a contentious relationship is about as helpful as a migraine.

"We have not identified the remains," I say simply. "We're looking at all missing persons cases now. DNA testing will be done, but as you know, that could take a while."

"How long have the bones been there?"

"We don't know."

"Have you been approached by any family members looking for loved ones?"

"No," I tell her, but I know the calls will come. People never give up hope when a loved one goes missing. "I'll be sending out a press release later this afternoon. If you leave your contact information, I'll make sure you get a copy. Excuse me."

I start toward my office, when I hear the front door slam open with a little too much force. I turn to see a thirty-something man walk in, not bothering to close the door behind him. I take his measure, not liking what I see. Six feet tall. About 160. Dark, receding hair. Brown eyes. He's wearing grungy blue jeans and a worn golf shirt, untucked. The tattoo of a horned devil peeks out from beneath the left sleeve. I don't see a weapon, but that doesn't mean he doesn't have a firearm or knife tucked into his waistband or boot.

I'm in uniform, my firearm strapped to my hip. I make eye contact with him and approach. "Can I help you?"

"You Burkholder?"

"I'm Chief Burkholder."

He's got a mean look in his eyes. The kind a man gets when he's spoiling for a fight. "I'll tell you what you can do for me. You can keep your goddamn motherfucking wallet handy is what you can do because I'm going to sue your fucking ass off. How's that for starters?"

"Sir, I'm going to ask you to watch your language." I glance to my left toward T.J. who's started toward us. "Do you understand me?"

He stares at me, saying nothing.

"What's your name?" I ask.

"You want to know who I am?" He huffs a belligerent laugh. "I'm the man whose baby you killed. The man whose wife you put in jail when she *complained.* That's who the fuck I am."

He moves closer to me so he's standing about three feet away. Too close; if he decided to make a move I wouldn't have time to defend myself, so I step back, keep my right hand loose over my sidearm. He smells like dirty hair and fast food. When he speaks I see stained yellow teeth and a canine tooth that's black with rot, and I think: *meth mouth.*

"What's your name?" I repeat.

"My name's Nick Kester, but you can call me 'sir.'" Spittle flies from between his lips with the last word. "That's who you're going to be making the fucking check out to."

"If you want to talk, I'll talk to you, but you need to calm down. You need to watch your language. I'm not going to ask you again. Do you understand?"

"Do I understand?" He looks around at all the people staring at us and laughs. "Hell, yeah, people! I understand! I got it! Your chief here? She killed my baby." He jabs two fingers at me, not touching, but close. "A little fuckin' girl, four months old. The only good thing I ever done in my whole life." He turns his attention back to me, and I swear I see raw hatred in his eyes. "And you took her away."

I stare at him, my vision narrowing into tunnel vision. Around me, the station has gone silent. Everyone is staring at us.

"If you're not going to calm down, you need to leave," I hear myself say.

"Don't tell me to calm the fuck down."

T.J. steps forward. "Mr. Kester, you need to leave. Now. Or I'm going to handcuff you and put you in a cell."

Kester turns his attention to T.J. and lets out a laugh. "All right. I get it. I'll leave." To the journalist standing next to me: "You want to ask her a hard question, blondie? Impress the hell out of your boss? Ask her what she did to Lucy Kester." His eyes slide back to me. His lips part, giving me a peek at teeth that look sharp enough to tear skin. "You'd better get used to calling me 'sir,' because once my lawyer gets finished with you and this Podunk town, you're going to be waiting tables—if anyone will hire you. Fuckin' baby killer."

He steps back, grinning an ugly smile, and walks backward to the door. There, he turns on his heel and leaves without closing it.

I stand there for a moment, my pulse thrumming hard, staring at the door. I'm aware of T.J. striding to it, closing it. The switchboard ringing incessantly. Mona's voice as she answers.

"Come on, folks," T.J. says. "It's over." He

130

looks over at me and frowns. "You okay?" he says in a low voice.

I pull myself out of my fugue, glance over at the young journalist, who's staring at me as if I've just become the story. She shoves the mike at me. "Chief Burkholder, do you want to comment on Lucy Kester or any of those allegations against you?"

"Leave your e-mail address," I tell her, "and I'll make sure you get a copy of that press release."

As I start toward my office, I hear her whisper to her photographer. "Did you get all that?"

Chapter 8

Two hours later I'm in my office poring over the files of the six missing persons from Holmes County. Throughout the morning, I've received calls from friends and family members of several missing individuals from as far away as Indianapolis. So far, none of them have matched the profile of my John Doe. Nineteen-year-old Jennifer Milkowski went missing in Cleveland four years ago. *No,* I told her mother; *this individual was male, but thank you for calling.* Forty-eight-year-old Raymond Stein disappeared from Montgomery County last year. *It's not him,* I told his father; *this individual was no older than thirty-five.* Twelve-year-old Caroline Sutton has been gone thirty years. *No, she's too young and female,* I tell her elderly mother. Seventy-seven-year-old Rosa Garcia wandered away from her daughter's home two years ago, and no one has seen her since. *No,* I told the weeping woman, *these remains are male. I'm sorry.*

I'm sorry. I'm sorry. I'm sorry.

How many times have these people heard those words from law enforcement?

Disappointment, delivered in massive doses over a period of years, has a unique sound over the phone. It's a silent echo with the power to crush the final, desperate remnants of hope. It's like a living, contagious cancer, and I feel it spreading and growing inside me with every call.

I read the six files multiple times. I look at every aspect of each case. Race. Gender. Age. The circumstances of the disappearance. Relationships at the time of their disappearance. Clothing. Jewelry. Dental work that may have been done. I look at old injuries with particular interest, because the one thing I know for certain is that this individual had a broken arm at some point in his life. It's the one element that could ID the remains and break the case wide open.

In the course of my career, I've worked several missing person cases—runaways and kidnappings mostly. The sheer number of missing never ceases to unsettle me. I honestly don't know which would be worse: knowing a loved one had been killed, or not knowing if they were dead or alive. With the missing, there's always hope. But the thing about hope is that with every day that passes without resolution, the heart is devastated a little more. It's a vicious cycle of hope and devastation. Family members left with a lack of closure. Too many never move on with their lives.

The families of these six missing persons have been interviewed dozens of times by multiple law enforcement agencies, including the local PD, the sheriff's department, and BCI. Still, I'm anxious to speak with them again. You never know when someone will mention some seemingly unimportant detail that ends up solving the case.

Using the contact information my dispatchers collected, I spend two hours contacting friends and family members of the six males missing from Holmes County. The instant I identify myself, I hear the hope leap into their voices. *Did you find him? Is he still alive?* Each time, I ask first about the broken arm. *No, he never broke his arm.* And I crush their hopes one more time.

I've just left a message for the final family, when my cell phone chirps. I glance down to see CORONER on the display, and I hit SPEAKER. "Hey, Doc."

"Don't get too excited," he tells me. "We're not finished with the autopsy. But we've found an irregularity I thought you might want to see."

"I'm on my way."

●●●

Ten minutes later, I arrive at Pomerene Hospital in Millersburg. I park outside the ER and take the elevator to the basement. The overhead lights buzz as I walk a narrow hall past the yellow-and-black biohazard sign and a plaque that reads MORGUE, AUTHORIZED PERSONNEL. At the end of the hallway, I push open dual swinging doors and traverse a second hall to the clerk's desk. Dr. Coblentz's assistant, Carmen, rises and offers a smile when I enter the reception area. "Hi, Chief. How's the storm cleanup coming along?"

"Slowly," I tell her, but I soften the word with a smile. "The good news is everyone's accounted for."

"Thank God they found that mission boy." She motions toward the door that will take me more deeply into the morgue. "Doc's expecting you."

I push through the double doors. Ahead, through the blinds of his glassed-in office, I see Doc Coblentz at his desk, leaning back in his big leather chair, his smartphone pressed against his ear. The sight of his feet atop his desk gives me pause. He's wearing his trademark scrubs with black socks and an unsightly pair of orange Crocs. Across from him is a studious-looking African American man with a salt-and-pepper goatee, horn-rimmed glasses, and close-cropped silver hair. I guess him to be in his mid-fifties.

Judging from the scrubs, he's a colleague, perhaps to consult on the bones.

Coblentz spots me and motions me in. His visitor rises and, offering a friendly smile, extends his hand. "You must be Chief Burkholder."

I smile back. "Guilty as charged."

He gives my hand a firm and lingering shake. "I'm Doctor John Harris, coroner up in Lucas County." He nods toward Coblentz. "Ludwig asked me to drive down to consult on your John Doe."

"I appreciate your coming down, Doctor Harris," I tell him.

"You just missed Doctor Stevitch." He sets his thumb and forefinger against his goatee, and in that moment he reminds me of a mathematician whose curiosity has been sparked by an abstract concept. "You have a very interesting case on your hands."

Doc Coblentz finishes his call. "Hi, Kate." His eyes flick to his colleague. "All I have to do is tell him we've found bones, and he drops everything and shows up."

"We went to med school together," Harris tells me.

"Back when dinosaurs ruled the earth," Doc adds.

"And we were more interested in poisoning ourselves with good Mexican tequila than dissecting cadavers."

"We killed a lot of brain cells in our early years," Coblentz says with a laugh. "In any case, Kate, John has been coroner up in Lucas County for . . ." He looks at Harris. ". . . Twenty-two years now?"

Harris nods. "Twenty-three next month."

"Good God, we're getting old." Coblentz shakes his head. "His subspecialty, however, is forensic osteology."

"The study of bones," I say. "I've been reading up on it."

Harris grins. "In other words, I didn't drive all the way down to Painters Mill to have a drink with an old friend."

"Although we may somehow work that in to our schedules," Coblentz adds.

I've known Doc Coblentz for about four years now, and this is a side of him I've not seen. More often than not he's cranky and grim and not always pleasant to be around. In light of his profession, I'm heartened to see this lighter aspect of his personality.

Doc Coblentz motions to his office door. "Shall we?"

We start down the hall, stopping at the alcove where packaged biohazard protection supplies are stored. As we enter, I notice Carmen has set out three sets of protective gear for us. The plastic wrappers crackle as we extract paper gowns, shoe covers, and hair caps. Once we're suited up,

Doc Coblentz hands me a pair of latex gloves and motions toward the autopsy room. "I think you know the way."

The autopsy room is about twenty feet square with gray ceramic tile walls and the acoustics of a cave. Despite the cleanliness of the place and a state-of-the-art HVAC system, the first thing I notice upon entering is the lingering smell of death and the equally unpleasant odor of formalin. Fluorescent light illuminates gleaming stainless steel counters. The backsplash is lined with a multitude of small buckets, plastic containers, and assorted apothecary-type jars. Butted against the far wall are two double sinks with arcing faucets. Higher, glass cabinets with stainless steel shelves are organized with bottles and instruments and other tools of the trade. A scale hangs down to about eye level, and I can't help but notice it's disturbingly similar to the kind used at the local grocery store.

There are two stainless steel gurneys in the room. Both are in use, the bodies draped with sheets. I've been here enough times, seen enough victims, to know neither body is that of an adult. I assume one is the bones, the other a child. Only then does it strike me that the second body is more than likely that of little Lucy Kester. Something goes cold inside me at the sight of the small, still form. I don't even realize I've stopped until I hear my name.

"Kate?"

I look up to see Doc Coblentz looking at me oddly, wondering why I've stopped in the middle of the room. "Is that Lucy Kester?" I ask.

He nods, his expression grim. "Always hate it when children come in."

I wonder if he knows I was one of the first responders. That I was one of the last people to hold her while she was still alive. That I may have inadvertently played a role in her death. "Have you done the autopsy?" I ask.

"Not yet."

"Let me know what you find, will you?"

"Of course."

My shoe covers and gown crinkle as I cross to the gurney containing the bones. Oblivious to my trepidation, Harris has already peeled back the paper covering. He's picked up an iPad and makes a note with a stylus, deep in thought, his brows knitting.

"We have the remains of a Caucasian male between the ages of eighteen and thirty-five," he begins. "From all indications he was healthy. Teeth are intact and present." He looks at me over his glasses. "So we should be able to get DNA." Then he goes back to his iPad. "This individual has had no dental work done. Not even a filling. There's no indication of disease or malnutrition. There is evidence of a completely healed fracture of both the ulna and the radius of the right arm. There's evidence that both bones underwent open reduction and internal fixation with plates and screws."

"Is there a serial number?" I ask.

He looks at Doc Coblentz. "Ludwig?"

Doc Coblentz hands me an index card. "We had to magnify it, but we got it." I put a call in to the manufacturer.

I take the card, drop it into my pocket. "Thank you."

Harris continues. "Interestingly, only one of the plates was recovered at the scene."

"There were *two* plates surgically implanted?" I say. "One of them is missing?"

"That's correct."

"The missing plate may still be at the scene," I tell him, feeling slightly alarmed because the scene was left unprotected.

Doc Coblentz shakes his head. "Kate, we discussed this at length with Stevitch. In addition to being a forensic anthropologist, he's also an expert in forensic geophysics. He went over that scene with a fine-tooth comb. The plate is not there."

"So if it's not at the scene, where is it?" I ask.

We fall silent. I'm trying to work through the logistics of the missing plate, when Dr. Harris speaks up. "I have a theory on that." He looks at me, his brows raised. "If I may continue?"

"Of course," I tell him.

"Everything's been photographed and processed," Doc Coblentz tells me. "Soil samples and those small bits of what appeared to be plastic were sent to the BCI lab in London, Ohio."

Harris picks it up from there. "Aside from the ring and a few scraps of clothing, there were no other personal effects found on scene."

"No one crawls around in the crawl space of a barn without clothes or shoes." I look down at the bones. Most are ivory in color with specks of dirt still clinging in areas. Some are stained brown and pitted. They've been arranged loosely in the form of a human skeleton, but even with my unschooled eye, I can see there are many missing. The orthopedic plate lies next to a long, thin bone. It's about four inches long and half an inch wide with a series of five oval holes evenly spaced along the length. The dirt has been removed, leaving it silver and shiny and looking out of place.

"Kate, we're missing approximately twenty-five percent of the bones," Doc Coblentz begins.

"We've got the occipital bone. The lower jaw." Harris indicates each bone as he names it, a scientist inventorying some project that has nothing to do with the death of a human being, but a puzzle that must be solved. "Both ulnas, only one of which is intact, and radius bones. The pelvis. Both femurs. Tibia and fibula are present.

140

Most of the spinal vertebrae. Scapula." He raises his gaze to mine. "Interestingly, the carpals, metacarpals, phalanges, tarsals, metatarsals, and lower phalanges are missing. Not just a few, but all of them."

"The hands?" I ask.

"And feet," Coblentz puts in.

"Is it possible they're still at the scene?" I ask. "They're small bones, and it seems likely they could be scattered. Maybe they're buried?"

Harris shakes his head adamantly. "I don't believe that's the case. However, depending on our findings regarding cause and manner of death, at some point the issue of missing bones may become a legal one, so Stevitch is going to go back out to the scene with GBR, or ground-based radar."

"To definitively rule out the possibility that something was overlooked," Doc Coblentz finishes.

"He won't find anything," Harris says. "Stevitch knows the soil properties. He knows what he's looking for. If there were bones in the ground on that site, they're here in front of us."

"Maybe animals carried the bones away over the years," I surmise. "Dogs or coyotes."

"Of course that's a possibility," Doc Coblentz says. "Anytime remains are unprotected, they are vulnerable to scavenger activity."

"But that doesn't explain the *markings* I found on some of the bones," Harris tells me. "Nor does it explain why so many of the smaller bones are missing."

"Markings?" Puzzled, sensing they're withholding the punch line to a private joke and I'm being left in the dark, I look from man to man. "Signs of trauma? What?"

"Well, basically, both hands and feet are missing," Doc Coblentz says.

I've heard of cases—homicides—in which killers removed the hands of their victims so the police were unable to identify the victims using fingerprints, but I didn't expect it on this case. "So we're dealing with a homicide," I say slowly.

"Probably, but we can't say for certain," Harris says.

"But if the hands were cut off—" I begin.

Coblentz interrupts. "Not cut off, Kate. *Chewed* off."

"Chewed?" It's the last thing I expected him to say, and for the first time I understand why they're so titillated. Not because they're macabre, but because their scientific minds have been confronted by a particularly challenging puzzle.

"By *what?*" I ask.

"We don't know," Doc Coblentz admits. "We're trying to identify the tooth marks now."

"*Tooth* marks? Seriously?" Incredulity rings hard in my voice. If the circumstances were different—if we weren't dealing with the death of a human being—I'd expect one of them to burst into laughter and shout, "Surprise!"

"Let me explain." With gloved hands, Harris picks up a bone that's slender and curved and about a foot in length. "This is the left proximal ulna, which is at the distal end of the forearm."

"Small bone in the lower forearm," Doc Coblentz explains.

"It's not unusual in cases like this for skeletal remains to exhibit postmortem carnivore and scavenger marks. In Ohio, for example, we would probably be dealing with coyotes or dogs or even a feral cat. The bones would show evidence of chewing, crushing, and gnawing. Sometimes the ends of long bones are missing altogether, which happens when the animals are trying to get to the marrow. This typically occurs if a body is dumped in a remote location and it remains undiscovered for an extended period of time."

Looking troubled, Harris indicates a long, narrow, carved indentation on the bone. "I can't be certain, but I don't believe these gouges were made by dogs or coyotes."

"By what, then?" I ask.

"We don't know," Doc Coblentz replies.

I think about that a moment, chilled by the possibilities. "Were you or will you be able to give me cause or manner of death?"

"Undetermined at this point," Harris says with a shrug.

"I'm not sure we'll ever know for certain, Kate," Doc Coblentz adds.

"No clothes or shoes. Hands missing. Chances are the body was disposed in a garbage bag and hidden in that crawl space." I look from man to man. "It's got to be homicide. But we need to be able to prove it, and we can't do that without an official ruling from you."

"We can only go by the facts," Harris tells me. "These bones are not going to reveal their secrets easily."

"So what's your theory?" I ask.

Coblentz nods at Harris. "John?"

"Let me preface by giving you some preliminary info on how we've arrived at this non-conclusion, if you will," Harris begins. "Typically, we have three types of bone injury: antemortem, which is an injury that takes place when the decedent is still alive. We can tell the injury occurred before death because there's some level of bone remodeling or healing. The second type of injury is postmortem, which takes place after death. In the instance of a postmortem bone injury, the edges of the bone will be rough or worn, if you will. And, of course, there's no remodeling.

"The third type of bone injury is perimortem. As with the postmortem bone injury, there is no bone remodeling. But with a perimortem injury, the edges of the damaged area are relatively sharp and crisp." Dr. Harris removes his glasses and looks at me. "We believe the injuries on the distal area of the ulna, as well as the lower extremities of both fibulas, occurred perimortem."

"You're going to have to explain that in English." But even as I say the words, in some small corner of my mind I already know, and a shiver hovers between my shoulder blades.

"The injury occurred at or near the time of death," Doc Coblentz tells me.

I stare at the two men, trying to get my mind around the repercussions of that. "Let me get this straight," I say. "The bone injuries you're referring to are tooth marks?"

"Correct," Harris says.

Coblentz meets my gaze. "These tooth marks, carved into those three large bones, occurred shortly before or shortly after death."

"Are you telling me this individual may have died *because* of those tooth marks?" I ask.

"I'm telling you it's a possibility," Harris says.

I look down at the bones, and the chill that had been hovering moves through me. "So this decedent could have been attacked by an animal and killed?"

"An animal or animals as yet unidentified," Harris tells me.

"Could that have occurred in the crawl space beneath the barn?" I ask. "Maybe he was working on the foundation and a coyote or dog attacked him? Or was he killed elsewhere and his remains moved and hidden in that crawl space?"

"We have no way of knowing for certain," Doc Coblentz says.

"And, of course, we don't yet know which species of animal," Harris points out.

I stare at him, searching my memory for someone I've come in contact with over the years who might be able to identify the tooth marks, but I come up blank. "Do either of you know of someone who might be able to identify the tooth marks?" I ask. "If that was the cause of death, I need to know."

Harris nods. "I worked with a guy over at the Columbus Zoo six or seven years ago. I'd performed an autopsy on a Franklin County man who'd been keeping a cougar illegally on his property and was mauled to death when he went into the animal's pen to feed it. Nelson Woodburn's specialty is wildlife biology. If anyone can figure out the source of those teeth marks, Woodburn can."

I address Doc Coblentz: "Can you forward images of those tooth marks to Woodburn?"

"Right away."

Harris looks excited by the prospect of involving his colleague. "I'll let him know to expect your call." He grins. "Nelson can't resist a good mystery."

I think about everything I've learned and realize that while it's crucial to determine the source of the tooth marks, there's still a possibility that foul play was involved. "So if those pieces of fabric or plastic found on scene turn out to be a garbage bag, then it's possible that while our victim may have been attacked by an as-yet-unknown animal, his body may have still been put into some type of bag and dumped in that crawl space."

"Bag aside, perhaps he was attacked and injured and crawled beneath the barn, trying to reach safety," Doc offers.

I nod, realizing that while I know a lot more about this victim than when I started, the list of things I don't know is much longer. "I guess I'd been hoping this guy had been working on the foundation or repairing a squeaky floor plank in the barn and had a heart attack or something."

"Unfortunately," Harris says with a sigh. "I suspect this individual suffered a much more horrific demise."

Chapter 9

Herb and Marie Strackbein live in a small Victorian that's painted a cheery yellow and set among mature maple and black walnut trees. According to the Holmes County auditor, they've owned the property on Gellerman Road since inheriting it when his mother passed away in 1978. The Strackbeins are in their sixties and live in Painters Mill.

I park in a shady spot at the curb and shut down the engine. Concrete steps draw my eye to a railed front porch, where blooming geraniums and petunias spill from a dozen or so terra-cotta pots. A red Volkswagen sits in the driveway in front of a one-car detached garage, also painted yellow. It's a pleasant-looking home with a cozy, welcoming countenance. I take the sidewalk to the door and ring the bell. When no one answers, I leave the porch and look in the garage, but there's no one there. I'm on my way back to the Explorer, when I hear the sound of a chainsaw coming from the backyard. I take the narrow sidewalk that cuts between the house and the garage.

"Hello? Mr. and Mrs. Strackbein?" I call out. "It's Chief of Police Kate Burkholder!"

I've just reached the chain-link gate, when a woman wearing a floppy straw hat peers around the corner of the house. "Oh. Hi. We're back here."

I open the gate and go through. "Sounds like someone's doing some storm cleanup," I say.

She takes off her hat and wipes her forehead with the back of her hand. "I worry when he gets that chainsaw out, so I came out to supervise and make sure he doesn't cut off his fingers. Almost as bad as when he gets up on that ladder. I swear the man is going to kill himself one of these days." But she says the words with a generous helping of good humor.

As if realizing I'm not there to shoot the breeze, she cocks her head. "We're not making too much noise with the chainsaw, are we?"

"No, ma'am. I wanted to ask you and your husband some questions about some property you own out on Gellerman Road."

"We saw that the barn was down." Nodding, she clucks her tongue. "It's just crazy how a tornado picks and chooses what it does and doesn't destroy."

She's a chatty, friendly woman with an amiable demeanor. But I know from experience that just because someone looks like your favorite aunt doesn't mean she doesn't have secrets.

"Can we help you?"

I look up at the sound of the male voice to see a sixty-something man approach. He's wearing dark work trousers and a white T-shirt that's damp with sweat at the chest and armpits.

"Mr. Strackbein?"

"That's me." He comes up behind his wife and sets his hand protectively on her shoulder. "What can we do for you?"

"I was just asking your wife about your property on Gellerman Road," I tell him.

149

"Knew that barn was going to go down one day," he says. "We inherited it from my mom when she passed in 'eighty-eight. Randy Smith leases it from us, puts in corn or soybeans every year."

"There was a Boy Scout troop cleaning up out there, and a couple of boys discovered human remains in the crawl space of your barn."

The man's eyes widen. "What?"

Mrs. Strackbein gasps. "A *body?*"

"I'm surprised you didn't hear about it on the news," I say.

"We were without power for two days," he tells me. "I heard something about bones on the radio, but didn't realize it was on *our* property."

"Who is it?" Mrs. Strackbein adds.

"We're trying to identify the remains," I tell them. "I'm wondering if either of you have any idea who it might be or how they may have gotten into that crawl space."

The two shake their heads. "No earthly idea," Mrs. Strackbein says.

I turn my attention to Mr. Strackbein. "Did your parents ever mention the crawl space?" I ask. "Did they ever say anything that might explain who died down there or why? Or did any friends or family ever go missing?"

Pulling a blue kerchief from his rear pocket, he blots sweat from his forehead. "No, ma'am. They never said a thing. That property's been in our family for as long as I can remember. I grew up in the house that used to be there. Played in that old barn, too."

"I understand the house burned back in 1982?" I ask.

"Mom was living there by herself back then. Couldn't take care of the place. Fire marshal said it was some kind of electrical fire."

"She moved in with us after that," Mrs. Strackbein adds.

"How long has . . ." He grapples for the right word. ". . . *it* been there?"

"Many years." I pause, watching for any signs of nervousness or discomfort, but I get neither. These people are genuinely shocked. "Did your parents ever quarrel with anyone that you know of? Did they have any enemies?"

"Not that I know of." Mr. Strackbein scratches his head. "My dad was kind of a crotchety old guy. You know, rubbed folks the wrong way sometimes. But that's just the way he was."

"What about your mom?"

"She was a real quiet gal. Nice, though. Baked a lot. Everyone really liked her."

"Didn't stand up for herself enough if you ask me," his wife puts in. "But everyone loved her."

"Have both of your parents passed away?" I ask.

"Dad in 1981. And mom in 'eighty-eight."

I nod, trying not to be disappointed. "Did you

ever see anything unusual or strange in the barn or on the property?" I ask.

He shakes his head adamantly. "I spent many a day exploring that dusty old place." He huffs a laugh. "Thought I knew every inch of it, but I never went down into the crawl space. I guess you never know about a place, do you?"

I swing by LaDonna's Diner for a coffee-to-go, and I've nearly reached the station, when my phone vibrates against my hip. A glance at the display tells me it's Nelson Woodburn, the wildlife biologist with the Columbus Zoo. I fumble with my Bluetooth and catch the call on the third ring. "Mr. Woodburn?"

"Yes, hello, Chief Burkholder. I understand you've got a mystery on your hands down there in Painters Mill."

"The more we learn about the remains, the more questions that arise."

"Well, I've never met a mystery I didn't enjoy, and I must admit with regard to this one my curiosity has bested me." He has a soft, scholarly-sounding voice with a hint of Kentucky. "Doctor Harris e-mailed me the images of the teeth marks in some of the large bones. I downloaded them immediately and set to work enlarging and trying to identify them."

"I appreciate your getting to this case so quickly." I have a whole new appreciation for science nerds. "Any luck identifying the tooth marks?"

He pauses with a smidgen too much drama. "I believe so, which I did mainly by ruling out the usual suspects, the domestic dog and the *Canis latrans thamnos*, a subspecies of coyote present in this part of Ohio." Another dramatic pause. "I looked at the dental formula of these mammals and I was quickly able to rule them out."

"So, if it wasn't a coyote or dog, what kind of animal was it?" In the back of my mind, I'm terrified he's going to tell me human, which would undoubtedly add another layer of creepiness to an already creepy case.

"Interestingly, I just finished writing a paper on livestock and animal predation identification. I believe those marks were made by one or more *Sus scrofa domesticus*," he tells me. "Or the common domestic swine."

"Pigs?"

"That's correct."

"Feral?"

"I'm afraid I don't have the answer to that. I can, however, tell you that there are very few feral hogs in this part of Ohio, if any. If this death occurred twenty or thirty years ago, chances are extremely low that feral hogs were involved."

I'm still trying to make sense of the information in terms of cause and manner of death, but it refuses to settle in my brain. "Doctor Harris, the coroner, believes that the hands and feet of the victim were chewed off. Is that kind of injury common to this type of attack?"

"In the course of my research, I learned that most often feral hogs aren't even looked at as predators with regard to livestock. But they are omnivores, and they will predate young or injured livestock. Typically when feeding in the wild, unlike other predators such as cougars or even bears, they leave nothing behind."

"So they would consume even bones?"

"It depends on how hungry they were and how much time they had. The jaw of the feral hog is certainly powerful enough to crush bone."

An unexpected chill sweeps through me. I can't think of a more unimaginably horrific manner of death than to be consumed alive by a large creature with jaws strong enough to crush bone. . . .

"In this instance, it looks like only the hands and feet were . . . consumed," I say.

"Of course, we have no way of knowing, but if I were to speculate, perhaps the attack was interrupted. And domestic swine aren't typically as aggressive as their cousins, the javelinas. That said, if domestic swine are left without food, they will certainly consume whatever food source becomes available in order to survive. In fact, there was a recent case in Oregon in which an elderly farmer went out to feed his hogs. When he didn't return, his family went out to check on him. The only thing they found was his watch."

The weight of Nelson Woodburn's words follows me into the station. I'm unduly relieved there are no media present. It's only when I notice my second-shift dispatcher at her workstation that I realize business hours have long since passed. Apparently, this story isn't sensational enough for anyone to be setting up tents. Yet.

"Hey, Chief," Jodie says cheerily.

"Hi." I cross to her desk. "You up to doing some research for me?"

"Always."

"Draft an e-mail to the Ohio Department of Agriculture. I need the names and contact information of every farmer in Holmes County who raised hogs from 1982 through 2005. Send it so they have it first thing in the morning. I'll follow up with a call."

She plucks a pen from her desk and jots my instructions. "I'll get right on it."

"I also need a list and contact info for all large-animal veterinarians in Holmes County who were practicing during that same time frame. Copy Lois and Mona on everything because I'm probably going to get them involved as well."

"Sure." Her brows knit, and she gives me a questioning look. "Is this related to those remains, or are you working on something else?"

"I'll let you know the instant I find out."

Once I'm behind my desk, I call Herb Strackbein, who tells me hogs have never been raised at the old barn on Gellerman Road. His father raised cattle years ago, but never had the proper fencing or facilities for hogs. I'll double-check his claim in the morning once I'm able to get in contact with the Department of Agriculture. For now, I have no reason to believe he's lying.

I spend an hour going over the files of the six missing men again, this time looking for any connection to farming or farm animals. Twenty-two-year-old Mark Elliott had just graduated from the College of Wooster and was newly engaged to his high school sweetheart. A young man just starting his life. No criminal record. No warrants. No connection to hogs. Thirty-five-year-old Raymond Stetmeyer, father of two young children, was married to Silvia Stetmeyer, an administrative assistant in Millersburg. Again, no connection to farming or farm animals. Thirty-one-year-old Ricky Maitland, no children, married to Gladys Morrison of Berlin, who remarried just last year. Nothing. Twenty-year-old Leroy Nolt. His is the only family I haven't yet spoken with, but a glance at the wall clock tells me it's after 10:00 p.m. Too late to make the call tonight. I'll need to pull employment records, but as far as I can tell from the information I have, none of the missing have any connection to farming or farm animals.

I'd told Tomasetti I'd try to be home in time for dinner. Not that he believed me; he knows I'm snowed under with this case, and he's okay with that. But I'm not being completely honest with myself. Or him. The truth of the matter is, I'm avoiding him. Tomasetti is an astute man; he knows I'm preoccupied with something. I'm terrified he'll look at me and somehow know. I have no idea how he will react to the possibility of my being pregnant.

The smart thing to do would be to stop by the drug store and buy a pregnancy test. At least then I'll know what I'm dealing with. Chances are this missed period is just a temporary manifestation of stress or diet.

Not allowing myself to take the thought any further, I gather the file, shove everything into my laptop case, and head for the door.

Forty-five minutes later, I arrive at the farm and let myself in through the back door. Tomasetti left the light above the stove on for me, which tells me he's already gone to bed. I cross the kitchen and see he left a note next to the coffeemaker. *Hi, guy.* Next to the note is a foil-wrapped chocolate Kiss. It's a silly thing, but it warms the cold knot of fear in my gut. It gives me hope that every-thing is going to be all right, no matter what the outcome of the test.

I go to the guest bedroom I've set up as an

office and set down my laptop case. Kneeling, I dig inside and pull out the pregnancy kit. I feel like a teenager sneaking a pack of cigarettes into the bathroom as I tuck the box into my shirt and take it to the half bath downstairs. It takes me several minutes to figure out how to use it. I spent a couple of extra dollars for the digital kind. It's pretty much idiotproof, and the results only take two minutes.

I take the test and set the stick on the counter next to the sink. I catch a glimpse of my reflection in the mirror as I wash my hands. A pale, worried-looking woman stares back at me. "You're not pregnant," I tell her firmly. "It's just stress. Crazy schedule. You need a vacation."

But I can't ignore the butterflies fluttering in my stomach or the way my mouth has gone dry. I don't want to look down at that tiny oval window.

I force my gaze to the test stick. I'm expecting relief. A moment I'll share with Tomasetti later and we'll laugh our asses off. The floor seems to drop beneath my feet, when, instead, I find myself staring down at that little oval window and the word PREGNANT stares back.

Chapter 10

I arrive at the station a few minutes after seven. I managed to avoid Tomasetti this morning, getting into the shower while he made coffee and then rushing out the door while he showered. He's probably wondering why I didn't at least touch base with him before I left, but there's no way I could look him in the eye without his knowing something's wrong.

I'm usually pretty good at compartmentalizing my life, doing my job without letting personal matters interfere. But I didn't sleep much last night. The reality of what I've let happen is like a hammer, pounding incessantly against my brain. This morning, I'm sick with worry. I don't know if my jittery stomach is from the pregnancy or the raw nerves that came with confirmation of it.

"Morning, Chief."

I enter through the front door to see Mona standing at the dispatch station with her headset on. The Black Keys belt out "Tighten Up" a little too loudly. I'm inordinately glad for the normalcy of the moment. A sense of stability and control washes over me, and I'm reminded that the world, that my position as chief of police, is much larger than my own problems. Women have been having babies since the beginning of time. I'll get through this. Tomasetti and I will deal with it. For now, I have to set it aside and concentrate on my job.

"Hey, Mona." Feeling calmer, I cross to the dispatch station and pluck pink slips from my message slot.

I scan them as I walk to the coffee station. Most are from media outlets wanting an update on the remains. There are two from Vern Nolt, the father of Leroy Nolt and the only family member with a missing loved one with whom I haven't yet spoken. Anxious to talk with him, I fill a mug with coffee, unlock my office, and slide behind my desk. While my computer boots, I make the call.

"This is Vern Nolt." The voice on the other end of the line has the froggy, slightly shaky quality of an old man.

Before I've finished identifying myself, he interjects, "Did you find my son? Did you find Leroy?"

"I don't know," I say quickly, not wanting to get his hopes up only to crush them if the identification process doesn't pan out. "Mr. Nolt, there were some human remains discovered here in Painters Mill. I'm talking with all the families in the area who've reported family members missing. I'd like to ask you a few questions if you have a moment."

"Of course I do."

I pull out my notes on the missing men from Holmes County and begin by verifying some basic information: name, age, the date of his disappearance. And then, "Mr. Nolt, do you know if your son ever had a broken arm?"

A quick intake of breath hisses over the line. Then the sound of a palm placed over the handset. He doesn't respond immediately, so I give him a moment. "Mr. Nolt?"

"Leroy worked at Quality Implement for a couple of years," he tells me. "There was a forklift accident. Pallet tipped over and a huge auger fell on him, broke his right arm nearly in half."

A sort of dark excitement surges. The kind that comes when I know a case is about to break. "Did your son have to have surgery to repair that broken arm?"

"Doctor Alan Johnson in Millersburg operated a couple of days after the accident. Had to wait for the swelling to go down. He put in some kind of pin."

"Mr. Nolt, I'd like to speak with you in person. Would it be all right if I drove over?"

Another short pause. The sound of a shuddery exhale.

He knows, I think.

"I'll let my wife know you're coming," he says and ends the call.

• • •

Vernon and Sue Nolt live in a nicely kept Craftsman-style home across the street from Sutton's IGA. I pull onto the asphalt driveway and park beneath the shade of an elm tree. Ahead, I see a detached two-car garage and a yard that's fenced with white pickets. A geriatric-looking mutt of dubious pedigree barks at me between the slats of the fence when I get out of the Explorer.

I'm ascending the concrete steps to the front porch, when the door swings open. An elderly man shuffles out. His eyes dart to mine, and in that instant I see a combination of anticipation and hope, and I know that after thirty years of not knowing the whereabouts or fate of his son, he's ready for the mystery to be solved, even if the news is bad. On his heels is a plump woman of about seventy. I don't realize they're Mennonite until I notice her print dress, the blue-and-white-checkered apron tied at her waist, and her head covering.

"Mr. and Mrs. Nolt?" I cross to them, my hand extended, and introduce myself. "Thank you for agreeing to see me on such short notice."

The elderly man's hand feels quivery and frail within mine. "I'm Vern." He steps aside to introduce his wife.

She's already moving around him, her eyes seeking mine. "Please tell us. Have you found him?" She looks down at my extended hand. As if it's an afterthought, she gives it a single, weak shake. "Did you find Leroy?"

"I'm not sure yet, but there were some human remains found here in Painters Mill. I'd like to talk to you about your son."

They stare at me, hanging on my every word, and I remind myself that I'm talking about a son they've hoped would return alive for thirty years now. "Mr. and Mrs. Nolt, can we go inside and talk?"

"Of course. Where are my manners?" The woman wipes her hands on her apron and then opens the door. "You can call me Sue. I made some iced tea. Come on inside."

Vern motions me through the door, and I follow her into the living room. The interior of the house is murky and cramped but not unpleasant. Dust motes fly where sunlight slants in between lacy curtains at the front window. The aromas of vanilla potpourri and recently baked bread add a comforting countenance. I didn't know my grandparents, but if I ever imagined walking into their home, it would have been like this one.

I motion toward the Amish quilt hanging on the wall above the sofa. It's heirloom quality, a stunning combination of mauve and cream and black with the iconic eight-point star in the center. "It's beautiful," I say. "Did you make it?"

Sue's smile is a sad twisting of lips. "It was a birthday present from Leroy a few weeks before he disappeared. I'd been looking for one with those colors." As if catching herself drifting back to a past that's long gone, she clucks her lips. "I'll fetch the tea."

Vern asks me to sit, so I take the brocade chair adjacent to the coffee table. Looking nervous, he eases himself onto an overstuffed sofa that's crowded with crocheted pillows, and I wonder how many nights his wife stayed up late, making those pillow covers, wondering where her son was, if he was alive, if she'd ever see him again.

"You have a nice home," I tell him. "How long have you lived here?"

"We bought it back in 1975." He smiles, and I notice that his teeth are still straight and white. "Leroy was ten. The first thing we did was build the tree house in the backyard. I can't tell you how many nights he spent out there with his friends, telling ghost stories and looking at the naked ladies in my *National Geographic* with the flashlight."

The thought makes me smile. "Do you have any other children?"

"A daughter, Rachel," he tells me. "Her name is Zimmerman now. Married a nice Mennonite man. They run the bed-and-breakfast out there by the winery. A Place in Thyme Cottage."

I pull out my pad and pen and write down the name. "You and your wife are Mennonite?"

He nods. "We left the Swartzentruber Amish

shortly after we were married." He waves his hand as if that part of his life is nothing more than a bad memory. "The bishop wasn't happy about it, and our church district basically excommunicated us. But their *Ordnung* was too strict for us." He grins. "I always liked cars a lot more than buggies."

Sue returns with a wicker tray containing three glasses and a paper plate heaped with oatmeal cookies. She sets the tray on the coffee table between us and looks at me. "We just heard about those Boy Scouts finding that skeleton," she says with a shake of her head. "And I knew."

"We're not certain it's your son," I tell her.

"It's him," she says. "A mother knows these things."

No one pays any attention to the tea or the cookies. They're a formality. Good manners. A minute or two for both of them to mentally brace for the discussion we're about to have. Or the news they're about to receive.

"Several agencies are involved in the identification process," I tell them. "The Bureau of Criminal Investigation may call you to make an appointment to take DNA samples. It'll entail a quick swab of the mouth. They need a close relative to match it to."

"Tell them to come any time," Vern says. "We want to know if it's him."

I reach for the tea and sip. It's cold and tastes

of mint, exactly the way my mother used to make it when I was a girl. "So your son had a broken arm a few years before he went missing?"

Vern nods, then leans forward and puts his elbows on his knees. "Like I said, he broke it at work." He looks at his wife, who's gone silent and still. "When he was about eighteen, Mama?" he asks.

"Seventeen, Papa," she says. "Folks at the farm store were so nice. Paid for everything, and his boss gave him a hundred-dollar bonus for being such a good boy."

"The remains found belong to a young man who could have been about your son's age when he disappeared. There's evidence that this young man had broken his right arm and had to have two plates with screws implanted to repair it."

Sue gasps, presses her hand over her mouth as if to smother it. "It's him. Oh, dear Lord."

Vern gives a single hard nod, then raises his gaze to mine. "What happened to him?" he asks. "How did he die? He was so young."

"We don't know the manner or cause of death yet."

Shaking his head, he looks down at the floor.

I give them a moment to digest the news and look around the room. On the end table is a framed photograph of an attractive young man with a mischievous grin, tousled hair and laughing eyes. "Is that your son?" I ask.

Vern nods. "Last picture we took of him."

"He looks happy," I say.

"Handsome, too." Sue smiles at the photo. "Took the picture on his birthday." A soft, sad sound squeezes from her throat. "Didn't know it'd be his last."

I pause, then go to my next question. "What's the name of the doctor who did the surgery on your son's broken arm?"

"Doctor Alan Johnson," Vern puts in. "He's a bone and joint doctor in Millersburg."

I write down the name. "There's a serial number on the plate, so we may be able to match it up with your son's medical records."

The old man nods. "I hope so."

"Did Leroy know any members of the Strackbein family?" I ask. "They owned the farm on Gellerman Road where the remains were found."

"Never heard him talk about anyone by the name of Strackbein," Sue tells me.

"Did Leroy have any enemies that you know of?" I ask.

"Everyone loved our son," she replies. "He was polite and conscientious. Had a good sense of humor. He was a hard worker, too."

I turn my attention to Vern, who's looking down at the cookies, his mouth working, and I sense he's holding something back. "Mr. Nolt?"

The old man raises his head and looks at his

wife. "He was putting in a lot of hours at the farm store. Trying to save enough money to go to the college in Goshen."

"It's an Anabaptist college," Sue adds.

Sensing there's more, I prod. "Did he ever get into any trouble?"

Vern sighs, and I hear something like resignation in that small release of breath. "Leroy was a good boy," he says adamantly. "But there was a time, a few years, when he liked to live his life on the fast road."

"Sometimes even good kids get into trouble." I shrug, hoping he'll elaborate, knowing that sometimes parents withhold details to protect their children. Or in this case, the reputation or memory of their child. "Sometimes that's part of growing up."

"Leroy went through a phase when he was drinking alcohol," Sue tells me. "Smoking cigarettes. And he ran around with a few English girls."

"Loose girls," Vern adds.

"Did he have a girlfriend?" I ask.

Another long look between the elderly couple, and I realize they've been together for so long they can practically read each other's minds.

"We don't know for sure," Vern says finally.

"Leroy was . . . quiet about such things," Sue adds. "You know, private."

"But we think he was seeing a girl."

"Any idea who she was?" I ask.

Vern shakes his head. "I asked him about it once. Leroy just grinned like he always did and said he'd tell me when he could. I'm not one to pry so I let it be."

"What led you to believe he was seeing someone?" I ask.

"Well," Vern says slowly, "his attitude changed mostly. He became a happy young man. Had a spring in his step, I guess. He stopped drinking and running around."

"He stopped seeing those loose English girls." Sue spits out the words as if they're a bad taste.

We fall silent. I sip the tea, everything they've told me about their son turning over in my head. "What about friends?"

"He used to run around with Clarence Underwood back in the day," Vern tells me.

"They were best friends," Sue agrees. "I never liked that boy. Had shifty eyes. But Leroy thought he was the berries."

I pull out my notebook and write down the name, but I'm familiar with Clarence Underwood. Three years ago, I busted him on a charge of manufacturing methamphetamine, which was a first-degree felony because there were two children in the home at the time. Just two months ago, I received notification from the Ohio Department of Rehabilitation and Correction that Underwood was about to be released after a two-year stint in Mansfield. I did my due diligence as chief and stopped by his rental house to welcome him back. He wasn't happy to see me, but the visit let him know I've got eyes on him. So far Underwood has kept his nose clean, but I'm certain the list of things he doesn't get caught doing is a lot longer than the things we in law enforcement know about.

"Is it possible your son was involved in drugs?" I ask.

Vern harrumphs. "I hope you believe me when I tell you the answer to that is no."

"Leroy might've been on the fast road for a while," his wife adds, "but, Chief Burkholder, he had no interest in drugs."

As a cop I know that even if Leroy didn't partake in drugs himself, the lucrative nature of the business can be a powerful draw. "How long did your son work at Quality Implement?" I ask.

"He started as a stock boy when he was still in high school," Vern replies. "Worked there up until the day he disappeared. He was always getting Employee of the Month, too. Putting in for overtime. Leroy was a hard worker."

"Did he ever do any work at any of the local farms? Or did he ever work around livestock?" I ask. "Hogs?"

"Well, as a matter of fact, he worked down at that big hog operation in Coshocton for a few months. Place closed down six or seven years

170

ago." Vern looks at me oddly. "Why do you ask?"

"Just trying to gather as much background information as possible," I tell him. "Was he friendly with anyone else who worked at the hog operation?"

"Not that I recall. He didn't work there long. Didn't like the conditions."

I nod. "During those years when he was drinking and running around, did he have any favorite hangouts?"

"That wild place out on the highway."

"The Brass Rail?"

"That's the one."

I nod, letting everything that had been said settle, and then I rise. "I appreciate your time, Mr. and Mrs. Nolt."

They rise, both of them looking surprised that I'm leaving. "Chief Burkholder, we need to know. Is the body his?"

I meet their gazes head-on and hold them. "Without DNA testing or a match on that surgical plate, I can't give you a definitive answer yet. I'm sorry; I know the waiting is extremely difficult."

"We need to know," Sue whispers. "Please."

"If I had to guess? I'd say there's a high probability it's him," I say quietly. "There are too many similarities. The broken arm. The timing of his disappearance. His age." I shrug. "I wish I had a better answer for you." The words feel pitifully inadequate.

"He is with God." The old man looks down at his shoes. *"Er hot en ewwerflissich lewe gfaahre."* He lived an abundant life.

"Don't worry, Papa." His wife pats his shoulder. "Once all the scientific stuff is done, we'll bring him home."

Chapter 11

There is a universal truth when it comes to violent crime: the deceased is never the only victim. The people who loved him—family members, friends, and lovers—continue to suffer long after the deed is done. With an unsolved missing person case, most loved ones never receive any kind of closure or find any semblance of peace again in their lifetimes. Too many take the grief, the loss, and that insidious lack of closure with them to the grave.

The tentacles of violent crime reach far beyond friends and family. Sometimes they extend to law enforcement as well; the detectives and special agents and investigators who spend countless hours over a period of months or even years talking to the bereaved, building a profile of the missing individual, trying to solve the mystery and, hopefully, bring them home. Contrary to common wisdom, cops invest a fair share of emotion. For some, too much. They lose sleep, time with their families, and peace of mind.

After my conversation with Sue and Vern Nolt, and despite my best efforts not to, I feel the weight of their sorrow pressing down on me. As I pull onto the street and head toward town, it occurs to me that learning of their son's death is not the worst news Sue and Vern Nolt will receive in the coming days. The circumstances and the details of his death will undoubtedly add to their misery.

I pull out my cell and hit the speed dial for dispatch. Lois picks up on the first ring. "Hey, Chief."

"Can you get me contact info on Doctor Alan Johnson? I believe he's an orthopedic surgeon in Millersburg."

"Sure."

"And the contact info on the hog operation in Coshocton."

"You got it."

"I need a ten-twenty-nine on Clarence Underwood, too." It's the code for "check-for-wanted." I spell the last name.

"Will do."

"Thanks. Give me a call." I hit my radio and hail Glock. "Can you ten-twenty-five me— four-two-six Gettysburg?" I recite Underwood's address from memory.

"I can be there in two minutes."

"See you there."

Clarence Underwood lives in a downtrodden

neighborhood of circa-1960s bungalows inter- spersed with double-wide trailer homes. A robin's-egg blue water tower stands sentinel, bracketed on one side by the railroad tracks, an abandoned gas station on the other. The best feature of the subdivision is the trees, a virtual forest of stately elms and maples, but any semblance of beauty ends there. Gettysburg Avenue is a narrow, pitted strip of asphalt with broken sidewalks and potholes deep enough to break an axle. A mishmash of vehicles, many of which are nearly as old as the homes, makes the street seem even narrower. To my right, someone has set up a basketball hoop in an abandoned lot, and six preteen boys eye me with suspicion as I idle past. I smile and wave, and I try not to notice when a kid with scraggly blond hair in baggy jeans jabs his middle finger at me.

Glock's cruiser is parked a few houses down from Underwood's place. I pull up behind him and hail dispatch. "Ten-twenty-three," I say, letting Lois know we've arrived on scene.

"Ten-four."

I get out and meet Glock on the street. "So what'd he do now?" he asks.

"Nothing that we know of." We amble to the buckled sidewalk, and I tell him about my conversation with Sue and Vern Nolt.

"You think Underwood had something to do with Leroy Nolt's disappearance?"

174

"It wouldn't be the first time drug money has come between friends."

We ascend the porch steps. The rail to my right is missing, the posts broken off at the base. The wood-plank floor creaks beneath our feet as we cross to the front door. It's older and bracketed by narrow sidelight windows. Standing slightly to one side in case some paranoid freak decides to shoot through the door, I knock.

I hear the blare of chainsaw rock coming from inside, the bass drum loud enough to rattle the glass in the window. I wait a full minute and then use the heel of my hand to knock a second time.

"Police!" I call out. "Clarence Underwood? Open the door, please!"

The door squeaks like a rat with its tail caught in a trap, and opens about halfway. I find myself looking at Underwood. He's in his mid-fifties now, with a full beard sprinkled with gray. He's wearing an AC/DC T-shirt, faded jeans, and a scuffed pair of Doc Martens. He's thin, but the T-shirt is stretched taut over a generous belly. His eyes are a striking blue, electric and intelligent, but they're shot with red and hostile when they land on me.

I pull out my badge and hold it up for him to see. "Mr. Underwood?"

"That's me."

"I'd like to ask you some questions," I say. "May we come inside?"

Bloodshot eyes sweep from me to Glock and back to me. "What about?"

"Leroy Nolt."

I can't be sure, but for an instant I think I see a smile in those eyes. But I can't tell if it's the smile of a man remembering an old friend, or a man who knows he got away with murder. "Do I got a choice?" he asks.

"I just want to ask you some questions about his disappearance. You're under no obligation to talk to me, but if you don't, I'll be back with a warrant."

He glances quickly behind him, an indication that he doesn't want us to see whatever lies on the other side of the door. "I'll come out there."

Glock and I move back simultaneously. Out of the corner of my eye, I'm aware of Glock keeping his hands loose and ready, maintaining a safe distance in case Underwood does something stupid.

The door swings open and he steps onto the porch. Even from two feet away I smell alcohol on his breath. He's not falling-down drunk, but he's not sober, either.

"I read about them bones found out to that old barn," he says slowly. "They belong to Leroy?"

The question shouldn't surprise me; news travels fast in a small town, especially if there's a dead body involved. But it's been my experience that when people have something to hide, the last thing they do is raise the subject I'm about to question them about. But then Underwood is smart enough to know how to play the game.

"We're not sure yet," I tell him.

"I reckon you wouldn't be here if you didn't think it was him." He shakes his head. "I'd always hoped he'd made it out of this shithole. Come back richer than God, and maybe share a little with his old buddy." He wobbles a little as he moves from the doorway, sets his hand against the siding to steady himself. "What do you want with me?"

"When's the last time you saw him?" I ask.

"Damn. Long time ago." He scratches his head, loosening a shower of dandruff onto the shoulders of his T-shirt. "A couple of days before he disappeared. I was working at Quality Implement at the time. We used to hang out on the weekends. Cruise around in his souped-up Camaro and drink Little Kings." His chuckle ends in a phlegmy cough. "He could put it away, that's for sure."

"Did the two of you ever argue?" I ask. "Have any disagreements about anything."

"Nope and nope. Leroy was easygoing. He was fun to hang out with, and we got on just fine."

"Did he have any enemies that you know of?"

Underwood shakes his head. "No way. Leroy was as laid back as they come. Funny as hell, too. Everyone liked him."

"Was he ever in to drugs? Any illegal activity?"

"That was me." His laugh is dark and unhappy.

"We did our share of drinking, but Leroy never got into anything else. Didn't even smoke weed."

"Was he seeing anyone? A woman?"

His brows knit. "We'd pick up chicks occasionally. Take them out to that old covered bridge and . . . you know." He shoves his hands into his pockets. "Damn, it's hard to remember. We was so young."

"You want to keep your hands where we can see them?" Glock says from behind me.

Underwood scowls at him but pulls out his hands, flashes his palms at us. "For fuck sake," he mutters.

"Clarence, relax," I say, putting a warning in my voice. "Just a few more questions, okay?"

"Whatever." He leans against the house, crossing his arms in front of him.

"So, was Leroy seeing a girl?" I ask again.

"I can't say for sure. He might've mentioned having a date once or twice. One thing I *do* remember is the last couple of months before he disappeared, he stopped going out to the bridge with me. He cut back on his drinking. It was like he found religion or something."

"Do you think he was seeing a girl?"

"Maybe. And not the kind of girls we took to the bridge, if you know what I mean. Someone he respected."

"Did he ever talk about her? Mention her by name?"

178

"Nope."

I nod. "All right." I offer a handshake. "Thank you."

He looks down at my hand as if I've just passed him a hundred-dollar bill and his hand isn't quite clean enough to snatch it up. "Yeah. Sure."

"Do me a favor, Clarence, and behave yourself, will you?" I ask.

His grin reveals a missing eyetooth and a lower one that's been capped in gold. "I'll do my best, but I ain't making any promises."

Back on the street, Glock and I are standing between our vehicles, watching the group of boys play Horse. "You think Underwood was involved in Nolt's disappearance?" he asks.

"I think he was up to no good for a lot of years," I reply. "But I don't think he knows what happened to Nolt."

"Do you have any idea who Nolt was seeing?"

I shake my head. "No, but I'm starting to get curious. Nolt's parents mentioned some mystery woman, too, but no one seems to know who she is."

"Married?"

"Maybe. I don't know. I sure would like to find her, though. I bet she could fill in some of the blanks." I pause. "Thanks for backing me up. You heading to lunch?"

He gives the group of boys a contemplative look. "I think I might shoot some baskets for lunch."

I want to hug him, but since anything so personal would be the epitome of unprofessional for a chief, I grin. "Have fun," I tell him, and start toward my vehicle.

After leaving Glock, I drive to the Roselawn Cemetery for the funeral of sixty-two-year-old Earl Harbinger, the Painters Mill resident who was fatally injured when his car was flipped over by the tornado. He was a retired dentist and had lived his entire life in Painters Mill, leaving behind his wife of thirty-six years and four sons, all of whom still live in the area.

The funeral of Juanita Davis was out of town. Lucy Kester's is tomorrow afternoon. I'd been thinking about her on and off all day, trying not to dwell too much. As chief, I'd wanted to attend the funerals of the dead to show my support for the families and the community. Because of the hostility displayed by the Kesters, I won't attend.

I walk in the door of the police station to find it blissfully quiet. Lois is sitting at her desk, eating a turkey sandwich from LaDonna's Diner. A glass of iced tea sweats atop a cork coaster next to her computer.

"What did you do with all the media people wanting to know about the human remains?" I ask as I pluck messages from my slot.

"I arrested them and put them down in the jail." She takes a bite of the sandwich and rolls her eyes.

"Any luck getting contact info for Doctor Alan Johnson in Millersburg?"

Nodding, she swallows. "The bad news is he retired in 2004. The good news is his son, Alan Junior, took over the practice." She passes me a handwritten note. "Phone number, address, and e-mail are there." She glances at the time on her monitor. "Said he'd be there until five o'clock or so."

"You're a lifesaver." I take the note and motion toward the sandwich. "Carry on."

Two minutes later I'm at my desk, punching in the number for Dr. Alan Johnson Jr. An overly enthusiastic receptionist puts me on hold, and Barry Manilow fills the line for a full two minutes. I'm about to hang up and try again, when Johnson comes on the line. Quickly, I identify myself and give him the fundamentals of the case.

"Was Leroy Nolt a patient of your father's?" I ask.

"I had my office manager check the archived records, and, yes, he was."

"Doctor Johnson, I spoke with Leroy Nolt's parents and they informed me their son had broken his right forearm and your father surgically implanted a plate to repair the fracture."

I hear rustling on the other end of the line, and I get the feeling he's not giving me his full attention. "What is it you need from me, Chief Burkholder?"

"I have the serial number of the implant," I tell him. "I'm wondering if you can look at your records and tell me if the plate recovered was the one used for Leroy Nolt's broken arm."

"How long ago was the surgery done, exactly?" he asks.

"I think the surgery was performed in 1982 or 1983."

"That's a long time ago."

"Do you have the records, Doctor Johnson? It's important."

He sighs. "Well, I don't have them on the computer, but I bet we have them in archive. My dad was pretty good at keeping records." Another sigh lets me know he's put out. A doctor who has no time for the dead. "Let me put Diane to work on this, and I'll have her call you."

I give him my cell as well as the number of the station. "The sooner the better," I tell him. "I'd like to positively ID this individual as quickly as possible."

"Everyone's in a hurry," he mutters.

An hour later, I'm sitting at my desk, a ham sandwich from LaDonna's Diner and an iced tea in front of me. Next to my dinner is the list of Holmes County hog farmers assembled by my dispatchers. Extracted from multiple government agency data, both county and state, as well as local veterinarians, the list encompasses the five-

182

year period before and after Leroy Nolt's disappearance. It consists of thirty-nine names with addresses and contact information. I doubt it's a comprehensive list; I happen to know that many of the local Amish are resistant to reporting information to any government agency. But it's all I have, and for now it's enough to get started.

If Dr. Nelson Woodburn's assertion is correct and Leroy Nolt's body was partially consumed by domestic pigs, where did Nolt come into contact with them? According to Herb Strackbein, the barn where the remains were found was never used for swine, so he had to come in contact with them somewhere else. The hog operation where he worked?

It may be something as innocuous as his entering a pen to feed the hogs and collapsing from some medical condition—an aneurism, for example. Over a period of hours, the curious— and hungry—hogs may have begun to feed on his body. Or maybe he fell and was knocked unconscious—with the same end result. All semblance of benevolence ends there, because if we're reading the evidence correctly—mainly the presence of the garbage bag—someone moved the body and made an effort to conceal it.

But it's the more sinister possibilities that haunt me this early evening. Did someone assault Nolt and throw his unconscious—or dead—body into the pen? Did they do it because they believed the animals would consume the body and in the process hide any evidence of foul play? Or did someone simply lock him in a pen with aggressive and hungry animals in an attempt to commit the perfect murder?

I think back to my own experience with hogs as a kid. We didn't raise them, but over the years we kept a few for butchering. My *datt* would buy the occasional piglet at the auction in Millersburg—cute little pink babies my ten-year-old self fell in love with on sight. But those pink babies grew quickly into four-hundred-pound animals, not all of which had amicable personalities. The boars in particular, which commonly weighed in at five hundred pounds or more, became aggressive. When I was eight years old, I remember one of our big sows finding a chicken in her pen. She chased the hen down, cornered it, and proceeded to eat it alive while I screamed for her to stop. In the context of Leroy Nolt's death, the memory makes me shudder.

It's been a busy, eventful day, and so far I've been relatively successful in keeping my personal problems at bay. Tomasetti has called twice; both times I let his call go to voice mail. I know it's stupid. I've been living with him for seven months now. I love him. I trust him. He's my best friend and confidante. Despite all of those things, I don't know how to tell him about my pregnancy. I want to believe it will be a happy moment for both of us, but I honestly have no idea how he'll react.

Setting the list aside, my appetite for the sandwich waning, I pick up my phone and dial his cell. I nearly hang up after two rings; in some small corner of my mind I'd hoped it would go to voice mail. Then I hear his voice, and in that instant I'm certain everything's going to be all right. Good or bad or somewhere in between, we'll deal with this.

"I was starting to think you were avoiding me," he says, but there's a smile in his voice.

Usually we share an easy camaraderie that includes a good bit of verbal jousting. But for an instant I can't conjure a comeback, and I feel a slow rise of what feels like panic because I don't know what to say. Finally, I land on the truth, hoping it comes out right. "I was."

"If it's about my eating that last Hershey's Kiss . . ."

"So you're the culprit."

"Busted." But his words are halfhearted. He's an astute man; he knows something's up.

We fall silent. I can practically feel his concern, gentle fingers coming through the line, pressing against me to make sure I'm all right.

"What is it?" he asks.

"I need to talk to you. I mean, in person. Tonight."

"Is everything all right?"

"Yes," I say automatically, then think better of it and add, "I'm not sure . . . exactly."

"Okay." A thoughtful silence ensues. "You want to talk now?"

"Not over the phone."

"Do you want me to drive into town? I can be there in half an hour."

"No," I say quickly. "I've got a couple of things to tie up here before I can leave."

He sighs. "Kate."

"Look, I've got to run. Seven o'clock or so?"

"Sure."

I disconnect before either of us can say anything more.

Chapter 12

There's no more beautiful place in the world than northeastern Ohio in the summertime. The drive to A Place in Thyme Cottage is as calming and picturesque as a Bill Coleman photograph. Rolling hills of farmland with big red barns and neat farmhouses interspersed with thick forests and ponds alive with weeping willow and cattails. By the time I arrive, I'm feeling settled and optimistic.

The cottage is nestled in a wooded area just off of Spooky Hollow Road. I take the narrow gravel drive and park next to a golf cart adjacent to a small garage. I emerge from the Explorer to a cacophony of birdsongs—cardinals and sparrows and red-winged blackbirds.

The Tudor-style cottage is storybook pretty with a steeply pitched roof, cheery yellow paint, and shutters the color of old brick. Red geraniums bloom in profusion at the base of the screened front porch. Flowers with delicate pink blooms overflow from earthenware pots set on concrete steps. A gingerbread picket fence surrounds the front yard. I'm walking through an arbor drip-ping with antique roses, when a voice calls out: "If you're looking for a rental, we're booked through August!"

I look to my left to see a plump woman in a floppy hat rising from her place on the ground where a flat of petunias are in the process of being planted. I guess her to be in her late forties. Clad in blue jeans and an oversize denim tunic, she pulls off leather gloves and starts toward me.

"I'm looking for Rachel Zimmerman," I say.

"You've found her." Her stride falters as she takes in my uniform. "You must be Chief Burkholder."

I cross to her and extend my hand. "Sorry to disturb your planting."

"Oh, I needed a break, anyway."

I look around. "This is a lovely bed-and-breakfast."

"Thank you. We love it here. My husband and I both have a passion for historical homes. When it came up on the market we couldn't resist. We've been running the place for almost five years now. And, of course, it's a bonus that the winery is so close. The tourists love it." She tilts her head, looking at me more closely. "My parents called me with the news."

"The identification won't be official until DNA comes back, but we think it's Leroy. I'm sorry."

"My poor brother. He was such a good kid. But kind of a lost soul, you know?" Putting her hands on her hips, she sighs. "I guess the good news is we know where he is now. He's no longer lost. At least now we can give him a decent burial."

"I know it was a long time ago, Rachel, but I was wondering if you could answer a few questions. I'm trying to piece together his final days and figure out what happened to him."

Her eyes sharpen on mine. They're an interesting shade of green and made up prettily with eye makeup. "Are you saying his death wasn't an accident?"

"The coroner hasn't ruled on cause or manner of death yet. In fact, we may never know for certain."

"If it was an accident, you wouldn't be here, though, would you?"

I don't respond.

We spend twenty minutes going through the

same questions I posed to his parents and his former best friend, but Rachel is unable to offer much in the way of new information.

"Do you know if he was seeing anyone?" I ask. "Did he have a girlfriend?"

Her eyes brighten. "I wouldn't have thought of it if you hadn't asked, but I *do* remember him seeing a girl. In fact, I walked up on them smooching in the woods across the street from our house, you know, before the grocery store was built. I don't know who was more embarrassed, him or her or me."

"What was her name?"

"I don't know. Leroy got all flustered and angry and just sort of shooed me away. But let me tell you, for a nine-year-old girl, I got an eyeful." Her thoughts seem to turn inward and she smiles. "I'd never seen two people kiss like that before. And I'd never seen my brother look at anyone the way he looked at that girl."

"What way is that?"

She pulls herself back to the present and nods her head. "Like they were in love. Big time."

"You have no idea who she was?"

"If it's any help, she was Amish."

It's the last thing I expected her to say, and my curiosity surges. "Are you sure?"

"Not positive, but pretty sure. We're Mennonite, you know. Mom and Dad left the Swartzentruber Amish when they were young. Right after they were married, I think. Mom still dressed plainly back when I was a kid. In an Old Order Mennonite kind of way." She smiles. "But I remember looking at that girl's dress and *kapp* and thinking how different it was than my mom's. So, yes, she was Amish."

I'm at my desk, looking down at the list of hog farmers my dispatchers collected. Orange marker in hand, I'm highlighting the names I know are Amish. Seven o'clock has come and gone. The clock on the wall taunts me with every tick of the second hand. I want to believe I haven't left for home because I'm busy with this case. Because I'm only halfway through the list and I want to finish before I pack it in.

I'm lying to myself. Again. Surprise.

Tomasetti hasn't called, but I didn't expect him to. He's home, waiting for me, trying to give me my space and wondering where the hell I am.

Way to go, Kate.

Finally, at just before 9:00 p.m., I pack my laptop into its case and head for the farm. Twenty-five minutes later I walk through the door. The television is on in the living room. I see the table set with two plates, a bottle of cabernet sitting untouched in the center, and guilt takes a swipe at me with big sharp claws. For not being here when I said I would, for being a coward. For not having the guts to face this head-on.

I make it through the kitchen and into the bedroom. I'm sitting on the bed, unbuckling my equipment belt, when Tomasetti comes to the door. For a moment, he doesn't say anything, just looks at me a little too closely, trying to figure out why I can't meet his gaze.

When I can stand the silence no longer, I put my elbows on my knees and look down at my boots. "I'm pregnant," I tell him.

It's the first time I've said the words aloud, and they shock me all the way to my core. This is the kind of thing that happens to other women. Women who have normal lives and normal jobs and live with husbands who've never taken the law into their own hands. Women who don't carry a gun and have never killed anyone.

The silence is deafening. I can't look at him. I'm terrified of what I'll see. Of what he'll see in my own eyes. There's no way I can protect myself or prepare for what he might say. Even after knowing him for over four years now, I haven't a clue how he'll react.

"How far along?" he asks.

"I don't know. Six or seven weeks. I have to go to the doctor."

"Okay, so you haven't been to the doctor yet?" He doesn't do a very good job of hiding the optimism in his voice. The hope that I'm wrong and all of this is a false alarm that we'll laugh about later. It pisses me off.

"I took a pregnancy test," I snap. "Last night. It was positive."

Another silence that goes on too long and then Tomasetti says, "I guess that explains why you've been avoiding me."

"Is that all you have to say?"

"I'm just trying to absorb all of this."

I raise my head and look at him, trying to decipher his frame of mind, discern any sarcasm or dark humor. In typical Tomasetti fashion, he gives me nothing. "I know. I'm sorry."

"How did it happen? I thought you were taking the pill?"

"I am." That I'd fail to do that one small, simple thing, more than anything, makes me feel like an idiot. "There were a couple of times when I missed a dose. I don't know."

"What do you mean you don't know? How could you not know?"

"I was busy with work. I pulled a couple of all-nighters." Misery presses down on me. I feel like crying. But I'm angry, too. Angry because he's not making this any easier.

"I take it you're not pleased," I say, after a moment.

"I'm not sure how I feel. I wasn't expecting this."

"Neither was I."

He's still standing at the door, his hands on the jamb on either side of him, looking at me as if I've betrayed him.

"I didn't mean for this to happen," I tell him.

"I know."

"I don't know what to do."

He leaves his place at the door. Instead of sitting beside me, he reaches down and takes my hand, pulls me to my feet. Hot tears sting my eyes when his arms go around me.

"I screwed up," I whisper.

"It's going to be okay."

"Tomasetti, I'm scared."

He kisses my temple, runs his hand down the back of my head. "Don't worry," he tells me. "We'll figure it out."

Chapter 13

Every couple of weeks I hold a roll-call type meeting with my officers. The department is small—only four full-time officers, including myself—and most days only one of us is on duty at any given time. Roland "Pickles" Shumaker is my auxiliary officer. He's a decade or so past retirement age and usually puts in about ten hours a week, most often working the school crosswalk. I communicate with my officers via e-mail as well as cell and radio, and we keep each other up-to-date on the goings-on in Painters Mill and Holmes County. But as chief, I feel face time is vital, especially for a small department whose members don't always see each other, for everyone to sit down and talk and maybe even do a little cutting up.

Tomasetti and I didn't get much settled last night. We didn't make any decisions or discuss the future or what this means in terms of our relationship. Still, I'm feeling more at ease this morning, and I realize the simple act of telling him the truth lifted a weight from my shoulders. I no longer have to deal with it alone.

I'm standing at the podium in our ragtag meeting room. Most of the reports I've heard this morning are about tornado damage and cleanup. We had a couple of instances of after-hours looting, mostly to businesses that sustained damage, and a couple of reports of fraudsters posing as home-repair companies trying to bilk the people whose homes were damaged by the storm.

I end the meeting with an update on the investigation into the remains found at the barn.

"Holy shit," Skid mutters. "Death by hogs."

"That's something out of a horror novel," T.J. adds.

The statement is followed by enthusiastic nodding of heads.

"Are we looking at foul play?" Glock asks.

"Even if the actual death was an accident—a fall into the pen, for example—an unknown individual may have made an effort to hide the body." I look at Skid. "Nolt worked for a while at that big hog operation down in Coshocton County."

"There you go," Glock says.

"Hewitt Hog Producers," Pickles puts in.

I nod at them and return my attention to Skid. "I want you to get me the name and contact info of everyone who worked there in the two-month period leading up to Nolt's disappearance. Check for criminal records and warrants, too."

"You got it."

"So if Nolt somehow ended up in the pen with those hogs," Glock says, "how did his body end up buried beneath that old barn?"

"That's a twenty-minute drive," Skid adds.

"Maybe Nolt had some kind of disagreement with one of his coworkers," T.J. says. "Maybe there was an argument or a fight and Nolt ended up in the pen. The coworker panicked. Dumped his body in the crawl space of the barn."

"If it was an accident, why not call the cops?" Pickles asks.

Skid grins at the old man. "Not everyone's as smart as you, Pickles."

"Maybe he had a warrant," Glock offers.

"Maybe the hog operation was breaking some law," T.J. says. "Pollution or some EPA regulation."

"We need to look at all of that." I glance down at my notes. "Almost every witness I've spoken with about Leroy Nolt thought he was seeing a woman. Interestingly, he didn't tell anyone her name or reveal her identity. Not to his family. Or his best friend. Or coworkers."

Pickles shrugs thin shoulders. "First thing that comes to mind is that she was married."

"Nolt's sister, Rachel Zimmerman, saw him with an Amish girl a couple of weeks before he went missing," I tell them. "Unfortunately, she can't identify the girl. We need to ID her." I pick up a photo of the ring Dr. Stevitch sent and hand it to Pickles. "The FA found this ring at the site. It looks like a woman's engagement ring. We think the deceased had it on his person at the time of his death."

Pickles tilts his head back and looks at the photo through his bifocals. "You know, there used to be a little jewelry store here in Painters Mill. Can't recall the name, but they used to sell cheap jewelry. Closed years ago."

My interest quickens. "How long ago?"

"Gosh, Chief, that place probably closed fifteen or twenty years ago. Only reason I remember is I bought Clarice a charm bracelet there once when she got pissed off at me." He slaps the photo against his palm. "Daisy's. That was the name."

"See if you can run down the owner," I tell him. "Show that photo and find out if they sold that ring. We need the name of the customer."

Pickles's chest puffs out a little. "I'm on it."

"Chief, do you think this mystery woman was involved in his death?" T.J. asks.

"I don't know," I tell him. "It's something we need to look at."

"Can't see a female moving a body," Skid says.

"Or body parts," Glock interjects.

"The whole hog thing doesn't sound like the kind of crime a woman would commit," Pickles adds.

"The Nolt family is Mennonite, aren't they?" Glock asks.

I nod. "If the girl was Amish, maybe he felt he couldn't tell anyone because her parents didn't approve."

"Or *his* parents." From her place at the door, Mona adds, "Could be a source of conflict between the families."

A thought pings at the base of my brain. Something I've seen or heard recently. Something to do with the Amish. I reach for the thought, but it slips away and then it's gone. "T.J., I want you to talk to the people who live near the barn on Gellerman. See if any of them were living there thirty years ago. Maybe someone remembers seeing something."

"You got it, Chief."

I tell them about my conversation with the surgeon who repaired Nolt's broken arm. "Hopefully, the serial numbers will be a match and we'll have a positive ID." I gather my notes, tuck them into the folder, and look out at my team. "Thanks for coming in, everyone." I glance over my shoulder at Mona. "Thanks for staying late to be here."

She grins and gives me a funky salute.

Folder in hand, I leave the meeting room and start toward my office. I stop at the coffee station, distracted, trying to recover the thought that left me, when I hear someone come through the front door. I glance over to see a short man with a scruffy salt-and-pepper beard approach the dispatch station. He's wearing a Hawaiian shirt and a slightly tattered fedora. He's familiar; I've seen him around town, but I have no idea who he is.

Lois stands and addresses him. "Can I help you?"

"Chief Burkholder?" he asks.

Her eyes slide toward me. She's wondering if I'm available. I set down the cup I've just filled and approach him. "I'm Chief Burkholder," I say. "What can I do for you?"

He shoves a large white envelope at me. The instant my hands close around it, he grins. "You've been served. Have a nice day."

I look down at the envelope. It's addressed to me with the return address of a law firm. Even before opening it, I know what it is. The parents of Lucy Kester have filed a wrongful death lawsuit against me and, possibly, the police department and the township of Painters Mill.

Around me, the reception area has gone silent. Vaguely I'm aware of Lois speaking to a caller. Mona is standing between dispatch and the coffee station, where she'd been texting, but now she's looking at me. Skid and T.J. and Pickles are standing outside their cubicle area, where they'd been talking. Even they have gone silent, all eyes on me.

Glock, who'd been at the coffee station, comes up beside me. "Everything okay, Chief?"

"Probably not," I mutter.

"I heard about Kester." He takes a sip of coffee as if all of this is routine. We both know it isn't. "You're aware that Ohio has a Good Samaritan law, right?"

He's the second person to remind me of that. While I appreciate the sentiment, I know that even with such a law in place, a lawsuit of this nature could cause problems. And it could be expensive, not only for the township but me personally.

I raise the envelope and smack my hand against it. "I need to take a look."

"Damn ambulance chasers," Pickles mutters.

Skid motions toward the door where the courier just left. "I knew I should have given that squirrely little son of a bitch a ticket the other day instead of a warning."

Leave it to my team to make me smile when

I'm facing a situation that's not the least bit funny. I appreciate it nonetheless. "I don't think that would help in this situation."

"Yeah, but it would have made all of us feel better," Glock says.

I'm no lawyer, but it doesn't take a law degree to know the lawsuit is going to become a serious issue. Not only is Kester suing the township of Painters Mill and the police department, but me personally. Despite Ohio's Good Samaritan law, I'll have no choice but to participate in the proceedings. I'll be forced to pay for a lawyer and invest the time and energy into defending my actions the day Lucy Kester died. Though I'll probably be cleared of any wrongdoing, there's always a chance that I won't, an outcome that would affect me not only on a personal level but could jeopardize my position as chief.

I skim the details of the lawsuit: *On or about the afternoon of June 3, Chief of Police Kate Burkholder, who was off duty at the time, entered the badly damaged premises of Paula and Nick Kester at 345 Westmoreland in Painters Mill, Ohio. Burkholder, who is a certified emergency medical technician, proceeded to assess the seriously wounded infant, four-month-old Lucy Ann Kester, and, against EMT training protocol, moved the child without the aid of a neck brace or backboard. As a direct result of Burkholder's decision to move the infant patient, Lucy Ann Kester expired four hours later at Pomerene Hospital in Millersburg. According to the Holmes County Coroner's autopsy report, the infant child, Lucy Ann Kester, had suffered from a fracture of the vertebra prominens. It is asserted that had the deceased infant been moved with the assistance of a backboard or neck brace, she would have likely survived the ordeal. . . .*

The lawsuit goes on for several more pages, but I don't read them. For the hundredth time I'm reminded that while Ohio's Good Samaritan law may protect me legally, it doesn't protect me from my own conscience.

I want to talk to Tomasetti and run all of this by him. It scares me how much I need him at this moment. It scares me because if the time ever comes when we're not together, I don't know what I'll do. Maybe I've come to rely on him a little too much. That scares me, too.

I dial Mayor Auggie Brock's office number from memory. He picks up on the first ring sounding perturbed, and I know even before asking that he's been served, too. I ask anyway. "Did you get served?"

"I did," he says. "You?"

"Unfortunately."

"The loss of a young life aside, Kate, this is not good PR for Painters Mill or the PD. We're a tourist town, for God's sake."

"I'm aware."

"Do you have a lawyer?"

"No." The thought sends a quiver of uneasiness through my gut. "Do we have someone on retainer?"

"Seitz and Seitz."

Hoover Seitz is a brilliant attorney, but it's common knowledge around town that he enjoys his happy-hour martinis a little too much.

Auggie sighs, already moving on to his next immediate problem. "We don't have the budget for a damn lawsuit."

I want to believe he's just venting his frustration, but in some small corner of my mind I know there's a possibility he won't back me on this. He'll be forced to pay for the legal defense for my department, but not me personally. It could wipe me out financially.

"Auggie," I say firmly, "I expect your support on this."

"Of course I'll support you, Kate. I'll do everything I can, but if the money isn't there, it isn't there."

I curb a rise of anger, even though I know there are already too many emotions tangled up in this mess.

"If you get any media inquiries, send them to my office," he tells me.

"All right."

"And for God's sake, call Hoover before happy hour starts."

After a brief conversation with Hoover Seitz, I'm feeling marginally better about the lawsuit. He assures me that the legal counsel for the Kester family—a firm out of Columbus known for taking cases like this one pro bono—is on a fishing expedition and using the bereaved parents' grief to earn a little blood money. Chances are they'll settle out of court, the cost of which will be covered by the township's liability insurance. Everyone gets a little money. Happy ending for everyone. Except, of course, Lucy Kester.

I spend an hour poring over every piece of paper and report I've amassed so far in my ever-growing John-Doe-aka-Leroy-Nolt file. I still don't have cause or manner of death, but when I look at all of the information as a whole, I believe it indicates he met with a violent end. The presence of a garbage bag where the bones were found tells me someone moved and/or tried to conceal the body. If Nolt's death was due to some innocuous farming accident, anyone with the common sense of a toad would have called the police—unless they directly or indirectly caused his death. But who would have a reason to murder a twenty-year-old Mennonite man?

Two possible motives come to mind, the first being drugs. Thirty years ago, methamphetamine was a rising star among dope dealers. Cocaine, marijuana, and an array of bootlegged pharmaceuticals were big business, too, even in rural areas like Painters Mill. If Nolt liked to "live his life on the fast road," as his parents had asserted, and he was anxious to make money, a drug deal gone bad is a reasonable scenario.

But the drug angle doesn't sit quite right. When parents tell me their child isn't "into" drugs, I invariably take that information with a grain of salt, because the parents are always the last to know, usually right after the local police department. In this case, however, I believed Sue and Vern Nolt. And I believed Clarence Underwood —despite his being an ex-con with a history of drug use himself—when he told me Nolt never used or sold drugs.

The second scenario lies with the as-yet unidentified woman Leroy had purportedly been involved with. The *Amish* woman Rachel Zimmerman saw him with. Was she underage? A minor? Was she married? Is that why they kept their relationship secret? Either scenario fits. Infidelity is a common motive for murder and has driven many a man to violence. Is that what happened in this case? Who was the woman? Does she know what happened to Nolt? And what became of her? Is she still living in the area?

I blow an hour looking through missing person reports for Amish and Mennonite females between the ages of fourteen and twenty-five who disappeared about the same time as Nolt, but I strike out. It isn't until I'm rereading the notes from my meeting with Leroy Nolt's parents that I'm finally able to put my finger on the thought that's been hovering just out of reach. The Amish quilt hanging on the wall at the home of Sue and Vern Nolt. According to Sue Nolt, her son gave it to her for her birthday shortly before he disappeared. Where did he get it? Amish quilts are extremely labor intensive—and they're not cheap, some costing upward of a thousand dollars. How is it that a twenty-year-old man, who's working at the local farm store and trying to save money, was able to afford an Amish quilt for his mother?

Energized by the thought of fresh information, I snatch up my phone and call the Nolts. Sue picks up on the third ring. "Oh, hello, Chief Burkholder."

"I'm sorry to bother you again," I begin, "but I was going over my notes from our earlier conversation and realized I forgot to ask you about the quilt."

"Quilt? You mean the one Leroy gave me for my birthday?"

"Do you know where he got it?"

"I don't know. Always assumed it was from one of the shops in town."

"Would you mind taking a look at it for me?

Sometimes the quilter will stitch her initials somewhere on the quilt."

"I've never looked, but I'm happy to check if you'd like. Hang on a sec."

I hear her set down the phone. Distant voices on the other end. I wait, tapping my pen against the folder. Two full minutes pass before she comes back on the line.

"Well," she begins, "I wasn't tall enough to reach the top two corners, so I had Vern take it down and, sure enough, the quilter embroidered her initials in the corner."

"What are the initials, Mrs. Nolt?"

"A.K.," she tells me. "They're embroidered right into the fabric in brown thread." She sighs. "Whoever it is, she does fine work."

I thank her for checking, end the call, and write the initials on a fresh sheet of paper. *A.K.* I search my memory for the names that have been mentioned in relation to this case, but I come up blank. I page through my notes and reports, looking for a name to match the initials, but there's nothing there. Is A.K. the girl Leroy Nolt had been seeing at the time of his death? Was she a quilter? Or is A.K. the mother or a relative of the girl? Or am I wrong about all of this and in the weeks leading up to his death, Leroy shelled out a thousand dollars to buy his mother a quilt for her birthday? The itch at the back of my brain tells me no.

I pull out the list of hog raisers my dispatchers assembled, and I scan it for Amish and Mennonite names beginning with the letter "K." But none of the Amish last names begin with that letter. Either there are none or, more than likely, the Amish didn't report in with their information.

Frustrated, I toss the list onto my desktop and sigh. That's when I realize there's one more resource I can utilize to find the name of the quilt maker, even an old quilt—and it's within walking distance of the police station.

En Schtich in Zeit is Pennsylvania Dutch for A Stitch in Time. It's an Amish quilt and sewing shop on Main Street just two blocks from the police station. I've driven past the place hundreds of times in the years I've been back. I don't sew, so I've never had reason to venture inside. One of the things I love about it is the display windows. Every holiday, the owner decorates the old-fashioned windows in creative and interesting ways, but especially at Christmastime.

The wind chimes hanging on the front door jingle merrily when I step into the shop. The aromas of cinnamon and hazelnut greet me, conjuring images of fresh-baked pastries and coffee. The space is long and narrow with plenty of natural light coming in through the storefront windows. The walls to my left and right are adorned with children's clothing—plain dresses, boys' shirts and trousers—hanging neatly on wooden hangers, the hand-printed price tags dangling and discreetly turned. Ahead and to my right are a dozen or more hinged wooden arms set into the wall. Each arm is draped with a quilt that's been neatly folded so that its best qualities are displayed. I see traditional patterns—diamond and star and peace birds. Farther back, twin beds are set up. Each is covered with an heirloom-quality child's quilt. Crib quilts and wall hangings are displayed on the wall above the beds.

At the rear, five Amish women sit at a long folding table that's covered with fabric, tools of the trade, and, in the center, an antiquated sewing kit. The women are looking at me as if I'm a stray dog that's wandered in. Their stares are not unfriendly, but I'm not met with smiles either, and I wonder if they know who I am.

"May I help you?"

I glance to my left to see a young Amish woman wearing a plain blue dress, a black apron, and an organdy *kapp* standing behind the counter. She's slender with a milk-and-honey complexion and liquid green eyes fringed with thick lashes. On the counter next to her is a platter heaped with what looks like homemade oatmeal raisin cookies.

"Hi." Returning her smile, I cross to her, pulling out my badge. "I'm Chief of Police Kate Burkholder."

"Oh. Hello." She cocks her head. "You must be Sarah's sister."

"I am. Do you know her?"

"Sarah comes into the shop every so often for supplies. In fact, she was here just yesterday for thread and some fabric. She's working on a wedding quilt for her neighbor." She looks away, uncomfortable now because she's aware that the other women are listening and she isn't sure how friendly she should be, now that she knows who I am.

"*Sie hot net der glaawe*," one of the woman says beneath her breath. She doesn't keep the faith.

"*Mer sot em sei Eegne net verlosse; Godd verlosst die Seine nicht*," whispers another. One should not abandon one's own; God does not abandon his own.

The young woman tightens her mouth and looks down at the cash register in front of her. Not speaking. Not meeting my gaze.

I lean close to her and lower my voice. "*Wer laurt an der Wand, Heert sie eegni Schand.*" If you listen through the wall, you will hear others recite your faults.

The young woman bursts out laughing, catches herself, and puts her hand over her mouth. But I can tell by the way her eyes are lit up that she appreciates good Amish humor.

"How can I help you, Kate Burkholder?" she asks.

"I probably need to speak with one of the other ladies, if they're not too busy," I say loud enough for the women to hear.

A plump woman of about forty anchors her needle and sets her fabric on the table in front of her. Scooting back her chair, she rises, her eyes holding mine as she starts toward me. She's a large, solidly built woman and moves like a battleship, shoulders back, chin up, her practical shoes clomping against the wood-plank floor.

"*Wei geth's alleweil*, Katie Burkholder?" How goes it now?

She's got a voice like a chainsaw. I've seen her around town, but I feel as if I'm at a slight disadvantage because I don't remember her name. "*Ich bin zimmlich gut.*" I'm pretty good.

She dismisses the younger woman with a cool look. The girl slinks from behind the counter and walks to the table, where she goes back to her stitching.

"I'm Martha Yoder," she says, sizing me up, not sure if she likes what she sees. "We met at the Carriage Stop a couple of years back."

"Good to see you again, Martha." We shake hands. "I'm working on a case," I begin, speaking loudly enough for the other women to hear. "I'm looking for an Amish woman, a quilter or seamstress with the initials 'A.K.' She made an heirloom-quality quilt back in 1985 and embroidered her initials in the corner."

"What'd she do?" whispers the young woman who'd been behind the counter when I walked in.

The question earns her a sneer from the woman sitting next to her.

"What was the pattern?" one of the other women asks.

"Center star," I tell her. "The colors are unusual, mauve and cream and black."

"A.K." Martha's brows knit. "Hmm. Let me think." She glances over her shoulder at the women and asks in Pennsylvania Dutch, "Who was it that used to use all that pink the *Englischer* tourists like so much? Anna? Ada? She's from down south, I think. Always got a pretty penny for her quilts."

A tiny woman with silver hair and rheumy blue eyes looks up from her needlework. "Little Abby Kline used to use a lot of pink. Been known to add her initials to her work, too. I've known her since the day the Lord brought her into this world. That girl's been making quilts since she was nine years old."

A second woman straightens and levels her gaze on me. "Almost forgot about little Abby. I made a wedding quilt for her when she married Jeramy Kline. Gosh, that's been thirty years ago now."

"Thirty years and four babies," another woman adds, as she leans forward and bites a thread to sever it. "All grown up now."

"She doesn't come into town much anymore," one of the younger women comments.

"Saw her at the grocery last week," says another woman as she pulls a needle through fabric.

Pennsylvania Dutch was my first language and even after so many years of speaking only English, my brain switches to my native tongue with surprising ease. "What was her maiden name?"

"Kaufman," one of the women says.

The last thing I want to do is start speculation or gossip, but I need information. Evidently, these women are well versed on goings on within the Amish community, so I take the risk. "Do any of you remember if Abigail knew Leroy Nolt?"

The eyes of the older woman—the one old enough to remember Nolt's disappearance—attach to mine. "Little Abby was always with Jeramy," she tells me. *"Always."*

The youngest woman's eyes go wide. "Does Abby have something to do with those bones?"

No one looks at her. I don't answer her question.

The eldest woman goes back to her sewing. "Little Abby never had eyes for anyone but Jeramy."

"Leroy Nolt was a Mennonite," Martha says. "Abby and her family are Swartzentruber."

"The two don't mix if you ask me," one of the other women says.

It's not the first time I've heard those words, and they annoy me as much now as they did when I was an angry and rebellious teen. While Mennonites and the Amish share a common Anabaptist heritage, the differences are vast and include everything from the use of electricity to the ownership of cars. The most significant difference, however, is the tenet of separation, which is central to the Amish but not part of the Mennonite way. Most Amish I know mingle freely with their Mennonite neighbors, but as in all cultures, there are those who are intolerant.

The old woman looks up from her needle and thread and levels a blue-steel gaze on mine. "Katie Burkholder, I think you'd be best served if you kept your feet under your own table."

Chapter 14

Abigail and Jeramy Kline live on County Road 19 just south of the Holmes County line. It's a hilly, curvy road that cuts through farmland and forest and is bordered by a guardrail that's seen more than its fair share of collisions. The house and barn are close to the road, by Amish standards anyway, and are set into a slope. At the mouth of the driveway, a hand-lettered sign tells me FRESH BROWN EGGS. AMISH QUILTS. (NO SUNDAY SALE!) Towering trees surround the plain farmhouse to my left. Ahead is a cornfield with razor-straight rows of corn that's already hip high. In the yard, a tractor tire on a rope dangles from the branch of a maple. The barn is white with a cinder-block foundation lined with a profusion of hostas. In a small pen adjacent to a shedrow, a sleek Standardbred mare reaches through a broken rail to nibble grass already shorn to dirt. Beneath the overhang of the shedrow, a black windowless buggy with wood-and-steel wheels is parked, its twin shafts resting on concrete blocks, and I'm reminded that this family is Swartzentruber.

I park adjacent to the house and take the sidewalk to the porch. I'm about to knock, when I spot the Amish woman hoeing in the garden to my left. I leave the porch and start toward her. She's so intent on her work she doesn't notice me, so I call out to her. "It looks like you're going to have a bumper crop of tomatoes this year."

She startles and nearly drops the hoe, pressing her hand to her chest and then laughing at herself. "Oh my goodness! I didn't see you pull up."

"I didn't mean to startle you." I reach her and show her my badge, nodding at the carefully staked tomato plants. "Looks like they'll be ripe in a few weeks."

"A month, probably. If the worms don't get them first." She smiles and then whispers

214

conspiratorially, "And if I didn't have such a weakness for fried green tomatoes."

"You and me both." Returning her smile, I offer my hand. "I'm Kate Burkholder, the chief of police up in Painters Mill."

"Hello, Kate Burkholder." Her grip is firm. She's got strong hands for a woman, and her palms are well callused from hours of manual labor.

I guess her to be in her late forties. She's got a tanned, youthful face with freckles on her nose and the quick, contagious smile of a woman who's comfortable with who she is and content with her life. She's wearing a homemade navy dress, black apron, and black sneakers, with an organdy *kapp*. She's a few inches taller than me. Despite the plainness of her clothes, I can see that her figure is trim and athletic.

"Do you have a few minutes to talk, Mrs. Kline?" I begin.

"Has something happened?" Her smile falters, pretty green eyes sharpening on mine. "One of my children? Has someone—"

"No one's been hurt," I assure her.

She breathes a sigh of relief. "I guess it's a mother's job to worry, even after they've grown up. Especially after they've grown up." She laughs at herself again. "And Jeramy's parents are getting up in years. I thought maybe . . ." She lets the words trail as if the notion is too unpleasant to utter aloud. "We've been trying to get them to sell their farm and move here with us, but—" She stops herself. "Here I am blabbing on, when you've driven all the way from Painters Mill."

"I'm here about an old case I'm working on," I tell her. "A young man who went missing back in 1985."

"Who?"

"A local man by the name of Leroy Nolt."

Abigail picks up the hem of her apron and begins to wring the material between her hands. "I can't imagine what that would have to do with me."

"Do you know him?" I ask.

Her hands go still. Her eyes remain level on mine. Her lips maintain the smile. There's no flicker of recognition. No outward sign of emotion. It's a completely normal and expected reaction of a woman who has no earthly idea who Leroy Nolt is or why I'm asking about him. But while everything about her is calm and relaxed, her white-knuckled grip on the hem of her apron gives me pause.

Her brows knit. She repeats the name, her eyes moving upward as if she's searching her memory. "The name is familiar, but I don't quite recall where I've heard it."

"Maybe you knew him a long time ago? Before you were married?"

"I don't think so," she says simply.

I nod, take a moment to look around and admire the peacefulness of the farm. "You and your husband have a beautiful home here."

"Thank you."

"Are you a quilter, Mrs. Kline?"

Her mouth opens as if she's wondering how I could know that, so I move to put her at ease. "I noticed the sign when I pulled in."

"Oh." She emits a chuckle. "I don't know where my mind is today."

"On the tomatoes, probably."

My response seems to put her at ease. "I do enjoy making quilts. God blessed me with the gift, so I do my best to put it to good use."

"Do you have any for sale?"

"I sold the last one a couple of days ago to a nice tourist from Cleveland. I hope to have another finished by the end of the month. Are you looking for a particular pattern?"

I shake my head. "Just something pretty. I'll have to come back, then." I wait a beat and then ask, "Your maiden name was Kaufman, is that correct?"

"Yes." Her eyes narrow on mine. "Why do you ask?"

"Do you initial the quilts you make?"

Her expression goes wary. "Sometimes. A lot of the Amish do."

"Did you ever make a quilt for Leroy Nolt?"

She opens her mouth to speak, but several seconds pass before the word comes. "No."

"What about his mother? Sue Nolt?"

"No."

"Are you sure?"

"Of course I'm sure." She takes a deep breath, and I realize she's making an effort to calm herself. "Why are you asking about people I don't even know?" she asks in a low voice, as if she doesn't want anyone to hear.

I pull out the photo of the engagement ring and show it to her. "Have you ever seen this ring before, Mrs. Kline?"

She stares at the photo. Mouth open. Eyelids fluttering. Then she seems to gather herself and shakes her head. "I don't think I can help you," she tells me. "I'm sorry."

I'm not sure I believe her, but I nod. "Is your husband home?"

"Yes, but he's in the—"

"I'm right here," a deep male voice calls out.

Refolding the photo, I tuck it into my pocket and turn. Jeramy Kline is about twenty feet away, crossing the side yard, closing in on us with long, purposeful strides. He's wearing black trousers and a gray work shirt. His beard is long, reaching nearly to his belly, thick and wiry, black shot with gray. He's a large man, well over six feet tall and weighing in somewhere around two hundred pounds, with a muscular physique and hands the size of dinner plates. His eyes are shaded by the black, flat-brimmed hat. Though I can't see them, I feel them on me.

"Is everything all right?" he asks as he reaches us.

"I was just asking your wife some routine questions about an old case I'm working on." I extend my hand. "I'm Kate Burkholder with the Painters Mill Police."

He gives my hand a thorough shake. "What can I do for you?"

"I'm wondering if you know a man by the name of Leroy Nolt."

"Leroy Nolt." His eyes narrow, crow's feet appearing at the corners. "The boy who disappeared way back. I remember the name."

"Did you know him?"

"I know *of* him. But I don't believe I ever met him. He was *Mennischt.*" Mennonite. He grimaces as if it pains him to say the word, and I'm reminded that many times in the Amish culture, the more liberal Anabaptists are frowned upon by the Old Order Swartzentruber Amish. "It was big news when he went missing all those years ago," he says. "I remember reading about it in *The Budget.*"

Beside him, his wife has gone silent. I glance at her to see that she's fingering her apron again, looking over at the tomato plants as if she's wishing she were anywhere but standing here talking to me.

"Are you sure?" I ask.

"Of course I'm sure." He tips his head. I can see his eyes now. They're blue and glinting with keen intelligence. "I'm wondering why you drove all the way down here to ask us about Nolt."

I consider telling him about the remains and the quilt emblazoned with initials the same as his wife's, but I decide not to. "I'm not at liberty to discuss the details of the case yet, Mr. Kline. I hope to be able to do that soon."

Before either of them can respond, I offer my hand for another shake. "I appreciate your time." I glance at Abigail and motion toward the garden. "Good luck with those tomatoes."

Ten minutes later I'm northbound on Ohio 83 just east of Lake Buckhorn, my mind going over my odd exchange with Abigail Kline. I'm pretty sure she was lying about Leroy Nolt. I think she knew him. I believe she made that quilt for him. And I'm damn sure she knew something about the ring. But why would she lie about any of those things? Does she know what happened to him? Was she somehow involved in his death? Has she been keeping the knowledge to herself for thirty years?

The questions tap at my brain like a reflex hammer against bone. There's something there—secrets, I think. But I don't know what they are or how they relate to the case.

Tugging on my headset, I call dispatch. "Jodie, can you get me the names of Jeramy Kline's parents?" I think about that a moment. "Abigail Kline's, too. Her maiden name was Kaufman." I spell the last names for her. "Get me addresses. Run them through LEADS, including Jeramy and Abigail. And check to see if any of the elders are on the hog-raisers list."

"You got it." She pauses. "You on your way in?"

I glance to my left, where Lake Buckhorn shimmers silver and green. Beyond, I see the lush rise of trees through the haze of humidity coming off the water. And I find myself thinking about Tomasetti.

"I'm going to call it a day," I tell her. "Just leave everything in the file, and I'll pick it up first thing in the morning."

The farm is beautiful at dusk. As I pull into the gravel lane, I'm reminded of all the reasons I've come to love this place. It's the kind of beauty that settles over you in layers. The old farm-house with its kind, grandfather face. The massive maple trees that stand like proud sentinels. Beyond, the lush green of the pasture and the mist rising from the pond. As I draw nearer, I spot the lilac bush Tomasetti discovered when he cleared away brush from a bramble in the side yard. The peonies we planted together a

221

few weeks ago. At some point in the last few days, he mounted a hammock between two trees, a chore I missed out on because I was working.

Usually, I'm looking forward to seeing him, no holds barred. That rise of pleasure in my chest when I spot his form on the dock where he's fishing, and I can't wait to tell him about my day and ask about his. Or that moment when I walk inside and he's standing at the kitchen sink chopping something, smiling at me, a towel thrown over his shoulder. This evening there is no quickening in my chest. No pang in my gut because I haven't talked to him all day and he thinks it's silly that I miss him. It's as if a fault line has shifted between us, opening a crevasse that's deep and dark, and neither of us is quite sure how to traverse it.

My pregnancy has been a constant in the periphery of my thoughts since the moment I found out. A weight that rests uneasily on my shoulders, on my conscience, on my heart. I know it's a cop-out, a delay tactic, but I haven't let myself think too hard about what I'm going to do. I'm not ready to be a mother; I'm not sure I'd be a good one at this point in my life. I work too much, putting in long hours and, sometimes, all-nighters. I take risks. I carry a gun.

My stomach flutters uneasily as I park next to Tomasetti's Tahoe and shut down the engine. I don't know if it's nausea or nerves or maybe a little bit of both. I take the sidewalk to the back door. I step inside to find him at the sink, washing dishes. He looks at me over his shoulder. His eyes are warm, but there's no smile. On the table, he left a plate for me. A napkin and silverware and a glass. No wine.

"Hey." I hang my jacket on the coatrack next to the door. "Sorry I missed dinner."

"It was just leftovers," he says. "I saved you some."

I unfasten my utility belt and drape it over the back of a chair. I want to get out of my uniform and take a shower. But something tells me this is an important moment. I need to stay out here and talk to him. "I'm starving."

He dries his hands on the towel and then goes to the refrigerator and pulls out a Tupperware container. "How's it going with identifying those remains?"

I relay the events of the day as I take the container from him. It's solid ground, and my nerves begin to settle. "I got an odd vibe from Abigail Kline. Like maybe she knew more than she was letting on."

"You think she's lying about knowing Nolt?"

"I do."

"You think she was the girl he was involved with?"

"Maybe. Her age is right. She's Swartzentruber; he was Mennonite. A relationship would have been a source of conflict for both of them and their families."

"That fits." He tosses ice into a glass and runs the tap. "Do you think she had something to do with his death?"

"My gut tells me she didn't, but . . . Nolt disappeared thirty years ago. That's a long time. People change. I need to talk to her again, away from her husband." I set the container in the microwave to warm it. "Maybe tomorrow."

"Did you get to the doctor?" he asks casually.

I shake my head. "I was busy."

"Did you call? Make an appointment?"

"No."

"Don't you think you should have made that a priority?"

The muscles at the back of my neck tighten as I open the microwave and pull out the food. I don't look at him as I pop off the lid, pick up my plate, and take both to the counter. "I was tied up most of the day. A lot on my plate right now with the storm cleanup and now these remains." I don't mention the lawsuit filed by the Kesters.

"You can't put it off, Kate. I mean, you don't have a lot of time."

I stop what I'm doing and look at him. "I'll go. I was just busy today."

"We need to know if you're pregnant. Get it confirmed."

"Tomasetti, it's been one day since I took the test. Time is not of the essence here."

He looks at me for a long time before speaking. "We need to know, so we can decide what to do about it."

The realization of what he's talking about creeps over me like ice, a glacier rushing down from the north to crush and freeze everything in its path. I stare at him, wanting to be sure, hoping I'm wrong. "What are we talking about here, exactly?" I ask.

"We need to know what we're dealing with. You can't stick your head in the sand and hope the problem will go away."

"The *problem?* Really, Tomasetti? Is that what this is to you? A problem?"

"You know what I mean," he growls.

"Maybe you should spell it out for me."

"Kate, don't read anything into this that isn't there. We have a situation on our hands. We need to talk about it. Deal with it. That's all."

"What are you suggesting?"

He says nothing.

"I didn't get this way by myself, you know. You were involved. You played a role, too."

His mouth goes tight. "I was counting on you to be responsible. I had no way of knowing you were playing it fast and loose with your birth control."

Anger sweeps through me with such force that

I feel it all the way to my bones. A shock wave that topples my balance, striking some vital part of me I thought was safe. I can't believe he would lay blame on me. "I may be a lot of things," I tell him through clenched teeth, "but I am not irresponsible."

"The only other scenario is that you meant for it to happen."

I step toward him, jab my finger at him. "There are some words that can't be taken back," I say. "I suggest you shut your mouth before you take that line of thought too far."

We're standing about four feet apart but it feels like a mile. For a moment, all I can hear is the blood rushing through my veins. Vaguely, I'm aware of our elevated breathing. The tension as thick and suffocating as glue.

"We owe it to each other to be clear, Kate. I'm not going to lie to you. I'm not going to dress this up all pretty for you. I don't want a baby. Not now. Maybe not ever."

The words fall down on me like hammer blows, so painful I can't take a breath. It hurts me to my core. I stare at him, not wanting him to see it. Not wanting to make myself that vulnerable.

"This isn't exactly optimal timing for me, either." I try to keep my voice even, but I run out of breath, and when I try to get oxygen into my lungs, it sounds like a gasp.

He stares at me for a too-long moment and

then he steps back, sets both hands on the counter, and leans heavily. "I don't want kids," he grinds out. "I can't love like that again. Not like that. I don't have the capacity."

My initial hurt augments into a powerful sadness, a sense of finality and loss as cruel and penetrating as a machete blade. "You're capable of love," I say quietly. "You love me."

"I do." He stares blindly at his hands as they grip the edge of the counter. "That's different."

"No, it's not. Love is love."

"No. Kids are different. They're . . ." He shakes his head. "My children. Kate, the way I loved them. It was . . . everything. When they died . . ." His mouth tightens, and his Adam's apple bobs as he swallows. "I can't do that again. I won't."

That's when it strikes me that while I'm light-years out of my element, Tomasetti has done this before. He's loved another woman. He's been through multiple pregnancies with her. Two births. He became a father. Loved his children. He watched them grow and experienced the ups and downs of being a dad. He'd loved two little girls for nine and eleven years, then they were taken from him—stolen from him—by violence when a career criminal decided to make an example of what could happen to a cop who dared cross him. Tomasetti has come a long way since those dark days. But he hasn't recovered. He may never recover completely.

"What do you suggest we do?" I ask.

"I don't know the answer to that."

"What do you want?"

He shakes his head again. "I want things to be the way they were," he tells me. "Before."

"You want me to get an abortion." The words are out, an ugly, unpredictable beast let out of its cage.

"I didn't say that."

"You're thinking it. I see it on your face. All this . . . urgency. As if this is a problem that must be dealt with quickly, before it turns into—"

"Don't," he snaps. "Just stop."

"Why? Because you can't deal with it? Because you don't *want* to? Because you're *afraid* to try? For God's sake, Tomasetti, I've never thought of you as a coward."

"Cut it out," he snarls.

"We're talking about the life of an innocent baby that has nothing to do with your baggage. Or mine."

He says nothing. He doesn't look at me. Makes no move to bridge the chasm between us. For an instant, I consider going to him. I need him. I don't understand why he can't open his mind. His heart. But something inside won't let me take that first, treacherous step.

"Have you bothered to consider the possibility that this isn't just about you?" I ask.

When he doesn't respond, I turn away, grab my

utility belt off the chair, my jacket off the coat-rack. He says nothing as I yank open the door and go through it.

As I run toward the Explorer, I'm keenly aware that he doesn't call out my name.

Chapter 15

"Well, Burkholder, you handled that with your usual eloquence and grace."

I'm southbound on Ohio 83 just out of Millersburg. It's past 9:00 p.m. and my police radio is quiet. T.J. made one stop about twenty minutes ago; a kid in a Mustang blew the stop sign out on Dogleg Road. On the west side of the county, the sheriff's office is working on getting a loose horse back to its pasture.

I'm loath to admit it, but I want to go home; leaving the house wasn't the most reasonable thing I could have done, especially when I'm exhausted and hungry and have a full day ahead of me tomorrow. I should have simply left the room, taken a shower, and gone to bed. I know Tomasetti well enough to know he would have given me my space.

But the fact of the matter is that this isn't merely a lover's spat that got out of hand and resulted in hurt feelings. The issues we're facing are serious and far-reaching. I've always known we would eventually arrive at this crossroad. That we would one day have to answer pressing questions about our future and having a family. Until now, we've been cruising along, happy and healing and enjoying all the things that, before we met, seemed out of reach. You never expect the brick wall when you hit it.

I've always planned on getting married and having children, but neither of those things were pressing issues or something that I consciously thought about. It was a happy, someday thought in the periphery of my plans for the future. A someday when I'd reach some miraculous pinnacle in my life when I wasn't so busy or so focused on my career. A point when Tomasetti wasn't so damaged. When we were both fully healed and ready to move on to a new phase in our lives. Honestly, I hadn't given the prospect of children much thought. But over the last months, I'd sensed Tomasetti's reluctance. Comments he'd made or looks he'd given me during certain conversations. I'd never given his reaction a second thought. I never pursued a definitive answer or pushed him on any of it. It was the sort of thing I made light of because I knew our love would prevail.

The future arrived with astounding swiftness, and I'm no more ready now to have children than I was a month ago or six months ago or a year ago. Yes, I love Tomasetti. I love him with a desperation that's so powerful it frightens me. Had he asked me to marry him, I would have said yes. But he didn't, and now we're out of time, and it breaks my heart that we're unable to embrace what should have been a happy moment for both of us.

The only thing I know for certain is that we're not going to get anything settled tonight. Better for me to spend it at my old house in Painters Mill. Give both of us time to cool down, do some thinking and maybe a little soul-searching.

I swing by the McDonald's in Millersburg for a burger, fries, and a chocolate milkshake and then I head south toward Painters Mill, sipping on the cold drink and plucking fries from the bag as I drive. A sense of homecoming rolls over me when I turn onto Main Street, with its pretty storefronts and antique lampposts. I consider pulling in to the police station as I idle past, but I'm in no frame of mind to talk to anyone, even if I am feeling a little lonely. Better just to get to the house, eat and shower, and get a good night's sleep.

I'm nearly there, when my cell phone emits a chirp. I glance down at the display, expecting to see Tomasetti's name. I'm surprised when I see Painters Mill Police. I shove my Bluetooth over my head and catch the call on the third ring. "What's up?" I say.

"Chief, I'm sorry to bother you at home," my

second-shift dispatcher begins, and I don't correct her. "I just took a call from a guy using that Amish community pay phone on Hogpath Road. He says your brother was in a buggy accident and he's hurt bad."

"*What?* Jacob?" I hit the brake and pull over. "Where?"

"Out on CR 14."

"What the hell is he doing out there?" It's nearly six miles from my brother's farm. "I'm on my way. Get an ambulance out there. County, too."

"Got it."

Glancing quickly in my rearview mirror, I make a U-turn in the middle of the street and hit the gas. I keep an eye out for pedestrians and other motorists as I speed through town, blowing the light at Main Street. The Explorer's engine groans when I floor the accelerator. Vaguely, I'm aware of the radio coming to life as the call goes out. I think of my brother and all the things we've left unsaid and unfinished, and a renewed sense of urgency strikes me dead in the chest.

"Be okay, Jacob," I whisper.

By the time I reach Delisle Road I'm doing eighty. I brake hard for County Road 14. My wheels screech when I make the turn. I drive a few yards, expecting to see lantern light or headlights or debris in the road ahead. But there's nothing. No buggy. No horse. No sign of an accident. No indication that anyone has been here. I hit my radio. "What's the twenty on that ten-fifty PI?"

"CR Fourteen, just off Delisle."

"I'm ten-twenty-three. There's no one here." I pause. "Where's the RP?"

"Reporting party didn't leave their name. Stand by."

My Explorer isn't equipped with a spotlight, so I reach into the seat pocket for my Maglite and set it on the passenger seat. When I look up, I catch a glimpse of something on the road ahead. A faint glint against the night sky. A vehicle with no headlights, or possibly a buggy two hundred yards away. I hit my brights and the emergency overhead lights and accelerate.

I speak into my mike. "I got it," I say, letting Jodie know I've found the location of the accident.

"Roger that. County's ten-seventy-nine."

I'm watching for movement, keeping an eye on the ditches on both sides of the road, doing about forty miles per hour, when a hole the size of my thumb blows through my windshield. At first I think I've struck a bird or an owl. But a second hole tears through the glass. A chunk of the dash hits the bridge of my nose, cutting me. Pain in my face. A thousand silver capillaries spread across the glass in every direction. Then the telltale *thwack! thwack!* of gunshots. The passenger window shatters. Glass pelts me. In my hair. Down the front of my uniform shirt.

I yank the wheel right. Stand on the brake. My headlights play over tall grass. The Explorer bumps over the shoulder. I glimpse a tumbling fence. The tree comes out of nowhere. I cut the wheel hard but not fast enough to avoid it. The impact throws me against my shoulder belt. The airbag explodes, hitting me in the chest like a giant fist.

For a moment I'm too dazed to move. My brain is cross firing. An engine working on one cylinder. I blink, try to get my bearings. The hood is buckled. There are two bullet holes in the glass. I raise my hand, but it's shaking so violently I can barely get to my shoulder mike. "Shots fired." I'd intended to shout the warning, but my voice is little more than groan. "Ten-thirty-three. Ten-thirty-three."

The radio snaps and crackles with renewed vigor. I unfasten my seat belt. Free myself of the deflated airbag. I see blood on the white fabric. I'm aware of pain in my face. I don't know if I've been shot.

Using my left hand, I try to open the door, but it's jammed. I press the window button, but it doesn't work. I crawl over the console. The passenger door won't open, so I slither through the window. Broken glass slices my left palm. I'm midway through, when it dawns on me that I have no idea where the shooter is. That I'm vulnerable here and not sure I have cover.

Then I'm through the window. I hit the ground hands-first. My elbows collapse. My shoulder plows into the ground. I roll and then I'm sprawled in grass that's wet with dew. "Shit."

Sirens wail in the distance. Crickets all around. The hiss of steam coming from beneath the hood. I get to my knees, draw my revolver. Then I'm crouched in the ditch. The road's shoulder provides scant cover, so I stay low. The three-quarter moon provides just enough light for me to see that whatever vehicle or buggy I'd seen earlier is gone.

Headlights wash over me. Blue and red emergency lights glint off the canopy of the tree I hit. I glance right to see a Holmes County Sheriff's cruiser glide to a stop.

"Sheriff's department! Identify yourself! Sheriff's department!"

"Painters Mill PD!" I shout. "I got shots fired!"

A Holmes County deputy, crouched low and holding a Maglite, his weapon drawn, approaches me. "Where's he at?"

"I don't know."

He approaches me, his eyes sweeping left and right. "Burkholder?"

"Yup."

He tries the passenger door, hoping to use it

for partial cover, but it won't open, so he kneels next to me. "You okay?"

"Hell if I know."

I start to get to my feet, but he sets a hand on my shoulder. "Whoa. You're bleeding, Chief. There's an ambulance on the way." He gives my shoulder an awkward little pat. "You need to get yourself checked out," he says, and then he speaks into his radio. "Ten-seven-eight." Need assistance.

A second cruiser arrives. I discern the Painters Mill PD insignia just as T.J. throws open his door and, using it for cover, draws his weapon. "Chief! Where's the shooter?"

"Unknown!" the deputy next to me calls out and speaks into his radio. "Suspect at large. We need a perimeter. Delisle Road. County Road Fourteen. Township Road Two. And Gaylord."

Another Holmes County cruiser arrives, engine groaning as it flies past T.J.'s cruiser. The ambulance parks several yards behind T.J.'s cruiser. All the while, the radio burns up the airwaves as law enforcement from miles around converge on an unknown shooter.

"What happened?" the deputy asks.

Quickly, I relay everything I know. "The caller said my brother was in a buggy accident." I hit my lapel mike. "Any sign of a buggy?" I say. "Casualties?"

"Negative."

The deputy and I exchange looks.

"Chief?"

I look past him to see T.J. trotting up to us. His stride falters when he spots my Explorer against the tree. "Shit." Then he's kneeling next to me. His eyes widen when he gets a better look at my face. "You hit? You're bleeding pretty good."

"Piece of the dash caught me, I think."

The deputy, still speaking into his radio, rises and goes to the front of the Explorer.

"You sure?" T.J. takes my arm as I get to my feet.

"I didn't get shot in the head, if that's what you're asking."

"You've got two bullet holes in your windshield." The deputy approaches, his expression grim. "I don't think he was aiming for the dash."

T.J. blinks at me. "Any idea who it was?"

I shake my head. "No clue."

The deputy curses. "We got no sign of the shooter. The son of a bitch booked. We'll take a look around, see if we can find some brass and tire marks." He turns his attention to me. "You get eyes on a vehicle? Lights? Anything?"

"I saw something. A vehicle or buggy. Then he started shooting." I frown at the front of my vehicle. "Don't know where that tree came from."

The men's laughter is interrupted by the arrival of two paramedics. I groan and the paramedic grins. "Don't look so happy to see us."

"I think I'm okay."

"Yeah, I can tell by all the blood streaming

down your face," he says, unfazed by my resistance.

I've met him at some point. He's competent and good-humored, and everyone calls him Fish. "Humor us, Chief. We're kind of sensitive about rejection, you know." Clucking his tongue, he frowns at the sight of my Explorer. "Anyone ever tell you you're tough on vehicles?"

"Yeah," I tell him. "Last time I wrecked one."

He whistles. "Town council's going to love you."

"They already do," I mutter, and I let myself be helped toward the waiting ambulance.

There are certain advantages to being the chief of police in a small town. Coffee on the house at LaDonna's Diner. Free apple fritters at the Buckhorn Bakery. The occasional dinner or lunch that comes without a check. The generosity of local merchants is a benefit I never take for granted and rarely partake in. Tonight, however, I don't argue when the doc at Pomerene Hospital gets me in and out of the ER quickly. I assure him I didn't hit my head or lose consciousness, but like most medical professionals, he's a stickler about the possibility of a traumatic brain injury, so they send me to radiology for a CAT scan. Then it's down to the lab for blood work. A young nurse cleans the cut on the bridge of my nose, deeming it superficial and predicting two black eyes before butterflying it and leaving me with instructions for an ice pack and Tylenol.

I've reached for my phone a dozen times to call Tomasetti, but I haven't yet made the call. I tell myself I'm too busy trying to stay abreast of the search for the as-yet-unidentified shooter. Besides, a few bruises don't warrant getting him out of bed at one o'clock in the morning . . . do they?

It's not until I'm alone in the ER, waiting to be released, when the seriousness of the incident hits home. An unknown individual fired at least four shots into my vehicle. I could have been killed. Was it random? Would the shooter have fired at *any* vehicle that happened to be driving down that particular road at that particular time? Were they targeting law enforcement? Or were they hell-bent on shooting me?

I'm sitting on a gurney, wearing a gown that looks as if it's been washed in a wood chipper, when I hear voices in the corridor outside the ER, and I think: *Shit.* I'd known the sheriff's department and SHP and about a hundred other agencies would want to talk to me about the incident. I'd only hoped to be out of here and dressed when it happened. There are few things that are quite so unnerving as talking to a bunch of guys when you're half-naked.

I glance down at my bare legs and feet. "Damn it." Snatching up the sheet at the foot of the gurney, I quickly snap it open and drape it over my legs.

"Chief? Knock-knock."

Sheriff Mike Rasmussen's voice calls out to me from behind the curtain. I roll my eyes and then paste a smile to my face. "I'm right here."

The curtain is shoved aside. Looking none too happy, the ER nurse offers me a commiserating frown as she walks the curtain around its track, opening my previously private space. "You have visitors," she says, handing me an ice pack. "I'll go check on your paperwork."

The sheriff is flanked by Glock and, of course, Tomasetti. The three men are staring at me, and I resist the urge to pull the blanket up to my chin. Instead, I look directly at Tomasetti and say, "I was just dialing your number."

"Uh-huh." Neither the tone of his voice or his expression give away his frame of mind, but I see him studying the bandage on the bridge of my nose. "You okay?"

"I'm fine. No stitches. CAT scan is fine." I shrug, trying not to wince because my shoulder hurts. "Kind of pissed about the Explorer, though."

"I put a call in to the mayor." Glock grins. "I figure I'd save you the headache and break the news."

I smile back. "You enjoy provoking Auggie."

"I'll take the fifth on that."

Rasmussen clears his throat. "You feel up to answering a few questions, Kate?"

I nod. "Did you get him?"

The sheriff shakes his head. "He beat it out of there quick."

"Did you find anything at the scene?" I ask. "Brass? Tire tread?"

"A single .22 casing." Rasmussen nods at Tomasetti. "We brought in BCI. I don't know if they'll assign John the case. . . ." His voice trails as if he's not exactly sure how to end it. "You know, personal relationships and all."

The sheriff knows we're involved; I'm pretty sure he knows we're living together, too. I don't, however, know if Tomasetti has communicated either of those things to his superiors at BCI. If he has, he won't be working this case.

"Even if I'm not officially assigned," Tomasetti says, "I can help expedite things, cut through some of the red tape."

"We appreciate that." Rasmussen turns his attention to me. "Kate, I know you've already been through this half a dozen times. Can you do it one more time for us? Take us through everything that happened this evening?"

"I was on my way to my house in town," I begin, thinking of the fight I'd had with Tomasetti, "and dispatch called, telling me my brother, Jacob, had been in a buggy accident out on County Road Fourteen." I look from

Tomasetti to Glock. "There wasn't an accident, was there?"

Glock shakes his head. "No accident. And no sign a buggy had been there. Your brother was home and didn't know anything about it."

"Do you know who called it in?" Rasmussen says.

"Dispatch said the call came in from the Amish pay phone on Hogpath," I tell them.

"We'll ask around. See if anyone saw anything," he tells me.

"One thing we do know," Tomasetti says, "is that whoever made the call wanted you out there, Kate. This wasn't random."

"Or they wanted a *cop* out there," I say. "Maybe any cop would've sufficed."

"They mentioned your brother specifically," he points out. "They used that information to lure you out there."

"CR Fourteen is pretty remote," Glock puts in. "Not many houses. Lots of trees."

"Perfect place for an ambush." Tomasetti scrubs a hand over his face.

I spend fifteen minutes taking them through everything that happened, from the moment I arrived on the scene until the Holmes County deputy showed up.

When I'm finished, the sheriff asks, "Do you have any idea what kind of vehicle was parked on the road?"

I shake my head. "I'm not even one hundred percent sure there *was* a vehicle. It was dark. All I really saw was the glint of something up ahead. I think it was my headlights shining off the hood or windshield. But I didn't get a good look at it."

Tomasetti glances at Rasmussen. "You're aware that Kate, the police department, and the township of Painters Mill were recently sued, correct? It's a contentious case."

"There's motive for you," Glock says. "Sounds like something that fuckin' Kester would pull."

Rasmussen nods. "I'll get someone out there to talk to Kester and his wife. Roll their asses out of bed."

"You might talk to Paula Kester's father, too," I tell him.

"A lot of animosity from all three of them," Tomasetti says.

Nodding, Rasmussen turns his attention back to me. "Any other disputes or arguments you've been involved in? I mean, as chief?" He clears his throat. "Or your personal life? Neighbors? Anything like that?"

It feels strange to be the recipient of such questions. Usually I'm the one asking them. "No."

"You piss off anyone in the course of your job?" he asks. "Maybe someone doesn't like the way you handled something? Got pissed off about a ticket?"

"Not recently." I say the words lightly, but no

one laughs. "The only other case I'm working on is the remains that were discovered under that barn," I tell him.

"Foul play involved?" the sheriff asks.

"It's possible, but we're not sure yet. We don't have a cause or manner of death. But I've been asking questions."

"To whom?"

I list the names and give the spellings. "Vern and Sue Nolt. Rachel Zimmerman. Clarence Underwood. Abigail and Jeramy Kline. The Amish women at the sewing shop in town." I go on to tell him about the possibility that domestic hogs were involved in the man's death.

"Holy shit," he mutters. *"Hogs?"*

"Figure that one out," Glock says.

"We have no way of knowing if it was a freak accident, if he fell into the pen and was killed by the animals or if someone pushed him," I tell them. "But even if it was an accident, from all indications, it looks like someone made an effort to conceal the remains."

"So it's not unreasonable to believe someone has something to hide," Rasmussen says.

Tomasetti looks at me. "As usual, Kate's been poking the bees' nest with a short stick."

I frown at him.

"Clarence Underwood was recently released from prison," Glock adds. "Former meth head."

"See if he has an alibi," I tell him.

"Yes, ma'am."

Tomasetti levels his gaze on me. "Might be a good idea for you to take a few days off."

"Probably not a bad idea," Rasmussen agrees.

Glock is smart enough to keep his mouth shut.

I sit up straighter, annoyed that they're ganging up on me. "I can't put this John Doe thing on hold—"

"Chief Burkholder?"

I look past my counterparts, relieved to see the ER doc approach. "Sorry to interrupt."

"As long as you're here to spring me," I grumble.

"In about two minutes." He looks at the men. "I need to have a word with the chief, if you're finished."

"I think we've annoyed her enough." Grinning, Rasmussen offers his hand, and we shake. "Glad you're okay, Chief. Let me know if you need anything or if you think of something else that might help us figure out who did this."

"I will. Thank you."

"Same goes, Chief." Glock gives me a small salute and heads for the door.

The doc and I look at Tomasetti. For an instant, he looks uncertain, as if he isn't sure if he should stay or go. When the moment gets awkward, the doc tosses me a questioning look.

I address the doc. "It's okay, Doc. We're . . . together."

"Oh. I see. All right then." He saunters to my bed and glances down at the clipboard. "We got the results back on your tests," he tells me. "CAT scan looks good. Blood work is within normal ranges." He grins at me. "I also had the lab run a qualitative hCG test. It's routine in case we need to do X-rays. You know you're pregnant, right?"

"I do now."

He grins stupidly at Tomasetti, who's standing beside him looking shell-shocked. "Congratulations. To both of you."

I mutter a thank-you. But my mind is reeling. I'd been harboring the hope that the pregnancy test was a fluke. That this whole thing was a blip in the radar and everything would get back to normal in a day or two.

"Any idea how far along?" I manage.

"You'll need to see your ob/gyn for that."

He's still speaking, but at some point I stopped hearing the words. I can't stop looking at Tomasetti, who's looking everywhere except at me.

Chapter 16

I'm certain I set my alarm clock for my usual 5:30 a.m. I'm just as certain that at some point after I fell asleep, Tomasetti turned it off. When I awoke in a panic at a little after eight, I wasn't sure whether to be pissed or pleased. He persuaded me to go with the latter, because I walked into the kitchen to find an omelet, toast, and juice waiting for me.

We didn't talk about my pregnancy last night. Instead, and in usual Tomasetti fashion, he grilled me about my personal safety and possible suspects. For once, I was happy to oblige. I'm not sure what it says about us as a couple that it's easier to talk about my near-death experience than the fact that I'm going to have a baby.

Over breakfast, he informed me that Rasmussen called earlier with news that Paula and Nick Kester, as well as her father, have alibis for the time of the shooting. Of course, that doesn't mean they didn't hire someone. They're not the hiring types, but it's not outside the realm of possibility that any one of them could have traded drugs for a favor. Tomasetti also confirmed that because of our personal relationship, he won't be assigned the case. But he reiterated that he will have access to information and will be able to expedite things that might otherwise take a while.

I didn't feel all that banged up last night; I didn't think I hit the tree that hard, but then adrenaline and anger can be effective analgesics. This morning, a headache the size of a *T. rex* rages between my eyes. Every muscle in my body feels as if it's been twisted into a knot. I down a couple of Tylenols with breakfast. A hot shower, and I'm feeling almost human.

Tomasetti puts up a valiant fight about my going to work, telling me I need to stay home to recuperate and give Rasmussen and my guys at least a day to get a handle on whoever might be behind the shooting. But he knows me well enough to know I'm not going to hide out. When I don't acquiesce, he moves on to plan B and suggests I take the .22 mini Magnum in my ankle holster as a backup weapon. I'm no fan of getting shot at, so I take his advice without argument.

He drops me off at the station at 10:00 a.m., before going to work in Richfield. I look like the walking dead. The bridge of my nose is bruised, and I'm pretty sure both eyes will be fully black by the end of the day.

Lois is at the switchboard with her headset on when I walk in. She gives me a double take, and gets to her feet. "Oh my."

Her expression makes me smile, which causes the bridge of my nose to hurt. "Whatever you do, don't say anything funny."

"I'll try not to." Her expression sobers. "I figured you'd take the day off."

"I thought this place might get kind of boring without me around to liven things up."

Lois hefts a laugh. "You guys have any idea who did it?"

"Not yet." I reach the dispatch station and pluck messages from my slot. "I don't want to alarm you, but I want you to keep a close eye on the door for suspicious visitors, will you?"

"You bet I will."

I go to the coffee station and find a mug. I feel her eyes on me as I pour.

"You need an ice pack, Chief? I think there's a bag of frozen peas in the fridge."

"That would be great." I touch the bridge of my nose. "I could use a loaner car, too, while the Explorer is in the shop."

"I'll call the garage and have them send one over."

I spend the morning rereading the file I've amassed on my John Doe aka Leroy Nolt case. An e-mail from Skid tells me Jeramy Kline's parents are deceased. Abigail Kline's parents, Naomi and Reuben Kaufman, sixty-four and sixty-seven years of age respectively, live on a county road outside of Charm. Neither has a record, although Reuben was cited multiple times for failure to display a slow-moving-vehicle sign on his buggy. The last ticket was issued three years ago. Either he's stopped driving the buggy or he's decided the slow-moving-vehicle sign isn't too ornamental after all.

Abigail has two sisters, both of whom are now married and living in Upstate New York. Her brother, Abram, still lives in the area. I make a mental note to pay him a visit, too, to see if he came into contact with Leroy Nolt.

I've just shut down my computer, when my

phone buzzes. I glance down to see SHERIFF'S DEPARTMENT pop up on the display.

"How're you feeling today, Chief?" Sheriff Rasmussen begins.

"Like the train conductor didn't see me standing on the tracks."

He chuckles. "I thought you'd want to know . . . that brass we found last night is, indeed, .22 caliber. Considering the distance, probably from a rifle. Crime-scene guy dug a slug out of your dash. Unfortunately, it's fragmented, so we're not going to be able to do anything with striations."

"Lots of people have .22 rifles around here." *Including the Amish,* a little voice reminds me.

"We may have gotten lucky, Kate. There's a partial print on the casing. We don't know if it's enough, but they're going to run it through AFIS and see if there's a match. Tomasetti's expediting everything for us."

AFIS is the acronym for the Automated Fingerprint Identification System. I feel a little swell of pride in my chest at the mention of Tomasetti. "Thanks."

"We stepped up patrols in all of Holmes County as well as Painters Mill proper. I've got my guys on mandatory OT."

"I appreciate that, Mike. Keep me posted, will you?"

"You know it. Take it easy today."

"I'll do my best."

Reuben and Naomi Kaufman live on a farm several miles south of Charm just off of County Road 600. It's a huge place with two big bank-style barns and a white silo in dire need of fresh paint. In the field that runs alongside the frontage road, two aging draft horses nibble overgrazed grass next to a mossy pond. I turn into the gravel driveway and park my borrowed unmarked Crown Vic beneath the shade of an elm tree and take the sidewalk to the front porch. The two-story farmhouse is plain with tall windows covered on the inside with dark fabric. Two rocking chairs sit on a porch that's been recently swept, but there are no flowerpots or hanging planters. Some Amish plant elaborate gardens, row after row of vegetables bordered by hundreds of beautiful flowers—petunias and daisies and geraniums. This garden is as plain as the house, with a dozen or more rows of tomatoes, corn, and green beans.

In light of the shooting last night, I'd considered bringing Glock with me, but Reuben and Naomi Kaufman are Swartzentruber, and I suspect they'll be more inclined to talk to me if I'm alone. That's not to say my being formerly Amish will open any doors. My fluency in Pennsylvania Dutch may help. But I've found that when dealing with Old Order Amish, especially with my being a cop, the fact that I left the fold trumps my heritage every time.

It's a beautiful day. The humidity adds a slight haze, but a breeze and the shade make the air feel good against my skin as I start toward the house. A mourning dove coos from the wind vane mounted atop the nearest barn. Sparrows chatter at me as I walk past a bird feeder filled with millet and crushed corn. I ascend the steps, open the storm door, and knock.

A moment later, the door opens and I find myself looking at a plump Amish woman in a dark gray dress that reaches nearly to her ankles. She's wearing the traditional *kapp* over steel gray hair that's thinning at her crown. "Can I help you?" Her inflection tells me she speaks Pennsylvania Dutch more often than English.

"*Guder nammidaag.*" Good afternoon. "Mrs. Kaufman?"

"*Ja.*" Her pale blue eyes sweep over me, taking in my uniform, and her nose wrinkles slightly, as if she's breathed in some unpleasant odor. "Is everything all right?"

"Yes, ma'am. Everything's fine." I show her my badge and introduce myself. "I'm working on a case, and if you have a few minutes, I'd like to ask you some questions."

"We're Amish. I don't see how we can help you with some *Englischer* case."

"May I come inside, Mrs. Kaufman? I promise not to take up too much of your time."

After a moment of hesitation, she opens the door.

I step into a rectangular living room with rough-hewn plank floors covered with a knot rug that's seen better days. The windows are covered with dark blue fabric, ushering in barely enough light for me to see a blue sofa against the wall, a rocking chair draped with an afghan, and a black potbellied stove in the corner.

I shove my sunglasses onto my crown. The woman's eyes narrow when she notices my black eyes. Smiling, I tap my right temple with my finger. "I was in a car accident last night."

"Oh." She nods, her expression telling me I probably deserved it for driving a motorized vehicle in the first place. "Would you like iced tea, Chief Burkholder? It's chamomile and mint, from the garden."

"Thank you, but I can't stay," I tell her.

The sound of the floor creaking draws my attention. I glance toward the kitchen to see an Amish man in a wheelchair rolling through the doorway. Reuben Kaufman, I think. He looks older than sixty-seven. He's wearing a blue shirt over narrow, bony shoulders. Black trousers. Suspenders. A flat-brimmed summer hat.

He makes eye contact with me. When he opens his mouth, I see he's missing a lower incisor. His face is slightly asymmetrical, with the left side sagging a little more than the right. His mouth quivers; I wait for him to speak, but he doesn't.

"This is my husband, Reuben," Naomi tells me.

I cross to him. "Hello, Mr. Kaufman." He raises a limp hand to mine. It feels cold and frail within my grip, and I shake it gently.

"Reuben has difficulty speaking sometimes," the Amish woman says. "He had a stroke, you see. Going on three years now." She looks at her husband. "Isn't that right, Reuben?"

He gives a subtle nod, but his eyes never leave mine.

Naomi moves behind her husband's wheelchair and sets her hands on the handgrips. "But we manage, don't we?"

She seems completely at ease with her husband's disability. They have their own unique mode of communication, and from the outside looking in, it seems as effective as words.

"*Sis unvergleichlich hees dohin,*" she says. It's terribly hot in here. "Let's sit on the porch."

I go to the door and hold it open while she wheels her husband outside. There, she sets the wheel lock and then lowers herself into a rocking chair. "*Sitz dich anne,*" she tells me. Sit yourself down.

"*Danki.*" The rocking chair has a wicker seat and creaks slightly as I lower myself into it. "You and your husband have a beautiful farm."

"Reuben's *mamm* left it to us when she passed. Been in the Kaufman family for years."

"I've driven by a few times. Didn't she used to raise hogs out here?"

Her eyes narrow on mine. "Never raised hogs."

"Have you and Mr. Kaufman ever raised hogs?"

"We've raised a few head of cattle over the years. Just enough to keep us in meat over the winter. Reuben prefers to work the land. Corn and soybeans, mostly. That's what his *datt* taught him. That's what he knows." She pauses. "What's this all about, Chief Burkholder?"

"I'm investigating a case involving some human remains that were uncovered by the tornado."

"I read about it in the paper." She shivers. "Such a horrible thing. Do you know who it is?"

"Not yet." I watch them closely as I speak, looking for any sign of nervousness or discomfort. "We're looking into the cases of several young men who went missing thirty or so years ago."

She cocks her head. "What does this have to do with us? We're not missing any family members."

"I heard your daughter, Abigail, used to see a young man by the name of Leroy Nolt." I don't know that to be fact, but I put it out there to see if it conjures a response.

"I don't know where you heard that, Chief Burkholder, but Abby never had eyes for anyone but Jeramy Kline."

I shrug. "Sometimes children do things without their parents' knowledge."

"Not Abby. She was a good girl." She looks at her husband. "In fact, I don't know anyone by the name of Nolt. That's a Mennonite name, isn't it, Reuben?"

He gives a barely discernible nod. But the old man's eyes are sharp on mine, and for the first time I realize that while his body was devastated by the stroke, his mind is crystal clear.

Naomi sips her tea, studying me over the rim of her glass. "What makes you think our Abigail knew this Nolt boy?"

"Since this is an ongoing investigation, Mrs. Kaufman, I can't get into the details just yet."

She laughs and pats her husband's hand. "Well, that's the police for you. Not as forthcoming as they should be." She cocks her head and her expression turns knowing. "I remember you now. You're the one who left." Nodding, she touches her temple. "Takes me a while these days, but I never forget a name."

I don't take the bait, instead, I turn my attention to Reuben. "What about you, Mr. Kaufman? Did you know Leroy Nolt? Did he ever do any work for you? Around the farm, maybe?"

The man gives a minute shake of his head and mouths a single word: *No.*

Naomi looks at me, triumphant. "See?"

Chapter 17

I take the long way back to Painters Mill and cruise past Abigail Kline's farm. I'm only mildly surprised when I see three Amish quilts hanging on the old-fashioned clothesline in the front yard. When I spoke to her yesterday, she denied having any quilts on hand. Did she think I wouldn't drive past and notice them? Is she selling them for someone else? Or did she make them? If so, why would she lie about something so seemingly benign?

I pull into the driveway and park in the same spot I did the day before. Instead of going to the front door, I start toward the quilts flapping in the breeze. The first is a traditional broken-star pattern with a striking color combination of sage green, teal, and purple on a backdrop of taupe. Even with my unqualified eye, I can see the required seven stitches per inch and the kind of intricate piercing that achieves perfect points.

I turn up corners of the quilt until I find what I'm looking for. The letters "A.K." embroidered in the fabric. The initials of the quilter. The initials of Abigail Kline. The same initials on the quilt I saw hanging on the wall in Sue and Vern Nolt's house. *Abigail Kaufman.* Are they one and the same?

"Are you looking to buy a quilt, Chief Burkholder?"

I turn at the sound of Abigail Kline's voice. She's standing between me and the Crown Vic, a bushel basket propped on her hip.

"I suspect they're probably out of my price range," I tell her.

"They do bring a pretty penny." After a brief hesitation, she starts toward me. She's dressed much the same as she was last time we spoke. Drab gray dress. Black sneakers. Head covered with an organdy *kapp*.

"My *mamm* taught me to quilt. Started when I was all of six years old. She told me I was born with the gift." She runs her hand over the quilt as if she's touching her firstborn child and gives a wistful smile. "I've had a needle in my hand since before I can even remember."

"I made one or two when I was younger," I tell her, "but I was never very good at it."

"It takes patience."

"And talent," I point out.

She smiles at the compliment. "By the time I was twelve, my *mamm* was telling all the women I was a better quilter than her." She laughs. "I was, too, though I'd never admit to it. I guess it's a good thing I love to sew. Keeps the hands busy and a little cash in the cookie jar."

She sets the basket on the ground at her feet. I look down to see it's full of dandelion greens with a few weeds mixed in. I motion toward it. "Now that brings back memories," I tell her.

"They're at their best in early spring, but still good now."

"My *mamm* used to make them with bacon and vinegar."

"Good on a salad, too, if you like them raw."

"I do."

We stand there a moment, admiring the quilts in silence, enjoying the breeze. "You told me yesterday you didn't have any quilts," I say.

She looks over her shoulder toward the house but doesn't respond.

I follow her gaze, and for the first time I notice the buggy is gone. "Your husband is away?"

"He went up to Keim Lumber for some wood." She laughs. "I suspect he'll come back with more goats."

Smiling, I move to one of the other quilts and run my hand over the fabric. "Is there a reason why you didn't tell me about the quilts, Mrs. Kline?"

She joins me, pretending to study her handiwork. When she runs her hand over the stitching, it quivers. "You were Amish once, weren't you, Chief Burkholder? But you left the fold during *Rumspringa*?"

That's not exactly the way it happened, but I don't correct her. "Yes."

"We're Swartzentruber. My husband and I.

My parents. I love being Amish. I love God, and living my life by the *Ordnung* gives me joy."

"I understand."

"The Amish have always been there for us. When Jeramy hurt his back two years ago, Big Joe Beiler and his friends cut and bundled our corn for us—when he had his own crops to harvest and eight mouths to feed." She looks out across the pasture, toward the pond where the two pygmy goats nibble green shoots near the bank.

"The Amish can be harsh, too," I say gently. "Judgmental."

"Sometimes."

"Sometimes that harshness is warranted. Sometimes it isn't."

When she says nothing, I turn to her, tilting my head slightly to meet her gaze. "Leroy Nolt's parents told me that in the weeks before he disappeared, he was seeing someone in secret. His sister saw him with a girl. An Amish girl."

The silence between us thickens. I see discomfort in her face. Her skin reddens above the collar of her dress. "You recognized the ring in the photo," I say gently. "I saw it on your face."

After a full minute, she whispers, "I knew Leroy." She utters the words as if she's afraid someone will hear and the repercussions will be severe.

"Do you know what happened to him?" I ask.

"No. I figured he left for the city. Columbus or Cleveland or, my goodness, he was always talking about New York City."

"Were you involved with him?"

"Involved?" She laughs but looks down at the ground. "I was just a girl with a silly crush."

"Is that all?"

"Of course."

"You must have missed him."

"Nooo." She draws out the "o" for emphasis. "I was happy for him. He'd followed his dreams, foolish as they were. And so different from my own."

My mind is already poking into all the dark corners of words that don't quite ring true. "Did anyone know about your relationship?"

"Chief Burkholder, we didn't have the kind of relationship you're insinuating."

"What kind of relationship was it, then?"

"We were . . . friends. More like acquaintances."

I nod, but I don't believe her. There's something there; something she's not telling me. "Did anyone know you and Leroy were friends?"

"We had nothing to hide."

"But you didn't tell anyone, either, did you?"

If there was an Amish word for "touché" she would have uttered it. "No one knew. At first, anyway. Then my *datt* saw us in the woods by the creek. Leroy was fishing. I'd gone down to pick raspberries for Mamm. My *datt* came down to seine for minnows." She shakes her head. "It was all very innocent."

"Was your *datt* angry?"

"He was . . . offended. You see, Leroy was *Mennischt.*" Mennonite. "And New Order at that. Datt . . . overreacted." She shrugs. "Forbade me to see Leroy."

"Because he was Mennonite?"

"Because he wasn't Swartzentruber," she corrects. "Datt told me I would be put under the *bann.* That I would have to confess my sins before the congregation."

"Did your mother know what happened?"

"We never talked about it."

"What about Jeramy?" I ask. "How did he play into this?"

"He didn't."

"Were you involved with Jeramy?"

Her smile is little more than a twist of her lips; her eyes are filled with something akin to nostalgia, only somehow sadder. "I've been in love with Jeramy Kline since I was a little girl. He's always been so handsome. So strong and hardworking and yet humble. All the Amish girls wanted to marry him."

"Your parents liked him?"

"They wanted me to marry him."

"Did you want to marry him?"

"Of course I did. I'm lucky to have him. He's a

good husband. A good father. A good provider."

I wonder if she's trying to convince me—or herself. "Abigail, if you know something about Leroy Nolt's disappearance, you need to tell me."

"That's all I know, Chief Burkholder."

I give her a full two minutes to say something more. When she doesn't, I lean closer to her. "I think something bad happened to Leroy Nolt," I whisper. "I'm going to find out what it was."

"Sometimes when bad things happen," she says, "the only one to blame is the person it happened to."

My office is blissfully quiet. From the reception area, I hear Jodie's radio grinding out an old Badfinger tune, interrupted only by the occasional crackle of the police radio. I'm sitting at my desk with the John Doe / Leroy Nolt file open in front of me. But it's all a blur. I've read it dozens of times, too many times to absorb anything new. A knock at my door draws me from my reverie. I look up to see Skid standing in the doorway.

"You got a minute?" He flicks the paper in his hand. "I've got the rundown on that hog operation you asked about."

"At least one of us isn't striking out." I motion him in. "Have a seat."

He takes the visitor chair adjacent to my desk and slides a single sheet of paper across to me. I can tell by the neatness of the typewritten page that he talked one of the dispatchers into typing it for him. Skid isn't exactly a neatnik.

"I take it you got nothing from the Kaufmans or Klines?" he says.

"A few lies, maybe." I tell him about my conversation with Abigail Kline. "I think she's the girl Nolt was seeing when he was killed."

"You think she knows what happened to him?"

"I think she knows more than she's letting on." Frowning, I look down at the sheet of paper he brought in. "I just have to figure out what it is."

"Hewitt Hog Producers was owned by Homer Hewitt from 1982 until they closed down in September 1997," he tells me. "Homer Hewitt filed for bankruptcy that same year. The company had amassed some EPA violations. Couldn't fix them and eventually went belly up. Leroy Nolt worked there from May of 1985 up until he disappeared."

"Interesting timing," I say. "What did he do there?"

"He actually worked in the office and helped out with some heavy machinery work."

"Any problems between Hewitt and Nolt?"

"Not that I could find."

"Anyone else?"

"No, ma'am."

I notice a Florida address for Hewitt. "When did he move to St. Petersburg?"

He glances down at his notes. "Four years ago."

I nod. "What's the status on the property?"

"Currently abandoned. There's been some talk that the new owner is going to turn it into a turkey farm, but there's nothing in the works."

"Thanks for giving up happy hour to put all this together."

He grins. "Anytime, Chief."

Movement at the door draws my attention. I glance up, half expecting to see Jodie. Surprise ripples through me at the sight of Tomasetti standing in the doorway. "Hi, Chief." He looks at Skid. "Skidmore."

"Agent Tomasetti." Skid rises and the two men shake.

"Anything new on your John Doe?" Tomasetti divides his attention between the two of us, including Skid in the conversation.

"I was just telling Chief Burkholder about that old hog operation down in Coshocton County."

Tomasetti arches a brow.

I fill him in on the highlights. "Considering the marks left on those bones, I thought it might be worth a look around."

"I agree." He gives Skid a pointed look. "Might be a good idea to take someone with you."

Skid clears his throat. "Sure, Chief, uh . . . just let me know and I'm there."

We fall silent. Realizing that's his cue to leave,

Skid moves closer to the door. "Let me know if you need anything else."

"Thanks."

He tips his head at Tomasetti and then he's gone.

For the span of several seconds, I stare at the door, part of me wishing Skid hadn't left so quickly.

"I'm sorry I've been such an egocentric son of a bitch," he begins.

"I don't know what to say to that."

"You could tell me I'm off the hook, or maybe let me know I'm being a little hard on myself." One side of his mouth curves into a smile. "Then we could go home and have makeup sex."

I return his smile, but mine feels halfhearted. "I know this has been hard for you."

"Harder for you, probably. I'm sorry."

I nod and look down at the reports spread out on my desk, not really seeing them.

"How are you feeling?" I look at him, not sure if he's referring to the shooting and ensuing accident last night or my pregnancy. Then he touches the place between his eyes to indicate the cut on the bridge of my nose.

"Better." The tension that had crept into my shoulders begins to unravel. "I've been wearing my sunglasses."

"For the record, you look good in purple."

"Tomasetti, you're full of shit."

"You're not the first person to tell me that."

"Probably not the last, either."

"Yeah." Sighing, he shoves his hands into his pockets. "I was in the area and I thought, if you have time, I'd take you to dinner."

"In the area, huh?"

"That's right."

"You have pretty good timing, because I'm starving."

"In that case, why don't you close that file and shut down your computer? I know just the place."

Two hours later Tomasetti and I are seated at Pier W, one of Cleveland's most elegant and renowned restaurants. Cantilevered atop the cliffs in Lakewood, west of the city, the restaurant offers a stunning view of a brooding Lake Erie and the skyline to the east.

After leaving the station, we'd made a quick stop at the farm, where I showered and spent ten minutes tearing through my closet, searching for something to wear that didn't include denim or have the Painters Mill PD insignia emblazoned in the fabric. I can count on one hand the number of times I've worn a dress in the last decade. Luckily, I kept the one I wore to my *mamm*'s funeral five years ago. It's a simple black shift with three-quarter sleeves and a hem that falls to the knee. I dusted off the pair of plain black pumps at the back of my closet. A touch of makeup, and I was good to go.

"No place for my mini Magnum," I'd told Tomasetti as I emerged from our bedroom.

"I'll keep mine handy." But his eyes swept over me. "You look nice."

"Can't do anything about the black eyes."

"They'll probably earn me some dirty looks."

I snorted. "You know, Tomasetti, you clean up pretty good yourself," I'd told him. "I mean, for an old guy."

He was laughing when we walked out the door.

I'd expected some overpriced steakhouse or seafood restaurant in Wooster. Not for the first time, Tomasetti surprised me when we hit the interstate and zipped north toward Cleveland. Now we're sitting across from each other at a round table draped with white linen. A votive candle flickers on the tabletop between us. To my left, a restless Lake Erie tosses whitecaps onto the rocky shore. Leaving us with menus, the waiter hustles away.

"So is this a date?" I ask.

"Yes."

"I'm not sure we've actually done this before."

"We haven't." He glances over at me. "We should have."

I look out across the silver shimmer of the lake. In the distance, I see the silhouette of a freighter against the horizon. Seagulls wheeling and circling overhead. Farther out, the hazy flash of lightning from a summer storm. I'm not easily dazzled. But tonight, with the mesmerizing power of the lake, and the man I love sitting across from me, I feel that rare sparkle inside.

"If you're trying to impress me," I tell him, "you're succeeding."

"I was still working for the division of police when I discovered this place. A lot of locals come here. It's low-key with great service." He glances down at his menu. "Damn good seafood."

I nod. "There's a whole part of your life I don't know much about. You don't talk about it."

"You know the important stuff."

The waiter returns and we order our food. Grilled walleye for me. Lake perch for Tomasetti. After refilling our water glasses, he leaves us again.

"Anything else come in from the sheriff's office today on the shooter?" he asks after a moment.

"The partial on the cartridge didn't match up with anything on AFIS."

"So he's never been arrested," he tells me.

"Nick Kester has a sheet as long as my arm."

"What about his wife? Maybe she loaded the rifle for him."

"She's not a match."

"Doesn't mean he didn't get someone else to do it."

"I know."

He nods, thinking. "What about the John Doe you're working on? The remains? Have you been pushing someone who might've pushed back?"

"I've been asking questions." I think about that a moment and shake my head. "Amish mostly."

"A lot of Amish have .22 rifles."

"True, but I can't see any of them doing something like that."

"No one ever does." He picks up his water glass. "Who are your suspects?"

Pleased to be on comfortable ground, I tell him everything I know about the case. "I'm getting some odd vibes from Abigail Kline. I'm pretty sure she lied about the quilt. She lied about not having any new quilts for sale, because she didn't want me to see that she embroiders her initials on them."

"People don't lie without a reason."

"I can't prove it, but I think she was the woman involved with Nolt when he disappeared."

"Why would she lie about it?"

"That's where things get complicated. Abigail Kline is Swartzentruber, which is one of the most conservative sects of the Amish. Leroy Nolt was New Order Mennonite, which is pretty much on the opposite end of the spectrum. It's generally frowned upon for Amish people to marry outside their church district, particularly if the person they choose is from a more liberal congregation. The gap between some of the church districts is huge, and a relationship between the two of them would have undoubtedly caused big problems, especially for Abigail."

"You think she lied simply because she doesn't want anyone to know she was involved with Nolt?"

I nod. "That's certainly a possibility."

"But you think there's more to it."

"I don't think she killed him," I tell him. "But she might know who did."

"She's protecting them?"

"Yes."

"How does Jeramy Kline fit into all of this?" he asks. "Or does he?"

"If Nolt's death was the result of some sort of love triangle gone bad . . ." I let my brain run with that train of thought. "Abigail Kline has known Jeramy since she was a kid. She always knew she'd marry him. Everyone expected it, and in the Amish community those kinds of expectations are taken very seriously." I look at Tomasetti. "What if Leroy Nolt came along and screwed it up for Jeramy?"

"I think you have a viable motive for Jeramy Kline to want Leroy Nolt gone for good."

"I've not been able to link them."

"You have the initials on the quilt. And didn't Nolt's sister see them together?"

"Maybe I could check with Rachel Zimmerman and see if she can ID Abigail. But it's been thirty years."

"Worth a shot."

The waiter returns with our food. Water for me. A nice sauvignon blanc for Tomasetti. Conversation lags while we dig in. I nearly groan at the delectability of the fish. "Tomasetti, you scored some major points tonight."

"I thought this might do it."

After several minutes, he goes back to the case. "What about Abigail Kline's father? If it's frowned upon to marry into a more liberal sect, he might have a pretty strong motive for wanting to get rid of Nolt."

I nod, finish chewing, and swallow. "I'm looking at him, too. He's old and frail. Had a stroke a few years ago."

"Was he raising hogs back then?"

"Naomi Kaufman told me they've never raised hogs."

"Even the righteous have been known to lie to get their necks out of a noose."

I tell him about the missing surgical plate. "Might be interesting to take a metal detector to the pens at their farm. If Nolt died there, the surgical plate could be there, too."

"You got enough for a warrant?"

"Enough to ask for one. Don't know if I'll get it."

"You could always ask for permission to take a look around. You'd be surprised the things people agree to when you ask nicely."

"I might just do that."

"Kate, is Jeramy Kline or old man Kaufman capable of pulling off the attack on you last night?"

"Kline certainly is, but I've talked to him. I don't think he knows anything about Nolt."

"Unlike his wife."

"Exactly."

"And Kaufman?"

I shake my head. "He's frail and in a wheelchair. There's no way he could pull off a decent shot and then get away so fast."

It isn't until after dessert that the conversation turns back to us. Tomasetti is no nervous Nellie—far from it. In fact, he's got the nerves of a steel building. But throughout dinner, I've sensed he was holding something back, or wanting to broach a subject and waiting for just the right moment to do it. By the time our waiter serves coffee, I'm more nervous than he is because I have no idea what he wants to talk about. If it's good or bad or somewhere in between.

The waiter has just laid the check on the table between us and wished us a good evening, when Tomasetti reaches across the table and takes my hand. "Kate."

"You're not going to blindside me, are you?" I ask.

"Probably." He tries to smile, but his lips twist into an expression that looks more like a grimace, and I think *Uh-oh.* "Probably going to screw it up, too."

We stare at each other for an interminable moment and then he asks, "Maybe we ought to consider making things a little more permanent."

"You mean, our living arrangements?"

"I mean us."

It's the last thing I expected him to say. I stare at him, my heart pounding so hard I can't speak. I do the only thing I can and choke out a laugh.

His brows go up. I see amusement in his eyes, and I'm glad he has a sense of humor, because I'm sure laughter wasn't the reaction he was anticipating.

"You know, Kate, I'm kind of putting myself out there." His words are lighthearted, but his eyes reveal a thread of uncertainty.

"I'm just . . . surprised. Tomasetti, we haven't talked about this."

"We should have." He shrugs. "Things are different now. I think we need to talk about where we go from here. Figure out where we stand."

"You sure you're not just stepping up to the plate because you knocked me up and you're a stand-up guy?" I say after a moment.

"I'm asking the woman I love if she wants to marry me."

I reach across the table and take his other hand. I haven't had so much as a sip of wine, but my head is spinning. "Tomasetti, I don't want you to propose marriage for the wrong reason. Just two days ago you weren't happy about my being pregnant. You weren't happy with me for letting it happen."

"It caught me off guard. That's all."

"I'm not sure I believe you." I smile, but my cheek quivers, giving away more than I intended. "Marriage is . . . a huge step. I want to be sure we do it for the right reasons."

"I know what I want."

"Contrary to popular belief, you're also capable of doing something completely selfless if it's the right thing to do and it involves someone you love."

"Are you telling me you don't want to get married?"

"I'm telling you that maybe we need to give this some time. A few days. A few weeks. I don't think we should rush into anything, especially now."

"You're not letting me down easy, are you?"

"Not a chance."

He nods slowly, holding my gaze. "Just so you know, Kate, I'm not going to change my mind. And I'm not going anywhere. You can count on me."

"I'm counting on that." Leaning across the table, I brush my mouth across his. "Let's go home."

Chapter 18

"Kate. Hey. Wake up."

I startle awake to gray light seeping in through my bedroom window. For an instant, I'm disoriented. Tomasetti is standing next to the bed. It feels like the middle of the night, but he's dressed. Button-down shirt. Creased trousers. Tie that's slightly askew. My phone in his hand.

I push myself to a sitting position. "What?" A glance at the alarm clock tells me it's past 7:00 a.m. "I overslept," I mutter.

"Your phone was ringing." He smiles and passes me my cell phone. "It's your dispatcher."

Because I'm accustomed to receiving middle-of-the-night calls, I always turn up my ringtone before going to bed. This is the first time in the history of mankind that I didn't hear it ring. "Thanks."

"You're welcome." Bending, he kisses me atop the head.

Clearing the cobwebs from my throat, I take the call. "Mona?"

"Chief, I'm sorry to bother you so early. But I thought you'd want to know. . . . I took a call from Abigail Kline last night. There was some kind of medical emergency out at their farm, and Jeramy Kline was transported to the hospital."

I swing my feet over the side of the bed. "What happened to him?"

"She said he got sick and had some kind of seizure."

"Is he all right?"

"The hospital wouldn't give out info, but one of the paramedics confirmed the seizure. I know you were just out at the Kline place, so I thought you might want a heads-up."

"Thanks for letting me know. I'm going to drive over to the hospital now."

Ask any cop if he believes in coincidence, and he'll respond with a resounding hell no. That's particularly true if said coincidence involves a current case. Normally, a citizen being rushed to the ER for some unexplained illness certainly wouldn't warrant the attention of the police. But Jeramy Kline isn't just an ordinary citizen. He may or may not be involved in a thirty-year-old mystery in which a man was killed. Is his jaunt to the hospital related in any way to the case?

While I'm not convinced either of the Klines were directly involved in the death of Leroy Nolt, they are not above suspicion. They're aware of my interest, and I know from experience that many times police attention can evoke a great deal of stress. If Jeramy is guilty of wrongdoing and fears I'm closing in, he wouldn't be the first to hurt himself to avoid arrest and prosecution.

I'm speculating, of course, and his trip to the ER might be as benign as a simple case of food poisoning. But I've learned to follow my gut, and this morning my gut is telling me the timing of this stinks.

It's after 8:00 a.m. by the time I reach Pomerene Hospital. I arrive at the nurse's station outside the ER to find a young woman in pink scrubs pecking at a keyboard with long French-tipped fingernails. "Oh, hi, Chief." She slants me a smile. "You're becoming a regular around here."

I smile back. Her name is Cindy, and she was on duty when I was brought in after the shooting two nights ago. "You guys are going to have to add me to your payroll."

"I'll get with the bean counters on that and see what they can do." She swivels in her chair. "What can I do for you?"

"I understand Jeramy Kline was brought in last night."

"Right. The Amish guy. We checked him in a few hours ago. Doctor Megason is looking at him now."

"Any idea what happened?"

"Let's see. . . ." She goes back to her keyboard and taps a few keys. "The patient wasn't conscious upon arrival, but it looks like the paramedics got some preliminary info from his wife." She squints at the monitor. "Seizures. Vomiting. Respiratory distress."

"Any history of epilepsy?"

"No."

"Head injury?"

"Wife says no."

"You guys check for the presence of alcohol or drugs?"

"It's routine in cases like this for the doc to draw blood, take urine, and send both out for a tox screen." She wrinkles her nose at me. "He's Amish, Chief."

"I'm not sure that matters, unfortunately." I sigh. "The wife around?"

"She's in the ER waiting area."

I make a stop at the vending machine for two cups of coffee and then head toward the ER waiting room. I find Abigail Kline sitting on an orange Naugahyde bench paging through a *Good Housekeeping* magazine.

She startles upon spotting me and rises abruptly. "Chief Burkholder. Is it Jeramy? Is he all right?"

Her face reveals stress piled upon a sleepless night. Her eyes are bloodshot, and the circles beneath them are the color of a bruise. I hand her one of the coffees. "I stopped by to check on Jeramy and see how you're doing."

"Oh." She looks down at the coffee and takes it. "Thank you. I'm fine. It's Jeramy I'm worried about."

"What happened?"

"He just . . . got sick last night. It happened so quickly. I've had four children who spent their fair share of time with fevers and whatnot. But this . . . I didn't know what to do or how to help him. I've never been so scared."

I nod. "Can you take me through what happened to him?"

"It was a normal evening," she tells me. "We had dinner and then we walked down to the creek. Afterward, we sat on the porch with some pie. We went to bed around nine thirty or so." She closes her eyes briefly. "He woke me around midnight. He was in the bathroom, throwing up and . . . you know. I went in to check on him, and he was terribly sick and shaking. I thought maybe it was the stomach bug that's been going around, so I fixed him some mint tea. It didn't help. Nothing would help. He got worse and worse. And then he just . . . fell to the floor and started convulsing. I thought he was going to die."

"What did you do?"

"He's too heavy for me to move. I couldn't get him to the bed, so I put pillows around him and I ran to the neighbor's house to call the emergency number."

"How's he doing now?"

"I don't know. The doctor came out and asked me a bunch of questions. I only got to see Jeramy for a few minutes. They put a tube in his mouth to help him breathe. He couldn't talk to me. He was so pale." Her face screws up, and she puts her hand over her mouth. "He couldn't breathe on his own."

"Does the doctor have any idea why he got sick?" I ask.

She shakes her head. "It's been hours and no one will tell me anything."

I nod. "What was his frame of mind last night?"

"He was fine. Same as always."

"Did you have any guests last night? Did the two of you see anyone else?"

"No, it was just us."

"Did you go anywhere?"

"No."

"I hope he's better soon." I touch her shoulder. "I'll check in on you later."

"Thank you, Chief Burkholder." She clasps her hands, her knuckles turning white. "I'm just praying to God it's nothing too serious."

I'm puzzling over Jeramy Kline's mysterious illness when I climb into my borrowed Crown Vic and start toward the station. It's probably an innocent case of stomach flu or food poisoning or maybe even the misuse of or allergic reaction to some prescription drug or unprescribed herb. But the timing of it niggles at my cop's sensibilities. Even if his malady doesn't have some benign explanation, I can't come up with a motive for why someone would want him out of the picture.

Unless, of course, the illness is self-inflicted because I'm about to find out about something he doesn't want me to know.

I'm barely out of the parking lot when I hit the speed dial for Glock's cell. "You up for an adventure?" I begin.

"I get to bring my gun?" he counters.

I try not to laugh but don't quite manage. "I want you to run by Axel Equipment Rental over on Third Street and rent two metal detectors for a couple days."

"Sure. I'm not too far from there now." He pauses. "Kind of wondering why we need them."

"I thought we might take them down to that abandoned hog facility and see if anything interesting turns up."

"You mean like a titanium plate?"

"And everyone says I hired you for your marksmanship."

"I'm sort of an all-around guy, I guess."

I grin. "Meet me there in an hour, will you?"

"Roger that," he says, and we end the call.

An hour later I'm southbound on County Road 24 northwest of Coshocton. On my right a cornfield stretches west to a precipitous hill and runs alongside the road. I descend a hill, cross a small creek, and the cornfield gives way to pastureland. A quarter mile past the creek, I come upon a wooded area of new-growth saplings and brush and small trees—nature reclaiming what's rightfully hers.

According to my GPS, Hewitt Hog Producers is on the right, dead ahead. I descend another hill and enter bottomland. The foliage thickens. Mature trees encroach, casting me in shadow. I'm looking for a sign or mailbox, an overgrown driveway or lane on the right. I've just crossed the creek for the third time when a barely visible path to the left snags my attention. I hit the brakes hard enough to lock up my shoulder harness.

I make the turn onto an overgrown lane. The Crown Vic bumps over old ruts and dry mud holes. Tree branches and scrub scratch the doors as I squeeze the vehicle through the cavelike entrance. A hundred yards in, the trees open to what had once been a large gravel lot. A huge metal building juts from the earth like primitive ruins. Streaks of rust the color of old blood give the building the look of a felled beast. Silos punctuate each end of the building.

I park in an open area, well away from hip-high weeds that could be concealing holes or snakes or God only knows what. I'm about to call Glock to let him know the map had it wrong, when I hear the crunch of tires. I glance toward the entrance to see his cruiser pull in. He parks behind my Crown Vic. I get out and retrieve the canvas bag in which I packed a couple of hand spades and a folding shovel.

I reach Glock as he's opening his trunk. "Hey, Chief."

"Any problem finding the place?" I ask.

"Naw." He lifts the first metal detector and leans it against the bumper. "Only drove by it four times."

Grinning, I look toward the main building. A dilapidated chain-link fence encloses what had once been the electrical box. The fence has been cut; the electrical box door has been pried off its hinges.

"Looks like the copper thieves have come and gone." He leans the second metal detector against the bumper and slams the trunk. "How long has this place been closed?"

"Around eighteen years. Give or take."

"Looks it." He straightens, his eyes skimming the trees and thick underbrush. He's not the uneasy type, but I sense his tension. I feel that same tension creeping into my own psyche. We're isolated here and surrounded on all sides by perfect hiding places. If you wanted to ambush a cop, this would be the perfect place to do it.

As if realizing my train of thought, he grins. "Keep expecting to see zombies walking out of those trees."

"If that happens, it's every man for himself." I lift one of the canvas bags and heft it onto my shoulder.

The front of the building is stucco that's

covered with green moss. The remainder is corrugated steel. From where I'm standing I see the remnants of what had once been huge roof fans, probably for dispersing heat and the stench in the summer. We don't speak as we weave through weeds and sapling trees toward the front door. Around us the woods are alive with the echo of birdsong and cicadas. A faded wooden sign dotted with bird shit is propped against a scraggly looking juniper that had once been part of the landscaping. I can just make out the faded print, HEWITT HOG PRODUCERS, and the logo of a smiling white pig. Next to it a faded NO TRESPASSING sign welcomes us.

"SO know we're out here?" Glock asks, referring to the sheriff's department.

I nod. "I called and let them know we were going to take a look around."

The front door hangs at a precarious angle by a single hinge and creaks in the breeze. The wood is naked of paint and warped from the elements. Beyond, I see what had once been a reception area of sorts and several offices.

Glock reaches the door first and slips inside. "What's the story on this place, anyway?" he asks as he enters the reception area.

"It closed down after some kind of problem with the EPA. Paid a big fine for dumping waste into a watershed." I follow him inside and am immediately met with the smell of rotting wood and the vaguely unpleasant odor of mildew. "Hewitt abandoned the business, didn't tell anyone there were a dozen or so hogs left behind. Agents came out and euthanized the animals."

Glock turns and looks at me. "Always hate hearing shit like that. People who abuse animals are fucked up."

"I agree."

"Bodes well for why we're here, though."

"Yes, it does."

We're midway through the offices. There's not much left. Except for a single swivel chair with a missing base, the furniture is gone. The office doors are nowhere in sight. Graffiti covers most of the walls. Some of it's colorful and creative, but most looks like the mindless work of paint huffers. I see a single glass meth pipe on the floor. Several aerosol cans strewn about. The tiny bones of what looks like a long-dead rodent. Dirt and lichens and other indistinguishable organic matter grow everywhere.

We reach another door. Someone has fired a shotgun into it, which left dozens of pellet holes and an opening the size of my fist. Glock muscles it open. We go down a short stairwell and find ourselves in the belly of a warehouse-type building with a loading dock and dozens of old pens. Most of the steel panels are gone. Some are rusted and broken down. I suspect the equipment and furnishings of this place were auctioned off a long time ago. What didn't sell was simply left behind, and over the years, people helped them-selves to whatever they needed. About half of the pens include concrete manure pits that are about four feet deep. Some have grates in place; others simply drop off.

Through a door on the far side of the warehouse, I see the facade of a dilapidated Quonset hut barn with a big sliding door and tiny square windows.

I take in the sheer size of the place and sigh. "A lot of ground to cover."

"You want me to call Skid or T.J.?" Glock asks.

I think about scheduling and overtime and shake my head. "Let's see how much ground we can cover. If it's not enough, I'll get them out here tomorrow."

He nods. "You know, Chief, with those remains showing signs that the vic was mauled by hogs, and he actually *worked* here, this is the place to look."

"The question is, did he leave that titanium plate behind?" I look down at my metal detector. "The guy at the rental place give any instructions on how to use this thing?"

"Yup." He reaches over and hits the power button. "There's your ON button. Sensitivity is set high, so it'll pick up just about anything, including beer tabs and crap. Since we're both a couple of amateurs, he thought that was best." He grins. "I think 'idiot proof' was the term he used."

"Not intended in a literal sense, I'm sure."

Another laugh, and then he offers instruction on technique. "All we have to do is set up a grid. Walk it. Sweep back and forth, like this." He demonstrates.

I pull out my phone and call up a photo of the titanium plate. "This is similar to the piece we're looking for. There may or may not be screws with it."

He nods. "I'll start on the north side, Chief. You want to take the south? We'll work our way toward each other?"

"Good plan."

He motions toward the Quonset hut barn. "If you don't mind, I'm going to check that out first."

"Remember what I said about zombies," I call out.

"Yeah, yeah. It's every man for himself."

We part ways. I go right, to the south side of the maze of pens. He descends the steps and starts toward the Quonset hut barn.

Two weeks ago I gave a talk to about forty seniors at the Painters Mill High School. Most of the students viewed police work as an exciting and glamorous career chock-full of high-speed chases, CSI-esque science, and dangerous under-cover work that nets millions in dirty cash and concludes with some scumbag drug dealer going to jail. A misconception perpetuated by movies and television. No one likes to burst the bubble of a young mind, so I was hard-pressed to point out that reality couldn't be further from the truth. But I did.

Sweeping a metal detector over a nine-thousand-square commercial hog operation is a prime example of exactly how unglamorous police work can be, especially when your efforts are hampered by steel panels, concrete manure pits, and falling-down feeders. So far my search has netted a screwdriver, six beer cans, spent shotgun shells, several nails, and a garter snake. It's hot and humid, and with the close proximity of the creek to the east, the mosquitoes are the size of bats and just as bloodthirsty. I'm two hours into my grid and working my way north, when I find the skull. I'm standing at the base of one of the manure pits atop a decades-old buildup of pig shit—that, much to my relief, has composted to soil—when I spot the curved globe sticking out of the dirt.

Propping my metal detector against the concrete wall, I tug the spade from my back pocket and squat for a better look. The skull is smooth and white and looks to be intact. Using the spade, I pry it from its nest. I'm no expert, but it looks very much like a pig skull. It's elongated and relatively flat from crown to nose, with small tusks jutting upward from the lower jaw. I glance down, see a glint of white from a second bone. I unearth several vertebrae. A dozen or so ribs. The blade of a shoulder. Picking up the metal detector, I slowly sweep the area. When no alert sounds, I leave the bones and move on.

I've only advanced a few yards, when a wave of nausea seesaws below my ribs. It's been happening on and off all morning. I attributed it to hunger, and so far I've been able to ignore it. But no more. I prop the metal detector against the fence. I barely make it to the edge of the concrete pen area before throwing up in the weeds. I'm bent at the hip with my hands on my knees, thinking I'm not quite finished, when I hear Glock behind me.

"Chief?"

Raising my hand, I wave my index finger and throw up again. I stay like that for another minute, embarrassed because I'm spitting and sweating. Finally, I straighten and tug a tissue from my pocket and wipe my mouth. "Sorry," I mutter.

"You need some water or something?" he asks.

"Nope." Pulling my chief-of-police face back in place, I turn to face him. "Just the heat, I think."

It's not a very good lie, because the temperature hovers somewhere around eighty degrees and there's a pleasant breeze. I wish I'd told him I'd tied one on last night.

"I'm used to it," he says easily. "LaShonda's

been throwing up for four months now. Her first trimester was—" He cuts off the word in mid-sentence.

A tense silence ensues, as if all the oxygen has been sucked away. I stare at Glock, willing him to take the words back. My mouth is open, but I can't seem to close it. All I can do is stand there, stupid and mute, certain my well-guarded secret is written all over my face.

Glock raises his hands. "Hey, it's none of my business."

My stomach is still quivering when I cross to him. "You find something?"

He holds up a baggie containing a dozen or so dirt-covered .22 caliber cartridges. "Looks like they've been here awhile." He motions to the place he'd been searching. "People have been shooting out here, but I thought these might be worth a look."

"You find bones?"

"A lot of them." He points to the corner of the structure. "Looks like whoever euthanized the animals just piled up the carcasses and left them to rot."

"Might be why all these cartridges are here." I think about that a moment. "Nolt's remains showed no sign that he'd been shot, but that doesn't mean it didn't happen. Let's bag them just in case."

We're interrupted by the crack of our

dispatcher's voice on the radio. "Chief, I've got a ten-ten over at McNarie's Bar."

Glock and I exchange looks. "Fight," he mutters. "We done here, Chief?"

"I just need to finish up that far north side." I cock my head, alerted by some inner voice that he's reluctant to leave me. "Go ahead and take the call. I'm out of here in a few minutes."

He hesitates.

"Glock, for God's sake, I'm a cop."

He looks uncomfortable, then sighs. "Look, Chief, I know you're as capable as the next guy, and I don't want to get in the middle of any- thing . . . personal, but Tomasetti asked me to keep an eye on you."

Now it's my turn to sigh. "Of course he did."

"In light of the shooting the other night, I thought it was a good idea. You know, buddy system."

I pat the .38 strapped to my hip. "And just between us, I've got a .22 mini Magnum in an ankle holster."

"Damn, Chief, I'm impressed. Kind of jealous, too."

I laugh outright. "Take the call before McNarie beats the shit out of someone."

"Yes, ma'am." Turning away, he jogs toward his cruiser, speaking into his lapel mike as he goes. "Ten-seven-six."

I'll be the first to admit the shooting left me

shaken. Still, I'm not sure if I'm irritated or appreciative that Tomasetti asked Glock to look out for me. Being a small-town chief of police isn't excessively dangerous. The risks of my position are minimal compared to the dangers faced every day by big-city cops, sheriff's deputies, and state highway patrol officers. Tomasetti has every reason—and every right—to worry. But do I want him speaking to my officers without my knowledge? Does it undermine my authority? How is he going to react when my pregnancy becomes more apparent?

I finish sweeping the north end of the building, finding nothing more than a rusted pair of pliers and an old horseshoe. I've just reached the loading dock and started toward the interior, when I hear the front door creak. Vaguely, I wonder if one of my other officers took the call at McNarie's and Glock has returned to help me finish.

I call out to him. "If you came back to help me finish, you're too late."

Looping the carry strap of the metal detector over my right shoulder, lifting the canvas bag with my other hand, I start toward the door. I'm midway there when it strikes me that he should have responded. Stopping, I set the canvas bag on the floor and lean the metal detector against the rail of a pen.

"Glock? You there?"

A minute sound makes the hairs at the back of my neck stand on end. In that instant I know it isn't Glock. "Painters Mill Police Department!" I call out. "Identify yourself!"

My words are punctuated by a gunshot. Adrenaline shoots like fire through my body. Crouching, I draw my .38, raise it, my finger twitchy on the trigger. A dozen thoughts slam into my brain at once. I'm not sure where the shot came from. I have no cover where I'm standing.

Hitting my lapel mike, I back toward the steps. "Ten-thirty-one E! Shooting in progress!" I shout out the address of my location.

A second shot pings off the concrete two feet from my boot. I can't see the shooter, but I'm pretty sure the shot originated from the front offices. I fire my weapon three times.

"Ten-thirty-three!" I shout into my mike. "Shots fired! Ten-thirty-three!" To the shooter: "Police! Drop your weapon!"

Another gunshot rings out, followed by the *zing!* of a ricochet. I need to get off the loading dock. I step back. My rear bumps the steel pipe that runs along the edge of the dock. A sickening *crack!* sounds as the steel posts give way. And then I'm falling backward into space.

Chapter 19

I land on my back hard enough to knock the breath from my lungs. The back of my head strikes the ground. I'm sprawled with my arms stretched above my head. I'm still clutching my .38, but I can't move. I can't speak or shout. I can't draw a breath.

I lie there, trying to suck air into compressed lungs. The ceiling of the building is a blur of steel beams, broken lights, patches of rust, and scraps of dry grass from birds' nests. An undignified sound grinds from my throat as I roll onto my side, wheezing. I glance at the loading dock, half expecting to see the shooter with a rifle shouldered, but there's no one there. The broken rail dangles by a single cable, still swaying. The steel post was rusted through and snapped when I leaned against it.

"Damn it. *Damn it.*" I'm aware of my radio cracking and spitting, urgent voices and codes I should know but can't seem to remember. I need to reply, but I'm still trying to get air into my lungs. My chest hurts. The small of my back. I move my legs and I'm relieved when they work. Propping myself on an elbow, I sit up.

Where the hell is the shooter?

I get to my feet. Crouching, I stumble to the

loading-dock wall and peek over the top. There's no one there. I raise my .38 and call out. "Painters Mill PD! Drop your weapon!"

My voice echoes wispy and high within the building. I listen for footsteps, for a door opening or closing, an engine in the lot out front, but I get nothing. I fumble for my lapel mike. "Ten-thirty-one E! Shots fired! Need assistance!"

"What's your twenty? What's your goddamn twenty?" comes a voice I don't recognize.

"County Road Twenty-four," I say. "Hewitt Hog Producers."

"Ten-seven-six," comes another. Glock, I realize. Calm. Determined. Capable. Glock. "ETA two minutes."

"Chief!"

I'm standing at the base of the loading dock, .38 in hand, listening to the radio traffic, when I hear Glock's voice.

"I'm here!"

He's standing just inside the door, sidearm at the ready, shotgun slung over his shoulder. Kevlar vest thrown on over his uniform shirt. I know from the radio that a Coshocton County deputy has gone around the back. Another is in his cruiser, circling the block.

I take the steps to the dock, trying to conceal the fact that my legs are shaking. "You clear the front?"

"No one there." He jogs toward me, his eyes assessing. "You hit?"

"No, I'm okay."

His eyes take in the dangling rail. "You fall?"

"Rail gave way." I brush bits of dried grass and dirt from my slacks. "I busted my ass."

"You need an ambulance?"

I shake my head. "Nope. I'm fine."

Sirens sound in the near distance. I know multiple agencies are responding. Coshocton County. Holmes County. I know they're already setting up a perimeter on the little-used roads surrounding the facility. Searching the immediate area.

"You get a look at him?" Glock asks. All the while his eyes scan the interior of the building, the door, the open area at the rear.

I shake my head. "No."

"Vehicle?"

Another shake.

"How many shots?"

"Three."

Shouts sound at the front of the building. "Sheriff's department! Sheriff's department!"

"Clear!" Glock calls out. "Painters Mill PD! Over here."

I glance over to see two uniformed Coshocton county deputies enter, eyes sweeping, sidearms drawn. One carries a shotgun.

"You think Kester is stupid enough to pull something like this?" Glock asks.

"I don't know. Maybe." I hold his gaze. "He was pretty pissed last time I talked to him."

His jaw clenches. "You sure you don't need to get yourself checked out?" He motions toward the busted rail. "That's a five-foot fall."

I don't like the way he's looking at me. Like he's worried and pissed off and once I'm out of the picture he might cut loose with something unbecoming a cop.

"I don't want you talking to Kester when you're half-cocked," I tell him.

"Chief, if that motherfucker's taking potshots at cops, someone needs to shut him down."

"Find out where he's living," I say. "Get a search warrant and pick him up."

The sound of voices from the front of the building draws my attention. Deputy Fowler "Folly" Hodges and a second deputy I don't recognize come through the door.

"I'm probably going to be tied up here for a while," I tell Glock. "If the judge gives you any shit, tell him to call me. Take Skid with you."

"Yes, ma'am." Giving me a mock salute, he turns to leave.

"Glock."

He stops and turns.

"And if it's not too much trouble, be careful."

For the next three hours, I put my best cop face forward, going over every aspect of the incident with Coshocton County Sheriff Arnie Redmon, while Deputy Fowler writes down every word. I yuk it up with the twenty-something paramedic who checks my vitals and my pupils and proclaims I have a few more years to live.

The woods behind the facility were searched by half a dozen sheriff's deputies, but they found nothing. In the dirt a few yards from the mouth of the driveway, a Coshocton County deputy discovered fresh tire tread marks that don't belong to my or Glock's vehicle, and the CSU technician from BCI proceeded to mix and pour a special plaster that will enable him to scan the image into a computer. From that, an analyst will try to determine the size and type of tire, which, hopefully, will lead us to the manufacturer, the retailer—and ultimately the person who bought it.

During a search, a Coshocton County deputy found two spent .22 caliber cartridges—the same type of cartridge that was found at the scene on County Road 14. We won't know definitively until ballistics is complete, but I know it's from the same shooter.

I've called Tomasetti twice, but his voice mail picks up both times. I leave two messages, letting him know there was an incident and that I'm all right. This is the kind of situation about which he needs to hear from me personally, but a message is better than nothing.

As the adrenaline wanes and post-incident jitters set in, my hands and legs begin to shake. Not for the first time today, I'm nauseous. My left wrist feels sprained—something I didn't notice while the paramedics were here and we were cutting up over something I can't even remember now.

I remind myself that I'm pregnant. That these sorts of things shouldn't happen to a pregnant woman, and an overwhelming rush of anger toward the shooter engulfs me. I keep my cool; I know what I'm experiencing is part of the process after a traumatic incident. But it's not easy, and by the time early evening rolls around all I want to do is go home and crawl into bed.

I wasn't expecting Tomasetti to show up on scene. Last I'd heard, he was at a meeting in Cleveland with some suits. I figured that was why he hadn't called me back. Little did I know he'd left the meeting and hauled ass down to Coshocton County.

I'm standing on the loading dock, talking to one of the deputies, when I see him come through the door. I'd know his silhouette anywhere. The way he moves. The way he holds himself apart. He's too far away for me to see his face, but I know it the instant he spots me. His body language changes. He descends the steps and starts toward me with long, resolute strides. I watch him approach, aware that I'm staring, but I can't look away.

My mouth goes dry. My palms are slick with sweat. I'm aware of my heart thrumming. My legs quivering. "Tomasetti."

"Chief." His face gives away nothing. No emotion. No concern. If I didn't know him so well, I might think he'd been sent down by BCI to look into some routine incident. But there's a coolness in his eyes that unnerves me. "Are you all right?"

"I'm okay." I want to go to him and let him envelop me in his arms, but there are too many people around, none of whom know we're involved.

He introduces himself to the deputy, and the two men shake hands. Tomasetti turns his attention back to me. "Sounds like you have a serial cop shooter on your hands."

"Glock and Skid are going to pick up Nick Kester," I tell him.

"That's a start." He looks at the deputy. "Can you excuse us?"

"Sure." The deputy tips his hat at me and then walks away.

"Are you here about the case?" I ask.

"I'm here for you," he says in a low voice. "You finished here?"

"I think so."

He motions toward the door. "I'll follow you home."

It takes us an hour to drive from Coshocton to Wooster. It's dark by the time we reach the farm. I called Glock on the way, and he informed me that while he was able to obtain the warrant, they've not been able to locate Nick Kester. They spoke to his wife, who claimed they'd had an argument and Nick went to the Mosquito Lake for some pike fishing. Since the Mosquito Lake State Park is out of our jurisdiction, I asked Glock to contact the state park officer on duty try to locate Kester at the park.

Considering the seriousness of the situation, I should be at the station. If it wasn't for Tomasetti, I would be, despite my aching body and throbbing head. But I know he's upset, and this is one of those times when my personal life must take precedence over my job. I don't know what to expect from him. The one thing I do know is that I want to fix it. If only I knew how.

I hear Tomasetti's car door slam as I let myself into the house through the back door. Flipping on the overhead light, I'm welcomed by my tidy farmhouse kitchen, the smells of vanilla and lemon-scented furniture polish, and a table that's somehow developed a thin layer of dust. I remove my .38 and set it on the tabletop. My equipment belt comes next. The .22 mini Magnum and the ankle holster. I drape all of it over the back of a chair. I try to shake off the apprehension creeping over me as I cross to the sink to wash my hands.

When Tomasetti comes in, I grab the towel off the hook and dry my hands. "Are you hungry?" I ask. "I didn't get lunch and I'm—"

"We need to talk about what happened," he cuts in.

Taking my time, I nod. "All right."

"Kate, this is the second time someone's tried to kill you. You don't know who it is or why they did it. You don't know how determined they are or if they're going to try again."

"I understand all of that," I tell him. "There are multiple police agencies working on it, including BCI. They were able to lift tire tread marks. Glock and Skid are going to pull in Nick Kester for—"

"You don't know that it was Kester."

"I don't know that it wasn't. He's a person of interest."

"The point, Kate, is that you're pregnant."

"Don't you dare throw that in my face," I say, surprised by the unintended attitude in my voice.

It isn't well received. I see anger overtake him—the way his mouth goes tight, his eyes go flat and cold—and I realize my mistake too late.

"You were out there alone," he snaps. "In

some barn out in the middle of fuck-all. Where the hell was Glock?"

"He was doing his job." I pull the towel off my shoulder and sling it onto the counter. "I know you asked him to keep an eye on me. Tomasetti, I'm his boss. I'm as capable as he is. It was inappropriate for you to do that."

Tomasetti doesn't even flinch at the accusation. "I don't care. Putting yourself in that situation was incredibly irresponsible." He gestures in the general direction of my abdomen. "It's not just you anymore, Kate. It's not even just about us."

I've seen Tomasetti angry many times over the years. Usually that anger is calculated. Conjured from that place where he keeps his emotions locked down tight until he needs it to make a point or he uses it as a tool to accomplish some goal. There's nothing calculated about this; it's raw and nasty, and I've never seen him skitter this close to losing control.

"I have a job to do," I snap. "People rely on me. I can't run away and hide until this is over. For God's sake, Tomasetti, I'm a cop."

"Maybe you shouldn't be."

Incredulity rises inside me, a flash flood churning and bursting its banks. "You have no right to ask me that. You can't do that."

"Don't preach to me about my rights or what I should feel. I didn't ask for this to happen. But it has, and now we have to deal with it."

"Tomasetti, Painters Mill is a small town. Crime is usually negligible here. It's a safe place to be a cop. What happened today is an anomaly."

"Tell the shooter that, Kate! Tell the guy who had you in his sights and pulled the goddamn trigger! All it takes is one bullet and one lucky shot!"

"It's part of the job! You know that. You have to accept that, or this isn't going to work."

"That's the problem! It's not working, Kate!"

"You're being unreasonable," I say, but my voice has gone breathless.

"Am I? Tell me you don't think about something happening every time you make a stop. When you're out on some back road in the middle of the fucking night and you have no idea who or what you're walking up on. Does he have a warrant? Does he have a weapon in the waistband of his pants? A shotgun on the floor? A knife on the passenger seat? Is he willing to use it to stay out of jail? Tell me you don't keep your hand over your .38. Can you tell me that? Honestly?"

"Of course I think about it. Every cop does if he's smart. It's called caution and training, and those are the things that keep us alive."

He stalks toward me. "Yeah, Painters Mill is a small town. It's safe. It's a regular fucking love-fest. But let me tell you something: It's the rural cops in towns like Painters Mill that don't have backup when they need it. Even if you can *get* to your radio, how fast can someone get there to help you if you get into a jam?"

"I'm aware—"

"You could have been killed today, god-dammit!"

I don't even realize I've taken a step back. I'm not afraid of him. I trust him with my life. But he's formidable when he's angry. "I wasn't."

"Is that all you have to say about it? 'I wasn't'?"

"You're out of line," I tell him.

"You're goddamn right I'm out of line," he says. "I'm worried about you." He taps his finger against his temple, snarling. "How can you not get that?"

Neither of us speaks for the span of several heartbeats. I absorb everything that's been said, and I struggle to settle my emotions and put my thoughts in order. "Okay, Tomasetti, everything you've said is true. I know sometimes things go bad. But it's a worst-case scenario. Chances are—"

"I don't want to take those kinds of chances!"

"This isn't just about me and my being pregnant. It's about you and your past and what happened to you. What happened to your family. You're letting that get in the way, and it's not fair."

His laugh is cold. "Don't bring them into this."

"You're overreacting—"

"I'm overreacting because I love you!" he shouts.

The tension snaps like a steel cable. The words deflate the anger that had been building in my chest. I look at him, loving him, wanting desperately for things to be right between us. But I don't reach out. This isn't going to be settled easily. Maybe not at all.

"Female police officers get pregnant and have babies all the time," I tell him. "It's not an ideal situation, but they don't quit their jobs or give up on their careers."

"You can compromise. Take light duty. Cut out the late-night patrols."

"You can't ask me to do that."

He says nothing, and the floor seems to crumble beneath my feet. I stare at him, flummoxed—and more upset than I've been in a very long time. "Tomasetti, don't do this to me. Don't make me choose."

"We've both been thinking about it, Kate. All I did was open the box and let it out."

I look down at my keys lying on the table. "I have to go," I say as I snatch them up.

Spinning, I yank open the door. Then I'm down the steps in a single bound. Running toward the Crown Vic. Aware that I left my equipment belt and weapons. The interior light comes on as I hit the remote to unlock the doors.

I hear the door slam behind me. The pound of Tomasetti's feet. "Kate. *Kate!*"

I reach the car, yank open the door. Out of the

corner of my eye I see him coming around the rear, gaze steady and latched on to me. Sliding into the car, I jab the key into the ignition, turn it.

"Don't go," he says.

I try to close the door, but he's standing in the way so I can't. Gently, he sets his hand on my arm and bends to me. "Please," he says. "I'm sorry. Don't go."

"Tomasetti, what the hell are we doing?"

"I think the official term is 'fighting.' "

I choke out a laugh. "Don't make me laugh, damn it. This is serious."

"I know."

I don't turn off the engine. "I don't know what to do."

Letting his hand slide down my arm, he takes my hand and steps back. "For starters, you can come here."

I turn the key and get out of the vehicle. He closes the door and then eases me backward until I'm leaning against it, and he falls against me.

"I was out of line," he tells me. "I'm sorry."

When I look away, he raises his hand and cups my chin, forcing my gaze back to his. "This scares me," he says. "I'm not very good at being scared."

"Neither am I." I stare at him, trying to untangle the emotions thrumming inside me and the words sticking to my tongue. "You're not having second thoughts, are you?"

"You mean about us?"

"I mean if you need some space, I'll give it to you."

"I don't need any goddamn space. I need you."

"Tomasetti, there's no easy solution to this."

"I know." He leans closer and kisses me, his mouth lingering on mine. "We'll figure something out."

Chapter 20

The call from Dr. Alan Johnson comes as I walk through the door of my office at just before 9:00 a.m. Setting my laptop case on the floor, my coffee on the blotter, I catch the line on the third ring.

"We finally received our archived records for Leroy Nolt," the doctor begins.

"Do the serial numbers match?" I ask.

"Yes, they do. That plate is the same one my father used to repair Leroy Nolt's broken arm."

I'd known that would be the case; there were too many coincidences for the remains not to belong to Nolt. Still, this makes it official. Now all I need is the cause and manner of death from the coroner.

"Thank you for checking on that for me, Doctor Johnson."

"Of course."

"I'd appreciate it if you'd keep this information confidential until I can notify the family."

"Certainly, Chief Burkholder. Good luck with the case."

I'm still on my first cup of coffee, thinking about Sue and Vern Nolt, when Glock calls me on my cell.

"Any luck with Kester?" I ask him.

"I hooked up with Trumbull County and a state park officer. We spent the night out at Mosquito Lake State Park, but Kester never showed."

"You search his place?"

"He and his wife are staying with his father-in-law, Chief. I got the warrant and Skid and I went out there. But Kester took his stuff and left. Wife's gone, too."

"Shit." I think about that a moment. "He own a .22 rifle?"

"We didn't find anything. No gun. No ammo. His father-in-law said he doesn't own a weapon, but you know how that goes."

"We have to assume he's armed and dangerous." I sigh. "I'm going to put out a BOLO on Kester."

"Probably a good idea at this point."

"Get some sleep," I tell him.

"Yes, ma'am."

I've just finished putting out the BOLO on Nick and Paula Kester, when T.J. peeks his

310

head into my office. "You got a minute?" he asks.

"Sure. Have a seat." I motion to the visitor's chair adjacent my desk.

Taking the chair, he raises the papers in his hand. "I know you're dealing with the Kester thing, Chief, but I was looking over some of these old police reports from around the time Leroy Nolt went missing." He flicks the paper with his index finger. "I think I hit gold."

I take the paper and read. It's a poor copy of a handwritten incident report for an "unknown disturbance" from the Coshocton County Sheriff's Department dated August 29, 1985. Deputy Mack Pelletier wrote:

Responded to disturbance call in the 3500 block of County Road 600 south of Charm. Concerned neighbor reported "screams and yelling" coming from the farm next door. Child witness reported an unknown individual falling into livestock pen with possible serious injury. Child's mother, SuAnne Ferman, heard nothing but stated child witnessed the accident at Kaufman farm next door and was frightened. Responding deputy arrived on scene and spoke with property owner, Reuben Kaufman, who stated the child sneaked onto property and became upset after witnessing the butchering of hogs. No citation issued. No further action required. End.

"That *is* interesting." I look at T.J. "Do you have an address for SuAnne Ferman?"

"I checked. Ferman passed away a few years back."

"Well, shit."

He grins. "Daughter's around, though."

"The kid who saw it?"

"Yep." He looks down at the paper in his hand. "Sally Burris lives in Berlin. She's owns a shop called Homespun."

I smile back at him. "How old was she when this happened?"

He checks the paper in his hand. "Nine, according to the report."

"Old enough to remember."

Homespun is located in the front half of a small cottage-style home just off of Main Street in Berlin. The bell jangles when I open the beveled-glass door. I'm welcomed by the warm aromas of sandalwood, bergamot, and patchouli, and find myself surrounded by old-fashioned wooden shelves jammed with handmade candles of every shape and size and scent. Mason jars, martini glasses, hurricanes—even seashells. The wall to my left is plastered with dozens of cuckoo clocks, some in the shape of the iconic red-and-white barn, others in the form of an Amish buggy. At the rear, a plump red-haired woman wearing a purple cardigan is ringing up a sale for a customer.

I browse salt and pepper shakers, hot pads, and homemade dog biscuit kits while the two women chat about the tornado. I find an amber-scented candle in a sea-glass hurricane I like. When the customer leaves, I approach the counter and set it next to the antique cash register. "You have some beautiful things," I begin.

The woman behind the counter beams a smile and picks up the candle. "Oh, I just love the sea glass. It's one of my favorite pieces in the whole store. And the scent is to die for."

"It'll look good on my dining room table."

"Look good anywhere." She's got dimpled cheeks and a gumdrop nose spattered with freckles.

I pull out my badge and identify myself. "I'm looking for Sally Burris."

"You found her." She gives me an exaggerated look of surprise. "What did I do?"

"I'm working on a cold case and ran across an old police report from the Coshocton County Sheriff's Office from 1985. Your mother had filed a complaint—"

"Oh! This must be about our old neighbors! Those Amish people, the Kaufmans."

"So you remember?"

"Heck, yeah, I remember." She gives a hearty belly laugh. "Gave me nightmares for a month. Nine-year-old kid doesn't forget something like that."

"Can you tell me what happened?"

She chuckles as if at herself, then looks at me from beneath her lashes. "Well, I used to sneak over to their farm. It was dumb, I know, but when you're nine and bored . . ." Rolling her eyes, she shrugs. "Anyhoo, I sneaked over there one afternoon. That old bank barn in the back. I climbed through the hay chute and I'm poking around on the second level, when these three Amish guys came out." She sobers and I can see the memories taking her back to a place that's not quite comfortable. "They were speaking in Pennsylvania Dutch, so I didn't understand what they were saying, but I could tell they were arguing."

"Do you know who they were?"

"I was down the hay chute with the hatch open a few inches, so I couldn't see their faces. All I could see was their legs and feet."

"What exactly did you see?"

Her mouth tightens. "At first the men were just talking. Then things got loud. They started yelling and there was some scuffling, and, oh boy, my heart was pounding like a drum. Then things got really weird. I mean, I always thought of the Amish as gentle and religious, you know? Well, let me tell you something, Chief Burkholder, that day they were neither. They were yelling like a bunch of drunken bikers. I heard cursing. There was some pushing and shoving and hitting. Then I swear I saw a guy fall out that big hay door in the back and into the hogpen below." She shivers. "I'll never forget the way his body sounded when it hit the pipe fence, then the concrete below. I'll tell you this: He didn't get up, and I swear all those pigs ran over to him and started crowding and squealing and God only knows what else. The whole thing scared me something awful."

"Did you see the face of the man who fell?"

"Just a glimpse."

"Can you ID him?"

"No, ma'am."

"What did you do?"

"I got the heck out of there. Ran home as fast as I could and told my mom. She called the sheriff. They came out to the house, asked me a few questions and wrote everything down. My mom told me later that Mr. Kaufman told the police that he was slaughtering hogs and that must have been what traumatized me."

"Is that what happened?" I ask.

She shakes her head. "No, ma'am, it's not. He lied to the cops. Those men were fighting. I saw someone fall into that pen, and I'm pretty sure he was pushed." She hugs herself as if against a chill. "And all those big hogs? I saw blood, Chief Burkholder. Either he cut himself in the fall or those hogs went after him." She huffs out a laugh, but it's a grim sound. "I never sneaked over there again, and to this day I can't drive past that old farm without breaking out in a cold sweat."

Chapter 21

In the course of a homicide investigation, one of the most important components a cop must establish is motive. Once he understands the *why,* he can usually come up with the *who,* and the rest of the case will eventually fall into place. The question of motive has been forefront in my mind since speaking with Sally Burris earlier in the day. Since, I've locked myself in my office, filled half a legal pad with supposition, and, after a lot of thought, drafted an affidavit for Judge Seibenthaler in the hope of getting a search warrant for Reuben and Naomi Kaufman's farm.

Is it possible that as a teenager Abigail Kaufman (Kline), a Swartzentruber Amish, became involved with Leroy Nolt, a New Order Mennonite? Is it feasible that their illicit affair educed the wrath of her father? I know from experience that some Amish are rigid in their belief systems and intolerant of those who differ. Some can be quite cruel to the fallen. But murder?

No one wants to believe a member of a group he or she admires and respects is capable of something so heinous. But as I gaze through the window and watch the Main Street merchants close up shop for the day, I realize that's exactly where my mind has gone—into that murky, dank place where fanaticism overrides religion, where hatred trumps tolerance, and something as sacred as the *Ordnung* is twisted into an unrecognizable and hideous command.

Rising, I leave my desk and stride to the reception area. My dispatcher, Lois, glances up from her computer screen when I enter. "You look troubled," she tells me.

"Call Judge Seibenthaler and tell him I'm on my way over."

"Yes, ma'am."

"Let everyone know there's a briefing in an hour." I glance at the clock on the wall and sigh. "And while you're at it, if you could throw in a little bit of good luck, I'd really appreciate it."

Ten minutes later I'm standing outside the chambers of the honorable Judge Harry Seibenthaler at the courthouse in Millersburg. It's just after five o'clock, so he doesn't keep me waiting. His administrative assistant ushers me through her office and into his inner sanctum.

"Chief Burkholder! What a pleasant surprise! What can I do for you?"

The judge is a corpulent man of about fifty with salt-and-pepper hair, a mottled complexion, and a gourdlike nose shot with broken capillaries. He weighs in at about 250, but he's not much taller than me. He's got a jovial personality and an appreciation for humor, but I know from experience he's a tough son of a bitch in his courtroom, and not only with regard to those who break the law. I've seen him take more than one cocky young lawyer down a notch. In the years I've been chief, he's denied more warrants than he's signed, and I have a sinking feeling this one won't make the cut.

"Thanks for seeing me, Judge."

"You caught me walking out the door. My granddaughter has a piano recital up in Wooster in an hour."

"In that case, I'll make this quick." I pass him the affidavit. It includes the highlights of the case, the information I gleaned from Sally Burris earlier, the location and reason for the search, and what I'm looking for—in this case the titanium plate missing from the remains of Leroy Nolt. I also give him a copy of the original crime report.

Slipping glasses onto his nose, he looks down at the affidavit, skimming, and then looks at me over the rims of his glasses. "Naomi and Reuben Kaufman, Kate? Seriously?"

Argument prepared, I launch into everything I know about the case. "I have a witness that saw a man fall into the hogpen. I have remains with marks consistent with the tooth marks of domestic swine."

"The Kaufmans are pillars of the community! The *Amish* community, which happens to be the

318

bread and butter of this town. For God's sake, Kate, my wife buys stuff from them all the time."

"I'm aware they're Amish."

Frowning, he turns to the second sheet of paper and then looks at me. "You're looking for a titanium orthopedic plate? What the hell is that?"

"It's an orthopedic implant," I tell him. "The decedent sustained a broken arm in which both the radius and ulna were broken. Two plates were surgically implanted. Only one was found with the remains."

"So you think this second missing plate is at the Kaufman farm?"

"I do."

Taking off his glasses, he sets down the paper. His leather chair protests when he leans back. "You don't have enough here for a warrant. You know that, right?"

"Abigail Kline—Reuben and Naomi's daughter —made the quilt Leroy Nolt gave his mother. When I asked her about it, she lied to me. She was involved with Leroy Nolt. Judge, I know there's something there."

"Have these bones even been confirmed as Nolt's? I mean, via DNA?"

"Not with DNA yet, but the surgeon who did the surgery on Leroy Nolt matched the serial number with the plate we found."

"Hmmm."

"Judge, Leroy Nolt went missing at about the

same time Sally Burris saw a man fall into the pigpen in the course of an argument at the Kaufman farm."

"It says here she was nine years old! I don't believe that's a reliable age, especially when it's been thirty years since the incident."

"She's reliable."

He removes his glasses. "Kaufman said he'd been butchering hogs. That's enough to upset any nine-year-old little girl." Spitting out a sound of skepticism, he taps on my notes with a stubby index finger. "And she didn't see their faces. She can't even identify anyone. Come on. You know that's not enough for a damn warrant."

"All I need is a few hours in the barn and pens with a metal detector."

"If you're wrong, do you have any idea what this will do to relations between the Amish and the rest of us? Things are already strained. We've already got them selling out and moving to Upstate New York. You go out there and start searching for body parts, and all hell is going to break loose."

"Judge Seibenthaler, with all due respect—"

He chops the air with his hand. "Not going to happen, Kate."

"What do you need?"

"For starters you can produce DNA that proves those bones are Nolt's. Until then, I'm not going to approve a search warrant for their farm or anyone else's. Without a positive ID, I just can't do it."

I tamp down annoyance, keep my voice level. "Judge, I believe Leroy Nolt was murdered. Someone has gotten away with it for thirty years. I think Jeramy Kline and Abram Kaufman are involved."

"You *think?* Kate, that's not good enough. For God's sake, we can't go around shaking down Amish families. Bring me some proof. Bring me something more concrete than a theory based on something a nine-year-old girl may or may not have seen thirty years ago. Otherwise, I can't help you." He looks at his watch. "Now I have to go."

Despite my best efforts, I'm still frustrated when I arrive back at the station. I make a conscious effort not to slam the door when I walk in.

"Everyone's here, if you're ready." At her dispatch station, Lois stands, eyeing me cautiously as I stalk past. "I take it your meeting with Seibenthaler didn't go well."

"That would be an understatement."

In my office, I snatch my notes off my desk, then make my way to the storage-room-turned-conference-room. My temper settles when I find my entire team assembled and waiting. I can't help but smile when I see Pickles sitting at the end of the table, a large McDonald's coffee steaming in front of him. I catch a whiff of English Leather when I walk past him. "Glad you could make it, Pickles."

He grunts as if it's business as usual for a seventy-six-year-old to be a cop. "Any word on who took a shot at you?" he asks.

"No." I hand him the mug shot of a grinning Nick Kester. "We're looking for this guy, though."

"Nice teeth," he mutters, passing it to Glock.

"For a meth head," Glock puts in.

I bring the briefing to order. "Nick Kester is a person of interest," I tell my team. "BOLO went out a few hours ago, but so far he's slipping through the cracks. Sheriff's office is running the investigation, but SHP as well as Coshocton and Wayne Counties are actively involved, too."

"Anything on the slug?" T.J. asks.

"It's a .22 cal," I reply. "Judging from the distance of the shot, probably from a rifle. Working in conjunction with the SO, we executed a warrant and searched the home of Kester's father-in-law, but it didn't produce a rifle or anything else of interest."

"Doesn't mean he doesn't have it with him," Glock says.

"Holmes County has stepped up patrols," Skid announces.

I nod, but I'd already known that was the case. When someone takes a shot at a police officer, it's serious business. Every cop in every juris-diction in the three-county area is champing at the bit to find him.

I take my place behind the half podium set up at the head of the table. "Until this shooter is apprehended, I want everyone in vests." I look at Pickles. "That means school crosswalk patrol, too."

He nods, looking a little too pleased at the prospect of vesting up.

I glance toward the door, where Lois is standing, listening for the phone. "Can you make sure we have inventory for that?"

"Yes, ma'am."

"If we don't have enough vests for everyone, see if you can get whatever we need on loan from the sheriff's office, Holmes or Wayne."

"Gotcha."

But all of us are well aware that a Kevlar vest won't protect anyone from a head shot.

"We do not have proof that Kester is our shooter. But he is a suspect. He's a known meth user and he's made threats against me personally and the Painters Mill PD." I pause. "I'm not going to get into the details, but you already know the Kesters have filed a lawsuit against me, the department, and the township of Painters Mill. That's something to keep in mind."

"So Kester's a man on a mission," Skid says.

"If this is about the kid, he might feel as if he has nothing left to lose," Glock puts in.

"Wouldn't be the first bozo wanting to go out in a blaze of glory," Pickles says.

I nod, making eye contact with each of my officers and, finally, Lois. "Effective immediately, I want an armed officer here at the station at all times. Mandatory overtime until Kester is either eliminated as a suspect or taken into custody."

I hear a couple of well-timed, exaggerated sighs, but not a smidgen of serious diatribe; every one of these officers would work around the clock without complaint if asked.

"I also want to brief you on some new developments on those remains found out on Gellerman Road," I say. "We were able to match the serial number of the titanium plate found at the scene to the plate surgically implanted in Leroy Nolt's arm. We don't have DNA yet, but I can say with certainty that those bones do indeed belong to Nolt."

"You notified NOK?" Glock asks.

"I talked to them, so they are aware," I tell him. "While I was cautious not to tell them something we don't have definitive proof of, I think they were able to draw their own conclusions. I'm going to wait for DNA before I confirm with them. So we need to keep this under our hats for now."

"Tough break for the parents," Pickles mumbles. "Always hate that."

"We have a person of interest with regard to the woman Nolt was seeing at the time of his death." I tell them about the quilt with the initials embroidered into the fabric. "Abigail Kaufman. She's Amish. Her last name is Kline now. She married Jeramy Kline a month after Leroy disappeared."

Skid grins. "Damn, those Amish girls work fast."

It's an offhand comment but drives home the possibility that if she was indeed involved with Leroy Nolt and then married so quickly after his disappearance, she may have had a reason.

Glock's eyes narrow on mine. "If there was some love-triangle thing going on between Jeramy Kline, Abigail Kaufman, and Leroy Nolt, there might be a motive there."

"She has a brother living in the area, too," I tell them. "Abram Kaufman. I haven't talked to him yet, but I plan to."

"So, is Jeramy Kline a suspect?" T.J. asks.

"He's a person of interest." I tell them about Kline's having been rushed to the hospital.

"What's wrong with him?" T.J. asks.

I shrug. "He got sick and had some kind of seizure."

"Interesting timing," Glock says.

"I think so, too," I tell him.

"Any chance he OD'd on drugs?" Pickles asks.

I shrug. "We can't rule it out, but at this point we have no evidence to support it."

"Maybe he knows the cops are looking at him and he tried to off himself," Skid offers.

"It's possible," I reply. "But I've talked with him and, honestly, he doesn't seem like the type."

"Maybe with the discovery of those remains, the wife added a little rat poison to his scrapple," Glock puts in.

"Hell hath no fury like a pissed-off Amish woman," Skid mutters.

The statement earns a few chuckles, including one from me, but I don't discount any theory this stage. "The ER doc ran a tox," I tell him. "Results will take a week or so, but I'll stay on top of it and keep you posted."

I turn my attention to T.J. "You want to give them the rundown on that SO report you found?"

The young officer clears his throat and recounts the details of the thirty-year-old police report from the Holmes County Sheriff's Department. "According to the report, a deputy was called to the farm of Reuben Kaufman after a neighbor reported witnessing some kind of accident or fall into the hogpen."

Simultaneously, Glock and Skid sit up straighter.

"The neighbor has passed away now," I tell them, "but the little girl who witnessed the incident still lives in the area. I talked to her earlier. Name is Sally Burris. She was only nine years old at the time, and apparently she'd sneaked over to the farm without her parent's knowledge. She didn't have a clear view of the incident but claims there were three men present and they were arguing."

"Was Kaufman raising hogs at the time?" Glock asks.

"He's not on the list, and he's denied it, but that doesn't mean he didn't have hogs," I reply.

Pickles leans forward and puts his elbows on the table. "Now that you mention it, Chief, I swear I remember them having hogs out there. Back in those days, they used those low sheds and kept them out in the pasture."

I look at Skid. "Lois and Mona and Jodie put together a list of large-animal veterinarians. Take a look at it, see who was practicing back then, and give them a call. Chances are at some point the Kaufmans had a vet come to their farm. For vaccinations. A sick animal. Castrations. A difficult birth. An injury."

"You got it."

"Chief," Glock says. "Any chance we could get a warrant?" he asks. "Get out there and take a look around?"

"Judge Seibenthaler shot it down."

"That old goat is more interested in tourism than crime solving," Pickles grouses.

I remind them of Nolt's broken arm and the missing titanium plate. "To put that into perspective: If Nolt was indeed one of the men

Sally Burris saw and there was an argument, it's possible he was either pushed or fell into the hogpen. It could be that the fall knocked him unconscious or otherwise incapacitated him, and the hogs—if they were hungry or aggressive or both—went after him."

"Sounds like whoever he was with wasn't too concerned about his health," Glock finishes.

"And they let the hogs kill him," I finish.

"That's one way to get rid of evidence," T.J. puts in.

"They put what was left into a garbage bag and buried it in the crawl space of that abandoned barn," Pickles adds.

Skid shakes his head. "That shit gives me the willies."

"What's the setup out at the Kaufman place?" T.J. asks. "I mean, the barn?"

"They have two barns. According to Sally Burris, the incident occurred at the one farthest from the road. It's a bank-style barn and built on a slope. In front, the door opens to the first level. The argument took place at the rear of the barn, on the second level." I think about that a moment. "I haven't seen the interior, but I know that a lot of those old bank barns have a hay door that looks out over the rear, for ease of feeding livestock, tossing hay, whatever."

"So that back door is ten or twelve feet from the ground?" Skid asks.

I nod. "If someone fell or was pushed, there's a decent possibility he'd be stunned or injured."

"Or unconscious," Glock says.

"If there were hogs below . . ." T.J. lets the words trail.

"Do pigs do that?" Skid's voice is incredulous. "I mean, would they attack and consume a human being?"

I tell him about my conversation with wildlife biologist Nelson Woodburn. "Domestic swine aren't as aggressive as their feral cousins or javelina, but if they're starved, there's no doubt they will attack and consume prey in order to survive. In this case, it's just the hands and the feet that are missing."

"That's brutal," T.J. whispers.

"Might be interesting to get out there with a metal detector," Glock says.

"Unless someone found that titanium plate in his pork chop," Skid mutters.

Pickles slurps coffee. "Shame about that warrant."

"Permission from the owner would probably suffice," Glock offers.

I give him my full attention. "That would be a best-case scenario."

"Wouldn't that be kind of like the fox asking the hens if he can come inside to borrow a cup of sugar?" asks Skid.

"According to Sally Burris," I say, "there was no female present."

"Not the kind of thing hubby mentions over shoofly pie," Glock adds.

"So, if the wife doesn't know what happened," T.J. says, "she has nothing to hide from the police."

I look at him and nod. "If she does and refuses us access to the farm, we're going to have to find another way."

Chapter 22

I arrive at the station early and spend two hours digging up everything I can find on Abram Kaufman. There's not much; law-abiding citizens tend to lead boring lives, especially when it comes to law-enforcement databases. He's married, never been arrested, pays his taxes on time, and he's never been involved in a lawsuit. Aside from a slow-moving-vehicle citation two years ago, he's kept his nose clean.

I find Skid in his cubicle, pecking at the keyboard of his desktop. "Any luck with veterinarians?" I ask.

"Not yet, but I'm only halfway through the list. Most of these guys are retired now. One has passed away."

"You up to making a trip out to Kaufman's place with me?"

"Which Kaufman?"

"Both," I tell him. "I'll fill you in on the way."

• • •

Abram and Frieda Kaufman live on a dirt road off of County Road 600, a mile or so from Reuben Kaufman's farm, not far from Charm. A good portion of the area is a floodplain, where the pasture is lush and dotted with dark pools filled with lily pads and moss. Massive old-growth trees—maple, elm, and black walnut—crowd the road on either side, casting us into dusky shadows. We crest a hill, and the trees open to endless rows of corn on both sides of the road, where hip-high leaves sway in the breeze.

I nearly miss the narrow mouth of the gravel lane. It's bordered on both sides by tall grass and tangles of raspberry bushes hugging the fence line. The plain mailbox is overgrown with weeds and easily overlooked. I make the turn, and the Crown Vic bounces over ruts and potholes.

"Bet the mailman loves delivering to this place," Skid mutters as we approach a small hill.

"Especially in winter."

The lane makes a lazy S, and then the corn gives way to a mowed shoulder. Ahead, I see a two-story brick house with a tin roof and the brooding facade of a place that's decades past its prime. The front porch wraps around two sides and tilts slightly on the north end. There are no hanging plants or clay pots. The windows are darkened with black coverings.

"They're Swartzentruber," I say as I park

behind a black windowless buggy. A second buggy with a handsome sorrel gelding still harnessed is parked beneath the shade of a tree.

"Is that good or bad?"

"We're about to find out."

We disembark and take the sidewalk to the front door. To my right I notice the big barn adorned with what looks like a fresh coat of white paint. The sliding door at the front stands open, telling me there's probably someone inside.

I hear Skid behind me as I cross the porch to the front door. I'm raising my hand to knock, when the door creaks open. I find myself looking at a stout Amish woman of about thirty-five with a round, ruddy face. She's wearing a dark gray dress that falls to mid calf, an apron, and off-brand sneakers. White *kapp* with the strings tied neatly beneath her chin. Her summer-sky eyes contradict a mouth that's disapproving and thin.

"Can I help you?" she asks, her accent heavy.

"Frieda Kaufman?" I ask.

"*Ja.*" She looks me up and down. "Who wants to know?"

I show her my badge and identify myself. "I'm working on an old case and was wondering if you'd mind answering a few questions."

"We don't know anything about any case."

The aromas of yeast bread and a house that's overly hot waft through the door. "I'm trying to find out what happened to a young Mennonite man who disappeared from Painters Mill back in 1985," I tell her.

She fingers the worn dish towel in her hands. "You're speaking of Leroy Nolt?"

"Yes, ma'am. Do you know him?"

"I met him once or twice. Way back. I heard he moved to Florida."

It's the first time in the course of the investigation anyone has mentioned Florida in relation to Leroy Nolt. "Did he tell you that?"

"Something I heard, is all. Don't recall who said it."

"Were you and Leroy friends? Was he friends with your husband?" I watch her closely for a reaction as I pose the questions.

She looks down at the dishcloth and dries hands that are already dry. "Leroy Nolt was no friend of my husband's and no friend of mine."

"Did you or your husband have some kind of falling out with him?"

She looks at me as if I'm dense. "Never was friendly to begin with. We're Swartzentruber. Leroy's *Mennischt*." The laugh that follows isn't pleasant. "He was *maulgrischt*." A pretend Christian. "Always had a lot of *Englischer* ways, if you know what I mean, with all the drinking and running around. Always smoking cigarettes and taking the Lord's name in vain." She clucks her tongue, then lowers her voice. "From what I heard, he liked his women, too."

"Any woman in particular?"

"Anything in a dress, I imagine. We didn't associate with the likes of Leroy Nolt. Florida can have him, as far as I'm concerned. Sure don't need him here in Ohio."

"What about Abigail Kline?"

The Amish woman's eyes sharpen on mine. "What about her?"

"Did she have a relationship with Leroy Nolt?"

"I suspect you'll need to ask her about that now, won't you?"

I nod. "When's the last time you saw Leroy?"

"Been thirty years or more. Don't rightly recall. Probably in town. He was always hanging out there, charming all those loose *Englischer* girls. Worked down to the farm store, so maybe that's where I seen him last."

I nod, realizing I'm not going to get anything useful out of her. "Is your husband here, Mrs. Kaufman?"

Her eyes flick toward the barn. "He's out there in the barn, castrating calves."

"Thank you for your help." I offer a smile. "I won't keep him long."

She closes the door without responding.

Skid and I take the steps to the sidewalk and then start across the gravel driveway. We're midway to the barn when he glances my way. "Did she really say 'castrating calves'?"

"I'm pretty sure she did." I look over at him

334

and grin at the discomfort etched into his features. "I take it you didn't grow up on a farm."

"City slicker from the word 'go.' "

"You want to sit this one out?"

"As long as Kaufman keeps his tools to himself, I should be okay."

The barn is huge and shadowy, the only light coming in through the open door, and it smells of cattle. There's a buggy just inside, but no horse hitched. A wagon filled with hay is parked farther in. Burlap bags filled with what looks like oats are stacked against the wheel. Voices coming from the rear of the structure draw me more deeply inside.

I hear a calf bawling from somewhere ahead. Skid and I go through another door and enter a large room with a concrete floor that opens to a small pen beyond. Two Amish men kneel on either side of a black calf lying on the floor, its legs secured with rope. The third man straddles the animal, a four-inch knife with a rounded tip in his hand. We stop a few feet away and watch as the Amish man deftly slits the animal's scrotum. A small amount of blood dribbles onto the concrete when he grasps the sac and squeezes the testicles through the opening. Quickly, he pulls out the cord, picks up emasculator pliers and snips. He's not wearing protective gloves.

Next to me, Skid makes a sound of discomfort. "That's fucked up," he mutters beneath his breath.

One of the Amish men holding the calf glances over at us and grins. "Looks like you have another customer," he says in Pennsylvania Dutch to the man with the knife.

The Amish man working on the calf chuckles as he uncoils the rope. Folding the knife, he snatches up a spray bottle and generously spritzes the incision with antiseptic.

"*Faddich*!" he proclaims. Done. Slapping the animal on the rump, he gets to his feet.

The two men on either side of the calf move away and rise. The animal clambers to its feet and gallops toward the pen, kicking up its heels.

"Abram Kaufman?" I say.

The man who'd cut the calf nods. He's tall and dark-haired with hawkish eyes and a steel-wool beard that reaches nearly to his belt. He's clad in black trousers, suspenders, and a blue work shirt. "I'm Abram." His eyes shift from me to Skid and back to me.

I offer a smile. "Did I catch you at a bad time?"

He doesn't smile back. "What can I do for you?"

"I'd like to ask you some questions about your relationship with Leroy Nolt."

"Nolt?" For an instant, he looks confused. "You mean the Nolt boy from years ago?"

"He disappeared in 1985. Do you know him?"

Wiping his hands on his trousers, Abram crosses to me. He's got blood on his right palm, dried blood that's gone brown beneath his nails. I'm relieved when he doesn't offer his hand for a shake.

"I saw him around back then," he tells me. "But I don't know him." Those hawk eyes narrow. "This got something to do with them bones found out on Gellerman Road?"

"I can't get into the details of the case just yet," I tell him.

He removes a kerchief from his pocket, lifts his hat, and wipes sweat from his forehead. "I don't know anything about any missing people. We're Swartzentruber, you know. We don't associate with the Mennonites, unless it's to hire one of them to drive us someplace."

"How do you know Leroy is Mennonite?"

He shrugs. "Must have heard it somewhere, I guess."

"Did you ever hire Leroy to drive you?"

"Always used that Yoder Toter up Dundee way."

"How well did you know Leroy?"

"Not at all. Might've seen him around town is all. Or up to the farm store in Painters Mill."

"Do you know who his friends were?"

"No."

"Did he have a girlfriend?"

He sighs. "Chief Burkholder, you can ask the same question twenty different ways, but you're always going to get the same answer. I don't know Nolt. I never did. If you want to know something about him, maybe you should talk to the Mennonites."

One of the men standing behind him chuckles, but I ignore him and focus on Kaufman. "What about your sister?" I ask.

"Abigail? What about her?"

"I heard she knew Leroy. I heard they were friends. *Close* friends."

His reaction is subtle—fingers opening and closing, mouth tightening into a more pronounced frown—telling me the mention of his sister hit a nerve.

"You misunderstood." His voice is level and calm, but he can't quite conceal the annoyance in his eyes. "Abby has been with Jeramy since they were kids."

I wait, but he says nothing, staring at me as if he's considering ordering me off his property.

"All right, Mr. Kaufman." Nodding, I move as if to leave, then I pause and look around the barn. "Did you ever raise hogs here on your farm?"

"Never cared for hogs." He motions with his eyes to the small herd of cattle in the pen. "Always had cows."

I look past him, where two more calves are in a tiny pen, awaiting their turn for castration. I see the outline of the knife in Kaufman's pocket. Bloodstains on his hands. "I'll let you get back to work then." I make eye contact with the other two men and start toward the door.

Skid waits until we're back in the Crown Vic before speaking. "I've seen some disturbing shit since I've been a cop, Chief, but I swear seeing that Amish dude cut off that calf's balls takes the cake."

I slant him a look. "I thought you were looking a little green around the gills."

"He didn't use an anesthetic. Seems kind of medieval."

"I take it you're not up for Rocky Mountain oysters for lunch? I know a place in Millersburg. . . ."

He groans.

A few minutes later, I make the turn onto County Road 600. Left and right, row after row of corn stretches as far as the eye can see. We pass an Amish boy walking barefoot along the shoulder, bamboo fishing pole in hand.

"Kind of reminds me of that movie *Children of the Corn*," Skid says.

I wave at the kid. He doesn't wave back. "If I recall, that one doesn't end well for the two main characters."

"Probably would have had a happier ending if they'd been packing."

I turn into the lane of Reuben Kaufman's farm, park in a spot that's just out of view from the house, and get out. Birdsong echoes off the treetops. The smells of fresh-cut grass and the faint odor of livestock rides a gentle breeze. A few yards away, half a dozen hens cluck and scratch at the ground. The house is built on a hill with views in all directions. From where I'm standing I can see the cornfields at the front of the property. At the rear, the land dips to a low area overgrown with saplings and brush and, farther, thick woods.

I take a closer look at the two barns as I start toward the house. The one nearest the house is the smaller of the two and not terribly old. The one in the rear is an ancient structure built into the side of the hill. The front sliding door stands open. Inside, I can just make out the silhouette of a wagon heaped with hay.

"You know, Chief, sometimes I swear I think the Amish have it right," Skid says.

"And then you remember how much you like tequila and realize it's just a pipe dream."

I'm smiling when I step onto the porch and knock. I hear footfalls inside. The door opens about a foot and Naomi Kaufman appears. She doesn't look happy to see me.

"Hi, Mrs. Kaufman," I begin.

"Hello." Her eyes slide from me to Skid.

He tips his head at her. "Officer Skidmore, ma'am."

She shifts her attention back to me without acknowledging him. "What do you want?"

"Do you have a few minutes, Mrs. Kaufman?

I'd like to ask you a few more questions about that old case I'm working on."

"What questions?"

"May we come inside, ma'am?"

"No, I don't think you can," she tells me. "I'm cleaning windows and I don't see how I can help you with something I know nothing about."

I remind myself that talking to her is secondary to getting inside that bank barn with a metal detector, so I'm not unduly perturbed by her refusal. "How is your son-in-law doing?"

She shrugs, her expression conveying worry. "He's very sick. The doctor's running tests and trying to figure out what's wrong with him. I've been praying for him. Abigail, too."

I nod. "I talked to Abigail."

Her eyes sharpen on mine.

"She admitted to knowing Leroy Nolt. I thought you should know." I pause. "In case you remembered something and wanted to tell me."

"A lot of young people get to know other young people, during *Rumspringa* and such. All that running around. I don't see what I could tell you about that."

"Did you ever meet Leroy?"

"No."

"Did Leroy ever visit you here at the farm?"

"No."

"What about your husband?"

"Not that I know of."

"Is your husband home, ma'am?"

"He's getting his physical therapy up in Wooster. Yoder Toter picked him up an hour ago."

Nodding, I look out across the cornfields, admiring the tranquil beauty of the place despite the sense of uneasiness between my shoulder blades. The leaves of the two giant maples in the front yard hiss in the breeze. A cardinal trills at us from a cherry tree near the fence.

I'm not above using my Amish roots to cozy up to someone to gain his or her trust. I don't fall to that particular device often, mainly because many of the Amish still judge me harshly for leaving the fold. But if the end result justifies the means, especially when it comes to a case, I have no qualms.

I address her in Pennsylvania Dutch. "I couldn't help but notice that old bank barn." I motion in the general direction of the rear structure. "They don't build them like that anymore."

She's not impressed by my fluency or my interest in the barn. "The barn on the farm where I grew up was nearly two hundred years old," I tell her. "They used wooden dowels, and some of the beams were as thick as a man's waist."

"The Amish certainly know how to build a barn to last."

I nod and I extend my hand for a shake. "It's been a pleasure speaking to you, Mrs. Kaufman. I appreciate your time."

She gives my hand a halfhearted shake, her expression telling me she's surprised to be rid of us so easily.

Skid and I turn to leave. Behind me, the hinges of the door squeak as she begins to close it. I reach the steps and then turn back to her. "Mrs. Kaufman?"

She pauses, glaring at me through the gap between the door and the jamb, a wily fox that hasn't yet escaped the trap.

"Would you mind terribly if I took a quick look in your barn?" I ask.

"Why on earth would you want to do that?"

I offer my best sheepish smile. "There aren't many like it left. Bank-style, I mean, and in such good condition. I'd love to see the interior, if it's no trouble."

She sighs. "I'll need to put on my muck boots. . . ."

"Please don't go to any trouble. I'll just have a quick peek inside. You don't have to come out if you've things to do."

Annoyed by my request but not seeing any reason she shouldn't grant it, she motions toward the barn. "Go on then. Just be sure to close all the gates. We've got goats in the pasture."

Muttering a thank you, I catch Skid's gaze and toss him the keys to the Crown Vic. He catches them with one hand and then crosses to the vehicle and unloads the metal detectors.

He meets me in the gravel area in front of the barn. "That was something right out of the *Columbo* playbook," he says.

"Let's hope it doesn't backfire," I say.

"Never backfired on Peter Falk."

"He never had to deal with the Amish."

The old barn is indeed a historical work of art, with access on two levels and the iconic gambrel roof. We enter via the open sliding door and are immediately swallowed by the shadows inside. I cross the dirt floor, where an antique-looking wagon sits, its bed piled ten feet high with hay. Beyond is a step up to a wood-plank floor. At the rear, a large square door looks out over the pasture. I can hear the red-winged blackbirds and the occasional *jug-o-rum* bellow of a bullfrog from the pond.

I motion toward the doorway. "Sally Burris said the man she saw fell from a second-story door to the pen below."

"That one fits the bill, Chief."

I take the steps to the wood floor and look around. Sure enough, from where I'm standing I see two-feet-square hay chutes cut into the floor. Generally, they're used to drop hay or grain to livestock housed in the stalls below. The chutes have wooden cover cutouts with leather straps so they can be easily lifted. I look at the chute to my right and imagine a nine-year-old girl sneaking into the barn to spy. She entered from the stalls on the underside of the barn and pushed the cover up from below. One chute in particular offers a decent view of the rear hay door, and I realize Sally Burris's story holds water.

My boots thud dully against the plank floor as I cross to the door. Below, a dozen or so rusty steel pens are set into concrete, forming a maze of sorts. Though the pens are designed to withstand the weight and strength of livestock, many are dented and bent from large animals and years of use.

"Let's get down there and put these metal detectors to work before we get busted," I tell Skid.

A quick look around reveals there's no way to reach the pen area without going back through the front. A route that would make us—and our metal detectors—visible from the house for a short stretch. I'm about to risk it, when I realize we can use the hay chute and get down the same way Sally Burris did the day she witnessed the incident.

Hefting my metal detector, I go to the hatch and kneel. The original leather grip has been torn off, but someone has affixed a loop of hay twine for a handle, so I use it to lift the hatch. Below, I see a dirt floor that's built up with decades of manure that's long since composted. I glance over at Skid. "I'm going down. Hand me the metal detectors, will you?"

"Sure." Taking my metal detector, he leans it against a support beam and then offers his hand. "Down the hatch."

I lower myself to a sitting position and dangle my legs through the opening. Taking Skid's hand, using my other to steady myself, I lower myself through the opening. I gasp upon spotting the hairy face staring back at me.

"You okay down there?" Skid calls out from above.

"Just a billy goat."

"Well, shit. Does he have horns?"

"Yup."

I look up to see Skid grin at me through the chute. Passing me the metal detectors, he deftly lowers himself through. I wander to the edge of the stall area and look out at the pens. The rusted steel rails are dented and covered with bird shit. Some lean precariously, held in place by posts set in concrete. The floor is pitted and chipped with a bumper crop of weeds sprouting through the cracks. The low areas and corners contain several inches of soil that has built up over the years.

"Looks like these pens haven't been used in a while," I say, stating the obvious.

Skid comes up beside me and I hear him inhale. "I swear it still smells like it, though."

He's right, and vaguely I wonder if the Kaufmans keep hogs in another part of the property.

I flip on my metal detector. "Let's get to work."

He pauses to motion at the billy goat that greeted me. "He gets too close, Chief, and I swear I'm going to plug him."

"We'll probably have to hide the body. . . ."

For the next fifteen minutes we hunker down and scan the ground as quickly and thoroughly as possible. Somewhere along the way the rest of the goat herd discovered us and, being the curious creatures they are, decided we're fair game for nibbling and, for the horned male, targets for some friendly head butting. The only thing we've recovered so far is a soda can and a rusty coffee can.

"That shifty-eyed son of a bitch butts me one more time and I'm going to—" Skid's words are cut off when a deep male voice sounds from inside the barn.

"What are you doing in my parents' barn?"

I look up to see Abram Kaufman glaring down at me. He's wearing the same clothes with the same bloodstains on his shirt and trousers. I see the outline of the knife in his pocket. He's holding a pitchfork in his right hand.

"Mr. Kaufman." Leaning my metal detector against the pen, I walk to the area directly below the doorway. "We talked to your mother earlier. She said we could take a look around."

His eyes narrow at the sight of the metal detectors. "Why would the English police want to look around an old barn? Don't you have better things to do?"

"It's related to the case we talked about earlier," I say vaguely.

He considers the metal detector at my side. "What are you looking for?"

"We were told Nolt visited here at your parents' farm a few days before he disappeared," I say, fishing.

The Amish man stares at me for a long while. His expression isn't friendly. "He might've come around once or twice, looking for work. Or a handout."

"Was he here the day someone fell into this pen?" I ask.

"I don't know what you're talking about."

"A little girl from next door claims to have witnessed an accident here at this farm. In this barn. She told her mother she saw someone fall into the hogpen." I make a gesture to encompass the pen where I'm standing. "The sheriff's department responded, made a report. Do you recall an incident like that?"

"Nothing like that ever happened." He shrugs. "That child was always sneaking over. Leaving the gate open. Making up stories."

"Gruesome stories?"

"I wouldn't know."

"What did she see that day?"

"Chief Burkholder, I believe it's time you

packed up your machines and left." His gaze rolls to Skid. "You, too. Hit the road."

"All right, Mr. Kaufman. Whatever you say." I make a show of switching off my metal detector. "Do your parents still raise hogs here on the property, Mr. Kaufman?" I ask as I sling the carrying strap over my shoulder.

"They've never raised hogs here." He points to the south side of the pen. "There's the gate. Make use of it. I'd appreciate it if you didn't come back."

Chapter 23

Since adulthood, I've considered myself an enlightened woman. I keep myself informed about issues that are important to me, including my health. That said, I'd rather stick my hand in a running garbage disposal than go to the doctor. Aside from a few trips to the ER for minor injuries sustained in the course of my job, I've managed to avoid that particular displeasure. But with my pregnancy looming large, it's no longer just about me, so when Skid and I arrive back at the station, I make the call and set the appointment for tomorrow at noon.

I'm packing my laptop into its case, about to call it a day, when my phone buzzes. I glance down to see POMERENE HOSPITAL blink on the display and I hit SPEAKER. "Burkholder."

"Hi, Chief. It's Doctor Megason over at Pomerene. I thought you'd want to know. . . . Jeramy Kline died about an hour ago."

Surprise takes a swipe at me. "What was the cause of death?"

"That's the thing, Chief. I don't know. He went into respiratory failure, so we put him on a ventilator. He suffered with uncontrolled gastric bleeding. We couldn't get him stabilized. Heart began to fail. He coded twice this morning. This afternoon, he coded again and we couldn't get him back."

"You ran a tox screen?"

"It came back negative. No drugs. No alcohol."

"Healthy middle-aged men don't fall ill and die without cause," I tell him.

"Rarely."

"Doc Coblentz is going to want an autopsy to determine cause and manner of death," I tell him. "So do I."

"I figured that would be the case, so I went ahead and notified him." He pauses. "Kate, we may run into some resistance from the family. When I notified the deceased's next of kin, his wife, Abigail, wanted to take him home immediately."

In the state of Ohio, the coroner doesn't need permission from the deceased's next of kin before performing an autopsy in order to determine cause of death. "I'll talk to her," I say.

"As you can imagine, she's pretty broken up."

"Is there someone there with her?"

"Nice Amish family arrived just a few minutes ago to take her home."

"Good." But my mind is already plowing through all the murky possibilities of what might have led to the untimely demise of Jeramy Kline. "Doctor Megason, if you had to take a guess on what killed him, what would you say?"

"I hate to speculate on something like that. But if I had to, I'd venture to say he came into contact with some kind of toxin. Something he ingested, more than likely. A pesticide perhaps. Whatever the case, it was very lethal. Jeramy Kline didn't stand a chance."

We chat for a few more minutes, then I thank him and end the call. The timing of Kline's death bothers me. He'd been a person of interest in the Leroy Nolt case. I'd connected the two men through Abigail Kaufman. Is it coincidence that he fell ill and died less than a week after the discovery of Leroy Nolt's remains? Or did someone *want* him dead and make it happen? If that's the case, what's the motive? Did Kline know something about Nolt's death? Was someone afraid he'd talk to the police? Or am I looking at this all wrong?

I pick up the phone and call Doc Coblentz. "I thought I might be hearing from you," he begins without preamble.

"Doc, I need to know the cause and manner of death of Jeramy Kline."

"You and me both. I've cleared my schedule and plan to perform the autopsy day after tomorrow."

I'd been hoping he could do it sooner, but I've learned not to push. "Doc, is there some type of comprehensive tox screen you can run?"

"Are you looking for something specific?"

"Not really. But Doc Megason thinks Kline may have come into contact with some kind of toxin."

"Such as?"

"Since Kline was a farmer, I thought we could check for pesticides. Or any farming-related poison that may have been absorbed, ingested, or inhaled." I think about Jeramy Kline's being Amish, their predilection for folk remedies, and add, "Is there a tox you can run that will isolate a toxin that's plant in origin?"

"I can send samples of tissues, blood, and urine for a poison screen." He pauses. "There are many toxins that don't show up if we're not looking for it. It would be tremendously helpful if you could be a little more specific."

"I wish I could," I tell him. "If you could just run everything you can think of."

"I'll do my best."

"In the interim, I'll talk to Abigail Kline and see if she can shed some light on the matter."

"Kate, there's one more thing: I performed the autopsy on the infant child Lucy Kester this morning, and I found some irregularities you need to know about."

For a terrible moment I think he's going to tell me that the little girl died at the hands of a first responder, after being mishandled, not knowing that first responder was me. "What did you find?" Closing my eyes, I brace.

"I don't believe the child died from injuries sustained from trauma related to the tornado, as we'd initially assumed."

"What do you mean?"

"The cause of death was a subdural hematoma—"

"What is that?" I interject.

"A hemorrhage between the dura mater and the brain."

"Brain injury?"

"Yes, but there's more to it than that. There were several irregularities I noticed right off the bat. In the course of my preliminary examination of the body, I noticed a slight protrusion of the anterior fontanelle—"

"Doc, in English . . ."

"The soft spot on top of the head," he says. "There was a slight bulge. So I had an MRI performed, and there was, indeed, a hemorrhage between the dura mater and the brain."

"Is it possible it happened in the tornado? Doc,

that mobile home was off its foundation and lying on its side. I found the baby beneath a playpen, but there was a sofa and television and a chair in the room. Any one of those things could have crushed that child."

The pause that follows tells me he's just realized I was a first responder. "Kate, normally under these circumstances I wouldn't look twice at something like this. There's no doubt that in the course of a violent storm the child had been tossed about inside her home. But the injuries I've described are not crushing injuries." He sighs unhappily. "I also discovered retinal hemorrhage in both eyes. X-rays indicated two healed rib fractures."

Terrible images flash in my mind's eye. The sweet face of a helpless baby girl. A tiny body in my arms, warm against my breast. Darker, disturbing images of an adult, a temper run amok. At the same time, the guilt that had been pressing down on me since the moment I heard of her death transforms into a slow, seething outrage.

"Doc, are you telling me that child was abused?"

"I strongly suspect the injuries present—both new and old—were sustained at the hands of a caregiver hours or even weeks before the storm."

I think of Nick and Paula Kester and I wonder

how a young mother or father could do something so heinous to their own child. "My God, she was only four months old."

He heaves a sigh. "Look, Kate, shaken baby syndrome is highly controversial, even within the medical community. In light of the circumstances of this infant's death, and before I can rule on cause or manner of death, I need to bring in a forensic pathologist for a second opinion."

Shaken baby syndrome. My God.

"Let me know the instant you get that second opinion," I tell him.

"Count on it," he says, and ends the call.

I leave the police station immediately after my conversation with Doc Coblentz. Our conversation follows me, his words taunting me with terrible possibilities.

. . . *the injuries present—both new and old— were sustained at the hands of a caregiver hours or even weeks before the storm.*

. . . *shaken baby syndrome is highly controversial, even within the medical community.*

I think of Lucy Kester, so tiny and vulnerable, and I wonder how anyone could inflict violence upon a baby. What kind of person does something like that? But the part of me that is a cop, the part of me that has dealt with individuals who've hit bottom—people who for whatever reason are incapable of exercising restraint or feeling even the most fundamental human emotions—knows those people are part of our society and things like this happen far too often.

It's dusk by the time I arrive at the Kline farm. Somewhere along the way I managed to put the news of Lucy Kester in some small compartment for later, so I can deal with the situation at hand with a clear head.

I'm surprised to find the farm deserted. When there's a death in the Amish community, friends and neighbors converge upon the bereaved in droves. The women clean and cook and care for the children. The men take over the running of the farm, feeding the livestock and taking care of any crops. When Big Joe Beiler's *datt* passed away a few years ago at the height of harvest season, Amish men came from miles away, most leaving their own crops in the field, to cut and bundle forty acres of corn.

I go to the front door and knock anyway. No one answers, so I stroll to the edge of the porch and look out over the yard and field beyond. A pleasant breeze caresses my face, bringing with it the smell of new foliage and the scent of honeysuckle, and I breathe in deeply. To my right I see Abigail's garden. Beyond, countless rows of corn sway in the breeze. Pulling one of my cards from my pocket, I go to the front door and slide it between the screen and the jamb, but it slips out and flutters to the floor. I've just stooped to pick it up, when I notice the wicker basket shoved against the wall, beneath the porch swing. It's the one Abigail was using to pick dandelion greens the other day. Oddly, it's still full of wilted greens.

I pick up the card. I'm about to rise, when something in the basket snags my attention. Not all the greens are dandelions, but the reddish stems of what looks like miniature rhubarb. Only it's not. My *mamm* grew rhubarb and regularly made strawberry-rhubarb pies, so I know what it looks like. I stare at the red stems, and a distant memory whispers unpleasant tidings in my ear. I remember my *mamm* telling me there are certain plants you don't ever pick when you're harvesting dandelions. *If it's red, put it to bed. . . .*

Kneeling, I pluck the questionable plant from the basket. The leaves are saggy and wilted, but the stem is still firm and red.

If it's red, put it to bed. . . .

I pull a small evidence bag from a compartment on my belt, tuck the stem into it, and drop it in my pocket. Leaving the basket, I rise and take the steps to the side yard. The grass is freshly mowed, probably by Jeramy before he fell ill. I cross the gravel driveway and head to the horse pen and barn. The grass is knee-high here with a profusion of goldenrod and thistle with lavender tops. Closer to the barn, I see another plant that's thigh-high with a reddish stem, egg-shaped, pointed leaves, and clusters of tiny white flowers. I go to it and kneel to study the stem. Sure enough, it's the same as the one in the evidence bag.

If it's red, put it to bed. . . .

Pulling on my gloves, I remove the small knife from my belt and cut off about a foot of the plant, capturing the stem, leaves, and flowers. An ink-like liquid the color of blood drips from the cut, and another quiver of uneasiness runs through me. I've seen this plant before. I was warned away from it by my *mamm* because it's poisonous. It's known by many names: nightshade. Cancer jalap. Pokeweed. There are certain times of the year when you can eat the new leaves safely, but they must be thoroughly boiled, the water tossed, and boiled again. Some Amish use the berries in pies and even harvest the tubers for canning, but you have to be very careful. My *mamm* never took the chance and forbade us to touch it.

Is it possible Abigail Kaufman harvested pokeweed with her dandelions and poisoned her husband? Was it accidental? Or did she harvest the green knowing fully they could kill him?

I met Chuck Gary when I was attending Columbus State Community College a few months after I left Painters Mill. I'd just earned my GED and enrolled in the hope of graduating with a degree in criminal justice. After what happened to me at the hands of Daniel Lapp when I was fourteen, I swore I'd never be a victim again. After a detective came to the college to speak about a career in law enforcement, I made the decision to become a police officer. It was a long and arduous journey for an Amish girl fresh off the farm. I was working part-time as a police dispatcher at a substation in a not-so-nice part of Columbus. I was broke, homesick, and lonely when Chuck, then my Biology 101 instructor, befriended me, helped me land a second part-time job in the campus bookstore, and somehow persuaded me to stick it out until I got my degree.

We lost touch over the years, though I still get Christmas cards from him, updating me on all the goings-on with him and his family. At some point he landed a tenured position at Kent State University and moved to North Canton, which is an hour or so northeast of Painters Mill. Last Christmas, he informed me that he was not only a grandfather for the first time but the senior research scientist in the biological sciences department and part-time professor of horti-culture. Hence, my call to him this evening.

"Katie Burkholder! Good golly, what a pleasant surprise. How are you?" His voice is exactly the same as I remember, as large and booming as a Broadway actor's.

I fill him in on some of the things I've been

doing over the last few years since we last spoke.

"I followed the Slaughterhouse Killer case from beginning to end," he tells me. "Dreadful business."

"Yes, it was."

"I always knew you'd make a fine police officer —and an even better chief." He makes a sound reminiscent of nostalgia. "I like to think I had something to do with that."

"You did. If you hadn't taken me under your wing, I'd have dropped out of school and gone back to Painters Mill with my tail between my legs."

"You don't do anything with your tail between your legs. But *had* you gone back, it would have been quite a loss to the English world now, wouldn't it?"

Though he can't see my face, I smile, and for the first time in years, I miss him. "Chuck, do you have a few minutes? I'm working on a case and I need your expertise."

"Ah, words like that will motivate an old curmudgeon like me, though I can't imagine what puzzle you couldn't solve on your own."

"Are you familiar with American poke-weed?"

"I saw Elvis Presley sing 'Polk Salad Annie' in Las Vegas in 1970. Does that count?"

I laugh.

"I coauthored a piece that was published a

couple of years ago in the *Horticultural Science* journal on the use of *Phytolacca americana* by herbalists and other nontraditional medicinal uses and folk remedies. It's a fascinating plant surrounded by an abundance of folklore."

"Is the plant poisonous to humans?"

"Very much so, particularly the tubers or root."

"And yet people eat it?" I say. "Poke salad?"

"That's one of the things that makes this plant so fascinating. The young leaves can, indeed, be eaten and enjoyed, but only if they're 'thrice boiled,' with the water changed between boilings. People have been known to use the berries for pies. Women used the ink to add color to their lips." He lowers his voice. "Just between you and me, I'd avoid the poke salad altogether."

"It's palatable?"

"I've heard it tastes like asparagus or spinach."

I think about that for a moment. "If a person were to mix pokeweed with dandelions or some other green, would it still be toxic?"

"Toxic as hell but a lot more tasty."

"What kind of symptoms would the victim have?"

"The patient would initially experience esophageal irritation. Within an hour he would develop severe abdominal pain and vomiting, followed by prolific bloody diarrhea. Later, he would suffer tachycardia. Elevated respiration. Once he was taken to the ER, the attending physician would note that the patient was hypotensive—"

"Low blood pressure?" I ask.

"Correct," he replies. "Due to the vasoconstriction of the large vessels, the physician would more than likely introduce pressor drugs to elevate blood pressure. If the patient was in respiratory failure, a ventilator would be introduced."

"What's the typical cause of death? I mean, even with medical attention?"

"A combination of maladies, any one of which could be catastrophic or fatal. Hypotension, cardiac arrhythmia, ventricular fibrillation, and severe respiratory depression."

"In the course of an autopsy and in terms of a toxicity screen, what specifically would the coroner need to look for?"

"That's beyond my realm of knowledge, Kate, but if I were to venture a guess, I'd say a general organic screen would pick up the toxins. In terms of the autopsy, bleeding and ulceration of the stomach and intestines would be found. Liver damage would be present." He pauses. "It sounds like you have another interesting case on your hands."

"If the tox or autopsy comes back with proof that my victim ingested pokeweed, how do I tell if the weed was picked inadvertently or purposefully included with the intent to poison?"

"As a fan of the classic mystery, I'd say it all boils down, so to speak, to motive."

Chapter 24

It's nearly midnight by the time I arrive home. As I pull around to the rear of the house, I notice that Tomasetti left the back porch light on for me, and something wistful and soft unfurls in my belly. I've missed him, I realize. I've missed the simple happiness of being with him. Of just loving him. Easy Sunday afternoons. Saturday mornings in bed. I'm midway down the sidewalk when the kitchen light flicks on and the door opens. Tomasetti, dressed in faded jeans and a Cleveland Division of Police T-shirt, steps onto the porch.

"You're a sight for sore eyes," he tells me.

I take the steps to the porch and stop a foot away from him. "You, too."

I expect him to pull me into his arms or maybe lay a kiss on me, but he doesn't. Instead, he steps back and opens the door to usher me inside. "Tired?"

"Yup." I step into our cheery, brightly lit kitchen, noticing the box of cereal on the table next to a bowl and spoon. "Another romantic dinner?" I quip, as I remove my equipment belt and drape it over the back of the chair.

"I knew you'd be impressed." He closes the door behind me. "Sorry, but we're out of food. I didn't have time to stop at the grocery."

"It's late. Cereal's perfect."

He's at the refrigerator, peering inside. I look down at the bowl in front of me and go to him. "Tomasetti."

He straightens, turns to me. Before he can say anything, I step close and put my arms around his neck. He smells of aftershave and shampoo and his own unique scent I've come to love. "I miss you," I whisper, and I press my mouth to his.

His arms encircle me, pull me close. He kisses me back, long and slow and with a certain reverence. After a moment, he pulls back and gives me a long look. "I think I'll serve up cereal for dinner more often."

My laugh feels good coming out. "I'm sorry I haven't been home much."

"I'm sorry I haven't been better company."

"It's just that this case . . ."

"It's okay," he says. "I get it."

I stop myself. "Tomasetti, it isn't about the case. I mean, not all of it."

He tilts his head as if trying to lift my gaze to his. "I think I got the other thing, too, Kate."

"This is new ground for me. I'm scared. I don't know how to do this. And I don't know how you feel."

"It's new ground for me, too. Having a kid . . . it's a big deal. It's okay to be scared."

Turning slightly, I run my arms over his shoulders and grip his biceps. "It's not only the pregnancy I'm afraid of. It's us. There's this . . . distance between us now that wasn't there before. It's like I can touch you, but I can't *reach* you."

"I know," he tells me. "It's my fault, not yours. Whatever gap exists, we'll bridge it."

"You didn't want this."

"I'm not going to lie to you. Right or wrong or somewhere in between, I didn't. That said, we both know life rarely serves it up just the way you want."

"I don't want this to get in the way of us."

"I'm not going to let it." He reaches for my hand. "Come here," he says. "I want to show you something."

Hand in hand, we leave the kitchen and take the stairs to the guest bedroom. It's a large space with tall, narrow windows that look out at the front of the property. Shortly after I moved in, Tomasetti added a bathroom and walk-in closet. The additions gobbled up some space, but there's still plenty of room, which includes a sitting area near the window.

The light flicks on and I find myself looking at a wooden bassinet. I recognize the Amish craftsmanship immediately: the dovetail joints and corkscrewed spindles. It's made of maple and stained the color of cherrywood.

"I found it at an auction in Geauga," he tells me. "It's Amish-made. The guy I bought it from said it's about sixty years old."

I can't stop looking at the bassinet. There's something about that solid piece of furniture, so sturdy and with so much history, that drives home the fact that all of this is real. That my life—our lives—are about to change in a very big way. The world is spinning out of control, and I feel the sudden need to hold on tight or else risk being flung off into space.

"I'm working on a case there," he tells me, "assisting the sheriff's office with the murder of a small-time meth dealer who's turning out to be not so small-time." He motions toward the bassinet. "There's a nick on the leg, and it's missing a caster wheel in the back. Both are easy fixes. I picked up a caster at the hardware store. And I think I've got some wood filler and stain in the garage."

It's not like Tomasetti to prattle. In fact, he's more likely to clam up. For the first time I realize he's nervous about what he's done. About how I'm going to react to it.

"Kate?"

I tear my gaze away from the bassinet and look at him. I see concern and uncertainty in his expression, and I realize this is an important moment. One that's going to define how we navigate this new turn in our lives.

"It's beautiful," I tell him.

He reaches for the bassinet and gently lays it over on its side. "Look at this." Beneath the crib section, carved into the wood are the words from an Amish proverb I hadn't heard or thought of in years.

A CHILD IS THE ONLY TREASURE YOU CAN TAKE TO HEAVEN.

I'm not a crier. I can count the number of times I've cried in the last five years on one hand. But the sight of those words inscribed in the wood and the knowledge that the man I love bought it for our child bring a rush of heat to my eyes.

I raise my gaze to Tomasetti's. "It's perfect."

"You sure? I mean, if you want something new, I can—"

"I love it." He starts to say something else, but I press two fingers against his mouth. "For God's sake, Tomasetti, if you say or do one more nice thing, I'm going to start blathering like an idiot."

"I guess there's a first time for everything."

"I'd rather it not be that."

"Okay." He wraps his fingers around my wrist and lowers my hand from his lips. Then his mouth is against mine and my back is against the wall. He leans into me and kisses me without finesse. A hundred thoughts scatter and fly, and I forget about everything except this moment between us and the promise of a future that, for the first time in my life, might just be within reach.

There are times when a case sinks so deeply into my psyche that I mull it even in my sleep. By the time morning rolls around, I'm convinced of two things: Jeramy Kline's untimely death was no accident, and his wife, Abigail, is responsible.

It's implausible to believe an Amish woman would mistake pokeweed for dandelion greens; the two plants are noticeably different in appearance and taste. If Abigail intended to include the pokeweed, she would have known it must be "thrice" boiled in order to cook out the toxins. I believe she purposefully poisoned her husband by serving up a toxic amount of under-boiled pokeweed mixed in with a batch of dandelion greens.

The problem, of course, is proving it. In order to do that, I need motive, which I believe is inexorably linked to the as-yet unsolved mystery of Leroy Nolt.

Tomasetti had an early meeting with the suits in Richfield and left the house at a little before six. He didn't wake me, which has become the norm since I found out about my pregnancy. It's a little after seven when I pad to the kitchen, still wearing my sweatpants and T-shirt. Outside, a summer storm has moved in. Thunder rattles the decorative plates hanging on the wall. The curtains above the sink billow in a breeze laden with humidity.

I'm pouring my first cup of coffee when I find the note tucked beneath the coffeemaker. *Let's go fishing this weekend.*

I laugh in the silence of the kitchen. It's the sound of a happy woman, and I pause to remind myself that that woman is me. That I laugh when I'm alone in the privacy of my own kitchen. And I will take to work with me today the knowledge that I am loved.

Pulling a pen from the drawer, I write: *Last to show baits the hook.*

I'm tucking the corner of the note under the coffeemaker, thinking about going upstairs for one more peek at the bassinet before jumping into the shower, when the back door creaks. I turn from the coffeemaker to see the door open a couple of inches, pushed by a gust of wind. Uneasiness flutters in my gut. Tomasetti is far too cautious to leave any door unlocked. Then I notice the sheen of rain on the floor. The sparkle of broken glass. A smear of mud on the tile. And I know someone's in the house.

Adrenaline ignites and spreads to my arms and legs with enough force to make me shake. My every sense flashes to high alert. The hum of the refrigerator. The din of rain against the roof. The slap of water against the ground. The hiss of the radio I left on in the bedroom upstairs. Outside, thunder rumbles like the footfalls of some massive primordial beast. My first thought is that Nick Kester found out where I live and has broken in. My second thought falls to my .38, which is lying on the night table upstairs next to the bed.

I set down the cup of coffee. My eyes dart to my cell phone charging on the counter a few feet away. I lunge at it, yank out the cord, and hit 911 with my thumb. Never taking my eyes from the door, I take a step back and look over my shoulder at the stairs. The living room is silent and dark, but that doesn't mean someone isn't there, intent on doing me harm.

I'm about to charge up the steps, when someone comes around from the front of the house. Even in the dim light I recognize Kester. He's wearing blue jeans. Pistol grip sticking out of his waistband. Dirty denim jacket. His hair is soaked and dripping, but he doesn't seem to notice. I smell the cigarette stench coming off him. For an instant, he looks surprised to see me.

"Nine-one-one. What's your emergency?"

He jolts at the sound of the tinny voice. His eyes dart to the cell phone in my hand.

"Sheriff's Department is on the way," I tell him. "You'd better run."

His mouth opens. I see jagged yellow teeth from within pale lips. A flash of uncertainty in his eyes. A glint of something ugly just beneath the surface. His right hand twitches, moves toward the pistol.

I hurl the cell phone, striking him beneath his left eye hard enough to open the skin. He reels back, hands coming up. "What the fuck!"

Spinning, I grab the banister, swing around it,

and fly up the steps two at a time. Kester bellows a curse. I reach the top of the stairs. My stocking feet slide on the hardwood floor. I scramble left and sprint down the hall, arms outstretched.

"Fucking bitch cop!" Kester pounds up the steps behind me. "I ain't going to jail 'cause of you!"

A gunshot snaps through the air. A hollow *thunk!* sounds as the bullet tears into the sheetrock to my right. Then I'm through the bedroom door, slam it behind me, slap the lock into place. Two steps, and I yank my .38 from the holster. Revolver trained on the door, I back toward the bench at the foot of the bed and snatch up my police radio. "Ten-thirty-one E!" I shout out my address. "Shots fired! Ten-forty!"

In a fraction of a second, Skid's voice snaps over the radio. "Ten-seven-six."

"Stand by," comes Mona's voice.

"Kester, I'm armed!" I scream. "You come through that door and I will fucking shoot you!"

"You got an ID?" Skid asks.

"Nick Kester," I pant. "He's armed with a handgun."

"Fuckin' MUTT!" Over the radio I hear the groan of his cruiser's engine as he cranks it up. "ETA two minutes. Hang tight."

"SO's en route," says Mona.

Never taking my eyes from the door, keeping the pistol leveled and ready, I back up and kneel beside the bed. I know it won't stop a bullet; the best I can hope for is that it will buy me a few seconds. If he comes through the door, I'll open fire until he stops moving.

"Anyone hurt?" Mona asks.

"No."

"Ten-twenty-three." Skid, letting me know he's arrived on scene. "Where's he at?"

"I don't know. Second level maybe. Be careful."

Holding my breath, I listen for movement in the hall. The only sounds come from the rain tapping against the window and the distant wail of sirens. I leave my position behind the bed and go right to avoid approaching the door directly in case Kester fires through it. I sidle along the wall and pause at the dresser.

"Nick Kester!" I shout. "The police are out front! Drop your weapon! Do it now!"

No response.

I wonder if his wife is with him. If she's somewhere in the house or sitting in a vehicle waiting for him.

I ain't going to jail 'cause of you!

And I realize he knows I had nothing to do with his daughter's death. . . .

Around me, the house is quiet. The silence unsettles me. Where's Kester? Where's Skid? My heart is pounding too hard. My hands are shaking. I edge around the dresser, set my left hand on the knob. A quick twist, and I swing open the door.

"Police!" I scream. "Drop the weapon! Get your hands up! Get on the fucking ground!"

A door slams somewhere downstairs. I can't tell if it's the front or the back. I don't know if it's Kester fleeing—or one of my own making entry.

"Skid!" I shout.

"I'm in the kitchen!" Skid's voice sounds from downstairs.

"I'm upstairs!" I shout. "Where's Kester?"

"Downstairs is clear!" shouts Glock, and another layer of relief goes through me.

Gripping my .38, I step into the hall. Skid bounds up the stairs, pistol leading the way. He makes eye contact with me and then enters the first bedroom. I pull open the hall closet, peer inside, find it empty. When I close it, Glock is coming down the hall.

"You okay, Chief?"

I jerk my head.

"Clear!" Skid exits the bedroom, nods at Glock, and then disappears into the bathroom.

I look at Glock and motion toward the remaining bedroom. "Let's clear it."

Nodding, his sidearm leading the way, he enters the room. I follow. While he checks the closet, I drop and look under the bed.

"Clear," he says as he emerges.

He looks at me closely as he holsters his weapon. I see his eyes fall upon the bassinet.

He stares at it a moment, then looks away as if realizing he's intruded upon my private domain.

"Fucker's gone." Ducking his head slightly, Glock speaks into his lapel mike. "House is clear. Suspect at large."

Skid stands at the door. He's also noticed the bassinet. He's not quite as good as Glock at concealing his surprise, but he's smart enough to keep his mouth shut.

I start toward the door. "You call Wayne County?"

Skid steps aside as I shoulder past. "They're setting up a perimeter now."

I look at Glock. "See if someone can get a K-nine Unit out here."

Nodding, he tilts his head and speaks into his shoulder mike. I start down the hall. My stride falters when I notice the hole in the drywall. Specks of plaster on the hardwood floor.

"Son of a bitch wasn't messing around, was he?" comes Skid's voice from behind me.

I stave off a chill, but I don't do a very good job of ignoring the little voice whispering in my ear: *That could have been you.*

"We need to find him," I hear myself say. "Pull out all the stops." I make eye contact with Glock. "You notify SHP?"

"Holmes County, too," he says. "BOLO is still active."

My arms and legs are beginning to shake in

earnest, so I keep moving down the hall. "He could still be on the property."

"I'll round up some guys and take a look around," Glock says.

"Those woods in the back are thick as hell," Skid puts in.

"Kester's got to have a vehicle somewhere nearby," I say.

"If there is, we'll find it," Glock tells me.

"Unless he already got to it and left," Skid puts in.

"You see anything when you pulled up?" I ask.

"No, but there are plenty of places to pull off the road and use trees for cover." Skid shakes his head. "Fuckin' meth heads can move pretty fast when you put a cop in the picture."

Glock and I chuckle, and I feel myself settling down, falling into cop mode, a frame of mind I'm much more comfortable with than traumatized homeowner. Or pregnant female who's just been shot at by an armed intruder.

I glance over my shoulder at Glock. "We need to get someone out to Paula Kester's father's house. Carl Shellenberger. Take a deputy with you. And wear your vest."

Touching the brim of his hat as he passes me, he jogs down the hall and disappears down the stairs.

Skid and I follow. At the base of the stairs, I

glance right to see a deputy kneeling next to the cell phone I tossed at Kester. He rises upon spotting me. "You okay, Chief?"

"Yup." I start toward my phone but realize it's probably evidence and may have Kester's DNA on it. "You contact BCI?" I ask the deputy.

He nods. "CSU is en route."

I think about Tomasetti, wincing inwardly at the thought of his finding out what happened from someone else.

"Just make sure everyone knows Kester is armed and dangerous." The image of him flashes in my mind's eye. "He looks like he's been up for a few days—"

The deputy nods. "We got people on it, Chief. Everyone and their uncle's out looking for this guy."

I nod and start toward the kitchen to call Tomasetti on the landline. He picks up on the first ring. "Kate?"

I can tell from the tone of his voice that he already knows. "I'm okay," I tell him.

"What the hell happened?"

"Kester broke in. After you left."

"You sure you're okay?"

"I'm fine."

"Was he armed?"

"With a handgun."

"Jesus Christ, Kate."

"Tomasetti, I'm okay." I hear static in the background and realize he's already in his vehicle. "Where are you?"

"Fifteen minutes away. Do me a favor and don't go anywhere."

"I'll be here," I tell him, and the line goes dead.

I'm standing on the back porch, talking with a Wayne County sheriff's deputy, when I hear the crunch of gravel beneath tires. I look up to see Tomasetti's Tahoe barrel down the lane, make a slight right, and then skid to a halt behind my borrowed Crown Vic. I have no idea how he made the drive from Richfield so quickly, but I don't care. All I know at the moment is that I'm glad to see him.

His face is grim when he exits the vehicle. He walks around the rear with long, assured strides, nodding at the deputy as he approaches. His face doesn't change when his gaze flicks to me. I think I see the flash of emotion in his eyes, but it's gone so quickly I can't be sure.

"You okay, Chief?" he asks easily.

I roll my eyes and sigh but don't manage the cocky attitude I'd intended to project.

He reaches me and stops a scant foot away. His gaze finds mine, and he runs his hands over my shoulders and down my arms as if he doesn't quite trust what his eyes are telling him.

"You got here fast," I say.

"One of the agents heard the call and recognized the address, then called me straightaway." He glances from me to the deputy and back to me. "They get him?"

I shake my head. "We've got three agencies looking. Glock and Holmes County went to talk to Paula Kester's father, but he says he hasn't seen them for almost twenty-four hours. Wayne County SO set up a perimeter. Skid and a bunch of deputies are searching those woods."

"Vehicle?"

"No."

"We think he got out before the perimeter was set up," the deputy interjects. "Nick Kester is the RO of a white 2008 Toyota Tacoma, so we added that to the BOLO."

Tomasetti glances toward the door, his eyes taking in the broken pane and beyond, the glass on the floor. "What happened?"

I tell him everything, hating the way it sounds, because a little voice inside my head keeps reminding me that I'm a cop and I should have been able to stop him. "It happened fast, Tomasetti. I just . . . walked up on him, in the living room. My radio and sidearm were upstairs. I couldn't do anything, so I chucked the cell at him and ran."

I can tell by the way he's looking at the door that he wants to go inside to see everything for himself. But until the CSU arrives and processes the scene, neither of us can risk contaminating any possible evidence.

"You didn't hear anything?" he asks.

"Nothing." But we both know I've been sleeping like the dead.

"Any idea how long he was in the house?"

"No."

He looks away, and I know he's wondering how much time elapsed between his leaving and Kester making entry and about all the things that could have happened in between.

As if realizing we need some privacy, the deputy slides his smartphone from his pocket. "Excuse me," he says and leaves the porch.

I watch him walk down the steps and stroll over to his cruiser to make his call.

"He fired one shot?" Tomasetti asks.

I nod. "It went into the wall. Upstairs hallway. CSU should be able to dig out the slug."

"Goddamn it, Kate." He scrubs a hand over his face. "Shooting at a cop? This guy's fucking nuts."

"I know."

"Any idea how he found out where we live?"

I shrug. "You can dig up just about anything online these days."

"Kester doesn't seem like the digging type." He thinks about that a moment. "You think he could have followed you home?"

I should have thought of that, but I didn't, and a creeping sense of dread slinks up my back.

"Tomasetti, I've been careful. I mean, I'm a cop. I would have noticed." But even as I say the words, I silently acknowledge that I've been distracted and probably not as cautious as I think.

Neither of us mentions my pregnancy, but the fact is as glaring and palpable as a physical presence.

I tell him about Doc Coblentz's assertion that Lucy Kester's injuries were more than likely a result of shaken baby syndrome. "He was going to get a second opinion, but that was his finding."

Tomasetti grinds his teeth. "That fucking Kester doesn't want to go down for that."

"He tried to blame me. His wife blames me. . . ."

"She probably doesn't know he abused the child, and he wants to keep it that way. It's a damn farce."

I try to smile. To let him know I'm okay. That I can handle this. All I manage is a twisting of my lips and a smile that feels like a lie.

Chapter 25

It takes five hours for the CSU to process the scene, which basically consists of the kitchen, living room, hallway, stairs, and bedroom. The largest piece of evidence recovered was the slug he dug out of the wall, which will be sent to the lab in London and analyzed. During a search of the woods at the rear of our property, Skid found a man's boot print in a muddy area. A Wayne County deputy discovered tire tracks in the dirt near a gravel pullover on the road just north of our property. The CSU successfully captured impressions of both. All the evidence will be analyzed and, if the case goes to trial, used in conjunction with my testimony to put Nick Kester behind bars. Of course, we have to find him first.

Despite the efforts of every law enforcement agency in the three-county area, Nick and Paula Kester have been eerily elusive. I suspect that after the shooting at the farm, Kester hightailed it to his vehicle and fled the scene before road-blocks could be set up. Some in law enforcement believe they fled the state. Tomasetti isn't buying into that theory; neither am I. I think they've found a safe haven and are hiding out nearby. Sooner or later they'll turn up. The question is when and whether anyone will get hurt.

Being a stickler for personal safety—especially mine—Tomasetti suggests we spend the night at the Marriott in Canton. We leave the farm at just after 4:00 p.m. and end up having a nice dinner at a steakhouse not too far from the hotel. After a stressful, frustrating, do-nothing day, it's a nice break.

This morning, however, it's back to reality. I'm a day behind on everything—no closer to determining the whereabouts of Nick Kester, solving the mystery of Jeramy Kline's death, or determining what might've happened to Leroy Nolt.

My third-shift dispatcher greets me with an animated "Chief!" as I come through the front door at just after 7:00 a.m.

"Hey, Mona."

She rises as I approach her station. "I heard what happened yesterday." I don't miss the hint of misplaced adoration in her eyes. "I'm glad you're okay."

I feel myself stiffen slightly when she throws her arms around me. "Thank you." Awkwardly, I hug her back. "I'm fine."

Pulling away, I pluck messages from my slot, trying not to notice the two-inch-wide streak of blue in her hair and the shadow of a reentry stamp from a bar in Akron on her left hand. She's wearing a black skirt that's a couple of inches too short and has paired it with a red bolero jacket. Despite her dubious wardrobe—and that unexpected show of affection—she is, as usual, all business this morning.

"Anything on Kester come in overnight?" I ask.

"Several people called the hotline with sightings, but nothing panned out."

I'm disappointed but not surprised. He's dug in somewhere, and sniffing him out isn't going to be easy. "I want you to send a message to the team. Make sure everyone is still wearing vests. Pickles, too."

"Roger that."

I glance over at the officers' cubicles. "You here by yourself?"

"Sorry, Chief. T.J.'s wrapping up an accident over on County Line Road."

But I sigh because my small department is perpetually undermanned. "If we don't have an armed officer here, I want you to keep the front door locked. Until further notice. If people want inside, they can knock and you'll have to let them in."

"No problem."

"Get T.J. on the radio and tell him I need him when he's finished."

"Okay."

I grab coffee on the way to my office and pull the file on the Nolt case. There's a message from the coroner, so I call him while my computer boots.

"I heard there was some excitement up at your place in Wooster yesterday," Doc Coblentz begins. "Everyone okay?"

"We're fine, but I've still got a suspect at large." Not for the first time I'm reminded of how fast word gets around.

"I just wanted to let you know I've got the Kline autopsy on the schedule for this afternoon."

I tell him about finding the pokeweed at the Kline farm and about my conversation with Chuck Gary. "Some Amish cook and eat pokeweed, but if it's incorrectly cooked, it can be toxic."

"That's why you were asking about toxicology."

"Yes."

"Interestingly, a few years ago, a young mother brought in a toddler that was critically ill with vomiting and respiratory distress. One of the first things I noticed was that the child's hands were stained red. After questioning the parent, I learned the child had wandered from the yard and into a weed-infested lot next door. The mother thought the child may have ingested some purple berries. She brought them in and I immediately couriered them to the lab, and they turned out to be American nightshade."

"So you have some experience with this particular plant."

"If memory serves me, the toxic components lie with the saponins. There's more to it than that, and I don't recall the specifics off the top of my head, but I'll look it up. Of course, the actual testing will be done at the BCI lab. Now that I know what to ask them to look for, they'll run an organic tox screen. If there's something there, they'll find it."

I think about my conversation with Chuck Gary. "I'll follow up with a call, too."

"Kate, it occurs to me that even if Jeramy Kline did indeed ingest some type of plant-based toxin, it may have been accidental."

I think about the wicker basket I'd discovered on the porch at the Kline farm. The one Abigail Kline used to gather dandelion greens and, evidently, pokeweed. "This might be one of those cases in which the cause of death is going to be a hell of a lot easier to prove than the manner of death."

I'm still thinking about the wicker basket when I hang up. Though it was in plain view and I had every right to be standing on Abigail Kline's doorstep, I couldn't confiscate it without possibly adversely affecting a potential case. Pokeweed is not illegal to possess. Had I appropriated the basket without first obtaining a warrant, it could have been rendered inadmissible in court and jeopardized the case, so I take the time to get my ducks in a row.

It takes me an hour to write up an affidavit and another forty-five minutes to obtain a search warrant from Judge Seibenthaler, which entails a call to Sheriff Redmon in Coshocton County and the stipulation that at least one deputy from his department accompany me to the Kline farm.

Once I have the warrant in hand, I swing by the

station and pick up T.J. "Where are we going?" he asks.

"We're going to search Abigail Kline's farm."

"We looking for something in particular?"

I tell him about the wicker basket. "Pokeweed is poisonous when prepared incorrectly. The BCI lab is going to run an organic tox on Jeramy Kline to see if that particular toxin was in his blood-stream when he died. I think they'll find it."

"Damn." Shaking his head, he whistles. "Never would have pegged her for murdering her husband. I mean with her being Amish and all."

"The Amish have all the same weaknesses as the rest of us," I say. "Including the human capacity for violence."

T.J. and I arrive at the Kline farm to find the place bustling with activity and a Coshocton County sheriff's cruiser parked on the shoulder a few yards from the driveway. I recognize the deputy immediately as Fowler Hodges and pull up next to his car.

"Hi, Folly."

"Hey, Chief. I just got dispatched. Sheriff said you've got a search warrant?"

I tell him about finding pokeweed in the wicker basket.

"So you think Mrs. Kline offed her old man?" he asks.

"I think it's a possibility."

"Well that'd be a shocker." His eyes slide toward the house. "You expect any trouble from these people?"

"No." I sigh. "Might be best if I serve the warrant, though. I'll keep it as low-key as possible."

"Sure thing, Chief." He motions toward the gravel lane. "After you."

Gravel crunches beneath my tires as I pull into the driveway. Ahead, four black, windowless buggies are parked in a row on the shoulder. The horses stand with their rear legs cocked and their heads down, grabbing a snooze while they have the chance. The teenage Amish boy tending them eyes me suspiciously as I park behind the buggies. I get out and give him a nod, but he looks away. I glance to my side to see Folly get out of his cruiser. He doesn't approach the house but saunters to the front of the vehicle and leans against the hood.

T.J. and I start toward the house. Four young children play on the tractor tire hanging from a tree branch in the side yard. On the other side of the front porch, two twenty-something Amish women kneel, chattering and tossing freshly pulled weeds onto a growing pile of compost. Two Amish men stand at the barn door, one with a pitchfork in hand, the other puffing a pipe, gray smoke curling into the air. Their eyes are in shadow from their flat-brimmed hats, but I feel their gazes follow us as we take the sidewalk to the house.

On the porch, I find a tiny elderly woman vigorously sweeping dirt into a dustpan. Her hands are misshapen with arthritis, her knuckles a mass of purple and white knots.

"*Guder mariye.*" I wish her a good morning as I ascend the steps.

The old woman straightens and gives T.J. and me an unhurried once over. "*Guder mariye.*"

I spot the wicker basket beneath the chair. The pokeweed is still inside. I try not to look at it as I address the woman. "Is Abigail home?"

She looks at me as if I'm dense. "What do the English police want with her at a time like this?"

"I need to speak with her. It's important."

The woman stops sweeping and, giving me a stern look, sets the broom against the siding and shuffles to the door. "Wait."

A few minutes later an Amish man of about thirty emerges from inside the house. He's dressed in black—trousers, suspenders, jacket, and hat—with a white shirt. His beard is the color of coal dust and reaches nearly to his belly. But it's his face I can't look away from. He's the spitting image of Leroy Nolt.

"You must be Abigail's and Jeramy's son," I say.

"I'm Levi Kline." His eyes slide to T.J. and back to me. "What can I do for you?"

"I need to speak with your mother. Is she home?"

"She's grieving." A pained look crosses his face. "Must you speak with her now?"

"I'm afraid this won't wait. I'm sorry."

His mouth tightens. For an instant, I think he's going to refuse to get her, then he gives me a nod and goes back inside.

When he's out of earshot, I look at T.J. "Why don't you go around to the back door in case someone decides to take a stroll?"

He's already midway down the steps. "Gotcha."

I wait several minutes, resisting the urge to pace. I'm about to knock again, when the screen door squeaks. Levi Kline steps onto the porch, looking slightly puzzled. "She's not in her room."

I cross to him and look past him to see the old woman hovering just inside, looking at me. "Where is she?" I ask, posing the question to both of them.

The woman turns away without answering.

I look at Levi and raise my brows. "Where is she?"

"I don't know. I thought she was in her room, lying down. She's not been sleeping well."

"Where did she go?"

"I don't know. I didn't see her leave. But . . . we were in the kitchen earlier." He looks perplexed. "Mrs. Beiler thinks she saw her go outside. . . ."

The elderly woman, I realize. "How long ago?"

"An hour or so."

"Is she somewhere on the property? Or did she leave?" I ask, the initial fingers of urgency pressing into me. I don't believe Abigail poses any immediate danger—not to others, anyway—but she is a person of interest in a possible homicide, and I need to know where she is.

"I can't imagine her leaving at a time like this. Maybe she needed some quiet time to think. You know, to be alone, and walked down to the pond or something. Datt used to go down there." Kline rubs his chin, shakes his head. "I'd like to take a walk down there to see if I can find her."

In the years I've been chief, I've worked hard to cultivate a positive rapport between the Amish community and the police department. While the relationship isn't yet where I want it to be, we've made headway. I'm loath to undo the progress, but I can't walk away from this.

I hand him the warrant. "I need to take a look around the premises. This warrant gives me permission to do so."

"What?" He stares down at the papers. "But . . . what is this? I don't understand."

"It's a search warrant that grants us permission to search the premises. I'd appreciate your cooperation."

"*Search* my mother's home?" His eyes widen. "But why? You think she did something wrong? You think she broke the law?"

"The warrant explains everything, Mr. Kline. Please read it." I hit my lapel mike and hail T.J. "Let's execute the warrant."

"Roger that."

Levi's eyes flick from me to Deputy Fowler, who's coming up the steps. "I don't like this," he says. "I don't think my mother would like it, either."

"We'll try to finish as quickly as possible. In the interim, you should probably find your mother."

One of the Amish men that had been near the barn has evidently heard the exchange and come over. Two little girls of about six or seven years of age trail behind him. He stops at the foot of the steps and eyes me with unconcealed hostility. *"Der siffer hot zu viel geleppert."* The drunkard has just sipped too much.

Ignoring him, I pull out the large garbage bag I'd tucked into my equipment belt and walk over to the wicker basket. While Levi Kline looks on, I pick up the wicker basket and place it inside the bag.

"I don't understand." He motions toward the bag. "Why are you taking that? What is the purpose?"

I hand the bag to Fowler, who tapes it closed and tags it with a label. I lower my voice and address the deputy. "The BCI lab is waiting for that. Will you have one of your guys courier it?"

I give Levi a nod and then descend the steps.

The older Amish man standing at the base of the steps glares at me as I walk past. I glance left and right and then head directly toward the boy charged with the buggy horses.

"*Guder mariya*," I tell him.

He's too polite to ignore my greeting but looks at me as if I'm some flesh-eating zombie with my sights set on him.

"Have you seen Abigail Kline?" I ask.

His eyes flick toward the house. "Don't look over there," I say. "Look at me. Have you seen her?"

His Adam's apple bobs twice. "She took the buggy."

"How long ago?"

"Less than an hour, I think. She asked me to harness the horse, so I did."

"Where did she go?"

His eyes slide toward the house, looking for someone to save him from having to deal with me. I move so that I'm blocking his view. "Answer me," I say. "Where did she go?"

"She didn't say."

I walk away without thanking him. I reach for my shoulder mike as I start toward the Crown Vic and hail Deputy Fowler. "Abigail Kline took the buggy and left. I'm going to look for her. You and T.J. okay here without me for a few minutes?"

"We'll be fine."

Frustration pushes a sigh from me. I'd wanted to be here while the search warrant was being executed, if only to answer questions and ward off any conflicts with the Kline family and the Amish as a whole. But with Abigail unaccounted for and the warrant in the hands of the Coshocton County Sheriff's Department, I feel my time would best be spent looking for her.

I spot Levi Kline standing at the base of the porch steps, watching me, and I walk over to him. "She took one of the buggies and left," I inform him.

"Are you sure?" For the first time he looks concerned. "I can't see her taking the buggy on her own at a time like this. I would have taken her wherever she wanted to go. Any of us would have. All she had to do was ask."

"Do you have any idea where she might have gone? Does she have a best friend? Her parents? The bishop?"

"If she was troubled or sad, she may have gone to see the bishop. Or maybe she went to Grossdaddi's farm." His brows knit. "Chief Burkholder, she should not be alone."

"What was her frame of mind last time you saw her?" I ask.

He considers my question for a long moment. "She was . . . in a dark place. Crying a lot. Shaken inside."

The last thing I want to do is needlessly worry

her family. Chances are, the situation is exactly as he theorized; Abigail needed some time alone or sought her parents or the bishop for counsel. But I've been a cop long enough to know that when people commit a crime as heinous as murdering their spouse, sometimes the next life they take is their own.

I'm trying to come up with a delicate way to ask him if his mother could be suicidal, but he beats me to the punch. "You think she's a danger to herself?" he asks.

"The thought crossed my mind."

The color drains from his face, and he takes a step back from me. "I'm going to look for her."

I consider asking him not to, but I change my mind. At this point, the more people we have looking for Abigail Kline, the better.

Chapter 26

As I pull out of the lane of the Kline farm, it occurs to me that if Abigail left an hour ago, she hasn't gone too far. Most Amish use Standardbred horses for their buggies because that particular breed is prized for its fast, working trot. Even so, they travel only eight to ten miles an hour. It's not an unduly long distance for me to cover relatively quickly in a patrol car.

Bishop Troyer and his wife live southwest of

Painters Mill, about ten miles from the Kline farm. If Abigail went to see him, she's still en route. I should be able to catch her before she arrives.

I take a right out of the Kline farm and head south on County Road 19 toward a secondary road that will take me to Highway 83. I drive slowly, keeping an eye out for telltale signs of the buggy—horse manure—and the side roads, in case she pulled over or opted for a shortcut. I pass an Amish wagon full of hay, but there's no sign of Abigail's windowless buggy. I cruise past Bishop Troyer's farm, but she's not there, so I loop around and take a less-used road south, back toward the Kline farm. It's possible that in order to avoid traffic, she took the county road.

I reach the Kline farm, pull onto the gravel at the mouth of the lane, and hail T.J. on the radio. "Any sign of Abigail Kline?"

"Her son walked the property, but she's not here, Chief."

"Damn it." I sigh. "You guys find anything else inside?"

"Folly found more of those greens in their refrigerator," he tells me, referring to the kerosene-powered refrigerator.

"Bag it and seal it," I tell him. "Get it to the lab. Make sure you guys follow chain of custody."

"Roger that."

"I'm going to head northwest to see if she went to her parent's farm."

"Ten-four."

Racking the mike, I back from the driveway and start in the opposite direction, going northeast on County Road 19. I've gone less than a mile, when I spot a pile of manure in the center of the northeast-bound lane. I have no way of knowing if it belongs to Abigail's buggy horse or if she even traveled in this direction. But this particular county road doesn't have much traffic. More importantly, Reuben and Naomi Kaufman's farm is only a few miles ahead, so I keep going.

Just past Beck's Mills, I hit County Road 119 and then make a left on County Road 600. A mile in, I come upon the Kaufman farm. There's no buggy in sight, but I pull in anyway and hail T.J. as I park adjacent to the barn. "I'm ten-twenty-three the Kaufman farm," I tell him. "No sign of Abigail's buggy, but I'm going to talk to them."

I rack the mike and get out. The farm appears deserted. A breeze has kicked up, rustling the leaves overhead as I start toward the front door. I knock and wait. I've just begun to pace, when Naomi Kaufman opens the door. "Chief Burkholder?"

The elderly woman holds the door open about a foot, looking at me through the opening. Her expression tells me she's surprised to see me. I look past her into the kitchen, where a dozen or so green tomatoes glisten with water on a cutting board. "Is Abigail here?"

"Abby?" The woman's brows knit. "She's at home. I'm making food to take out there now. Why?"

"She's not at home, Mrs. Kaufman. Are you certain she's not here?"

Opening the door wider, she steps onto the porch. "You checked the farm? With Levi? I can't imagine her leaving at a time like this."

"I just left her house. Abigail took the buggy and left. I thought maybe she came here to talk to you."

"How odd." She gives me a perplexed look. "Abby's not one to leave and not tell anyone. She doesn't care much for driving the buggy, either, especially with all the traffic."

"Do you have any idea where she might've gone?"

"My goodness, no." Her brows knit, and then she gives me a nod. "Why are you looking for her, Chief Burkholder?"

Several thoughts enter my mind simultaneously. First, that she hasn't asked about her daughter's well-being. Secondly, that she should have already been at her daughter's farm. And last, that she's a decent liar for an Amish woman. "Do you mind if I come inside?" I ask.

"What? You don't believe me? You want to see for yourself that she's not here?"

"Maybe your husband has seen her."

"He's not here."

"Where is he?"

"Not that it's any of your business, but he has his physical therapy today in Wooster. For his legs, you know." She cocks her head. "What do you want with Abigail, anyway? Has she done something wrong?"

"I don't know, Mrs. Kaufman. But I need to find her and make sure she's all right."

Her expression becomes concerned. "You think something's happened to her?"

"I don't know. Can I come inside?"

Sighing, she opens the door. "Come on."

I brush past her and go into the living room and look around, but there's no sign of Abigail or anyone else. The house smells of coffee and fried bacon, with the slight aroma of vinegar.

"You can look all you want, but there's no one here."

I trail Naomi to the kitchen, where she goes to the sink and hangs a towel on a hook set into the cabinet above. A cast iron Dutch oven sits atop the stove, the lid rattling as the steam escapes. A plastic glass filled with what looks like iced tea sits on the table, sweating droplets onto the blue-and-white-checked tablecloth. I open the back door and glance around the rear porch, but there's no sign anyone has been there. Naomi follows me out of the kitchen and back to the living room. I go to the stairs, take them two at a time to the second level. The Amish woman calls out to me, but I don't stop.

Something nags at me as I check the three upstairs bedrooms and the bathroom, as if I've missed something. I stop in the hall, trying to call forth the niggling sensation stuck in the corner of my brain, but nothing materializes. I go back to the bedrooms and check each closet. I look under the beds. I even check the linen closet, but there's no one there.

Naomi is waiting for me at the foot of the stairs. "I don't know what you hoped to find up there," she snaps. "Aside from all the laundry that needs doing."

"Is it possible she's on the property some-where?" I reach the base of the stairs. "Maybe she needed some alone time?"

"If she came to our home," Naomi says, "she'd come inside like a normal person."

I give her only half an ear as I head toward the small bathroom off the living area. The shower curtain is closed, so I shove it aside. The tub is empty. The sense that I've overlooked something important jabs at me. Where is Abigail? What have I missed?

I stop in the living room. Naomi is in the kitchen, standing at the stove. I watch as she removes the lid on the Dutch oven. The aromas of bacon and cider vinegar and the green, mustardy scent of dandelion greens taunts my olfactory nerves. The dish has a distinctive aroma. . . .

I stride into the kitchen, look down at the pot. "What's in that pot?"

Naomi looks at me as if I've lost my mind. "Greens, for goodness sake. I can't see how that's any business of yours."

I take the lid from her. "Where did you get these greens?"

"Abigail brought them over a few days ago. I don't see what that has to do with—"

"Has anyone eaten any of this food? Tasted it?"

"*What?* I might've sampled a green or two."

"Mrs. Kaufman, I have reason to suspect this food is contaminated."

"Contaminated? What are you talking—"

"Poisoned."

"*Poisoned?*" She cackles. "That's just pure horsefeathers."

Nudging her aside, I turn off the stove and slide the Dutch oven off the hot burner. The greens smell good with bacon and cider vinegar. They were a summer staple at my house when I was a kid. Jacob and Sarah and I spent many an afternoon gathering dandelion greens with our *mamm*. But I suspect there's pokeweed mixed in with these. Pokeweed that was not properly prepared. But why would Abigail want to hurt her parents?

"Mrs. Kaufman, I believe Abigail added pokeweed to these greens. You know that if pokeweed isn't prepared properly, it's toxic."

"That's just crazy talk, Kate Burkholder. She wouldn't do that to us or anyone else. Everyone knows you got to cook the pokeweed three times. . . ." But she doesn't look quite so sure of herself now, and I know that for the first time she's considering the possibility that I'm right.

My cell phone vibrates. Annoyed by the interruption, I snatch it up and check the display. I'm surprised to see STARK CO SHER. I make eye contact with Kaufman. "Hold on a sec." Turning away from her, I answer with my usual, "Burkholder."

"This is Detective Tom White with the Stark County Sheriff's Department. I wanted to let you know we got a line on Nick Kester."

My interest surges. "You have him in custody?"

"No, but we're pretty sure we know where he is. Three women on horseback in Whitacre Park near Waynesburg reported seeing a couple matching the descriptions of Paula and Nick Kester, camping in a remote area near some equestrian trails. One of the women recognized him from a photo in the newspaper. I'm dispatching deputies now. Since your department is involved, I wanted to give you a heads-up before the shit hits the fan."

"I appreciate that, Detective. Do you need assistance?"

"Well, you never know how these things are going to go down. If Kester's armed—and we're assuming he is—I figure we can use all the officers we can get. I'm going to give Wayne County a call, too."

"I'll dispatch one of my officers now."

I release the call and speed-dial Glock. He picks up on the first ring. "Hey, Chief."

"Stark County Sheriff's Department thinks they have Kester," I tell him.

"Shit. Stark County?"

"They received a tip from some horseback riders. A woman recognized Kester from a news-paper photo. They're camping in a remote area up in Whitacre Park near Waynesburg."

"You want me to head over that way?"

I lower my voice. "Glock, I'd go with you, but I'm tied up here at the Kaufman farm."

"You find Abigail Kline?" he asks.

"No, but I think she's somewhere on the property." I pause. "I think she may have tried to poison her parents."

"Shit. You need an ambulance out there?"

"No one's hurt. But I'm going to take a look around. If she's here, I'll get on the radio. But I'm probably going to be tied up for an hour or so."

"Roger that, Chief. I'll keep you posted on Kester."

"Be careful," I say, but he's already discon-nected.

I clip the phone to my belt. Naomi has gone into the kitchen. I find her at the sink, washing dishes and stacking them on a strainer. "Mrs. Kaufman, I'm going to need to take that pot with me."

"Do what you must, Chief Burkholder. But I think it's just silly to think Abby would put poke in there on purpose. If it's in there at all, it was an accident."

"I hope you're right." But I know she's not. I find two mismatched pot holders in a drawer, grab the hot Dutch oven, take it through the living room, and elbow my way through the front door.

Naomi trails me as far as the porch. "You're wrong about Abby."

Ignoring her, I go down the steps, pop the trunk of the Crown Vic, and set the pot inside. That's when I notice the buggy wheel marks in the moist ground next to the gravel. I kneel for a closer look. I'm no tracker, but the marks look recent.

Naomi stands on the porch, watching me, her arms crossed in front of her. "Mrs. Kaufman, how does Mr. Kaufman get to the clinic?"

"That Yoder Toter from Dundee picks him up and drives him up to Wooster," she says.

"Has there been a buggy here today?"

"She drives a van."

I look around. There are plenty of places to hide on this large farm. There are cornfields, impenetrable woods, and two huge barns.

"Mrs. Kaufman, I'd like to take a look around. Is that all right with you?"

"Let me put on my muckers." The Amish woman turns and goes back inside.

I don't wait for her. Ever present in the periphery of my thoughts is the knowledge that when someone reaches the low of murdering family members, sometimes suicide is the next step. A sense of urgency pushes me into a jog. I cross the gravel to the barn and slide the big door open several feet. Shadows play hide-and-seek in the murky light. I get the impression of a large area with a dirt floor and a low ceiling strung with cobwebs. The smells of old wood, rotting hay, and damp earth tickle my nose. I look down, seeking buggy wheel marks, but there are none.

"Abigail Kaufman!" I call out. "It's Kate Burkholder with the Painters Mill PD! I need to talk to you!"

I listen, but the only reply is the moan of the wind. I venture more deeply into the shadows. To my right are the bony ribs of a hay rack that's pitted with rust. A child's Radio Flyer wagon that's missing both front wheels lies on its side. To my left, half a dozen bags of feed are stacked against the wall. On the rear wall ahead, three grimy windows, some with broken or missing panes, stare blankly at me like dead eyes. I go to the nearest one and squint through the cobwebs and grunge. The pasture beyond is hilly and lush with a wet-weather creek where cottonwoods and elms jut fifty feet into the air.

Turning away from the window, I go to the wooden steps and take them to the loft. It's a small mow with a dozen or so bales of hay stacked haphazardly. Some of the bundling strings have broken open, spilling loose hay onto the floor.

"Abigail Kaufman!" I call out.

But I know she's not here.

Disappointment presses into me as I take the steps back down to the first level. I've just reached the ground, when Naomi comes through the sliding door. "I told you she's not here," she says, looking triumphant.

Ignoring her, I walk past her and leave the barn through the sliding door. I break into a jog and go around the side of the barn, where I'd seen a gate earlier. The area is overgrown with weeds as high as my chest. I'm about to turn away, when I notice some of the weeds are laid over. The thought of ticks and other unsavory insects crosses my mind as I wade in. Some of the stems are broken and bent. Renewed interest flares when I discern the wheel marks of a buggy in the damp earth. They go through the gate and into the rear pasture. But why would she take the buggy back there?

Naomi Kaufman calls out my name. I glance

around the side of the barn to see the elderly woman slowly making her way down the incline toward me.

"Are there any other structures on the property?" I ask.

She stops a few feet away. She's breathing hard. Sweat beads on her forehead and upper lip. "Only thing standing is that tumbling down old barn where we used to butcher years ago. I don't even know if the thing is standing anymore, especially after that storm."

I almost can't believe my ears. In the back of my mind, I recall Sally Burris's words: *That old bank barn in the back.* I'd assumed she meant the second barn within sight of the house. But she hadn't; she'd meant a third structure set farther back on the property. . . .

"Where is it?" I ask.

"It sits on the property line between our place and Abram's farm. About half a mile thataway." She motions toward the earthen dam that bridges the creek. "Used to be an old two track that ran along the fence line."

I point in the direction of the house. "Go back inside, Mrs. Kaufman."

"Abigail wouldn't go back there." She glares at me, angry because she knows she won't be able to keep up with me and I'm not going to wait.

Turning away, I jog toward the dam, my eyes on the buggy tracks in the soil. The *jug-o-rum* bellows of bullfrogs echo within the canopy of the trees as I cross the dam. I feel the humidity rising off the mossy surface of the water, smell the mud baking on the bank. It's so quiet I can hear the flies and mosquitoes buzzing. Pig frogs grunt from within the cattails.

On the other side of the dam, the ground is soft and spongy beneath my boots, and I find the shod hoof marks of a horse bracketed on either side by wheel ruts. The tracks are fresh, and though the path is overgrown, the trail is easy to follow.

The terrain is rolling and crowded with saplings, brush, and mature hardwoods, which makes it difficult to see more than fifty yards in any direction. The sun beats down with merciless intensity, and I find myself wishing I'd looked at an aerial view before venturing out, but of course I didn't realize I was going to be tromping through an overgrown pasture this afternoon.

I crest the second hill, and the rusty tin shingles of a roof loom into view ahead. I traverse a dry creek bed, elbow my way through a patch of reeds on the other side, and get my first good look. The structure is a dilapidated bank barn with a swaybacked roof and wooden siding the color of old bone. Several shingles have been peeled back by decades of wind. Much of the wooden siding has fallen to the ground, where the earth is slowly reclaiming it. The rear portion of the gambrel-style roof has collapsed. Through the opening, I see the top of a tall concrete silo with a missing dome.

I'm looking down at the faint trail through the weeds, when I hear the snort of a horse. Thirty feet away, through a stand of saplings, a bay horse is looking at me, its ears pricked forward. The animal is still hitched to the buggy. I've startled him, and I can tell he's thinking about bolting.

"Whoa," I whisper as I approach. "Easy."

I reach the buggy and peek inside. A crocheted afghan is draped across the seat. An empty bottle of water lies on its side on the floor. There's no sign of Abigail. I walk to the gelding and set my hand against its rump, then slide my fingers beneath the harness leather. The place where the leather presses against the horse's coat is wet with sweat, telling me it hasn't been standing idle long. Oddly, one of the leather driving reins is missing. I look around, but it's not on the ground.

I nearly call out for Abigail, but a small voice warns me that stealth may make for a safer approach. I don't know what her state of mind is. I don't know if she's armed. In fact, I don't know if she's the one who's been taking shots at me. Concentrating on keeping my feet silent against the ground, I go to the front of the barn. The sliding door is closed, but I don't need it to enter; several pieces of siding have fallen away, leaving plenty of room for me to slip through.

Giving my eyes a moment to adjust to the dim light, I thumb the keep strap from my holster. I don't believe Abigail intends to harm me; more than likely she's come out here to end her own life. But I know the lengths to which a desperate individual will go to get the job done.

Light slashes in through hundreds of gaps in the siding, illuminating dust motes and flying insects. Ahead, a large flatbed hay wagon sits front and center. Above it, a set of massive grappling hooks holds several hundred pounds of loose hay that smells relatively fresh. I can just make out the pulley-and-cable system that runs the length of the roof at the ridge board. Vaguely, I wonder if the Kaufmans lease this part of the property or allow one of their neighbors to store hay.

I step over fallen boards and other debris. A shovel handle. A broken cinder block. A leather strap that was once part of a harness rigging. Mounds of loose hay. Cobwebs droop from every surface like silver moss. Rodentlike squeaks from the rafters overhead tell me there's a healthy population of bats. It's not until I've walked a dozen or so steps that I notice the smell. A strong, unmistakable stench I recognize from my youth. *Hogs.* I'd approached the scene upwind, so I didn't notice until now. Naomi had said no one used this barn and no one had been back here for years. I wonder who owns the hogs, who's taking care of them.

Straight ahead, a large hay door looks out over the pasture beyond. I can hear the pigs grunting and moving around in the pen below.

Something splats against my arm. At first I think it's an insect, but when I glance down, I see the black smear of guano on my forearm. I look up and see dozens of bats hanging from the ridge rafter at the roof's peak. "Shit."

I'm looking around for something with which to wipe my arm, when movement to my right snags my attention. I startle and find myself looking at a disheveled Abigail Kline. She's wearing a gray dress with a black apron. Her *kapp* is untied and slightly askew. Her sneakers are covered with mud. She's holding the leather rein from the buggy in her left hand. In her right, she's clutching a knife the size of a machete.

Chapter 27

"Abigail."

She's standing about fifteen feet away. Butcher knife in her right hand. Buggy rein clutched in her left. I'm aware of her body language, and I keep a close eye on her hands. I wonder if she was planning to use the leather to hang herself.

"How did you find me?" she asks.

"It wasn't easy." With deliberate slowness, I tilt my head and speak into my lapel mike. "Ten-seven-five," I say, letting dispatch know I've made contact with her. But I never take my eyes off of Abigail.

"What are you doing out here?" I ask.

She's staring at me as if I'm an apparition that's arrived to drag her to hell. In the light slanting in through the door, I discern dull eyes and a flat expression. She's a pretty woman with a wholesome smile and easy-to-read expression. Today, her face has transformed into something I barely recognize. Dark circles beneath her eyes. Hair that's greasy at her crown. The crow's feet at the corners of her eyes seem deeper. Lips that had once smiled so easily are dry and cracked.

"I just . . . want to be alone for a while," she says quietly.

I nod toward the knife in her hand. "Will you do me a favor, Abigail, and put down the knife?"

She doesn't comply, doesn't acknowledge my request, and she doesn't release the knife. "How did you know I was here?"

"I was looking for you," I tell her. "I saw the buggy tracks. I need you to put down the knife so we can talk about what's bothering you."

She offers a smile, but it conflicts with the hollowed look in her eyes. "I don't think I have anything to say, Chief Burkholder. To you or to anyone else."

I nod, taking my time, not rushing her. "I know you're upset. I think if we could just sit down and talk for a few minutes, I think we could get all of this straightened out."

"Some things can't be straightened out," she whispers. "You don't understand what's happened. You don't know what's been done. You don't know what *I've* done."

"I know you poisoned Jeramy," I tell her. "I know you tried to poison your parents. What I don't know, Abigail, is why."

She raises her gaze to mine. It's not guilt or sadness I see in the depths of her eyes, but righteousness. The expression of a woman who's righted a wrong and in doing so made the world a better place. "He that smiteth a man, so that he die, shall be surely put to death."

I recognize the quote. It's from the German Martin Luther Bible and has been interpreted a dozen ways over the centuries. But it's not the origin or meaning of the quote that interests me. It's the intent behind her utterance of it.

"Exodus," I say.

"I'm impressed, but then you used to be Amish, didn't you? Of course you know the Bible."

This barn is far from the ideal location to question a suspect, particularly with regard to a serious crime. I'd much prefer to have her in an interview room with a camera rolling and at least one other cop present. But my instincts tell me that if Abigail is going to talk—if she's going to tell me anything even remotely useful—it's going to be here and now and on her turf.

"Abigail, why don't you explain that quote to me?" When she doesn't respond, I push. "Does it have something to do with Leroy Nolt?"

"Leroy." A sound that's part sob, part sigh escapes her, and she presses a hand to her mouth as if to prevent another. "They betrayed me. All of them."

"Jeramy?"

"Yes."

"And your parents?"

Her hand trembles. She looks at me over the top of it, her eyes filling with tears. "How could they?"

"What did they do?"

She shakes her head, her hand clamped tightly over her mouth. "I can't."

"Were you involved with Leroy?" I ask.

An odd laugh bubbles out of her. "I married Jeramy when I was seventeen years old, Chief Burkholder. I've always been with Jeramy. *Always*. Since I was a girl."

"But it was Leroy Nolt you loved, wasn't it?"

"*Sell is nix as baeffzes.*" That is nothing but trifling talk.

"I know you gave him that quilt, Abigail. It's got your initials on it. I know you initial your work."

"It doesn't matter now," she says. "It's gone.

Everything. He's gone. All of his dreams. They're . . . dust."

I look through the hay door. I can't see the hogs below, but I can hear them moving around, grunting, rubbing against the steel pens, cloven hooves tapping against concrete.

I choose my next words with care. "I met your eldest son earlier," I tell her. "Levi."

"Do not speak of him." She raises her hand as if to prevent me from continuing, as if she already knows what I'm going to say.

I don't stop. Instead, I take a step closer and lower my voice. "He's the spitting image of Leroy Nolt. The eyes. His smile."

"No . . ."

"Levi is Leroy's son. You were pregnant with Leroy's child when you married Jeramy."

"That's not true." Turning away, she moves closer to the wide door at the back of the barn.

I follow, hoping she doesn't intend to jump. She's armed with a knife. I have my sidearm, but I know from experience her frame of mind is such that it won't matter. You can't threaten someone with deadly force when they want to die.

"Abigail," I say softly, "Tell me what happened to Leroy."

She stops at the door that looks out over the pens and the overgrown field beyond and takes a deep breath. My attention is honed on Abigail, but I'm ever aware of the hogs below. Several of the animals—the boars—are huge and probably weigh in at three or four hundred pounds. They have a feral, intelligent look about them. Some of the smaller animals are wallowing in a mudhole in the corner of the enclosure. Others, having noticed us, are standing below the door, their beady eyes trained on us as if expecting us to drop feed to them.

"Did Jeramy do something to him?" I ask. "Was he there the day Leroy was killed? Is that why you poisoned him?"

Her face screws up. "I can't speak of it."

"What about your parents? Were they involved? Do they know what happened? Is that why you tried to poison them?"

"They murdered him." Her voice is so low, I have to lean close to make out the words.

"What did they do to him?"

"They hated him." She sucks in air as if coming up for a breath after a long underwater dive. "Because of me. Because I loved him."

"What happened to Leroy?"

"We were in love. The kind of love a young girl's heart can barely contain. We'd been meeting secretly for weeks. We were going to run away and be married. Have children. A happy life together." Her eyes glaze, and I know she's riding her memories back to the past. "We planned it for weeks, and I was so happy. I wanted to tell everyone, but of course I couldn't say a word.

You see, Leroy was New Order Mennonite. We're Swartzentruber." She sighs. "My *datt*'s hatred for Leroy was an ugly thing. Monstrous. I think on some level, Datt knew I would choose Leroy over him. Over the church."

"What did he do?"

"The day Leroy and I were to leave, Leroy asked me to meet him at the covered bridge. He had a car, you know. He'd been saving his money. For the future. *Our* future." She smiles the brilliant smile of a girl in love, and I know that in her mind she's no longer standing in this old barn with me. She's seventeen years old and waiting for her lover.

"I'd never been away from home before," she whispers. "I was so scared. What would my *mamm* do? Would the Amish speak of me behind my back? And what of my *datt*, who was so very strict? He'd told me I'd marry Jeramy Kline, after all. But my love for Leroy was much more powerful than the fear." She shrugs. "I packed my little satchel. I waited until dawn, and after my *datt* left for the day, I walked to the bridge and I waited for Leroy." She lowers her head, her brows coming together in anguish. "I waited for two days. I spent the night at the bridge because I was afraid if I went home, Leroy would come for me and I wouldn't be there. He never came."

"Why didn't he show?"

Her eyes meet mine. I see knowledge in their

depths. Words too painful to utter aloud, but a story that must be told. "It was Jeramy who finally came for me. That second day. He found me sitting there, crying and near physical collapse. He told me Leroy had left town. And then he asked me to marry him."

"Jeramy knew about your relationship with Leroy?"

"I didn't tell anyone, but a young girl wears her heart on her sleeve. That kind of love is difficult to conceal. Looking back, I think he must have known. My *datt*, too." She looks off in the distance, and her eyes glaze. "I was too young and naive not to believe Jeramy. I believed Leroy had left without me. All these years, I believed he'd left to chase all those crazy dreams he had. I was happy for him. I was secretly rooting for him to find the success he'd craved for so long and worked so hard for." She looks down at the leather rein in her hand as if not quite remembering why it's there. "I think Jeramy knew I was with child. Even as I cried for Leroy, he asked me to marry him.

"But I never forgot about Leroy. It was my secret." Her smile is wistful. "I'd picture him in the city, in some fancy car or restaurant or just walking on the sidewalk in a flashy suit. I'd fancy him thinking of me. Wishing I were there with him. Some days I believed I'd go. I fantasized about it. I'd just start walking and never come back. Better yet, he'd write me a letter, begging me to join him, and I would. Oh, how I fantasized about that. How I'd join him in some big city and we'd live happily ever after. . . .

"But the babies came and life intervened." She falls silent, thoughtful. "Thirty years have passed, and my life has been a lie. All of it. A life based on deceit. And secrets. And sin. So much sin."

"Abigail, what happened to Leroy?"

"It was his own doing, but I can't fault him. He couldn't have known it would cost him his life." A sound of despair squeezes from her throat. "The day before Leroy and I were supposed to run away together, while I was away cleaning house for a neighbor who'd just had a baby, he came here to ask my *datt* for permission to marry me. Jeramy was here. My *datt*. My brother. Mamm. Can you imagine?" A breath shudders out of her. "But there were too many hard feelings. Too much hatred. The men argued, especially Jeramy and Leroy. So much that my *mamm* asked them to leave the house. And so they came here, to this barn, to talk." She spreads her arms to indicate the very building in which we're standing. "But the talk quickly turned to an argument. Jeramy and Leroy fought. Somehow, Leroy fell from the loft into the pen below. Struck his head on the concrete." As if envisioning the scene in her head, she looks down at the pen. "He never woke up."

"How do you know all of this?" I ask. "Did Jeramy tell you?"

She nods. "When I read about the discovery of those bones and the ring, I knew it was Leroy. And so I asked Jeramy. Finally, after all these years, he told me the truth."

I think about the remains and evidence of tooth marks on the bones, and I wonder if she knows the hogs fed on her lover's body, possibly while he was still alive.

"Jeramy and Leroy fought about you?" I ask.

"And ideology." She offers a sad smile. "I was a pretty girl back then. Both men were in love with me. I supposed I loved both of them, too, but in different ways. Jeramy was the stable one. Handsome. Upstanding. The one everyone respected." Her smile shifts; the secret smile of a woman in love. "But it was Leroy with all of his crazy dreams that set my seventeen-year-old heart on fire."

"Was Leroy's death an accident?"

"I honestly don't know."

"After Leroy fell into the pen, did anyone try to help him?"

"Jeramy said they did, but . . . who really knows? People lie to suit their needs." Slowly, she uncoils the leather rein, letting one end fall to the floor. "After Leroy fell, Jeramy, my *datt*, and my brother ran down to help him. But Leroy was gone. Hit his head. Jeramy said he wanted to call the English police, but Datt forbade it. Instead, they buried him in the crawl space of that old barn." Kneeling, she loops the leather rein around a support beam and runs the free end through the loop. "Right where those Boy Scouts found him. He'd lain there all these years. Alone."

"You said Leroy had a car," I say. "What happened to it?"

"After dark, Jeramy and my brother drove it down to Beach City. They found a back road and drove it into the lake."

I look out the door at the beautiful rolling hills beyond, and I'm surprised by the twinge of melancholy in my chest. Such a sad story. A young life lost. And many more ruined. "That's why you poisoned Jeramy?" I say. "Why you tried to poison your parents?"

"Yes."

"What about your brother?"

She looks down at the floor, shakes her head. "I couldn't—"

A sound from behind turns me around. Alarm reverberates through me at the sight of Reuben Kaufman standing twenty feet away, a .22 rifle leveled at my chest.

Chapter 28

For an instant, I'm not sure if I'm more shocked by the image of Reuben Kaufman out of his wheelchair and standing on his own power—or the sight of the rifle. His finger is inside the trigger guard. The muzzle is steady. Next to me, Abigail goes perfectly still. We stare at him in silence. Tension knifes the air.

"Mr. Kaufman, put down that rifle." I'm keenly aware of the .38 against my hip. My lapel mike at my shoulder. Either would only take an instant to reach, but there's no way I can do it before he gets off a shot.

"I need you to put down that rifle," I repeat. "Right now. Before someone gets hurt." I motion toward Abigail. "Your daughter."

Never taking his eyes from me, he addresses her in Pennsylvania Dutch. "Go to the house."

Abigail doesn't move. Instead, she looks at her father as if recognizing him after a long separation. "I know you were there. All these years . . . you knew . . . about Leroy, and you never told me."

"He was a *maulgrischt*." A pretend Christian. "I protected you. I saved your soul. Now go to the house with your mother and let me take care of this."

She moves toward him.

He doesn't take his eyes off me. "You. Get over by the hay door."

I'm ten feet from the door, but I have a clear view of the pen below, where a dozen or so massive hogs mill about, sows and boars, and half-grown piglets. More of them have noticed our presence and lift their heads to look up at us.

"Mr. Kaufman, people know I'm here," I tell him. "The police are on the way. You can't possibly get away with this."

He jabs the rifle at me. "Do it!"

His voice booms through the structure. Until this moment, I'd seen him as a frail, sickly old man confined to a wheelchair and in need of constant care by his long-suffering wife. All of it was a lie. The wheelchair. His failing health. All to protect him from what he'd done. To keep his secrets from coming to light. The thought sends a chill through me.

"Put down the rifle." Hoping to buy some time, I raise both hands and sidle toward the door. "I'll do whatever you say." I look at Abigail, urging her with my eyes to obey him and get back to the house. She's standing slightly behind Kaufman, so that the old man is between us, forming an irregular triangle of sorts. She stares back at me, her expression chillingly blank.

Kaufman tilts his head, looks at me the way a

scientist might look at some small animal he's about to slice open. His face is devoid of emotion. There's no tension. No fear. Just the cold resolve of a man determined to save his daughter, his family, and his own neck. In that instant I realize I'm not going to be able to talk him down.

Keeping my hands at shoulder level, I sidestep closer to the door and try another tactic. "Abigail told me Leroy Nolt fell into the pen. I know it was an accident. I know she wasn't there. I know you had no part in what happened. No one's going to hold either of you responsible for something you didn't do. If you put down that rifle, both of you can walk away from this."

The Amish woman's head jerks toward me. "They murdered him, Chief Burkholder. All of them. Jeramy. My brother. My father."

I don't look at her, keeping my eyes on Kaufman, waiting for an opportunity to pull my sidearm and stop the threat.

Kaufman shifts his gaze to his daughter. "*Sei ruich.*" Be quiet.

"The truth has been kept quiet long enough," she tells him.

"Leroy Nolt was *Mennisch.*" Mennonite. He hisses the word, but his hatred echoes with crystal clarity.

"And you're a *maddah.*" Murderer.

"I did it to keep you from burning in hell."

"*Leeyah.*" Liar. "What about your bastard

grandson?" she hisses. "How are you going to save Levi's soul?"

Kaufman opens his mouth, his lips quivering. The rifle quivers in his hands. "*Sei ruich*!"

In the instant his attention shifts away from me, I yank out my revolver and fire twice, center mass. Kaufman jolts, red blooming just above his hip. The rifle clatters to the floor. He goes to one knee. I'm in the process of holstering my .38 when he launches himself at me, catching me off guard. His shoulder rams my midsection. I reel backward, nearly go down. With stunning speed, he snatches up the rifle, brings it up. But I'm faster, and I grab the barrel and stock with both hands, ram him with it. He's not much bigger than me. Despite his age and at least one gunshot wound, he's stronger. I yank the rifle toward me, try to topple his balance. He stumbles forward but doesn't fall. I twist the rifle right, try to wrench it from him. He counters by twisting left. I lose my grip on the muzzle. He swings it toward me. His finger slips into the trigger guard.

In the periphery of my vision, I see Abigail moving. I hear a shout, but I can't make out her words. A high-pitched *zing!* sounds from the rafters above. I glance up, see the hay pulley quiver.

Kaufman looks up. Too late, I see the massive load of hay barreling toward us. I try to get out of the way, but I'm not fast enough.

The hay plows into us like a giant battering ram. It strikes me in the face and chest and knocks me off my feet. My boots leave the floor. And then I'm falling backward into nothingness.

Chapter 29

The first thing I'm aware of is the sounds of the hogs all around. Wet concrete against my back. Not quite knowing where I am. The stench of manure. The shuffle of cloven hooves against the ground. I'm cognizant of pain, but I can't pinpoint its exact location. My head. My left wrist. The small of my back . . .

I open my eyes. For an instant, I'm not sure what I'm looking at. But as my senses return, I recognize the load of hay dangling twelve feet above me. Around me, hogs scamper about, rooting around and eating the fallen stems. My presence has caught the attention of the animals. A big boar with a single tusk. A large sow with a bloody stump for a tail and a chunk of flesh taken out of her rump.

I grew up around farm animals—cattle, hogs, horses, and sheep—and I've never been afraid of them. But I don't like the looks of these hogs. They're skinny and feral looking. Judging from the enthusiasm with which they're eating the fallen hay, they're hungry, too.

A groan escapes me when I push myself to a sitting position. Pain knifes up my left wrist. I glance down, try to move it, and I'm rewarded with another jolt. Broken, I think.

I glance at the loft door above, but there's no one there. I look around for my .38, but it's nowhere in sight. The pen is about forty feet square, poorly kept, and crowded with dozens of hogs. The volume of the grunting and squealing is deafening. Several of the animals are scuffling over fallen bits of hay.

I get to one knee and struggle to my feet. Dizziness sends me sideways, but my balance quickly levels out. I look around for Kaufman. He's lying on the concrete ten feet away, not moving. There are several hogs between us. I can't see his face; I don't know if he's conscious. I don't even know if he's alive.

I speak into my shoulder mike. "Ten-thirty-three. Ten-fifty-two. Kaufman farm," I add and recite the address.

The radio crackles as several agencies respond to my emergency call for assistance. "Ten-seventy-six."

Relief rushes through me at the sound of Skid's voice, and I know the first responders are on the way. When a cop gets into trouble, jurisdiction ceases to matter. You drop everything and you go.

I speak into my shoulder mike. "Abigail Kline may be armed."

"What's her twenty?"

"The old barn at the rear of the property. Half a mile in. Send an ambulance."

"Ten-four."

I start toward Kaufman. I've only taken two steps, when one of the hogs bumps my leg hard enough to knock me off balance.

I lash out with my boot. "Back off!"

I miss and the animal shies away. The boar trots past, snuffling, watching me. Its tusk juts two inches from its lower jaw. Most hog farmers trim the tusks once a year. The teeth can get caught on fences and cause injury. Without trimming, the teeth can grow to several inches in length. The animal becomes a danger not only to other hogs but to its handlers.

Trying not to agitate the hogs, I sidle through the herd. The animals' bodies are hard against my legs. My knee brushes against one of the sows. Squealing, the animal spins and nips my calf. Pain shoots up the back of my leg.

Bending, I slap the hog hard on the back. "Get back! Go! Get out of here!"

The sow grunts and shuffles away. I glance down at my leg, dismayed to see blood seeping through the fabric, and a chill lodges at the base of my spine. "Shit. *Shit.*"

I reach Kaufman and kneel. His eyes are partially closed and rolled back white. His mouth hangs open. Blood from a broken tooth that's pierced his lower lip trickles down his chin. At first glance I think he's dead, then I notice the rise and fall of his chest. Blood coming through his shirt on his left side just above the waistband of his trousers. A gunshot wound.

"Don't try to move," I tell him. "There's an ambulance on the way."

His lids flutter. His eyes focus on my face. "*Heeda der saus*," he whispers.

Beware the hogs.

The back of my neck prickles. I look over my shoulder. The larger hogs are devouring the fallen bits of hay, threatening the younger animals with snapping jaws when they dart in to steal a scrap.

"What the hell's wrong with them?" I ask.

He doesn't answer. But I already know. They're starving. And the reality of the situation sends a quiver of fear through my gut.

"Can you walk?" I ask.

He tries to sit up. His face contorts with pain, and he only manages to flop around like a fish. "My legs . . . broken, I think."

"Mr. Kaufman, we need to get out of this pen."

"The gate." He motions to a steel gate secured with a chain. "There."

I look around for his rifle, but it's nowhere in sight. Bending, I grab his right wrist and start to drag him across the concrete. Kaufman cries out, but I don't stop. He's not a large man, but he's dead weight, and it takes every bit of strength I possess to move him. Progress is excruciatingly slow. I try to avoid the pigs and the patches of stinking black muck, but the pen is crowded and filthy and I don't quite manage.

I'm fifteen feet from the gate when a shot rings out. I look toward the loft door to see Abigail Kaufman with the rifle to her shoulder, her eye on the sights. Releasing Kaufman's wrist, I duck down. "Abigail! No! Put down the rifle!"

She doesn't comply. Gives me no indication that she even heard me. Another shot cracks. A ricochet *zings* off the concrete inches from Kaufman's head.

I have no cover. She's at a high vantage point, thirty feet away, close enough even for someone unaccustomed to firearms to hit their mark. "Put down the gun!" I scream. "Do it now!"

Bending, never taking my eyes off her, I reach for Kaufman, grip his wrist, and pull. "Help me, damn it," I tell him.

Face contorted, he scrabbles with his left leg. When he looks up at me, I see pain and terror in his eyes. "My legs . . ."

I drag him another couple of feet. I'm only a few feet from the gate when one of the hogs rushes me from behind. Its snout strikes the back of my leg. Tilting its head, it chomps down on my calf. Pain streaks up my leg. The animal shakes me. My balance totters. I drop Kaufman's hand and barely maintain my balance.

"Get off me! Get away!" I punch the animal hard. The sow releases my leg and continues past, then turns to stare at me with bold, intelligent eyes.

Five feet away, the boar watches me, chomping its teeth.

"Kaufman!" I shout. "Get up!"

The boar charges. Despite its size, the animal is agile and fast. Shoving its snout beneath Kaufman's shoulder, it roots upward with so much force that the man is flipped onto his side. It's not until I see blood that I realize he's been slashed with the tusk.

The old man screams. "The gate! Open it!"

The sow circles for another pass. I step back, keeping her in sight. Another shot rings out. I hear the bullet strike flesh. Kaufman jolts. Vivid red blooms on the fabric of his sleeve and dribbles onto the concrete. His scream rents the air.

I risk a look at the loft door to see Abigail lining up for another shot. "Drop the rifle!" I scream. "Drop it! Right fucking now!"

Another gunshot, followed by a ricochet a foot from where I'm standing. Specks of concrete hit my trousers. Spinning, I run toward the gate. I've only gone a few feet when the boar rushes me, rooting the air, its tusk flashing white. I kick it in the snout with my boot. The boar bellows but retreats.

I vault over the top of the gate. A curse grinds from my throat when my injured wrist slams against the ground on the other side. I roll and lie still. For an instant the only sound comes from my labored breaths. The grunting and squealing of the hogs. The wail of a siren in the distance.

Using the gate for support, I get to my feet. Abigail Kline stands at the loft door, staring into the pen below.

"Abigail, drop that rifle!" I shout. "Do it now! Drop it!"

A muffled scream sounds from the pen. Bending, I look between the rails of the gate to see that the hogs have surrounded Kaufman. The larger animals dart in, rooting and slashing. The smaller animals squeal and vie for position. The old man is sitting up, slapping at the animals with both hands. Terror on his face. Mouth open in a silent scream. A big sow lunges at him, slashing at him with her mouth. The scream that follows is horrific. The sow retreats, a bloody scrap in her mouth. A strip of material from his shirt. Horror burgeons inside me when I realize they're mauling him. . . .

"Shit. *Shit!*" My hand shakes as I grapple for my shoulder mike. "Man down! In the pen! The hogs are mauling him!"

I step onto the lowest rail of the gate and scream at the animals. "Get back! Get away!"

But the animals are frenzied now. Injured and

on the ground, Kaufman makes a feeble attempt to fend them off, slapping at them. For a split second I consider going in to help him. But I know the animals would turn on me, too.

"Back off!" I shout. *"Back off!"*

The Amish man's screams are a horrible, high-pitched keening that opens a fist of revulsion in my gut. I look around for a weapon, something to throw, and I spot a piece of broken fencing on the ground. Part of a busted cinder block. I snatch up both, throw them one at a time as hard as I can at the hogs. Both objects hit home, but neither is large enough to stop the carnage.

Unhooking the chain, I swing open the gate. Several of the hogs swing their heads my way. One of the smaller animals starts toward me. I turn and run toward the barn. Kaufman's screams follow me. The dreadful sound of a man being eaten alive . . .

I scale the first fence I come to, putting as many obstacles between me and the hogs as possible. Then I'm in an old stall on the underside of the barn. I spy the hay chute ahead, shove off the cover, and climb through.

A deputy with a shotgun and flak jacket rushes toward me. "Where's the shooter! *Where's the shooter?*"

"Loft," I tell him. "Female. She's got a rifle."

He sprints toward the stairs that will take him up a level. I get to my feet and hit my lapel mike.

"Man down! He's being mauled! In the hogpen!"

"Ten-ninety-five." A voice I don't recognize tells me he's taken Abigail Kline into custody.

"Chief!"

I turn at the sound of Glock's voice, see him come through the front of the barn, face grim, moving fast.

"You hurt?" he asks.

"Kaufman's down. In the pen. For God's sake, the hogs are killing him!" I don't wait for a response. Cradling my injured wrist, I go back to the hay chute and drop down to the stall below. Quickly, I jog to the aisle and rush to the pen. I know immediately something has changed. Kaufman has gone silent. The hogs have quieted.

I reach the gate, startling when a juvenile hog careers past and scurries toward open pasture. I look in the pen. Most of the pigs have fled. Shock and revulsion rise in my chest at the sight of Kaufman—what's left of him—lying in a pool of blood.

"What the fuck?" Glock whispers behind me.

The Amish man lies unmoving in a prone position with his face turned away. His arms are spread wide. Hands gone, the sleeves of his shirt shredded and blood soaked. One leg is bent at the knee and crossed over the other. A massive pool of blood has been trampled by dozens of cloven hooves.

I tilt my head to my lapel mike. "What's the

433

ETA on that ambulance?" But I know it's too late.

"Paramedics just arrived at the house, Chief," comes T.J.'s voice. "Want me to send them back?"

"That's affirm. Make it fast."

I don't want to go into the pen. I don't want to see what the hogs did to Kaufman. I don't want the sight branded onto my brain. I don't have a choice. I'm a first responder and EMT certified. It's my responsibility to take every action necessary to preserve life until help arrives.

The gate squeaks when Glock swings it wider. We start toward the fallen man. The stench of manure is powerful, but I barely notice. I can smell the blood now. Too much of it for anyone to have survived.

"This is going to be bad," Glock mutters.

I stop a few feet away and look down at Kaufman. His shirt and suspenders are shredded and have been torn away from his body. His torso is riddled with bite marks. The flesh on his abdomen is torn, and something gray with blue veins protrudes from the gash. Bile rises into the back of my throat when I look at his face. His eyes stare sightlessly into space. His right cheek has been torn open, exposing the gums and teeth and part of his jawbone. His right ear is gone. His hands are gone. The stumps of his wrists are jagged flesh and the pink-white of protruding bone.

"That's some disturbing shit," Glock mutters.

I don't know what to say to that. I'm not sure I can speak even if I try.

Digging into his equipment belt, he digs out a latex glove and slips it onto his right hand. Kneeling, he presses his index finger against Kaufman's carotid artery.

After a moment, he lowers his head and gives a single shake. "He's toast."

The next hours pass in a blur. Abigail Kaufman is taken into custody and transported to the Holmes County Jail in Holmesville. The county prosecutor will have to sort through an array of charges, ranging from the attempted murder of a peace officer, attempted murder for what she did to her parents, and first-degree murder for the poisoning death of her husband. That's not to mention Kaufman. Since she implicated her brother in the death of Leroy Nolt, two additional Holmes County deputies were dispatched to Abram Kaufman's farm to bring him in for questioning.

Doc Coblentz pronounces Reuben Kaufman dead at the scene. It's premature to rule on the cause or manner of death, but in an off-the-record conversation, the coroner tells me that if my bullet had killed Kaufman he wouldn't have continued to bleed once the hogs went to work on him. By all indications, while the fall and the bullet incapacitated him, he more than likely died of massive trauma and blood loss caused by the mauling that followed. At some point a local animal-protection organization is called in and the hogs are rounded up. I don't know what will happen to them. I'm not sure I want to.

I recount the incident a dozen times to several law enforcement officials affiliated with two agencies. The case is officially assumed by the Holmes County Sheriff's Department. I give another statement along with the pertinent information on Abigail Kaufman to the lead detective. I physically walk him through the scene, which is being sketched, videotaped, and photographed. I try not to look at any of it.

Once Kaufman's body is transported to the morgue, the CSU from BCI goes to work. The rifle is confiscated. Since I fired my service revolver, my .38 is also taken for testing "just to cross the t's and dot the i's," according to the detective. The CSU is looking for the slugs from the .22 when Tomasetti calls.

He begins with his usual: "Are you all right?"

"I'm okay." But I tell him about my wrist. "Might just be a sprain."

He makes a sound that's part dismay, part disapproval. "That's not code for 'compound fracture,' is it?"

I can't help it; I laugh. It feels good after the things I witnessed this afternoon. It reminds me that I'm alive. That I still have my life and a future with the man I love.

As if understanding, Tomasetti falls silent and listens as I take him through it.

"Tough scene," he says when I'm finished.

"I don't think I'm going to be eating pork chops any time soon."

Now it's his turn to laugh, but it's short-lived. "Nick Kester and his wife were taken into custody. Kester had a handgun in his possession, but not a rifle."

"Reuben Kaufman did."

"He knew you were getting close to figuring things out."

"Ballistics will probably confirm he was the shooter, not Kester."

I want to add something about closure and justice, but I'm not sure either of those things is the case. While a killer was taken into custody and three cases were closed, none of them entailed a happy ending for anyone involved. Especially little Lucy Kester, who was the only innocent in the bunch.

"Kate, have you been to the hospital?"

"I'm going to head over that way in a few minutes."

He just sighs. "Look, I can drive down there if—"

"Tomasetti, I'm okay. Really. You can't leave work to rescue me every time I get into a scuffle."

"This was more than a scuffle. The fall alone—"

"I'll have Glock drive me over to Pomerene.

437

A quick X-ray, a wrap for my wrist, and I'll be good to go."

He falls silent. I know he's not happy with the situation. But this is ground already covered, and I know he doesn't want to rehash it, especially over the phone.

"I'll be home before dark," I tell him. "What do you say we meet out at the pond and catch a few fish?"

After too long a pause, he says, "I'll buy the bait."

"In that case, I'll meet you at the dock," I tell him, and disconnect.

Chapter 30

If someone were to ask me in January or February if I'm planning to spend the rest of my life living in northeastern Ohio—or anywhere in the Midwest for that matter—my answer would be something along the lines of *Hell no! Are you nuts?* Ask me the same question on an evening like this one, when the breeze is like silk on your skin, the frogs and crickets and the last of the birds launch into their end-of-day serenade, and the moon is a pale yellow sphere rising above the treetops to the east, I'd respond with *Why would I ever want to live anywhere else?* It's evenings like this one that make those long winters worth the wait.

It's dusk and I'm sitting in a lawn chair on the small wooden dock, looking out over the pond, and there's no place else in the world I'd rather be. The cattails on the far side teem with dragon-flies and a few early evening lightning bugs. A turtle snoozes on a rock a couple of feet from the bank. In the cottonwood tree on the north side of the pond, a male cardinal laments the end of the day. A glass of iced tea sweats atop the cooler next to a citronella candle. A six-pack of Killian's Irish Red chills inside. I brought the bamboo fishing poles, both affixed with the requisite red-and-white bobbers. On the outside chance Tomasetti wants to show off his casting prowess, his rod and reel with the lure most likely to catch the big bass that's been taunting him for weeks now is lying on the dock alongside the poles.

"Looks like you started without me."

I startle at the sound of Tomasetti's voice and turn to see him striding toward me. Long strides. Eyes intent on me. *Worried about me,* I think, but he doesn't want me to see it, so I let it go. There's enough light for me to see that he's still wearing his work clothes—slightly wrinkled button-down shirt, creased trousers, and one of the ties he bought at Milano last time we were in Columbus. The tie is askew, telling me I'm not the only one who's had a long day.

"Did you bring the bait?" I ask.

"Of course." He holds up a container very much like one for Chinese food takeout. "Night crawlers." He grins. "Nothing better for catching bass at night."

"Does that mean we're going to fish all night?"

"We could."

"And play hooky tomorrow?"

"Best idea I've heard all week."

I rise from my chair, open the cooler, and hand him a Killian's. "You look like you could use this."

"I can." He takes the beer.

I see him looking at the wrap on my wrist, and it makes me feel self-conscious. "I think the big one has your name on it."

"Hopefully, he's hungry and feeling reckless tonight." He sets the beer on top of the cooler without opening it. "Kate."

Before I can speak, he strides toward me. His arms go around me and he pulls me close. "God, I'm glad you're okay."

"Me, too."

"How's the wrist?"

I fall against him, set my face against his shirt, breathe in his scent, and sigh. "Hurts like hell."

"Well, that's just like you to milk it, isn't it?"

"You're on to me, I guess."

"Broken?"

"You know by now that I never do anything halfway."

He pulls away slightly, putting just enough space between us to make eye contact with me. For an instant I avoid his gaze, then I look into his eyes.

"Bad scene today?" he asks.

"Yeah."

He nods. "So what aren't you telling me?"

I promised myself I wasn't going to cry, but I feel the burn of tears rising in my eyes. "I lost the baby."

John Tomasetti is one of the most guarded people I know. But I don't miss the ripple that runs the length of him. I see that same ripple play across his features. Surprise. Concern. A quick flash of pain.

"Aw, Kate." He makes a sound that's part sigh, part groan. "I'm sorry. I'm sorry. . . . What happened?"

"The doc couldn't say for certain. Trauma, maybe. I fell about twelve feet." I shrug. "I don't know. Sometimes miscarriages happen and you never really know why."

He averts his gaze but not before I see the pain slice across his features, as raw and unwanted as a knife wound. "Are you sure?"

"The doc checked my hormone levels when I was in the ER. I mean, I had to have my arm X-rayed . . . a CT scan . . . my hormones fell. . . ."

"Did you lose consciousness? I mean, in the fall?"

I nod. "I think so. For a few seconds."

"I guess you forgot to tell me about that," he says dryly.

"I didn't want to worry you."

"Do you have a concussion?"

"No."

He blinks rapidly, then closes his eyes. Trying to figure out how to react, how to feel. Good luck with that.

"Are you sure you're okay?"

"I'm fine. CT was normal. Aside from the broken wrist . . ."

We both know the pain of a broken bone is nothing compared to the heartache of losing something precious.

He puts his arms around me again and pulls me closer. His lips brush against my temple. I feel the warmth of his breath on my face. Wet tears on my cheek. I don't know if they're mine or his.

"Tomasetti, we weren't exactly ready to bring a child into the world."

"I know."

"So why does it hurt so much?" I whisper.

He doesn't answer for the span of a full minute. He just holds me snugly against him. So close I can hear the thrum of his heart. The steady rhythm of his breathing. I can feel the tension in his shoulders, vibrating beneath my hands.

"When you love a child," he says slowly, "you're at the mercy of your heart."

"I don't know the first thing about raising kids."

"Somehow we would have bumbled through."

I smile, but my cheeks are wet. A thousand more tears wait at the gate. "Tomasetti, this was ours. Something innocent and precious and good. A new life we created together. Even if we weren't quite ready . . . I didn't want to lose that."

"I know. Me, too." Finally, he pulls away, looks down at me, and for the first time I see tears on his face. "We would have made it work, Kate. And we would have been good at it. But I was afraid, too. That kind of love . . . for God's sake, it takes over your life. I wasn't sure I had the courage to lay myself open like that again." He grimaces, grapples for the right words. "But I did," he whispers finally. "I did."

I put my hands on either side of his face, bring his mouth down to mine. I taste the salt of tears on his lips. "I'm sorry."

He straightens, gives me a stern look. "You have nothing to be sorry for."

"If I hadn't gone into that loft . . ." I shrug. "If I'd waited for backup. Let Skid or Glock do it . . . If I hadn't tried to do it by myself. If I hadn't fallen. If I wasn't a cop—"

"Kate. Stop." He steps away, slides his hands over my shoulders to my biceps and squeezes gently. "You don't know any of that for sure.

You can't blame yourself for something that might've happened anyway."

"You told me I shouldn't be a cop. Maybe you were right."

"Or maybe I was being an overbearing ass."

I choke out a laugh. Some of the pressure compressing my chest releases.

He offers a half smile. "What? No argument?"

"Well . . ."

We fall silent, trying not to think or feel too much, failing on both counts.

"Are we going to be okay?" I ask.

"We're going to be fine."

"What about the future?"

He lifts his hand and sweeps a strand of hair from my face. His eyes search mine. His knuckles linger against my cheek. "Might be a good idea to keep that bassinet handy. I mean, just in case."

"It *is* beautiful. One of a kind . . ."

"And old. Kind of like me." His eyes burn into mine as he recites the proverb inscribed into the bottom of the bassinet: "A child is the only treasure you can take to heaven."

"I love that." Fresh tears fill my eyes and course down my cheeks. "And I love it that you remembered."

"The proverb might be Amish, but I've known it for a long time."

Raising up on my tiptoes, I press a kiss to his

cheek, then wipe the tears from my face. "Tomasetti, if we're going to get any fishing done, we should probably get started."

"I think you're right."

Stepping away from him, I bend and pick up one of the bamboo poles. "Do you think you could bait my hook for me?"

He takes the pole. "You're kind of squeamish for an Amish girl."

"I'd appreciate it if you didn't spread that around. I have a reputation to uphold."

"Hey, your secret's safe with me." He steps away, spots the flashlight lying against the cooler, picks it up, and turns it on. I watch as he takes it to the edge of the dock and sets it down so that the beam shines out over the water to draw insects —and fish.

"So what's going to happen to Abigail Kline?" Bending, he opens the tackle box containing hooks, lures, bobbers, and fishing line, and begins to rummage.

"She admitted to poisoning her husband. She could be charged with first-degree murder, but I suspect the county attorney will strike a deal and go with second-degree. I mean, she found out Jeramy had murdered her lover. He'd lied to her for thirty years. If the case goes to trial, the jury will probably be sympathetic. Better chance of a conviction if she's prosecuted for a lesser charge."

"What about the Kaufmans?"

"There's a lot we don't know yet, but Abram may be charged with the murder of Leroy Nolt. We don't know how much Naomi knows, but she'll be thoroughly questioned. If it's determined she knew, appropriate charges will be filed. The thing is, we don't know if Nolt's falling into that pen was premeditated or accidental."

Nodding, he threads the hook, then leans forward and bites off the excess line. "I heard they didn't find a rifle at Kester's father-in-law's place."

"Abram Kaufman owns a .22. Deputy found it hidden in the barn during a search." I pick out my hook and tie it onto the line of my own pole. "I'm betting it's going to be a match."

Tomasetti usurps my pole and finishes. "So Kaufman's our sniper."

"Looks like."

Leaning close, he reaches for me, pulls me close, and presses a kiss to my cheek. "I'm glad he's a bad shot."

I grin at him. "Me, too."

Pole ready, he rubs his hands together and picks up the box of bait. "What do you say we catch us some fish?"

"Last one to reel one in has to scale them."

"You're on, Chief Burkholder. You're on."

Center Point Large Print
600 Brooks Road / PO Box 1
Thorndike, ME 04986-0001 USA

(207) 568-3717

US & Canada:
1 800 929-9108
www.centerpointlargeprint.com

WITHDRAWN

37	**Wade Boggs** . . . .**44.4** *
	Charlie Gehringer 44.4
39	Ed Delahanty 44.3
40	**Bobby Grich** **44.1**
41	Bob Gibson 44.0
42	Ed Walsh 43.3
43	**Robin Yount** **43.1**
44	**Ozzie Smith** . . . .**43.0** *
45	Roberto Clemente 42.9
46	Reggie Jackson 42.8
47	Roger Connor 42.7
48	Lou Boudreau 41.3
49	Hal Newhouser 40.8
50	Luke Appling 40.7
	Bobby Wallace 40.7
52	Dan Brouthers 40.6
53	Gabby Hartnett 40.1
	Bid McPhee 40.1
55	Hoyt Wilhelm 40.0
56	**Dave Winfield** . . . .**39.7** *
57	**Ron Santo** **39.5**
58	Joe Cronin 39.4
59	Carl Hubbell 39.2
	Cal Ripken . . . .**39.2** *
	Arky Vaughan 39.2
62	Frankie Frisch 39.1
63	**George Brett** **39.0**
	Bobby Doerr 39.0
65	Amos Rusie 38.9
66	**Ryne Sandberg** **38.8**
67	**Tony Gwynn** . . . .**38.5** *
68	**Joe Jackson** **37.5**
69	Whitey Ford 37.2
	Tim Keefe 37.2
71	**Roger Clemens** . . . .**36.9** *
	Bob Lemon 36.9
73	Ted Lyons 36.7
74	Willie McCovey 36.5
75	**Bill Mazeroski** **36.3**

* Does not include 1995 season

Note: Bill Mazeroski ranks #75 among 14,000+ players; among position players (non-pitchers), he ranks #55.

Since there are 174 players in the Hall of Fame, and only 54 rank ahead of Bill, this Total Baseball Ranking strongly suggests that Bill belongs there too.

There is a yawning gap -- twenty years -- between Hall-of-Fame second basemen Red Schoendienst (born 1923), and Joe Morgan (born 1943). Bill Mazeroski, the finest representative of this missing generation of second basemen, was born in 1936. Talented enough to play with adults in mine leagues as a youth, at 19 he was a second baseman in the National League, at 21, the youngest All-Star at second in league history. He would be selected an All-Star seven times.

At 22 he won his first of eight Gold Gloves. At 24 he hit the only home run to end Game 7 of a World Series. At 30 he turned 161 double plays in a season; no one has come close since. At 36, after seventeen seasons and a record 1,706 double plays, he retired.

At 59, in March, 1996, Bill Mazeroski will be eligible for induction into the Hall of Fame by a vote of the Veterans Committee. He richly deserves the honor.